YOU ONLY NEED ONE

LAUREN CONNOLLY

For Mom & Dad
Thank you for reading to me every night and telling me Real Life Stories.
You are both the reason I hear voices in my head.
(That's a good thing)

Visit my website at www.laurenconnollyromance.com
Cover Designer: Okay Creations
Editor: Jovana Shirley, Unforeseen Editing, www.unforeseenediting.com

This book is a work of fiction. Names, characters, places, and incidents either are products of the author's imagination or are used fictitiously. Any resemblance to actual persons, living or dead, events, or locales is entirely coincidental.

ISBN-13: 978-1-949794-02-1

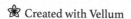 Created with Vellum

PROLOGUE

HOLLY

"IF YOU DON'T TALK to me, I swear, I'm gonna go crazy. Like *punch a hole in the wall* crazy."

The room is quiet, except for the scratch of a pencil and the occasional crackle of stiff paper as I shift uncomfortably on the examination table. Luckily, I'm just getting the results of my blood test today, so I've got on jeans and a cotton T-shirt rather than the revealing gown that opens up in all the private places I don't want my brother to see.

Marcus sits in the only normal chair in the room, foot crossed over his ankle, notepad propped on his knee, pencil skittering across the paper. In his own world, like always. Normally, I'd leave him to it, but today, I need a distraction.

"Which wall?" He keeps sketching.

"Which wall? *Which* wall? Does it matter?" I throw my hands up at the ridiculousness of his question.

"Only if you're strong enough to break through the drywall." Finally, he stops drawing, instead using his pencil like a professor would use a pointer during a lesson. He even sounds like one of my instructors. "Three of these walls"—he points them out—"you'd likely just get empty space behind. So, you're good to go. But this one"—he reaches back to tap the one behind his head—"is a load-bearing wall. So, there are beams. I'm guessing steel. Punch one of those, and you'll break your hand." Finished with his lesson, Marcus goes back to his work.

I roll my eyes, a common occurrence around my big brother. "You architects. Think you know everything, don't you?"

"When it comes to walls? Yeah."

I snort and try to leave him alone.

He didn't have to come with me today. I've been going to the doctor alone since I was fifteen. But this isn't a normal yearly checkup. And I think it'll be better to hear the news together. If it's good, then plans can be made immediately. If it's bad ... well, at least I won't need to repeat it.

Marcus huffs in what I can tell is frustration. He flips his pencil over and erases the offending mark with a glare. I smile as I watch him work. Doesn't matter if he makes a mistake or two; the final drawing will be amazing. Everything Marcus creates blows my mind.

I can feel my smile fall when the door clicks open, and my doctor walks in. It's not that I don't like Dr. Williams. I really do. She's perfectly nice and always professional, and she gets straight to the point.

Even when her news sucks.

"We've received the results of your blood test. I'm sorry, Holly, but you are not a match for Marcus. You won't be able to give him your kidney."

A buzz fills my ears, and the room gets fuzzy for a second.

You are not a match.

You are not a match.

You are not a match.

A broken record flicks those words over and over in my head.

I thought I just needed to wait.

"When you're eighteen, then you can check. But I'm not letting you go before then."

Marcus told me that for a year. Ever since his kidneys got so bad that he needed constant treatments—aka dialysis. No matter how much I begged him, told him that age didn't matter if I could save his life, he never gave in.

Today was supposed to be the day.

But today is just a new person telling me that I have no control.

A warm hand gives my knee a squeeze. When I glance up from my lap, Marcus smiles at me in sympathy. As if I were the one living with a death sentence. This man doesn't deserve the crappy genes he was dealt. I just want to fix it.

"Don't worry about it, Holly. We knew there was no guarantee. I mean, we're only half-siblings." He pats my leg before standing and offering Dr. Williams his hand. "Thank you for checking. And for being gentle with my sis."

Her face stays serious as she shakes his hand. "No one is a fan of needles. I'm just sorry I couldn't give you better news. You're still on the donor list though. And there are other options, such as exchange programs."

"Exchange programs? What're those?" I sound desperate, but I don't care.

Marcus grimaces but keeps quiet when I shush him.

Dr. Williams makes sure to face both of us as she explains, "An exchange program, also called a paired donation, is when two or more people with kidney failure have willing, medically able, living donors who are incompatible"—she gestures at me—"with their loved one"—she points to Marcus—"but are compatible with another in need. If a pairing match is found, that means you would be donating to a stranger, Holly, with the understanding that their family member or friend would be donating a kidney to Marcus. With your brother's rare blood type, I can't guarantee we will find one of these situations, but it doesn't hurt to enter into the program. If you think you would be comfortable with that situation?"

I choke out a disbelieving laugh. "Are you kidding? Sign me up!"

"Holly, don't—"

I turn to my brother, pinning him with a glare and giving his chest a firm poke. "If you think for one second that I'm not doing this, you're in for a rude awakening, bro. You'd better get ready because I'm finding you a kidney if it's the last thing I do."

Silence fills the room before Marcus sighs in defeat. He knows when I'm armed and ready for battle.

Turning to the doctor, he gives her a shrug. "If it's what she wants, then I'm on board."

Dr. Williams nods and writes herself a note. "Okay. I'll put your information into the system."

"Good."

We might have gotten some bad news today, but there's still hope. And I'm going to cling to it like a rabid raccoon.

Marcus ruffles my hair as we exit the office. "I still can't believe this is how you wanted to spend today."

I shrug. "You're the one who made me wait."

He shakes his head like I'm the weird one and tosses me the car keys. "Now that the depressing portion of the festivities are over, let's go get you some birthday cake."

1
___

BEN

Three Years Later

THESE WAITING ROOMS always smell the same. Not bad exactly, but distinctly sterile. If this smell were a person, it'd be that guy who ironed his dress shirts before he hung them up and then again right before he wore it, and then he would glare at your wrinkled T-shirt, as if you'd somehow offended him.

It's giving me a headache.

But I push past it because today is a good day. Today, I meet *her*. My donor.

My kidneys are shit. My fault. I can't curse at my parents or a stranger for this situation. Maybe the universe, but I'm not a fan of yelling into the void. Nope, I screwed my body up all on my own.

Still, all my family members and friends got tested to see if they could help me out. Maybe give me one of theirs. No luck there. Every time they called with a negative, I would try to convince myself that it didn't matter, but then I'd have to hook up to the machine again.

Each treatment with the needles in my arm, sucking my blood out to be cleaned and then piping it back in, pushed me closer to crazy town. The only thing that kept me going was the hope that my wait on the organ donor list wouldn't be longer than the life left in my body.

Today's the big day.

My parents are late, but I don't care this time. Without them here, I can people-watch. Maybe catch a glimpse of my donor before the official meeting.

I only know her name and her brother's, who needs a kidney just as bad as I do. My doctor said a name is all he could give me without their permission, and some people don't even get that.

Holly and Marcus Foster. My superheroes. I half-expect her to burst in here, sporting a Wonder Woman getup. Getting a kidney from Gal Gadot would be a bonus.

That's just wishful thinking though. I've got my eye out for a man and a woman more my parents' age or older. Kidney failure isn't something people as young as me normally deal with. I'm an outlier.

Yay me.

My glasses slide down my nose as I bend over the book in my lap. I should've brought one of my textbooks, but studying political science isn't as interesting as reading a novel. Normally, I can get lost in a good story, but today, I can't get through a paragraph without glancing at the door.

Finally, it opens, and in walk a middle-aged man and woman.

They're obviously here together, her hand wrapped around his forearm. She has her dyed blonde hair pulled back from a round face, making it easy to see her thin lips pinched together. The man looks like any military movie drill sergeant with buzzed hair and steely eyes.

They have to be the Fosters.

I almost jump up and introduce myself, even consider kneeling and kissing Holly's feet. But I don't do that because Mr. Foster looks like a man who throws punches first and asks questions never. Better wait for the doctors to call us in.

I've no idea if they'll even be interested in talking to my cousin, Fred, and me over the next few months. They might be good with a quick hello and then radio silence until surgery day.

The Fosters sit down on the other side of the room in the only two remaining empty chairs.

It's depressing how crowded the waiting room is. When I got here, I ruled everyone present out as possibly being Holly and her brother. A few older men with varying shades of gray hair are scattered around. An elderly woman sits with a young girl, clasping her hand and holding tight to a rosary. A father whispers in Spanish to his preteen boy. A guy with darker skin, who I'd guess is in his thirties, has a sketchpad propped in his lap. And then a young woman sits on her own, next to Holly.

Staring at the two people I've been waiting for, while creepy, makes sense. Staring at the mystery girl beside them is only reasonable if you ask my dick for input.

She has a textbook on her lap, and she taps the end of a highlighter on her full bottom lip, like she's trying to draw attention to it. What man wouldn't want to get a closer look at that pouty mouth? Of course, I'm making up the invitation. She only has eyes for her book.

Most people here are obviously sick. It's in the way their skin looks or a smell they have. Or the fear mixed with depression on their faces.

This girl should be on a billboard advertising health. And swimsuits.

Silky brown hair waves slightly, brushes against her cheeks, and ends just below her chin. She's got on a conservative white blouse, buttoned to her slim throat. I want to pop a few of those buttons open, see more of that skin flushed with a healthy glow. A black skirt covers her to the knees but still lets my eyes trace down her toned calves to where they disappear into a pair of heeled black boots. The whole outfit makes her look like she's heading into a job interview, but I find the professional look sexy as hell.

I'm curious.

Why is she here? This girl can't be dying ... can she?

7

A surprising surge of panic has me clenching my hands.

With a deep breath, I push the strange reaction away because it's not rational. I've never spoken to her, so why should I care about her medical issues?

My imagination has too much free rein when I'm stuck in these uncomfortable situations. Like a coping mechanism, to avoid my own problems, I make up fake issues for other people that I can worry about. That has to be it.

I'm being ridiculous. I don't know why she's here, who she is, or even what her name is.

She hasn't even looked at me.

And, like I yelled that thought across the room, my mystery girl glances up from her book, her gaze connecting with mine.

HOLLY

Why did we get here so early?

This is supposed to be a good day, but I'm still a jittery mess. I think it's these sitting rooms. Maybe the chairs with their poor back support and lack of cushioning or the lighting, always fluorescent. But, really, I think it's the smell. Brings back bad memories.

I've been stuck reading this same page for the last five minutes, trying to focus enough to get the words to stay in my brain.

It's no use. I'm too excited. Too scared.

Will things finally work out this time?

I glance out the side of my eye to check on Marcus. He grumbled about me staring at him earlier, so now, I have to be covert.

As usual, he's busy with his designs. Just last year, a prestigious architecture firm in NYC made him a decent job offer. So good in fact that he was willing to leave his beloved Philadelphia to relocate. I might have given him a shove or two, making sure he didn't let a dream slip through his fingers. I miss him, but at least he's just a train ride away.

When I'm sure he's not freaking out, I refocus on my homework for digital marketing. Normally, I'm all about this subject. I carry half of the class participation on my own shoulders.

I still can't concentrate.

But, this time, it's not my worries throwing me off. There's a weird pressure brushing against my skin. Like I'm being watched.

With that creepy thought itching over me, I put my finger on the sentence I last tried to read and tilt my head up to view the room.

Immediately, I lock eyes with a guy sitting against the opposite wall.

He's staring at me, though he does jerk in surprise when I first look at him. But, instead of doing the usual thing where you dramatically glance around, putting on a show that says, *Oh no, I wasn't staring at you. You just happened to catch me as I was looking at everything in the room*, the guy keeps on watching me.

Weirdo.

I scan my clothes, looking for a giant stain or something else that would make me worth examining. But the crisp linen shirt I ironed this morning is spotless. When I brush my hand across my mouth, I don't feel any stray crumbs. A quick finger-comb of my hair assures me that nothing is sticking out at a strange angle.

So, what's this guy's issue?

Flipping my eyes back to his side of the room, I find him still looking my way, only now he has a half-smile. Like he found my self-examination amusing.

Well, he's not the only one here who can gawk at strangers.

I place my highlighter down, angle my body toward him, and set to staring.

Then, I make my list.

1. Strawberry-blond hair with a touch of a curl in slight disarray. Probably did that on purpose with styling products.
2. Wire-rimmed glasses sitting on a straight nose, making him look like a young professor. Bet they're not even prescription.

3. Blue-checkered dress shirt, neatly tucked into corduroy slacks. Preppy much?

4. Can't tell how tall he is, as he's sitting down, but I bet he's obnoxiously tall. Like *break my neck to look him in the eye* tall.

5. Holding a book. Okay, I guess that's hot.

6. Overall, too attractive for his own good.

As I reach my conclusion, his half-smile morphs into a full-on smirk.

Now, I'm annoyed. I'm over here, worried about my brother's health, trying to stay sane during this wait, unable to tell which of these older men is Benjamin Gerhard—the person I'm getting myself cut open for—and Mr. Handsome Face is practically laughing at me.

He wants something to laugh at? I'll give him something to laugh at.

I start with a fierce glare made to wither even the strongest of men. Then, without warning, I cross my eyes and stick out my tongue like the grown woman I am.

There, that should teach him to stare at strangers.

When my eyes settle back into their proper direction, I'm satisfied to find his mouth has popped open in shock.

Situation handled, I go back to my textbook, prepared to lose myself in the technical writing.

But then the chuckling starts.

With the self-control of an Amazon warrior, I keep my eyes on my book, even as the stranger's choked laughter fills the room. I comfort myself with the knowledge that everyone else here probably thinks he's crazy.

"Making new friends?" Marcus's murmured question has me glancing up at him. Now, he's the one with a half-smile.

Did he see my immature exchange with the stranger?

He grins and crosses his eyes at me.

Yes. Yes, he did.

"He started it," I mumble back.

The laughter dies off.

Dagnabbit.

10

The silence is more tempting than the noise, and I can't hold back the urge to check on Mr. Annoyingly Attractive. His smile is gone. Instead, he appears puzzled as he glances between my brother and me.

I don't have time to wonder about him any longer because the door beside reception swings open.

A woman in watermelon-colored scrubs appears and reads off her clipboard. "We're ready for the Gerhards and the Fosters now."

As I stand, I scan the room, trying to get my first look at Mr. Gerhard. But the only person who stands up besides Marcus and me is Mr. Getting-on-My-Nerves Gorgeous.

Oh no.

"You?" I can't hide my disbelief. I shake my head to clear it. Or to deny the truth.

He's too young!

I just stuck my tongue out at him!

This can't be right!

The guy looks just as confused as I am, gaze flitting between me and the woman sitting in the chair next to mine. I'm still convinced that he is joking and will sit back down. But then he says one word, and my fate is sealed.

"Holly?"

~

BEN

I do my best to play catch-up as our group settles around the conference table. I stared like an idiot in the waiting room, but now, I try not to gawk at the girl sitting across from me.

No, not *the girl.* Holly. Holly Foster.

Apparently, I was way off base, thinking my donor would be a middle-aged woman. Instead, I've got this little brunette, sexy in a girl-next-door kind of way, with heart-shaped lips and the ability to sass me without speaking a word.

I'm not sure if she's going to save me or destroy me.

Dr. Stevens and a woman I expect is this lovely girl's physician both lean over a laptop. They're probably getting the Skype session set up, what with my cousin joining us long distance. I take advantage of the free moment to force the blood back to my brain, so I can avoid making an ass of myself.

Other than her hilarious exchange with me and the first moment of recognition when our names were called out, Holly hasn't glanced my way. I should be grateful, but instead, I miss having those coffee-brown eyes glaring at me.

Okay, so our first interaction was slightly awkward. But that doesn't change things. Now, I have a face to pair with the name. Now, I know who is willing to undergo surgery to save my life.

And I have to admit, kissing *this* Holly's feet is more appealing than doing so with my first assumption. Kissing other parts of this Holly is tempting, too. Like the delicate hand she's tapping on the table. Or maybe the soft cheek that blushed red when she realized who I was. Possibly that pouty bottom lip she's nibbling on at the moment.

Whoa. Pump the brakes. Put it back in your pants.

I give myself a firm mental shake and try to dump a proverbial bucket of ice water on my overly excited brain.

I *cannot* fantasize about making out with my organ donor. There has to be a rule somewhere that says that. Like in the Bible or something. I definitely feel like I should go to hell for the thoughts of what I want to do to her mouth.

Trying to take my mind off of forbidden fantasies, I turn my attention to Holly's brother, Marcus. I'm guessing they aren't full siblings, based on the differing skin tones. Holly is the color of whipped cream, light and pale. Marcus's skin is much darker. If I were painting them, I'd use alabaster for her and russet for him. I can see the relation more in the shape of their faces and the set of their eyes.

"You've probably guessed by now, but I'm Marcus."

Shaking the hand he offers me, I smile in response to his amused grin. He probably saw his sister's antics in the waiting room.

"Good to meet you. I'm Ben." Under the pretense of being polite but really because I need to hear her speak, I turn to hold my hand out to his sister. "And you must be Holly Foster. My knight in shining armor."

She blinks and then gives me her hand, rewarding me with a smile even though it does appear tight around the edges. "At your service."

If only.

Just as I'm trying to brainstorm ways to hear that sweet voice again, my parents are ushered into the room.

"So sorry we're late," Mom says before giving me a kiss on the cheek while my dad pats me on the back. "Are these the Fosters?" She turns hungry eyes on the siblings, who stand up to greet my parents.

"Yeah, Mom. This is Holly Foster and Marcus Foster." I try to meet Holly's eyes, but she's shifted her attention away from me. "And these are my parents, Victoria and Benjamin Gerhard."

More handshakes are exchanged, and everyone takes their seats. Dr. Stevens lets out a noise of satisfaction, and the large TV screen at the end of the room emits the ringing of a telephone. A few seconds go by before my cousin, Fred, appears on the screen. He grins through his thick beard and waves. Next to him is a well-dressed man with more hair on his upper lip than the top of his head. Introductions resume, and I find out that Fred's companion is Dr. Gupta, and Holly and Marcus's is Dr. Williams. After everyone says their hellos, the doctors get into the details.

"Now, I want to reiterate to Holly and Fred, this is all voluntary. You are under no obligation to complete this donation if, at any point, you feel uncomfortable with proceeding."

I swear that Holly flinches slightly at Dr. Williams's words.

Does she not really want to donate? Is her brother forcing her into this?

I should talk to Holly alone at some point. To ask her about the donation, of course. Definitely not because I want to try to get a real smile out of her.

"Over the next few months, you will undergo multiple tests to ensure you are healthy enough to donate. You will also submit to mental evaluations, so we know you are emotionally ready to take on this task. You will be counseled on the procedure as well as the potential risks and the recovery period. Do you understand all of this?"

Both Holly and Fred nod.

"Good. Once we finish with those steps, assuming everything goes well, we will schedule your surgeries. Now, you've all introduced yourselves to one another, but we like to provide you with this time to get to know a little more about each other. Also, you can decide on how much communication you'd like to have during this process."

"How much is there normally?" This is from my mother, who keeps smiling at Holly, likely just a step away from hopping over the table and planting a kiss on the girl's mouth.

Get in line, Mom.

"It differs from case to case," Dr. Stevens says. "Some decide that meeting once is all they need and don't converse until the day of surgery. Maybe not even then. Others exchange contact information and actually spend time together. They like the idea of having that connection. It's really up to you all."

Well, I know what I want, and it doesn't involve leaving this room and never getting to see Miss Foster again.

In a strange reflection of my mom, my donor now wears a huge smile. Unfortunately, I'm not on the receiving end of it. That lucky bastard is cousin Fred, who grins right back.

After a beat of silence, I'm about to open my mouth when Holly takes the words from me.

"I understand if you all would prefer not to, but I'd really like to keep in touch. Even if it's just texting. Or a phone call every so often." She directs all these words at Fred.

I get the strong urge to remind her that it's *me* she's giving her kidney to.

Then, I notice her hand. It's not tapping on the table anymore or fiddling with her highlighter. Instead, she has it wrapped around her brother's wrist, gripping hard. As if to reassure herself that he's still sitting beside her.

I glance back at my parents and find them both staring at Holly like she's a magic genie, here to grant them a wish. In a way, she is.

My parents gaze at Holly the same way she's looking at my cousin, and I can't fault her for ignoring me.

But I decide that, when she's done thanking the universe for the gift that is Fred's kidney, I'm going to make her notice me again.

"You want someone to talk to? I'm your man." I lean over the table toward her, trying to catch her eye.

Holly hits me with the full weight of her attention. "Regular phone calls and everything?" The hope in her voice gives me all the opening I need.

"Why stop at phone calls? Other than Fred, we're all in Philly. You wanna hang out, then just give me a place and time."

I know I've said the right thing when her soft mouth curls up at the corners. The sweet smile does strange things to my chest, and suddenly, every inch of my skin heats up.

I'm so screwed.

~

HOLLY

Mr. Distractingly Devastating is getting back on my good list.

The idea of exchanging good-byes with this family today and then Marcus having his new kidney in a few months, no problem, is not something I can trust. I don't need tabs on Fred twenty-four/seven or anything, but forming some sort of friendship could only help the situation. Same thinking when it comes to Mr. ... okay, I should probably start calling him Ben.

"I'll hold you to that. But Marcus just moved to New York City, so it's really just me who's local."

Not that my brother is pushing for a get-together. Marcus is invested, but he has always been a bit of a loner. He trusts me to handle the human interactions most times.

"Yes, tell us about yourselves. All we really know are your names, that Marcus needs a kidney, and that you're willing to donate one." Ben's mom stares at me, her gaze as fixed as a missile target.

I'm not intimidated. Mrs. Gerhard is my kind of woman. Straight to the point.

"Okay, sure. So, Marcus"—I wave my hand at my brother, knowing that he wants me to take over the introductions—"moved because he was offered a job at an architecture firm. That's what he does for a living. Designing buildings and spaces. He's pretty much a genius at it."

"Holly." Marcus uses his chiding big-brother tone, but I just roll my eyes at him.

"And, unless he's trying to get you to hire him, he's annoyingly modest about how amazing his work is." Now, he's the one rolling his eyes, but I just ignore him, as is mandated in the little sister's guidebook. "As for me, I'm a student at Wharton, the business school at—"

"The University of Pennsylvania," Mrs. Gerhard finishes my sentence with a surprised look.

I don't know why though—unless she's shocked that I made it into an Ivy League school.

"How long have you been at UPenn?" That's from Ben's father.

"I just started my third year. I'm working on a BS in economics and hoping to qualify for the fast-track MBA program."

"That is a wonderful coincidence." Ben's mother smiles at me, so some of my defensiveness melts away.

"What is?"

"Well, we were excited enough to learn that there was a donor living in Philadelphia who was a match for Ben. But then to find out that you two attend the same university? It's a small world!"

My eyes flick to Ben, and for the first time since the waiting room, I give his face a thorough examination.

1. Strong jawline with a clean shave.
2. A slight cleft in his chin.
3. Red-gold hair still maintaining its skillfully tousled appearance.

4. Broad shoulders filling his shirt out to perfection.

5. Straight white teeth bump his genuine smile up a notch. Probably flosses like a champ.

6. Still too attractive for his own good. And for my state of mind.

I'm completely sure I've never seen him before in my life. "What's your major?"

"Political science." Ben watches me studying him, unmoving, as if he knows I want him to keep still during my perusal.

"He'll be applying to law school next year," Mr. Gerhard adds, smiling at his son.

"So, you're a junior?" I'm not completely sure how the whole pre-law situation works.

"Really, I should be a senior, but I've had to go part-time the past two years. You know ... medical issues." He gives a general wave to take in our surroundings.

I nod in understanding. It took Marcus an extra year to get his degree because of classes conflicting with treatment times.

"Maybe we can be study buddies." Now's a good time as any to reach out the hand of friendship. "I don't understand a word of that legal mumbo jumbo, but I can hold up flash cards like a pro." I use my most braggy voice, and Marcus snorts at my antics.

Ben grins broadly.

My goodness, that's a smile that could run a car off the road.

"Sounds like an offer I can't refuse."

"Obviously, I can't meet up with you all, being out here in Colorado. But I can give out my phone number. Text me anytime." That offer comes from Fred, the image on the screen a half-second behind the audio.

After he's done with his, we all rattle off our phone numbers, including Ben's parents.

I think it's sweet that they're here with him. Our dad tends to keep a relatively hands-off approach to the situation, trusting us to update him on any new developments. Secretly, I think my adoptive father is self-conscious about his lack of a college degree, as if he'd only hold back the discussion by being here. I'd try setting him straight if it wouldn't embarrass him more. Someone who can disassemble and rebuild a car engine and then rewire an entire house could never be considered uneducated.

"Well, if you've no further questions for us, then I think we're done for today. Fred, you can talk to your doctor about setting up all your pretests in Denver. Holly, you can stop by the front desk to arrange your appointment times." Dr. Williams ends the videoconference after we wave good-bye and stands to lead us from the room.

We file out, and I head toward the front desk but stop when I feel someone grip my hand.

Mrs. Gerhard lingers and clutches my palm. "Miss Foster—"

"Holly," I correct her.

Victoria Gerhard lets a smile trace over her serious face. "Holly. I just wanted … I needed …" She huffs out a frustrated sigh, and I get the impression that this is a woman who normally knows exactly what to say. "What you're doing for my son … thank you." She gives my hand a soft squeeze before releasing me and hurrying after her departing husband.

I stand still for a moment, recognizing in her a reflection of my own gratitude. If Fred were in this room with us, I would have bruised his ribs from my death-grip hug.

When I go to turn to the desk, I'm stopped again, this time by a gentle brush on my arm. I glance back to see Ben, his cheeks turning faintly red.

Would his skin be hot to the touch if I pressed my fingers there?
Stop thinking about touching the guy's face. His face is off-limits.

"Sorry about my mom. She can be a bit intense at times, but she means well."

"Oh no, it's fine. I totally get it. You're her son, and she's just happy that you're going to be healthy again. And, believe me, having a mom like yours is nothing you should ever be sorry for."

At his quizzical look, I realize that I'm babbling and tripping close to a topic I don't even like talking to my brother about. Good time to cut and run.

"Nice meeting you, Ben. I'll see you around campus."

"Yeah, see you."

I hear his response as I briskly walk away, front desk in sight.

Do not look over your shoulder. Do not look over your shoulder.

The internal mantra is useless. When the office door creaks open, my eyes flit toward the sound, finding Ben Gerhard paused in the doorway. As if waiting to get my attention again, he grins and waves, and then he finally walks out of my sight. Marcus sits in a chair by the door, waiting for me to schedule my appointments, so we can head out.

I love spending time with my brother. But, today, there's a tug of regret that he's the one I'm leaving this office with instead of a bespectacled man with a propensity for staring.

2

BEN

WHEN I GET home from the doctor's office, only one of my two roommates is around.

"You said Holly Foster? Wait, does she have short brown hair?
Cute face? Nice ass?" Jasper asks while his eyes stay locked on the TV.
He bought some new video game that's been taking up an unhealthy
amount of his free time.

"Dude, that's my donor you're talking about ... but yeah. Do you
know her?"

He pauses his game, and I'm the lucky receiver of his full attention. "I think she's the Holly in my digital marketing class. You said
she's an econ major, right?"

I nod.

"Well then, I think I know your donor."

"That's crazy. You have a fucking class with her? What's she like?"
I sit down heavy on the chair across from him. Lately, my body seems
to tire out quickly, and when I get tired, I get cranky. I never used to
be this weak.

Jasper grins like he's remembering an inside joke. "Let's just say, it's a good thing I know what I'm talking about in that class."

"What's that supposed to mean?"

He taps his controller on his chin for a second and then grins. "Okay, so a week ago, the professor gives us a topic to discuss. A few of us give some input. Then, Holly talks, and she's got a great point, referencing the readings and everything. Then, right after her, this guy, who barely shows up to class anyway, basically repeats what Holly said, except he switches a few words around. Now, most people would just roll their eyes and let it go. But not Holly." He pauses to chuckle, his gaze unfocused, like he's watching it all play back.

Suddenly, I'm jealous. Jasper already has stories about this girl, and I'm not sure I've said more than ten words to her.

"So, what'd she do?"

"Oh hell, it was great. Holly stands up like she's about to give a speech and says"—Jasper tries out a higher-pitched voice—"'Excuse me, but no. We're not doing this. You read the book, you come up with your own ideas, and you show up to class to talk about them. You do *not* take my words and pass them off as your own. Do the work; don't try lying about it. Understood?' Something like that. And she actually waited until the guy nodded his head!" Jasper is laughing for real now, and I can't keep from smiling either. "The professor didn't even know what to do. He just pretended like it hadn't happened and moved on. But, yeah, don't mess with Holly. She's nice though."

"How so?"

The girl he just described sounds more intimidating than nice.

"She lent me a pen one time when I forgot mine. And I've seen her explaining concepts to people when they seem lost. I think she only gets angry when people are being dicks." Jasper appears thoughtful for a moment and then gives a firm nod. "I think you've got a good one. I can't see Holly backing out of something. If she said she'd give you her kidney, then she meant it."

The idea of her backing out didn't even occur to me.

"Cool. That's cool. So, do you know anything else about her?"

"Like what?" Jasper has his game back on, so I only have half of his attention, if that, which might work to my advantage.

"Uh, I guess other classes she might have? Or who any of her friends are? Does she have a boyfriend?"

Apparently, I'm shit at being subtle.

Jasper pauses his game and turns to fully face me. "You've gotta be kidding."

I avoid his eyes. "Kidding you about what?"

"About what? You're asking if this girl is off the market. So, tell me, Benny boy, do you have a boner for your donor?"

Jasper cackles at his own joke while I grimace. Partly because that joke is horrible, but also partly because I think he's right.

"Just forget it."

Game back on, attention off me. "Yeah, right. And I have no idea. I've got one class with her. I don't know her whole life story."

"Thanks." As I head to the stairs, I hear him call after me.

"My marketing class is Thursday morning in Huntsman Hall. Ends at nine a.m. Just FYI."

～

HOLLY

The dream always begins the same way.

The door looms tall before me.

I reach up, turn the knob, and push. The hinges squeak as the door swings wide, revealing the dark room beyond. My feet move forward on their own.

Everything in the room is familiar. The worn dresser cluttered with knickknacks and jewelry. The ironing board pushed off into the corner. The large bed with its simple wooden headboard. This is Grams's room. A place to snuggle for bedtime stories or to find comfort after bad dreams. She should be asleep here, in her bed.

Someone is under the covers, but when I pull the sheet back, it's not my grandmother.

It's Marcus.

My brother lies still, lids closed, like he's sleeping, but his chest doesn't rise. I put my hand on his shoulder and find him ice-cold.

The darkness around me shifts and moves, closing in on us. Marcus begins to sink into the bed, as if the mattress were quicksand. He's disappearing from my sight, and he doesn't respond when I scream his name.

There's a pressure at my back, pushing me toward the sinkhole in the bed where my brother has vanished. Terror seeps from the black space.

I turn away, looking for the door. It stands there, closed again.

With fear scraping its way down my spine, I run. The darkness slows my legs, pulling me back, but I push my way through. My fingers clasp the doorknob, wrenching with a mighty tug—

I'm awake.

I gasp and pant, trying to slow down my breathing. My shirt is soaked through with sweat, sticking to me. I shiver uncontrollably.

"Just a dream ... just a dream ... just a dream ..." I mutter the words. A mantra to slow down my frantic heart and to push the terror from my mind.

I know I shouldn't call him. Sleep is so important for him. But I need to hear his voice or else the panic won't leave. The hardwood next to my bed is cool on the early fall night, and my fingers slide over the floor until they grasp my phone. My thumbs tremble as I type in the number I know by heart.

"Holly?"

A sigh flows out of me, taking with it most of the tension in my stiffened muscles. "Yeah, it's me. Sorry to call so late. I just ..."

"Are you okay?" My brother's voice, which started out as a sleepy slur, now sharpens to full awareness.

"Yeah. It was the nightmare. I just needed to make sure you were okay."

"I thought you stopped having that dream."

Marcus spent plenty of nights comforting me when I was a kid. Seems things haven't changed much.

"I thought so, too. Guess it wasn't done with me though."

A sigh drifts from his end of the line. "You need to stop putting all this pressure on yourself. This exchange won't go like the last ones. And, if it does, we'll get through it."

"Yeah, okay. I'm okay." The words sound false to my own ears, but I let the lie go. Marcus should be sleeping, not reassuring me that a dream isn't real when I already know that. "I'm gonna let you get back to bed. Sorry I woke you."

"It's going to be fine. I'm doing okay. Stop worrying. I love you, sis."

"Love you, too, bro."

"Night."

"Night."

After he hangs up, I shut down my own phone. Luckily, in my loft, my clothes are all an arm's length away, so it's no trouble to shuck off my damp shirt and grab a clean one. The dry fabric does a great deal to help distance me from my former terror.

I snuggle back into my mattress, pulling my blankets up to my chin. "Just a dream."

The claim might work better if it were true. Why my brain chooses to morph the events of that night from my childhood is a question for a therapist.

∽

BEN

I should be heading to my car, not to Huntsman Hall. But my feet said a big *screw you* to that, and now, I'm walking in the opposite direction. Straight toward the girl I haven't been able to get out of my head.

I shouldn't be doing this.

It hasn't even been a week since we met at Dr. Williams's office.

I haven't texted Holly to see if she wants to hang out.

She doesn't know that I know she's in this class.

I've made it to the front of the building when the full weight of my weirdness registers.

What is wrong with me? When did I turn into a stalker?

I turn to head back the way I came and make it two steps before someone shouts my name. I'm caught, betrayed by my own.

"Benny! Look who I found!"

There's no question in my mind who's going to be next to my overly helpful friend when I shift to meet his grinning face. There, walking at his side, is Holly Foster, organ donor and unhealthy crush of mine. Luckily, she doesn't appear creeped out by my sudden appearance. Instead, she wears a small smile as her eyes travel between Jasper and me, like she's trying to figure us out.

"Aren't you glad I told you to meet me here? I was totally right. I have class with your Holly." Jasper gives a dramatic flourish of his hands, as if he were a magician introducing his assistant.

"I didn't call you *my* Holly."

I need to get new friends.

She just chuckles and shakes her head, making her soft brown hair swish against her cheeks.

"Well, I'll leave you two. I've got ten minutes to make it across campus." Jasper waves before sprinting off, leaving me standing awkwardly with my hands in my pockets while Holly watches me.

"You're really uncomfortable right now, aren't you?"

Her question takes me aback, and I fumble on a response. "What? Me? No. Of course not. I'm so comfortable right now. I'm practically a Lay-Z-Boy recliner."

And I'm also an idiot.

She laughs. "Oh, Ben. I knew it."

"Knew what?" I brace myself.

"You're weird."

Holly is full-on grinning at me now, and it's hard not to smile back when she gazes up at me with that joyful expression on her face.

"I'm not weird." There's no conviction behind my words because they're definitely a lie.

"Oh, sorry. My mistake. You're totally normal, and you did not just compare yourself to furniture." She's still staring up at me, clearly enjoying herself.

And, suddenly, I want to be weird. I want to be so weird for her.

"Not just any furniture. A Lay-Z-Boy. That's a high-quality chair. Someone weird would pick a crappy piece of furniture, like a desk."

Holly breaks then. One hand on her hip, the other covering her mouth, she lets her laughter spill out, and the sound is something I could get drunk off of. I step in closer, so I can soak up as much as possible.

"So weird. I love it." She shakes her head, eyes squinting with her smile. "So, you decided to ambush me, huh?"

Ashamed, I hang my head, maybe putting on a bit of a show for some sympathy. She gives my shoulder a light shove, and I have to fist my hands in my pockets, so I don't grab her wrist to pull her in closer.

"Don't worry. I'm not mad."

"Yeah, sorry. Jasper said you were in his class. And I guess I just wanted to see you again, so I thought casually dropping by would be the cool thing to do. But, now, I'm realizing it's more stalkery."

"Well, as long as you realize that. And you seem sorry, so I'll forgive you."

Holly steps closer to me, and I get teased with the scent of her perfume. It's kind of sweet, like honeysuckles. I breathe deeper.

"So, do you want to do something? My next class isn't for a few hours."

She's asking me to hang out. Hell, I want to say yes so badly. A normal guy could.

But I'm weird. It burns in my stomach that I only got these few short minutes with her.

"I want to, but I've got somewhere to be soon. Can I take a rain check?"

Please say yes. Please say yes.

She doesn't answer right away. Instead, her eyes travel down to where I'm unconsciously rubbing my knuckles on my forearm. I stop the moment I realize it but not before Holly's face shows understanding.

"You have a dialysis treatment?"

I get over my surprise fast when I remember that her brother probably has a fistula in his arm in the exact same place I do. Holly obviously knows the basics of treatment for kidney failures.

"Yeah, I'm supposed to be there in twenty minutes. So, about that rain check—"

"I'll go with you."

My mouth hangs open for a second, and then I shut it fast when I realize how stupid I must look. "Go with me?"

"Yeah. If you want some company?"

She stares up at me with those fucking adorable brown eyes, and all I can think about is being alone with her for an extended period of time. But a dialysis treatment isn't like grabbing a cup of coffee.

"You know it takes three hours, right? Just sitting there."

Her smile heats my chest—and maybe some other places.

"I know. Marcus was always bored out of his mind, so I went with him a lot. Just so he'd have someone to talk to or play a card game with or something. Do you get bored?"

Hell yeah, I do. Sometimes, I want to peel my skin off; I'm going so crazy from sitting in that chair with the needles in my arm.

"Yeah. I usually just watch TV or try to study. But, if you want to entertain me, then be my guest."

That earns me another grin. I'm about to keep a tally of all the times I've made her smile because each one makes me feel like a badass standing on the gold medalist podium after an Olympic game.

I indicate the direction of my car, and we start walking.

Three hours with Holly Foster. My day just got interesting.

～

HOLLY

When we reach Ben's SUV, he tries to act like a gentleman and open the passenger door for me. Instead, while he's distracted, I climb into the driver's seat. He leans down to peer at me through the car with a baffled look. That expression, paired with the sight of his glasses sliding down his nose, is so endearing; I can't help my grin.

"Sorry, Ben. I never ride in a car I'm not driving. But look at it this way; now, you have a chauffeur!"

I pat the passenger's seat in an enticing manner. Hopefully, he's not the type to make a stink over this. It might seem like a joke, but I am completely serious.

Ben slides in and hands over the keys. "You'd better have a stellar driving record."

"The only tickets I've gotten are parking. But that's Philly. I'm pretty sure they change the rules overnight without telling anyone."

This city is hell for people who own cars. I'm all about public transportation.

"Fine. But I get to DJ."

He reaches for the preprogrammed buttons, and I wonder what's going to come out of the speakers. Is he a hard rock, screamo kind of guy? Or maybe he's got a bit of country in him. He could be top forty or gospel. Punk? Jazz? R & B?

Turns out, I'm wrong on all counts. The station number 93.3 flashes on the screen, and multiple voices fill the car.

"Oh my gosh, are you serious?" That definitely came out as a squeal, but his choice is so perfect.

Misinterpreting my reaction, Ben frowns. "You've got a problem with Preston and Steve?"

"No way! They're only the best morning show ever." I reach over to turn up the volume. "Good choice, Benny. I approve."

He groans. "Not you, too. Jasper won't let that nickname die."

Despite his grumbling, when I glance to my right, Ben has on a smirk. The expression sets off little sizzles in my stomach, like I consumed the forbidden combination of Pop Rocks and soda. A good comparison, seeing as how getting tingly about my organ recipient is even more off-limits.

I'm allowed to have only friendly, non-fluttery feelings about him.

Reminding myself of this, I decide it's time to focus on driving.

When a gap appears in traffic, I pull out of the parallel spot and onto the busy street. We're past the heavy morning rush, so even though there's traffic, we're still moving through the city at a decent crawl.

"So, where are we headed?" All of the treatment centers I know are in west Philly, but we're in Center City, so I need some direction.

"Just go toward Rittenhouse Square. It's only a few minutes past there."

Fancy. I wonder what a dialysis center in the most expensive section of the city will look like. Maybe it'll be like a spa where everyone is getting pedicures and shoulder massages while their treatments are happening.

I chuckle at the image. Ben smiles at me again, probably thinking the radio show has me laughing.

We don't talk for the next fifteen minutes other than when Ben directs me to turn at certain lights. The Preston and Steve crew make us both crack up. They're the funniest people on the radio in Philly, possibly the world. Listening to them takes my mind off the unwanted reaction I had to Ben.

"Make a left here and then park in the first spot you find. The building is on the right."

This street is lined with townhouses. Huge, fancy, beautifully built townhouses. Not somewhere I'd expect to find a dialysis treatment center. Of course, I've been to only a handful, so what do I know?

I luck upon a nice stretch of open street, so I don't even have to go through the tango of parallel parking.

Score.

We get out, and as I reach into the backseat to heave out my hefty backpack, I search for any sign of the center, but all the buildings seem residential.

"Holly, over here." Ben stands on the front steps of one of the million-dollar townhomes.

"What are you doing? I thought you had a treatment."

He reaches behind his head to scratch his neck, a grimace marring his tan face. "I do. I get them done here. This is my parents' place." He pulls out a key and unlocks the front door before holding it open for me.

This is an interesting turn of events. I climb the steps and enter the most expensive residence I've ever been invited to.

My attempt not to stare around like a country bumpkin is only partly successful as Ben leads me through the house.

Just past the entryway is a gorgeous living space. The floor plan is open with tall ceilings, and the furniture somehow appears both expensive and comfortable. The kitchen is magnificent with large stretches of white marble countertops.

I sigh at the thought of my cramped apartment's kitchen where it's almost impossible for two people to stand at one time. How much easier my Sunday meal prep would be if I had space to turn around.

I do like my apartment. But, with both my roommate, Terra, and me living there, it can sometimes get claustrophobic.

"How many people live here?" My question echoes around the magnificent room.

I wonder if Ben has ever hosted a karaoke party here. The acoustics are fantastic. I could go to town on some Kelly Clarkson in this place. Or bust out some P!nk. I can just imagine standing in front of that giant fireplace with a mic in my hand, going full diva.

And the crowd goes wild!

"Just my mom and dad." Ben's answer brings me back to reality.

"Not you?"

"Nope. I rent a place closer to campus with Jasper and our friend Sammy."

Ben heads up another flight of stairs, and I follow, leaving my stadium behind.

We pass some bedrooms before I spot a familiar setup. Beside a large leather recliner is a hemodialysis machine. Even though I understand the mechanics, I still think the thing looks like it belongs in a sci-fi movie with all its buttons and tubes and knobs.

"So, you hook yourself up and everything?" I let my bag drop with a heavy thud in the far corner where it can't get in anyone's way.

Ben doesn't meet my eyes. "Yeah. I went through the training and all that. I tried out the centers for a while, but trying to get a good appointment time was crazy hard. Then, if I needed to shift one ... it just wasn't working."

He shrugs and scratches the back of his neck again. I have to admit, the pose does wonderful things for his biceps, but I think it's his go-to nervous tic.

"My parents installed this here, so I can make my own schedule. And I can have it done more often. So, there's less buildup." He still won't look at me.

I realize he's embarrassed. Talking to a stranger about his fluid buildup probably doesn't top his list for fun times.

"That's good you've found what works for you. Why's it here though? Instead of your place?"

Ben shrugs again. "More space here. And I just ... I don't want the guys to see. To see me like this." He gestures at the machine.

My heart aches. Marcus felt that way, too. He never wanted Pops to go to the treatments with him. Didn't want me to either, but he was never able to stop me from tagging along.

With a dismissive wave, I give him a piece of my mind. "If your friends judge you for getting medical treatment, then they can go fall in dog poo for all I care."

Ben smiles at me, looking both amused and confused. "Fall in dog poo?"

"Have you ever fallen in dog poo?"

He shakes his head.

"Well, it sucks. Smelly, embarrassing, and definitely not something you forget. I know I haven't." Worst day of middle school ever.

Ben opens his mouth like he's about to ask more questions, but the doorbell cuts him off.

"That's probably Dr. Stevens. He comes by once a month for a checkup. Give me a second." He jogs down the hall.

With a slow spin, I take in the whole room. Other than the chair and the machine, there's a window with a plant on the sill, a sink, a cabinet that probably holds all the medical supplies, a large TV mounted on the wall, and a small side table with a lamp and remote control. My guess is that Ben doesn't like spending any more time in here than he has to. There's not even another chair for someone else to sit in.

"Hey, Holly. You remember Dr. Stevens?" Ben stands in the doorway next to a familiar middle-aged man with faded black hair and deep lines around his eyes.

All that identifies him as a doctor is the stethoscope around his neck and the classic physician's bag grasped in his left hand.

He reaches out his empty palm to shake mine. "Nice to see you again, Holly. I just wanted to say that what you're doing for Ben is wonderful. And really brave of you."

I shrug, trying to ignore the queasiness in my stomach when I think about the part of this process that requires me to be brave. "Happy to help."

"That's good to hear. Now, sorry to do this, but would you mind giving Ben and me a few moments?" Dr. Stevens sets his bag down by the sink.

Ben's smile is tight and apologetic.

"No problem." I move to back out of the room. "I'm just going to go root through all your stuff and find out all your dirty secrets."

I wink, and he gives me a nice, deep laugh. Seeing a real smile back in place makes it easy for me to retreat. I shut the door behind me and get ready to explore.

Maybe rifling through his things was an exaggeration, but I still plan on checking this swanky place out. The current floor is mainly bedrooms.

Peeking my head in one, I guess it's his parents'. There's a lived-in quality, even with the bed neatly made. Books sit on each nightstand, and a makeup table is covered in perfume bottles and a bunch of cosmetics. A cracked door reveals a walk-in closet that I am pretty sure is the same size as my roommate's bedroom. I don't go any further than leaning in through the doorway. I'm not a total creep.

Down a bit farther, I think I've found Ben's old room. It's the only other one with some personality. The rest are all pastel, places you'd have a guest sleep.

I take a careful step into the space, vowing I won't touch anything. Only look.

This isn't the TV version of a high school boy's room with posters of half-naked women next to pictures of sports idols. Instead, there's artwork, mainly paintings of landscapes. Gorgeous nature scenes with trees and rolling hills. Even some mountains.

I examine the bookshelves and find a decent amount of sci-fi novels. Looks like Ben is a bit of a nerd. But, on closer inspection, I realize he actually has a wider range of tastes. There are classics, like *Dracula* and *The Jungle*, along with nonfiction authors like Malcolm Gladwell. I have to smile when I find all seven Harry Potter books in hardback. Good to know he's not opposed to a bit of magic in his reading.

His bed is perfectly made up. I go to peek beneath the covers, only to be disappointed. I was hoping that he might have fully committed to a fandom with a set of Star Wars or Batman sheets.

Oh well.

Back out in the hall, I realize that the stairs go up another floor. When I head up them, I come out in a sitting room. This one seems warmer than the space downstairs. Like the first floor is for show, and this floor is for living. Floor-to-ceiling bookshelves line the walls. Seems like the Gerhards are big readers. More couches are spread around, paired with dark wooden coffee tables. On the far wall, there's a set of glass doors.

When I push through them, I walk out onto a large rooftop patio. Metal furniture with thick cushions sits around an empty firepit. In the corner is a covered hot tub big enough to seat eight.

But the best part is the view. The Philly backdrop makes this a city dweller's paradise. I can imagine having strings of lights hung around, burning bright after the sun goes down. People laughing and drinking fancy cocktails as they discuss their extravagant lives. Just like a scene from a movie.

I've never been in a house this nice before. My grandma's place was a decent size with three bedrooms and a yard. But things always felt a bit cramped. There was a short time, after Marcus moved out, that the place seemed vast but for all the wrong reasons. Pops's house was better; Marcus was there, and I had my own room. But neither come close to this towering townhouse.

My brother would probably love this place, maybe even try to design something similar. Me, I'm a little overwhelmed. Should've just stuck to one room or one floor. Piling it all together at once is like trying to read an entire textbook in one sitting.

I let my thoughts trail off at the sound of the glass doors opening. Dr. Stevens steps out to join me, and we gaze across the top of the city.

"They really have a great view here." I gesture to the sight, as if he needed any help in finding the sprawling scene.

"Mmhmm." He glances over at me. I'm not sure what he sees, but he gives me a kind smile and a pat on the shoulder. "They're nice people."

From what I can tell, he's right. And that's a good thing because it means Fred is probably nice, too. Less likely to have a change of heart. The exchange shouldn't be in jeopardy.

I want to be friends with Ben and Fred. Friendships connect you. And they're easy. Uncomplicated.

That's all I want. No flutters. No sparks.

Just friends.

Dr. Stevens clears his throat and turns to leave. "Ben has started his treatment. You're good to join him whenever you're finished exploring."

I follow after him. "I'll walk you out."

"Oh, you don't need to do that."

"It's no problem. I've got to grab something anyway."

BEN

Holly passes by my room with only a quick wave as she and Dr. Stevens head down the hall.

Is she leaving? Without even saying good-bye?

That doesn't make any sense. She offered to come. And we took my car.

Tubes stick into my arm, holding me in the chair. I want to rip them out and follow her.

For a moment, I seriously consider it.

But what if I do and then find she's just in the bathroom? How crazy will I look if I stop my treatment right after I started just because I want to know where she is?

So, instead, I clench my teeth and turn the TV to some random channel. At least, this way, I won't look like I've been sitting in silence, waiting for her to come back. If she comes back.

A few loud thumps echo up the hallway. Then, moments later, Holly stumbles through the doorway, hauling one of the large padded chairs from my parents' dining room table. Apparently, she carried the thing up the flight of stairs because, being the horrible host that I am, I forgot there was nowhere else to sit in this room.

Except for my lap, which I would've been happy to offer up.

"Shit, Holly. I'm sorry. I'm an idiot. I can't believe I forgot another chair."

She flinches, and I wonder if I hurt her feelings. But then she gives me a sweet smile, and I'm back to admiring her mouth.

"You kidding me? This worked out perfectly. Now, I don't have to lift weights today." Holly arranges the chair, so she can see both me and the TV before settling into it. "Oh, good. You're not a show-er."

I glance at my fly and then back at her with a raised eyebrow. "What do you mean?"

"Oh gosh, not like that! I mean—and please don't take this the wrong way—I'm glad you covered your arm." She gestures to the cloth I have draped over my forearm where I'm hooked up.

Embarrassment makes my neck itch as I nod stiffly in understanding and avoid her eyes. I wish Holly weren't seeing me here, in this chair, dependent on a machine.

She grips my free arm. "Ben! I told you not to take it the wrong way! It's got nothing to do with you. It's all me."

When I glance up, she's pressing a palm against her chest, eyes begging me to understand. But I don't.

"It's just that, ever since I was a kid, I've had this irrational fear of needles. Seriously, they freak me out. So, the less I see of them, the better." She gives a gentle shudder.

"But you said you went to your brother's treatments all the time."

"Yeah. I'd cover my eyes till they were done sticking him. Marcus would always warn me."

I watch as she chews on her bottom lip, eyes unfocused.

"But there were some people who just had their arms out in the open for everyone to see. And that's totally fine. They shouldn't have to cover up if they don't want to. But I just couldn't look around while I was there."

"How's that going to work with the testing? They have to draw your blood all the time. And then there's the surgery."

She gives me a small shrug before she answers, "Yeah, I know. I'll just deal with it when the time comes."

I'm an even bigger leech than I thought. Not only am I asking Holly to give me her organ, but I'm also making her repeatedly live through her fear. My stomach twists, and she must catch some of the self-disgust on my face because she gives my shoulder a pat before leaning back in her chair.

"Don't worry about it. That's future Holly's problem." Before I can push her on it, she changes the subject. "So, home makeover shows are how you distract yourself, huh?"

Not wanting to upset her, I let my worries go for the moment and follow the direction of her eyes. Apparently, the random channel I picked was HGTV, and there's a couple on the screen, having a meltdown about wallpaper.

"You know it. Love the subplot."

"Subplot?" She grins at me, obviously seeing right through my serious tone.

"Oh, yeah. See, most viewers think this is about two happy people finding their dream home together."

"And it's not?"

36

"Oh, no. That's just what the producers tell them to get them on the show. I know the truth. What's really going on." I'm using my intense conspiracy voice, and Holly plays right along.

"Well, now, you have to tell me."

I lean in close, mock whispering, "It's marriage Hunger Games. They're lucky if they make it out alive. And without a divorce."

She snorts out a laugh, eyes crinkled, fist against her mouth, like she's trying to stifle the noise. I want to see what she looks like when it breaks free.

"See? I was right." Her smile is triumphant.

"About what?" I can feel the grin creeping across my face.

"You're weird." She shakes her head, still smiling, and then tucks her legs into a crossed formation, balancing on the seat, as if she were on a yoga mat. "So, you said just your parents live here, right?"

I nod.

"Do you have any brothers or sisters?"

"Nope. I'm an only child."

"Oh no. I guess that means you're a spoiled brat, huh?"

"Of course not. I just know that I'm always right, and everyone else thinks I'm the greatest thing that's ever walked this earth."

"Wow. How have you remained so modest?"

"It's definitely a struggle, seeing as how I'm totally awesome. But I manage."

We've both got straight faces, but I notice hers start to crack.

"I wouldn't want you to strain yourself."

"Only a normal person would strain themselves. Luckily, I am abnormal."

That does her in. Holly covers her face as the giggles spill out. She's still holding herself back, but I'm getting closer.

Once she calms down, she starts digging deeper. "Okay. Real question though. So, if you can have this whole setup in the house, why haven't you gone to peritoneal dialysis?"

Back on my kidneys again. At least, when Holly asks me questions, all I pick up on is genuine curiosity, not morbid pity. And it's a valid question. Peritoneal is more portable and can happen while I'm sleeping. If I had the choice, I'd switch to it in a second.

"I tried, but I kept getting infections. So, it just made me sicker. This works best for me. And, besides, now, I get to sit around for hours at a time. It's the American dream." My joke falls flat, only earning a polite smile from Holly.

What I wouldn't give to not have to be reminded of my physical failures almost every day of the week.

"Do you mind ..." Holly hesitates before going on. So far, she hasn't seemed like someone who'd censor herself, and I'm not disappointed. "Can I ask how you ended up on dialysis?"

I don't talk about it much. But again, Holly looks at me in a different way than everyone else. Others tend to stare at the machine like it's a magnet, even when I'm having a conversation with them. Holly waits for my answer, eyes on my face. It's refreshing and disconcerting at the same time.

Then, there's the fact that she's my cure. She deserves to know how I got sick.

"Have you ever heard of the Pacific Crest Trail?"

At her eyebrow raise, I can tell she's got an idea about it.

"I saw that movie *Wild* with Reese Witherspoon. About the woman who hiked on her own. Are you saying you did that?"

She seems impressed, but before she can build up an image of me in her mind, I set the record straight.

"That was my plan. Fred and I were supposed to go after my freshman year of college. We were actually both putting off college for at least a semester to do the whole thing."

That was one of the worst fights I'd ever had with my parents, and I'm pretty sure Fred's mom cried for a week straight when he told her.

"Then, he broke his ankle and had to back out at the last minute. I'd been planning everything for months, so I decided to go alone." Didn't know how much that decision would change my life. "I hiked for three weeks before I started having this really bad pain. It was a kidney stone."

She gives a sympathetic wince.

"The next town was days away, and with the pain, it was hard to hike the normal distance. Then, it didn't pass right, and I got a UTI." One of the most physically painful experiences of my life. "I was feverish and alone. I could barely crawl out of my tent. Much less hike any farther. So, I stayed where I was for close to a week before three guys found me. They were hiking, too. They helped me get to a section of the trail that crossed a road, flagged down a car, and took me to the nearest hospital. I got treated for the infection, but the damage to my kidneys was done. They've gotten worse over the past few years, and I had to start dialysis a little over a year ago."

I don't want to look at Holly. The way I ended up here was all my fault. Just stupid decision after stupid decision, and now, I'm permanently damaged.

Her warm hand slides into my relaxed palm. "That must've been terrifying. I don't know if I would have survived that. Being alone out there and being so sick." She clutches my hand, and when I glance up, there's real fear in her gaze. "I'm glad you made it back okay."

"Well, not completely okay." I roll my eyes toward the machine.

"So what? You're alive, and I've got a spare." She beams at me. "It's going to work out fine."

There's that warmth again, seeping through my chest. Holly's hand is still in mine, and I want to raise it to my lips. But I know I shouldn't, so I simply enjoy the touch of her skin against mine.

A light vibration sounds over the TV. Holly uses her free hand to reach into the back pocket of her jeans and produces a battered cell phone. Whatever she reads has her leaping from the chair, leaving my hand empty.

"Oh, freaking dagnabbit!"

Dagnabbit? Was that English?

"What's wrong?"

Holly starts scooping up her things. "I can't believe I forgot. It's on my list and everything! My adviser, I'm supposed to meet with her in twenty minutes! Do you know where the closest bus station is?" She stares at me.

"Sorry. I don't."

She groans and tries to lace up the shoes I didn't realize she'd slipped off.

"You can't reschedule?"

"I've already done that twice, and she's going to be gone all next week. I don't know the next time I can sit down with her. How far are we from campus? Like jogging distance?"

Her boulder of a backpack swings dangerously as she heaves it onto her shoulders.

"Holly, slow down."

"I can't! This was great, Ben, but I've gotta go!" She's almost to the door.

I'm not ready to see her leave, selfish as I am.

"Holly, wait!" I don't think she's going to listen. "Holly! Take my car!"

Out of sight, I hear her sneakers squeak to a halt on the hardwood floor, and then she's back in the room.

"Take your car?"

"Yeah. You'll never get there on time with the bus. Use my car."

"Are you sure? How will you get back to your place?"

"I'll call Jasper. I'm serious, Holly. Take my car." I fish the keys out of my pocket and dangle them off my finger, as if to tempt her with their jingling.

"Okay, okay. You're a lifesaver." She grabs the keys, but instead of immediately turning to sprint out the door, she leans in and presses her warm lips against my cheek. The caress is over too soon as she backs up with a wave. "I owe you!"

Then, she's gone.

I'm left in my chair, the phantom of her kiss haunting me.

How did something so simple make my skin so hot?

And how can I get her to do it again?

3

HOLLY

"SEE? I told you the coffee was decent." Roderick holds his Styrofoam cup up and grins at me.

"I've had worse." That's honestly the best compliment I can give it. Not that I had high expectations. It is hospital coffee after all.

What I'm really surprised by is my agreement to meet Roderick here. A hospital cafeteria is not our usual spot. Normally, it's his apartment. Specifically, his bedroom.

Roderick works as a resident doctor, and I met him during one of my visits a while back. He's handsome and nice. He also understands the concept of a no-strings-attached relationship, which is exactly what I want.

Or what I wanted.

Honestly, right now, I'm just searching for a way to get a certain person out of the part of my brain where I keep my spank bank. Ben Gerhard should not be spending time next to Sam Claflin, James McAvoy, and Joseph Gordon-Levitt.

Roderick should be there instead. So, when he suggested a coffee get-together during his break, I agreed. I thought normal interaction with the guy I'd been sleeping with might kick my brain back into gear.

No such luck.

"This is nice. Seeing you with your clothes on."

He gives me a winning smile, but my responding chuckle comes out forced. I didn't have to force a laugh with Ben.

Stop it. He's off-limits. No flirty fraternization allowed.

If I'm hoping to get romantic with someone, Roderick is right in front of me, and he's a willing participant. Time to actually put some effort into this.

"So, how's life?"

Wow. What a stimulating question. I should be a moderator at a political debate.

Roderick doesn't seem to mind. "Busy. But that's the life of a doctor. Still have a good portion of my residency left, but they all love me here."

He grins and winks at me, and I try for a genuine smile.

"Well, that's good." I sip my coffee and wonder where my ability to come up with conversation went. Things flowed so easily yesterday with Ben.

No, this is not Ben time. This is Roderick time.

"Any interesting patients lately?" *There, that's decent.*

"Of course. Loads of them. This one woman had pus—"

Nope. My brain shuts down at that word, and I check out for the rest of his story. I'm tempted to ask him if there's a broom closet we could make out in. Not because I'm particularly turned on at the moment. I just don't want to have to talk to him anymore, and that's my go-to solution for occupying his mouth.

"So, Holly"—my name has me focusing back on him—"I was thinking that, sometime—"

His beeper cuts him off, and I praise the universe for the quick save. Roderick grimaces when he glances at it.

"Sounds like someone needs you." My coffee sloshes around as I stand, ready to make my escape. "I should head out anyway. Gotta get ready for my shift."

"Oh, yeah. You still working at that bar?" He stands up next to me, putting his hand on my lower back as we walk toward the door.

"Yep. Pays the bills." My voice comes out squeaky as Roderick moves his hand lower.

When we get to the point where we part ways, he's fully cupping my ass, and I'm coming to the conclusion that our year-long fling has reached its end.

"I'll text you later." He gives my behind a squeeze and leans in for a kiss.

I let it happen but break things off before tongues come into play.

"See ya!" I practically yell as I power-walk away, wanting to get out of this place as fast as possible.

If this had been the end of his shift, then I probably would have let him know we were done. But I'm not going to be responsible for putting him in a pissy mood right before he has to treat some random patient.

I rifle around in my bag until I find my cute striped notebook. After flipping it open to the right page I run down my list of things to do today.

Coffee with Roderick. Check.

I turn to the next page where I've already begun Saturday's list. Time to write in another item.

End things with Roderick.

Decision made. No more doctor booty calls.

Problem is, now, I don't have anyone to distract me from my inappropriate thoughts about a certain pre-law student who shall remain nameless.

Maybe getting sexed up by another guy isn't the answer. I pull out my phone and search for the university's fitness class schedule while I walk toward the bus stop. There's a spin class tomorrow morning.

Perfect. Instead of a guy, I'll straddle a bike.

After digging out a pen, I add the new solution to my list.

Spin class 10:15 a.m.

Now, I just need to make it till then without doing something stupid.

43

~

BEN

The lined paper should be filled with notes. That was the whole reason I shut myself in my bedroom with my textbook. Instead, my pencil has been creating doodles that are now morphing into full-scale drawings.

This is how it always happens. I plan on being productive, but my hand has its own ideas.

At first, it's a few swirls and shapes here and there. Then, my eye catches on something in the room, and I start translating it onto the paper.

So far, I've got my discarded sneakers and the cover of the textbook I'm supposed to be reading chapters from. But I've moved past distraction and on to full-blown procrastination.

I'm stuck on a portrait of Holly laughing. It's a rough sketch of her sitting cross-legged in that chair she dragged into my treatment room. My memories bring back all the little details, like how her tight jeans showed off the smooth curve of her calves and the V-neck T-shirt that shifted enough to the side to reveal a simple white bra strap. My pencil traces her neck in the way I want my mouth to, bringing me up to those petal-shaped lips. The sight of her laughing, eyes closed, hand in her hair, is burned in my brain. I bring it all back to life on my notebook paper.

Then, I crumple the picture in a ball when there's a knock on my door.

"You decent?" Jasper calls out.

"Yeah!" I respond after shoving the evidence of my obsession under a pillow.

He pushes the door open and leans against the frame. "When do you wanna head out?"

When I texted Holly this morning to ask about my car, she suggested I visit her at work. Some bar called Both Ways. I've recruited Jasper to give me a lift again.

"Can you give me twenty minutes?"

"Sure. And I think we need to get Sammy to come with us."

"Is something up?"

Jasper gives me a laugh with little humor. "Something up? Yeah, there is. His fucking blood pressure. I don't know what those professors are saying to them this semester, but he's on edge. Has been for weeks. You haven't noticed?"

"I mean, yeah. But Sammy is always really intense."

I try to think back on the recent times we've talked. There haven't been many. Even though we're the same major, he's a year ahead of me, and he has twice the course load. Doesn't leave much time for chitchat.

"It's gotten worse though. He doesn't do anything other than shove his head in books all day. He needs to take a break. By trickery or by force."

I move to stack my unopened textbooks off to the side of my bed. "Okay. I'm on board. What's the plan?"

Jasper takes a beat before answering, "Well, we're already heading to a bar, so that's a start. We just need to get him to come with us." He pauses again before continuing, "I'll think of something. You just be at the car in twenty minutes and go along with whatever I say. Got it?"

"Aye, aye, captain."

He grins at my mock salute, flipping me off before walking away.

I pull on a clean shirt after reapplying deodorant. Because I'm not likely to fall asleep at a bar, I opt to put in my contacts. Run a comb through my hair, spray on cologne, and I'm good to go.

Tonight should be interesting. Bars aren't my normal hangout, seeing as how I don't drink anymore. Alcohol messes with my delicate hydration balance. Not to mention, I don't want to put strain on any of my other organs. That goes for my liver.

When I walk out to the driveway, Sammy is already sitting in the front seat of Jasper's Mustang. I have to admit, he looks like a different person without a textbook in front of him. His fingers drum impatiently on the dashboard. I wonder what story Jasper came up with.

The moment I slide into the backseat, Sammy turns to throw

questions at me. "What do you know about this speaker? Jasper said that he's discussing corporate law, but that's all he said. Do you at least know his name?" Sammy already has the internet browser up on his phone, ready to Google whatever answer I give.

I've never met a person who loves to research as much as Sammy.

Unable to lie as smoothly as Jasper, I decide to play the ignorant card. "Sorry, I don't know any more than you do. Didn't know there was a speaker until Jasper told me. Where is he anyway?" I'm proud of my smooth subject change.

"Looking for his wallet."

"He's going to take forever. He left it on the back of the upstairs toilet. Why was he even taking his wallet out then?"

I've lost Sammy's attention, as my roommate explores the university's news updates, likely looking for tonight's fictional speaker. Worried we'll be found out, I text Jasper the location of his wallet.

Another minute or so passes before he slides into the driver's seat.

"I can't find anything on this guy. Are you sure tonight is when he's coming to talk?" Sammy holds up his phone as evidence, but Jasper ignores it, turning the car on and backing out of the driveway.

"Trust me, Sammy."

"It's not that I don't trust you. I just think you were misinformed."

"So, just because you can't find anything on it means it's not happening?"

Since I'm in the backseat, I don't have to fight the grin pushing at my cheeks. Jasper loves messing with Sammy.

"It doesn't make sense that they wouldn't put anything on the university's events calendar."

"Maybe you didn't look closely enough." His voice is steady, as if he's not lying straight out of his ass.

"I looked close. Maybe you didn't look close," Sammy mutters the words as he returns to scrolling through his phone.

I can't help a snort that escapes, but I quickly cough to cover up my lapse. Fortunately, Sammy is too absorbed in proving Jasper wrong to notice, but I meet J's eyes in the rearview mirror and watch them crinkle with a hidden smile.

Getting to the bar doesn't take long; it's the parking that's hell. As we're circling another block, I spot a familiar vehicle.

"There's my car!"

"Why is your car here? And why aren't we on campus?" Sammy glances between the two of us, obviously suspicious.

I'm sure we're found out, but Jasper is a manipulative ninja.

"We have to make a pit stop first. Ben lent Holly his car."

"Who's Holly?"

"*Who's Holly?* Are you serious? She's giving Ben her kidney! And she's so cool. You've gotta meet her."

"Meet her? I mean, sure. I'll meet her at some point."

"Nah, we can do it tonight. And check it out!" Jasper slides his car into an empty space. The bar is right around the corner. "Can't waste a primo spot like this. We'll just pop in with Ben, say hi, maybe grab a quick drink, and then head out."

Before Sammy can take the moment he needs to catch up, Jasper jumps out of the car and jogs toward Both Ways. Sammy stares back at me, as if I might explain what is happening, but I just grin and open the door to chase after my friend.

I wonder if Sammy will stay behind in the car in protest. My question is answered when I hear a car door slam and am soon joined by my confused roommate.

Jasper gets in the back of the line by the door, but I wave for him to follow me to the front. When I reach the bouncer, I smile at him in what I hope is not a douchey *I expect to be let in immediately* kind of way. The guy is huge, muscles bulging in his tight black T-shirt, and he has that classic security-guy frown.

"Hi. I'm a friend of Holly's. She said I should give her name at the front door."

A silence extends between us as the guy runs his eyes over me, then Jasper, and then Sammy. I start to worry she never got around to letting him know we were stopping by. After an uncomfortable amount of time, he gives a slight nod.

"IDs."

We all pull out our licenses, which he scans with a handheld device before stamping each of our hands.

"Check the second-floor bar."

I thank him and move through the door before he can change his mind and throw us back out. The first floor has a decent crowd of people all centering around a square-shaped bar. I don't see Holly passing out drinks, so I take the bouncer's advice and look for a set of stairs.

"Back left." Jasper points, and past his finger, I spy our route to the next floor.

"You been here before?"

"Maybe." That and a shrug are all I get.

"Come on. Let's get your keys and head out." Somehow, Sammy is now in the lead, heading for the stairs.

Jasper and I grin at each other and follow along. Poor guy still thinks this is just a side trip.

As we move upward, the background music swells until it fills the air around us. Apparently, the second floor is for dancing. A DJ booth sits back against the wall, leaving a large, clear area for the mass of writhing bodies.

I don't spot the bar right away, and again, Jasper hands out directions. Across the dance floor is an archway leading into another room. That's where we head, weaving through the crowd of sweaty dancers in our own individual ways. Jasper just cuts a straight path. I maneuver and dodge, rather smoothly might I add. When I check to make sure Sammy is still following me, I find my previously surly roommate bopping his head and swaying his hips. He uses his dance moves to jump from partner to partner on his way across the floor.

Through the archway, we find the second-floor bar. I expect the seating up here to be just as crowded, but it looks like most people grab their drinks and head back out to dance. The first bartender I see has thick black hair falling over her shoulders, some dusting the top of her generous cleavage, which is practically resting on the bar as she leans forward to hand two women their drinks. She's the type of person to draw stares with her stunning curves and dark eyes. But she's not the one I'm looking for tonight.

48

Walking farther into the room, I finally find Holly at the other end of the bar, shaking a tumbler as she grins at two guys, laughing at whatever they're saying. I've never been the macho, alpha type, but I have a strong urge to elbow them out of the way and steal Holly's smile for myself. Instead, I move up behind them and wait until they're done getting their drinks.

She's quick, smoothly pouring the liquid into martini glasses and garnishing them with a flourish. "You boys have a good night. Come back and see me when these are empty."

"You know we will!" They clink their glasses together and then saunter away, leaving an empty stool for me to swing myself onto.

"Ben! You made it!" Holly reaches across the counter and gives my forearm a squeeze while smiling at me. Then, she glances behind me to where I assume my roommates are standing. "Hey, Jasper. How's it going?"

"It's good now. Have you met our other roommate?"

"I don't think so." She lets go of my arm and holds out her hand for him to shake.

"This is Sammy."

"Nice to meet you." He grips her hand, but I'm glad to see the shake doesn't linger. Not that I have any reason to expect it would.

At the start of the night, I was excited for the three of us to be hanging out, but now, selfish bastard that I am, I kind of just want to talk to Holly on my own. I'm not rude enough to say that out loud though.

"You'll be wanting your keys, I'm guessing?"

I watch her slide her hand into the back pocket of some high-waisted shorts she's wearing. Up until this moment, I never realized how much emphasis that style puts on a girl's waist. I wonder if I could span my hands completely around her there. Maybe, one day, she'll let me try.

My inappropriate thoughts are cut off by the jingle of keys in my face.

"I might have to draw some directions on a napkin for you to figure out where I parked."

49

"Don't worry; we saw it when we were driving in."

My eyes lock on a bead of sweat running down Holly's neck. I have a clear view because she's pulled her short hair up into a pony-tail with only a few strands falling down in the back. The drop of perspiration traces its way from her shoulder to her collarbone and then disappears beneath the neck of her tank top, straight into the valley between her breasts. My dirty imagination is back in full force as I picture letting my tongue follow the same path.

"Now, who are these handsome gentlemen you have congregating down here, and why don't they have drinks yet?" These husky words come from the other bartender, who has meandered her way to Holly's section.

I wonder if there's competition for customers and tips, but Holly's smile is genuine when she glances at the other woman.

"This is Ben."

The girl's face shows a flash of recognition at the sound of my name. I'm not ashamed to admit, I'm filled with a swell of happiness, knowing that Holly has mentioned me to other people.

"This is Jasper, from my marketing class. And then Sammy here is Ben and Jasper's roommate. Everybody, this is Terra, my roommate slash coworker slash butt-saver for getting me a well-paying job, so I can actually afford rent."

Terra wraps Holly in a one-armed hug at the praise as she waves at us all.

"Now, because of Ben's generosity, you are all lucky enough to receive one free drink of your choice. What'll it be, my good sirs?"

Terra leaves Holly to take our orders as more customers appear.

"Holly, you don't owe me anything. Seriously."

"I'll take a whiskey, neat. Jameson, if you've got it." Apparently, Jasper isn't above cashing in my favors.

Holly smirks and reaches for a bottle on the shelf behind her. Not five seconds later, he's sipping from his glass, a content curve to his mouth.

"And you, Sammy?"

"Huh?"

This whole time, my roommate has been glancing back at the dance floor, an expression of longing on his face. I've never been to a club with him before. Seems like he's a fan. Jasper and I share grins that we keep turned away from him.

"What drink do you want? First one is on the house." Holly waves at the wall of liquor bottles behind her.

"Oh ... I probably shouldn't. I think ... aren't we leaving soon?" He glances at the glass in Jasper's hand.

"We've got time for one drink. Tell the lady what you want." My tricky roommate swirls the amber liquid, as if trying to hypnotize him into misbehaving.

He still looks uncertain.

"Hey, Sammy." All our eyes turn to Holly, who somehow appears both serious and amused. "Terra and I like to play a game sometimes where we guess the drinks people are going to order. How about you let me make you a surprise drink, one I think you'll like? And then you can tell me if I'm wrong or right. Sound good?"

After a moment, he nods reluctantly.

"Okay, prepare yourselves, boys. This is going to be fun."

HOLLY

I only need to observe Sammy for a few seconds to diagnose him.

This man needs tequila.

The recipe is simple.

1. Orange juice
2. Tequila
3. Grenadine
4. Garnish

As my hands move with precision, I try not to let my attention stray back to Ben.

The second he walked through the doorway, I knew he was in the room.

Some people fill the air with energy, like Terra. It can be exhausting, although it does help when working in a dance club. Ben is at the opposite end, giving off a sense of calm steadiness that centers me.

All traces of tension drained from my neck when he leaned against the bar. It's not that I'm super stressed or that I hate my job. Some nights are just louder and more demanding than others. Tonight was one of those until my new friend walked in.

At least, I think he's my friend. What do you call the person you are giving a kidney to and have hung out with once and have borrowed their car and are now giving his roommates free drinks? The closest word I can think of is *friend*.

And that's all we are. Just friends. No need to be admiring the tempting curl of his lips or the unruly hair falling over his forehead, begging me to finger-comb it back into place.

I tear my eyes off Ben, focusing on the task at hand. "There you go, Sammy boy. Take a sip and tell me what you think." I slide the glass across the smooth wood with the exact amount of pressure to ensure it lands directly in front of him.

He hesitates, and I'm guessing it's the colorfulness of the beverage. Tequila sunrises are accurate representations of their name. I pop a cherry in the red-yellow liquid and raise my eyebrows, hoping my expression conveys that I will not back down until he at least tastes it. With a sigh, he picks up the glass, places his lips to the rim, and gives a tentative sip.

He's a goner.

"Holy hell, that's delicious. What is it?"

Success.

"Why don't you finish it, and I'll tell you when you come back for round two?" I lean over the bar and lower my voice, so he has to come in close to hear me. "Now, I've seen you eyeing that dance floor since you walked up to my bar, Sammy. I think you need to take this delicious drink I made you out there and dance your heart out before your wet-blanket friends make you leave."

For a second, I worry I might have read him wrong, but then a reluctant smile spreads over his face.

"I mean, as long as we're not leaving right away."

Then, we lose him as he dashes through the archway, back to the sea of dancing bodies.

"Good team effort! Now, maybe he won't die from stress over-load." Jasper settles onto a free stool at the bar. "So, what made you choose that drink for Sammy?"

"Easy. Tequila, for the dancing. Delicious fruity disguise, so he doesn't realize how drunk he is until it's already happened. And by then, he won't care."

Jasper lets out a roar of laughter while Ben chuckles into his closed fist.

"You're like a bartender therapist. But, seriously, Holly, you've gotta let me pay for the drinks. You really don't owe me for the car."

I shake my head. "Stop it, Ben. You're not supposed to refuse gifts. And, now, it's your turn for a drink!"

"Don't worry about me."

He's gone stiff, and I think I know why.

"I'm not going to give you alcohol. And don't worry; I don't imbibe either. Making sure I'm handing off quality equipment." I wink at him.

Jasper snickers into his whiskey.

Ben's smile returns, but he still shakes his head. "I'm a tough customer. Don't think you can read me as easy as Sammy."

The gauntlet has been thrown.

I lean over the bar and whisper to him, "Silly Ben. Haven't you figured out yet that I know exactly what you need?"

BEN

Holly's flirtatious whisper has me discreetly adjusting myself. I can't tell if she knows the effect she has on me.

At first glance, Holly is an enticing combination of sweet and cute. Then, she takes a string of words that should be innocent and makes them sound like a promise of naughty things to come. Pair that with the fact that she's basically saving my life, and I'm having a hard time with not lusting after her.

Some part of my brain shouts at me that pursuing my donor is wrong. It's a very minor part, and the pounding music from the next room easily drowns it out.

I watch as Holly creates what she claims to be exactly what I need. I hope she's right because I doubt I could decline anything she went through the effort to create.

First, she brings out a stone bowl and fills it with some green leaves, which she grinds up with another stone implement. Then, in one of those drink shakers, she pours in water from a newly opened bottle and then squeezes in a bit of lime. Holly shakes the container with a few flourishes.

"It's more for the effect." Her smile is cheeky, and I don't know how every guy in this bar isn't lined up behind me, clamoring for her attention.

Holly scrapes the mashed leaves into the same type of glass she served Jasper's whiskey in. Then, taking a shot glass, she fills it to the brim with her water-lime mixture, pours the liquid over the leaves, and repeats the action once more. Apparently, this is the end product because she adds a sliver of lime to the rim and pushes the concoction across the bar to me.

"For you, we have wonderfully refreshing lime water with muddled mint leaves. Exactly three ounces." She leans in close again, no longer wearing her showman bartender persona. Instead, she has serious eyes and an encouraging smile. "If you've already reached your daily fluid intake, I won't be offended if you don't drink it. But it's always nice to at least be holding a drink when you're hanging at a bar with your friends."

Before I can say anything, another customer appears, waving for Holly's attention. Back is her friendly grin, and Jasper and I are left alone for the moment. Luckily, he's people-watching, so no one notices me coming to grips with the strange combination of emotions mixing in my head.

Again, my illness was a factor in something as simple as whether I could even order a drink. That was enough to shame me. Then, Holly figured out exactly what I needed. She knew, likely from her brother, that keeping my body fluids balanced was imperative while on dialysis, so she gave me a small, precisely measured drink. And not just a glass of water. No, she found flavors and elements that were acceptable for my strict diet. The kindness of this gesture, delivered right when I felt like crawling into a hole, floors me.

Just to give my mind something else to focus on, I reach for the glass and take a sip.

It's delicious. The taste is fresh and clean, cooling my mouth on its way down. I want to chug the whole thing and ask for another. Instead, I savor the treat.

"You've got a good one there." Jasper takes a break from scanning the room, observing me instead.

He's a sharp guy; he reads people well. No doubt, he knows exactly how gone I am on Holly. We glance down the bar to where she's popping the caps off a couple of beer bottles.

"Problem is that I don't actually have her." I fidget in my seat, trying to shrug off my infatuation. "Besides, I just want us to be friends. She shouldn't have to give her kidney to a complete stranger. She should know me."

Jasper snorts. "Whatever you say."

"What's that supposed to mean?"

"I'm just interested to see if you can actually be around her for months and not try anything. It'd be impressive, is all." Jasper appears so smug.

To prove I don't have to hover near Holly, I get up to search for Sammy. Just to check on the guy. A couple steps past the arched doorway, and I spot him. He's hard to miss.

Sammy owns the dance floor. I had no idea he had any sort of rhythm, but he moves with the beat, lost in his own world. I can't even tell if he's dancing with anyone. Watching my normally rigid roommate let loose and actually enjoy himself has me grinning.

Jasper was right. Sammy's been wearing himself into the ground. And it's not even like he needs to. The guy is insanely intelligent. Whenever someone points this out, he always shrugs off the compliment, claiming he has the typical Asian parents who drive him to overachieve. I've met the Ches, and they are definitely hard customers to please. But, even without their pushing, I don't think Sammy would have any trouble maintaining his 4.0. He doesn't seem to agree most days, which is why nights like tonight are so important.

I'm still pondering the change in him when Sammy opens his eyes and finds me through the crowd. Wearing a huge grin, he weaves his way over to me.

"This place is great! And this drink is delicious!" The glass he holds up is already empty. Realizing this, he frowns and pulls me with him as he beelines for the bar. "Time for round two!"

I laugh at his eagerness and indulge in another sip of my own Holly creation.

HOLLY

I don't know how Sammy is still standing. After his fourth tequila sunrise, I cut him off. There is no part of me interested in cleaning his colorful puke off my bar.

Midnight is approaching, and the guys have been here for hours. Talking to them in between serving drinks makes work more enjoyable than usual. Ben and Jasper stay near the bar, conversing with each other and occasionally throwing out jokes, while their roommate acts like a kid on holiday out on the dance floor.

It's also funny to watch Ben slowly realize what type of establishment he's in. It takes three different guys offering to buy him a drink before understanding flashes on his face. This is an important moment. I want to know how he'll react to the knowledge that I work in a gay bar.

Each time he's approached, Ben politely declines, which is a point in his favor. A lot of insecure men would feel the need to rage and huff, informing all those closest to them that there was no way in hell a man could ever give them a boner.

Yeah, buddy, no one really cares about that, except you and the bigoted people who raised you.

So, Ben earns my approval with his kind but firm refusals.

Getting hit on is one thing; finding out that the entire clientele tends to be homosexual is the next level up. He scans the room, coming to focus on a generously tattooed woman ogling Terra's chest as she slides her a very generous tip.

Sorry, lady, she's taken.

Terra is a fantastic flirt, but that's as far as it goes. She has an iron-clad commitment to her girlfriend, Faith, who's currently stationed in Afghanistan with her Army unit. Terra's just working for the tips, and most nights, she comes home with at least fifty bucks more than me. I'm plenty friendly, but patrons come to me when they want drinks made quickly and with precision, and they go to Terra for a gorgeous rack to admire. You don't have to be a straight dude to love boobs.

Ben turns to look at me, and I can see the question on his face. Suddenly, I get the urge to clarify that I am *very* interested in men.

"No, it's not a requirement to work here."

He flinches at my called-out comment but then smiles ruefully. "Just wondering."

I collect the payment for the three beautiful blow-job shots I just crafted and then sidle back to Ben and Jasper.

"No problem. As long as you don't have an issue with people who are." I don't miss the way Ben's eyes flick to Jasper.

On occasion, I've seen Jasper in here, but I wasn't sure if Ben knew. Seems like he does. Another good sign.

"Nope. Not at all."

I've known Ben for only about a week, but everything I've discovered so far indicates that he's a decent guy. I'd still give him my kidney even if he were a jerk. It's not like having a bad attitude means you should get a death sentence. Still, knowing that my donation will help out a good person eases a stressful clench in my chest that I just realized was there.

My self-reflection is interrupted by the appearance of a very cocky Sammy. "Read 'em and weep, losers." He throws down a handful of trash on the bar before taking a sip of a drink I definitely did not serve him.

"Sammy"—I use my most motherly tone—"where'd you get that drink?"

He grins around his straw and taps the trash pile. "I have many new friends. They like to give me things."

Ben picks through the crumpled napkins and paper scraps. "These all have phone numbers on them."

"That's right." Sammy grins and takes another tug on his straw.

"But all the names are guys' names. Sammy, you're straight. Remember?" Ben explains in a voice you'd use with a child.

Jasper snorts behind his fist.

Sammy glances at the numbers—I count six—that he's collected. He appears thoughtful. After a moment, he shrugs and smiles wide again. "Doesn't matter. Conclusion is still the same."

"And that is?" Ben's voice comes out strained, like he's trying to hold back laughter.

"That Sammy Che is hot!" he declares while flexing some arm muscles that aren't too shabby.

His buddies both crack up but give him some friendly slaps on the back.

"Okay, we've reached the *talking in third person* threshold. I think it's time to call it a night." Jasper pulls out his wallet to pay for the one other whiskey he drank.

"What? Nooo ..." Sammy moans while glancing back to the dance floor.

"Yes. Time to go. Actually, it's time to find you some food to soak up all that fruity liquor you've been sucking down. What do you say to a cheesesteak, buddy?"

This gets his spirits back up. "Geno's?"

Jasper grumbles, "You know I'm a Pat's guy."

"But, please ..." Sammy gives a very convincing, sad puppy-dog face.

Jasper sighs in defeat. "Fine. But, if you puke in my car, we're going to Pat's. Got it?"

"Deal."

"Okay, now, pay Holly for your drinks." Jasper talks to him like a dad would to his toddler. It's adorable.

I already have Sammy's tab closed out and his receipt ready to be signed, which he does with a dramatic flourish.

"Nice to meet you, Holly. Thanks for the drinks. And the kidney." He bends at the waist in a low bow, catching me off guard. The formalness of the gesture is effectively ruined when he pops up, shoves Jasper, and yells, "Race you to the car!" before sprinting away.

"Goddamn it, Sammy! Wait up!" Jasper throws a bill on the bar and runs after him.

When I glance at Ben, he's just shaking his head and chuckling. He's probably used to their shenanigans.

"I like your friends. They're fun." I'm still smiling as I collect their payment but stop short when I see the amounts. First off, Jasper paid me twenty bucks for one drink, and secondly, Sammy gave me a one hundred percent tip. "Shoot. You might want to text them to come back. They both way overpaid me."

Ben glances at the receipt and bill when I show him but just gives a shrug. "Don't worry about it. That's normal."

Ah, apparently, Jasper and Sammy are just as well off as Ben's family. Still, I hesitate.

"Are you sure? I meant to treat you, not swindle your friends out of money." Even if accepting it would take a good chunk out of this month's electricity bill.

"Seriously, Holly. It's not a big deal."

Maybe not to him. Reluctantly, I slip the receipt into the register and cash out the tip.

"Do you want another?" When I look back at Ben, he's covering a jaw-cracking yawn.

The poor guy notices me watching and smiles apologetically. "Sorry. I'm not bored, I swear."

"Come on, Ben. I get it." I reach over and pat his arm. "You're doing better than Marcus. I'm not sure I've ever seen him stay up later than eleven. Even on New Year's Eve." As I retract my hand, I take his glass with me. "I'm going to have to cut you off and send you home. Driving while tired is as bad as driving drunk." My stern voice returns, but I take road safety very seriously.

The slow curve of his lips causes a strange clenching sensation in my abdomen. That's been happening a lot tonight. First was when I met his eyes and found no glasses barricading me from the smooth dark green of his irises. Then, there was the moment when he ran his fingers through his red-gold hair as he laughed at one of Jasper's jokes. And, now, that sleepy smile is triggering it again.

Interesting.

Dangerous.

This is something I need to address when I am alone.

"You're probably right."

"You'll find, I usually am."

His smile grows wider at my retort.

Ben slides off his stool, and now, I'm kicking myself for saying he should go. Getting through the last part of my shift seems like torture now that I won't have my distraction here.

"Thanks again. For the car, I mean. But also for hanging out with me. You made the night go by faster."

Ben leans his arms on the bar. The fabric strains over his fore-arms, and I'm tempted to reach out and touch him. Instead, I pick up an empty glass and pretend to dry it off just to keep my hands busy.

"You're welcome. I had fun." He stands up straight but hesitates, drumming his fingers on the bar surface.

I don't want him to go. He should though. I think I need him to.

"So, I guess I'll see you around."

A couple of people approach the bar with intent. A good reason to take my eyes off his. I put my glass down and move to help them.

"Holly." Ben saying my name jerks my focus back to him. "Text me. If you want to hang out. Even if you just need a ride somewhere. Or, you know, a car to drive with a person in the passenger seat."

His smile holds laughter, and there goes that darn clenching again.

"Will do, Ben. Have a good night."

"You, too." Then, he surprises me by scooping up the hand I left resting on the bar, bringing it to his lips, and giving my knuckles a light kiss. "See you soon."

Then, he's gone almost as fast as Sammy, and I'm left wondering why the guy I'm planning on giving my kidney to has such a strange effect on the rest of my body.

4

HOLLY

"You're doing too much."

I glance up from my textbook to the simmering soup on the stove-top. "No, I'm not. I'm just studying until it's ready."

Pops shakes his head at me as he leans on the doorframe between the kitchen and the front hallway. He's still got on his uniform, the jumpsuit covered in grease stains from all the cars he's been under during the day. Mondays are usually his long days, trying to catch up with the weekend drop-offs.

"That's not what I meant. Well, yeah, it kinda is." He lets out a deep sigh as he runs his hand over his face and sits at the kitchen table across from me. "You've got too much going on. School, your jobs, the clubs, and the kidney donation. Pile on top of that, you coming here, cooking for me? It's too much, sweetie. You need to slow down."

"I'm fine." That comes out more defensive than I meant it to.

"Maybe right now. But this'll wear you out fast."

I breathe in deep through my nose, reminding myself that he's just trying to take care of me. It's been his job since I was ten, so it's probably hard to let go. "Trust me, Pops; I've got it all under control. Look." Reaching into my bag, I pull out my striped notebook, my day planner, and my monthly calendar. "See? I've already organized all my days. It's all set." My fingers run over the lovely color-coded schedules, and I find myself relaxing at the sight of the organization.

Pops pinches his bottom lip between his fingers as he scans everything. "And which of these colors is for fun?"

"Huh?" I turn the calendar toward me, not understanding what he means.

"Where's your break? When do you relax? Spend time with your friends?"

He stares at me, eyes sad, and I shift in my seat.

"I see Terra every day." I'm back to defensive.

Pops starts using my fantastic scheduling skills against me. "Look here. Class. Class. Work. Club meeting. Doctor appointment. Study. Class." He ticks each off like they're offensive. "Right there. Saturday. You should be doing something fun, but you just made it a whole day of studying and work. Come on, Holly. I want to see you give yourself a break." His Southern accent is starting to get thicker, which means he's actually getting agitated.

Pops moved from Atlanta to Philly to live with his uncle when he was fifteen after his parents died. He tried really hard to get the twang out of his voice, so he could fit in, but it's never gone away completely.

"I do."

"When? Write it in this fancy schedule. I want to see it here or else."

He scowls at me, but I give it right back.

"Or else what?" I don't live under his roof anymore. I'm my own woman, and I can live my days however I please.

"Or else I'll tell your brother."

Crap.

"You wouldn't."

Pops raises his thick eyebrows, daring me to test him. He'll do it. I know he will. And he knows one of the things I hate most in this world is worrying my brother. Marcus should be focusing on his own health, not whether or not I'm overextending myself.

Grumbling under my breath, I pull the calendars back to my side of the table. I guess Saturday doesn't have to be *all* studying. It pains me to write over the neatly drawn boxes. I use colored pens once I have everything mapped out, and now, it's like a toddler scribbling on a Monet.

After adding *Break* to all my Saturdays, I go to set my pen down, but Pops's voice stops me.

"And?"

"And what?"

He taps the calendar. "Sometime during the week, too." When I just glare, he pulls his phone out of his pocket. "Wonder if Marcus would agree with me."

"Fine!" I throw my hands up and then scan the week. Thursday is the only other day with a huge chunk set aside for studying. Going with Ben to his treatment the other week didn't throw off my schedule, even with my meeting oversight, so I take a chunk out of that day, too. "Happy?"

My adoptive father looks over the calendar, and I swear, I'm ready to scream when he goes to point at something else. It's the Monday evening box labeled *Make Pops dinner/Study*.

"Change that. Now, it's *Takeout with Pops and gin rummy*."

He grins at me, and I melt. How can I stay mad when all his meddling comes from love?

"Okay, you win." I make the change.

He stands up and pulls a deck of cards out of his pocket. "Not yet, but I will."

～

BEN

Holly only came with me once, over a week ago, but walking into my parents' house without her depresses me. The idea of sitting in that chair for hours with only a TV to distract me is torture.

To put off the inevitable, I search the house for my parents. I find them in the sky library. That's what I named it when I was ten, and it stuck. The way the bookshelves are only broken up by windows revealing the tops of buildings always gives me the sense of sitting above everything. Floating in the sky.

Muted light spills from the lamps, just bright enough to read by. Dad sits in his work clothes. He's removed his shoes, tie, and jacket, and rolled up the sleeves of his shirt. When I was younger, I knew this meant I could climb into his lap because he was out of work mode. Tonight, he has some papers in front of him, glasses sitting low on his nose as he reads.

His file is propped on top of my mom's feet, which rest in his lap as she stretches lengthwise on the couch. She's wearing one of her silk nightgowns, but she still has a string of pearls around her neck. Her fingers run over the smooth beads as she reads a well-worn novel.

This is classic Mom and Dad. I'm one of the lucky ones with parents who've found a way to battle their issues and maintain their love, even after twenty-six years of marriage. Watching them together warms my chest but also brings focus to an empty section inside me.

What is that kind of love like? How do I find something that fits so well?

I've dated plenty, all nice girls I should've been happy with. But it never felt right. There was always a gap between us, a fake face I wore like a mask. Even before I got sick. Now, it's worse. I can barely stand myself in the mirror, imagining what other people see.

Sick. Dying.

That's got to be why I'm hung up on Holly. It's not that I'm attracted to her really. She's just the answer to my health issues. Once she heals me, I can be comfortable with myself again.

"Oh! Ben, you scared me!" My mom clutches her chest, smiling and shaking her head at me. "Why are you lurking in the doorway?"

I shrug. "Just thinking."

"Everything all right?" Dad scans me from feet to forehead.

Searching for any indication that I'm not well. At least, more not well than usual.

"Yeah. I'm fine. Guess I'm just putting it off."

Like synchronized performers, they frown simultaneously. The pity does nothing but make my neck itch. I shouldn't have said anything.

"Honey, do you want me to come sit with you? We can watch a movie together."

She offers to keep me company all the time, even saying she'll work later on the mornings I get my treatment done. But, no matter how cold and calculating Victoria Gerhard is in the courtroom, she can't hide the devastation of watching her only son hook up to a machine in order to continue living the semblance of a healthy life. It's better for both of us if she keeps her distance.

"Nah. That's okay. I'll leave you to …" I lean forward to read the title of the book in her lap and give a scoff when I make out the words.

"Don't you dare insult *Jane Eyre*." Mom waves a scolding finger at me, and Dad chuckles as he returns to his papers.

My hands rise in surrender as I back out of the room. "Of course not. Charlotte Brontë can do no wrong."

"That's right. Don't you forget it."

From the shadows of the hallway, I spy on them a bit longer, not ready to leave the peacefulness of their presence for the cold hum of a machine.

Dad lets his hand rest on one of the bare feet cradled in his lap and gives a gentle squeeze.

"Benjamin Gerhard." Mom always refers to my dad as Benjamin, so I know she isn't calling me back.

"What?" His shoulders rise and fall, but I catch the sneaky curl of his lip.

"Just know that my foot is in a very precarious position if you decide to try anything."

Dad grins, but he retracts his hand. "Yes, dear."

Like stepping from the warmth of a bonfire into a frigid winter night, I descend the stairs.

Once I'm plugged in, I try watching a movie. Maybe *Die Hard* will do the trick. But, every time I start to get absorbed, my arm throbs, and I'm pulled right back out. A groan of frustration leaks from my throat. Luckily, my parents are still a floor away and don't hear me.

If only Holly were here. Treatments seem even harder now that I know what it's like with her next to me. Holly didn't pity me or look at me like I was less of a person. The needles grossed her out, but she put that on her fears and issues. Not me.

Around her, I forget the discomfort.

Not giving myself time to reconsider, I lean to the side, so I can slide my phone out from my back pocket.

Over the past week, we've exchanged a few texts. Just the basics, like me telling her I got home safe after the bar and her asking how Sammy's hangover was treating him. I've wanted to see her again, but if I show up outside of her class, I'll feel like I've crossed over from friendly acquaintance to stalker. Just because I can't stop thinking about her doesn't mean she wants to spend time with me.

But texting her isn't a big deal. Friends do it all the time.

Ben: *How do you feel about Die Hard?*

There's no guarantee I'll hear back anytime soon.

I wonder where Holly Foster is on a Monday night. Class? Studying? Working? Or maybe she's hanging out with her boyfriend. It seems unlikely that someone as kind and sexy as her would be single. Selfishly, I want that to be the case. I almost asked her at the bar but held off for two reasons. First, I reasoned she might get uncomfortable if she thought I was hitting on her. Second, I was afraid of her answer.

My phone vibrates.

Holly: *One of the best holiday movies I've seen.*

Damn, this girl keeps getting better.

Ben: *Of course. So much better than A Christmas Story.*
Holly: *Definitely. But everything is better than A Christmas Story.*
Ben: *You don't like A Christmas Story? It's a classic!*
Holly: *That classic gave me nightmares of ginger-haired bullies and getting my tongue frozen to a lamppost. It took me weeks to get over it! No, thank you.*
Ben: *Guess I won't be giving you a sexy leg lamp for Christmas then.*
Holly: *Only if you want to get smacked in the face with it.*

I snicker at the thought of Holly chasing after me, waving that iconic lamp as a threat.

Holly: *So, whatcha doin'?*
Ben: *Dialysis. I'm bored. Entertain me!*

A few minutes pass, and I wonder if I was too demanding. Then, my phone buzzes repeatedly.

Holly is calling me.

I sit up straighter and fix my rumpled shirt. As if she could somehow see me.

"Hey."

"Hey there," she speaks softly, and I hear some rumbling in the background.

"How're you doing tonight?"

"I'm good. On the bus. Coming back from my dad's. So, you're bored, huh?"

"To tears. Tried watching *Die Hard*, but it's just not working for me tonight. Thought I'd see what's up with you."

"Well, I just got soundly beat in a game of gin rummy, so my pride's a bit dinged up. And I've still got a chapter to read for my class in the morning."

"Digital marketing, right? With Jasper?"

"Yeah. Thank the universe he's in that class. Everyone else drives me crazy." Even over the phone, I can hear the smile in her voice.

If I were a good guy, I'd be happy the two of them were close. Instead, petty jerk I am, I get the urge to give her a detailed recounting of the morning our freshman year when I found my roommate passed out outside our dorm room, wearing a tube top and booty shorts with half of his head shaved. With effort, I keep it to myself.

"Yeah, he told me about the time you put someone in their place. Gave him a verbal beatdown?"

Her chuckle is low, sending goose bumps over my chest and down my legs. "Well, that's what happens when you get on my bad side."

"I'll keep that in mind."

"Oh, Benny boy," she sighs out the nickname, and I'm shifting in my seat, suddenly restless. "You are so far from my bad side; you'd have to take a weeklong road trip just to catch sight of it."

Her confession knocks me on my ass. I swallow multiple times while I try to come up with some witty response.

"Same." *Nailed it.*

Holly laughs again. "So, are you at the beginning or getting to the end of your session?"

"Pretty much exactly halfway. Been here for an hour. One more to go."

"Only two hours?"

"Yeah. Two hours on Mondays and two hours on Tuesdays. Then, I get three hours on Thursdays and Saturdays."

"And it's working for you?"

"As much as it can. Can't wait to get all this time back though." The moment I say it, I realize how that could stress her out. "Sorry. I know you've still got all the checkups. No pressure. Seriously."

"It's okay. I get it. Actually, I've got one of my first appointments tomorrow."

"You nervous? 'Cause of the needles and everything?"

"Ugh, don't remind me." The humor leaves her voice, and I miss it. "I've had blood drawn before, obviously. So, I can do it."

Holly sounds off now. And it's all my fault.

"You definitely can." Wanting to get the happiness back in her voice, I change the subject. "Anything interesting happen since I saw you last?"

"Hmm ... let me think." Through the phone speaker, I hear her humming to herself. "Oh, yeah! I almost got into a fight at work on Saturday!"

"Really? What happened?"

Holly proceeds to tell me a story of a bachelorette party with a bridezilla to rival all others.

"Then, when I told her I had to cut her off—and this is after four tequila shots and three Long Island iced teas, I remind you—she literally jumped up on the bar to get at me!"

"No!"

"Yes! And, the whole time, she was yelling about how I was ruining her special day."

I'm too shocked to laugh, but Holly punctuates the story with her sweet chuckles.

"Did she reach you?"

"No. Terra saw what was happening, so she was already on the other side of the bar, ready to call for security. When this lady started climbing, Terra grabbed her by the hair and pulled her off. You do not want to mess with Terra. She held her until Jimmy, our security guy, came to carry her out."

"That's insane." Knowing that Holly got out okay, I give in to the urge to laugh along with her.

"Well, that's what I get, working in a bar."

"Do you like it there? When you're not getting attacked by drunken bachelorettes?"

That earns me another chuckle, but then her tone turns thoughtful.

"Yeah, I do. For now. The pay is good, and the people are nice. Curt—he owns the bar—lets me help him with the books at the end of the night, so I can get an idea of what running a business is actually like. Honestly, I think that's been more helpful than half of my classes."

"So, that's what you want to do? Own a bar?"

"Not a bar. But, yeah, I definitely want to own a business one day. I haven't figured out what yet, but I don't think I want anything to do with food service. The hours are just too crazy."

"I could see you running a business."

"Really? You've known me for only a few weeks."

"Yeah. But you have that kind of presence. People listen to you."

"Most people say I'm bossy." Her voice betrays her dislike of that description, and I make a note never to call her that.

"I'd call you confident and commanding. But those are good things." I really can't think of any bad things about Holly.

"You're sweet, Ben. I—"

My breath stops, on pause until I hear her speak again.

"Sorry. I just realized my stop is next. I should go."

My good mood dims, but I keep the disappointment out of my response. "No problem." And, because I'm fucking stuck on her, I tack on what I hope sounds like a casual thought. "The offer about my car still stands. If you don't want to take the bus next time."

"Noted. Night, Ben."

"Good night, Holly."

She cuts the call off on her end first. I lay the phone on the armrest and stare at the TV screen, not really watching. Instead, I replay our conversation, remembering how her laugh sounded and the warmth her voice brought to my chest.

How is it that Holly can take my mind off a shitty situation like no one else can?

The second half of my treatment is almost over, and I didn't even notice being hooked up once her voice was in my ear.

This is bad.

Holly is starting to feel like a lot more than just my donor. I want her around me all the time, not just on the day of my surgery.

I don't just want her kidney. I think I want all of her.

5

HOLLY

AIR WHISTLES in and out through my nose because my teeth are clenched too tight for me to gasp in through my mouth the way my lungs want me to.

1. Don't cry.
2. Don't throw up.
3. Don't panic.
4. Repeat.

Over and over, I run down the list in my head as Dr. Williams draws multiple blood samples from my inner elbow. My mind reels at the pinch of the tiny metal needle sliding through my skin. I have a *living inside a horror movie* amount of fear coursing through me.

Rain pounds on the window, pairing perfectly with the torment in my head and chest. Maybe, if I can focus on the streams of water flowing down the glass, I won't feel the sharp, cold needle puncturing my vein.

Nope. Not working.

1. Don't cry.
2. Don't throw up.
3. Don't panic.

"Deep breath, Holly. We're all done," Dr. Williams speaks kindly as she secures gauze to my arm with a bright purple wrap.

I try to do as I was told, but my jaw locks up.

"You did good. We'll give you a call in a week or so when we get your results back from the lab, but as long as nothing has changed since last time, we can move to the next step."

I should say *thank you* or smile. All I can manage is a nod before I stiff-leg my way out of the exam room, down the hall, through the waiting room, and straight into the restroom where I lock myself in a stall. I don't even take a second to wipe down the seat before I collapse onto it and stick my head between my knees, fighting off the dizziness and nausea.

After a slow count to sixty, I'm able to stand and leave the stall. My hands still shake as I splash cold water on my face. Knowing that I would be soaked in stress sweat, I packed my deodorant in my purse this morning, which I now reapply generously.

In the mirror, I'm the worst version of myself—helpless and scared. There's no makeup on my face because I didn't want it to run and smear if I ended up crying. But this also means there's nothing to cover the dark bags of a sleepless night or to smooth out the blotchy redness of my anxious cheeks.

Needles always do this to me.

"It's not the same thing. This isn't like Mom. You won't disappear." My voice rattles over the words. "You're in control."

But saying it doesn't make it true.

I bend at the waist, pressing my forehead into my palms as I grasp at composure.

"It's worth it. It's all worth it."

I'm saving Marcus. Well, really, I'm saving Ben, but it's all connected.

Still, knowing that the reason is altruistic doesn't remove my animalistic fear. That tiny metal device destroys me. It makes me feel dirty.

I slide my trembling fingers into my purse, pull out my phone, and navigate to Marcus's number. My thumb hovers over the Call button.

I want my brother to talk me down, to calm my shattered nerves. That's always been his job.

He got me ice packs for my bruises and covered my eyes during scary movies. He hugged me when I was crying and defended me when I was bullied. He made my meals and picked me up from school. His steady presence was the anchor in a stormy childhood.

But I don't press the button. He has a real job now, and it's not taking care of me. Every day, he suffers because of something real, and here I am, falling apart because of a standard checkup.

It's time to stop putting my irrational fears on him.

Unfortunately, deciding not to bother my brother doesn't make leaving the restroom any easier. The idea of walking three blocks in a torrential downpour, so I can catch a bus that will in turn drop me off another four blocks from my apartment is depressing. Even though I'm successfully holding the tears back right now, I'm not sure that miserable commute wouldn't put me over the edge.

I need to be calm. I need to be in control.

Maybe it's not the healthiest solution, but I've recently found one way to get both of those things.

My phone practically dials itself, and he picks up on the second ring.

"Hey, Holly! What's up?"

"Hey, Ben. Are you busy right now?"

"Not really. Just got out of class and was about to grab lunch. Why?"

"Is that offer for a ride still on the table?"

"Send me your address. I'll leave now."

Ready at a moment's notice, like he's Superman. Pairs well with my current damsel-in-distress situation.

"I'm at Dr. Williams's office. Do you remember where that is?"

"Yeah. I'll be there in fifteen. Twenty at most."

"Okay. Text me, and I'll come out to your car. Thanks for doing this. I owe you."

"Stop saying you owe me. If anyone is in debt, it's me. See you in a few."

He hangs up before I can think of a response.

I attempt to smooth out the shaking in my hands and fix the mess that is my hair. Sometimes, I tug at it to calm my nerves.

Almost exactly fifteen minutes after I called him, Ben texts me that he's outside.

When the front glass doors slide open, he's waiting with an umbrella. "Not sure if you brought one."

"I could kiss you, Ben."

He gives me a funny look, but I just latch on to his arm, so we can both stay dry. The doctor's office has a small parking lot, so his car doesn't have to loiter on the street. Without even reminding him, Ben opens the driver's door for me before collapsing the umbrella and rushing to the passenger side.

When we're both ensconced in the warm, dry car, I take a moment to appreciate the firm steering wheel gripped in my palms.

I'm driving the car. I'm in control.

"You okay?" he speaks carefully, and I hate it. I'm not made of glass.

"Yeah. It's just ..." I let out a heavy sigh because I know how ridiculous my explanation will sound. "The needles. They get to me." My head falls back against the seat, and I do my slow-breathing exercises.

"Can I do anything?" He sounds lost.

"I don't know. I guess, talk to me about something. Anything." Simply being around him is helping. My pulse isn't racing anymore, just taking an energetic jog.

"I blew up a toilet once."

I choke on unexpected laughter.

"What?"

When I turn my head to glance at him, he's nodding.

Ben is wearing his glasses again today. I like the way the wire rims frame his eyes. His hair is damp from the rain, which brings it to an almost auburn hue. He's man-spreading in the passenger seat, taking up all the space available to him, and he's shifted slightly to face me.

"My cousin snuck some firecrackers into school one day. He showed them to me in the restroom, and I decided it'd be cool to light one. When it started going off, I panicked. Threw it in the toilet." He's grinning at me as my mouth gapes open. "But it kept going. The whole toilet bowl cracked. Water was spraying everywhere. It was bad."

Hilarity builds in my chest and busts out of me. "That's idiotic!"

Ben's chuckling right along with me. "I know. We were so stupid. They suspended us for a week. Lucky we didn't get expelled."

I cover my face as I snort. An image of a wide-eyed younger Ben next to a gushing toilet fills my mind, and it just sets me off more.

As my giggling rolls out, my anxiety fades.

BEN

Watching Holly crack up helps ease my guilt.

But it's not gone completely because this is all my fault. Normally, people have to get blood drawn maybe once a year, and then they can forget about needles and injections until that time cycles around again.

Holly's just getting started.

If this is what she goes through from a quick needle stick, how is she going to deal with an IV in her arm come surgery time?

It's enough to make me want to tell her to back out.

But would she listen?

And would I see her again?

She lets out a long sigh after her giggles trail off.

"Okay, I'm better. Where are we headed?"

Maybe she's good to drive, but she still seems rattled. Her hands clench the steering wheel with a white-knuckled grip.

"What do you think would make you happy? Something we could do right now."

Surprise flashes over her face, and then she turns thoughtful. After a few seconds, Holly gifts me with one of her sweet smiles. "Almond croissants."

I can't help but laugh at her tone, filled with longing and reverence.

"You have a place in mind?"

She nods vigorously, and I chuckle some more, mostly from relief.

"Then, by all means, take me to these glorious pastries."

Holly goes to pull the car out of the parking lot.

"So, Ben, tell me about yourself."

The request sounds forced, but I don't mind distracting her.

"What do you want to know?"

I wait as she clicks the blinker on for a left-hand turn.

"Why are you pre-law?"

Of course. *The* question. It always comes up, and I always give the idealistic answer about challenging myself and serving the public. But I don't want to bullshit Holly. Also, I'm pretty sure she'd see right through me and call me on it.

So, I give her a bit of the truth.

"It's the family business. Both my parents are lawyers, and so was my grandfather, Benjamin the second, and his father before him, Benjamin the original. I grew up around legal talk. I understand it. It's a safe bet for me."

"Wow. That's a lot of Benjamins. And lawyers. You find it easy then?"

I lean back in my seat, letting Holly's questions sink in. "I wouldn't say easy. Even going part-time, my days are pretty full of studying and writing papers. And this is just undergrad. From the stories I've heard, law school is when the real grind starts." I try not to grimace as I think about it.

"Do you enjoy law?"

Do I enjoy law? I think back, trying to remember if I've ever been asked that before. Nothing comes to mind. It's always been whether or not I'm good at it, which I'm sure I can be.

"Some of it is interesting. And, if you work at a successful firm, then you can make a pretty good living."

Holly snorts as she merges into another lane. "Way to give me a non-answer, Ben. I wasn't asking how big your salary would be. I want to know if you enjoy it. If you look forward to becoming a lawyer one day. Does it excite you? Make you happy?"

"Not everyone is going to be super over-the-top happy about their job. Making a decent living is important."

When did this turn into a debate? And why do I feel like I'm arguing for the wrong side?

"Yeah, I get that. For a lot of people, making enough money to support their family is what makes them happy. But that's usually because they come from a place of financial instability. You come from a well-off family, so you have the freedom to explore multiple avenues."

I open my mouth, on the verge of speaking, when I realize that I have nothing to say. Luckily, Holly stops me with a shake of her head while still keeping her eyes solidly on the midday traffic.

"Sorry. I'm attacking you. Let's just table that. Instead, answer me this; if money and career stability weren't issues, what would you choose to do?"

That has my mind stumbling, and I blurt out my question without thinking, "No family expectations?"

We're at a red light, so she can safely take her gaze off the road and examine me. Those dark eyes of hers see more than I want them to.

"No family expectations." The light turns green, and she smoothly moves us forward.

Again, I debate on giving a false answer, saying, *I don't know,* or, *I've never thought about it.*

But how could I lie to a girl who called for my help when she was vulnerable? That's a dick move.

With a deep breath, I make a decision. "I can show you."

~

HOLLY

"Show me?" I flick my eyes over to his side of the car but only for a second because Philly traffic is not something you can navigate on instinct.

Still, my nanosecond glance catches Ben's fingers reaching for the top button on his shirt. Another quick peek and another button undone.

"Dude, if you want to be a stripper, then go for it, just not while I'm driving."

Ben's hands stop. "Hmm. That's an idea. Probably make some decent cash at it. What would my stage name be?" He taps a finger against his chin like he's in deep thought. "Ben the Pre-Law Player?" I snort, and he grins. "What about the Dirty Dialysis Dancer?"

I chew my lip as I think and then start bouncing in excitement. "Oh, oh, I know! Benjamin Get-Hard the Fourth!"

There's a pause, and then the joyous sound of his laughter booms through the car. It's infectious, and I find myself grinning along with him.

Once he catches his breath and wipes the tears from his eyes, he returns to the task of unbuttoning his shirt.

"Seriously, Ben, why are you ..." My question peters off because I finally catch a glimpse of what he's revealing. Then, I get an eyeful.

A car horn honks, and I flinch, realizing I've slowed down at a green light.

"Okay, wait. I can't drive while you're doing this. Just give me a second."

Thankfully, he nods, and I check for open spaces along the sidewalk. Once I've pulled into an empty spot, I put the car in park and turn to face him.

"Are those tattoos?"

Ben nods again and releases a few more buttons until he's revealed close to half of his chest.

Like the ink on his skin is magnetic, I can't help reaching over to touch the designs. My fingers hesitate before they land on his skin because, even if we're friends, that doesn't mean I can start feeling him up without his permission. Instead, I meet his wide eyes.

"Do you mind?"

Tight-lipped, he shakes his head, so I finish my gesture, fingering the first tattoo I caught sight of. From what I can see, it appears to be the bow of a ship, and when I push his shirt open further, the rest of it is exposed along with more pictures. There's a shovel with a pair of shoes dangling from the handle, a bat in flight, a castle surrounded by trees, and the head of a blue dragon.

The tattoos are not a continuous scene, but somehow, the shapes and lines of each seem to complement each other. Ben has a colorful collage on his chest, and it's all I can do to keep from undoing the last few buttons to discover how far it goes.

"These are amazing! How many do you have?"

"I stopped counting after twenty." His voice sounds weird.

When I take my eyes off his ink, I find Ben watching me with his lips pinched tightly between his teeth.

Does he think I'll judge him?

Honestly, I'm just trying to let my mind catch up.

Never would I have guessed that glasses-wearing Ben with his pre-law status and rich family would reveal this. Sure, tattoos are becoming more popular, and if he'd told me he had one or two, I wouldn't have thought much about it. But this is a different level.

"How far do they go?" I brush my hand down his warm chest to emphasize my question.

He shivers under my touch.

We're getting close fast, but I can't seem to retract my hand. I want to see more.

Ben clears his throat. "My whole chest and back. Shoulders. My upper thighs and ... my ass."

Normally, curse words put me on edge and make me flinch. But, when Ben lets that one slip, my cheeks warm as I imagine what kind of ink he might have on those firm mounds.

I need to stop touching him before I ask for a private show.

With the will of an Amazon warrior, I pull myself back and settle into my seat, hands tucked in my lap, fingers laced so that I won't stretch them out for another caress. There's been enough time spent touching my new friend. He's not a goat in a petting zoo.

"So, you made sure you could cover them up?"

"Exactly. Tattoos might be more mainstream now, but no one wants a lawyer who's sporting visible ink. Also, my parents ..." He lets that sentence trail off as he pops the buttons back in place.

As his chest disappears, I want to protest, but I can't think of a logical reason to demand that he not wear a shirt.

"Your parents don't know about them?"

Ben gives a half-shrug, half-headshake. "They know I have a few. But they've never been fans, so I stopped telling them."

He reaches up to scratch his neck, and I'm suddenly very annoyed at Mr. and Mrs. Gerhard.

"I'm sorry. I think they're beautiful."

"Beautiful?" He looks at me like I'm talking crazy.

"Yeah, Ben. Your tattoos are beautiful. Deal with it." I lightly punch his shoulder, trying to be playful. And also maybe because I'm having a hard time with not touching him. "Do they mean anything?" The pictures seem personal.

"Each one is a book I've read."

"Really?" I want to rip his shirt open for a chance to guess which ones. "What's the ship for?"

"*Treasure Island.* My granddad read it to me when I was a kid." His voice has gone heavy with memory.

"The shovel and shoes?"

"*Holes* by Louis Sachar."

"Nice. I loved that one, too. The bat?"

"*Dracula.*" He actually puts on a Romanian accent for that, and I roll my eyes while smiling.

"The dragon?"

"*Eragon*. Well, the whole Inheritance Cycle series actually."

"Hmm, never heard of it. I'll have to look it up. Okay, and the only other one I saw during your striptease"—he snorts—"was the castle."

"Ah, yes. Have you ever heard of this magical place called Hogwarts?"

"Of course! You're speaking to a certified Ravenclaw."

"Well, I'm a Hufflepuff. But we can still be friends."

We grin at each other like the geeks we are. But then I get a pang in my chest when I try to think back on the last book I read for pleasure. It's been months, maybe even over a year.

"Hey. What's wrong?" His hand cups mine, and I realize I'm frowning.

"Nothing. Just ... you're reminding me of some good books. And I used to love reading, but I feel like it's been so long since I did it for fun." I sigh and press my fingers to the growing ache in my forehead. "My schedule is so full. And, when I do have free time, I feel like I should be studying or working."

Maybe Pops has a point.

"Careful you don't burn yourself out." Ben massages my fingers.

I'm surprised by how comfortable it is to have someone to hold on to.

But this is straying toward serious again. I want the lightheartedness back.

"Wouldn't want your organ donor crapping out on you, now would we?" My lame joke falls like a cement block between us, and I immediately regret it.

Hurt clouds Ben's emerald eyes. "Holly—"

"No, I'm sorry!" I wave my hand to cut him off. "Bad joke. My humor is off today. Back to tattoos. You don't have one for *every* book you've read, do you?"

Ben watches me for a moment before answering, "No. I'd be completely covered. These are books that I've loved or that meant something to me."

"Even on your butt?" That slips out before I can think about what I'm asking.

Ben just laughs. "Yes, Holly. Even on my butt. Ask me nicely, and maybe I'll show you one day."

He winks, and I have no response other than to stick my tongue out at him. His smile grows.

"Okay. So, you've got a load of hidden tattoos, and while they're fun to look at and I'd definitely like to get a peek at more, I'm not seeing the alternative career path here."

His humor fades, and I watch discomfort rise to the surface. But he doesn't shut down. Instead, he shares another hidden piece of himself with me. "I drew all of the designs myself."

So, that's it. Ben has an artistic soul, but he's living an analytical life.

"Wow, really? That's so amazing!"

He grins when I shove his shoulder.

"Do you only draw tattoos? Or do you draw pictures and then decide to get them tattooed on you later?"

He shrugs. "A bit of both. I started out just drawing. Then, I got interested in the skill and technique that went into tattooing. I wanted to see if someone could translate my drawings onto skin. And they could." He's quiet for a moment, but I get the sense he has more to say. "I wish *I* could."

"You want to learn how to tattoo?"

"I mean, yeah. In an ideal world where I'm not sick and I don't have to get a real job to support myself."

"Tattooing is a real job. Plenty of people do it. Probably don't make as much as lawyers, but I'm sure they make a living wage."

Ben nods noncommittally. He's lost his happy amusement, withdrawing his hand from mine.

I decide to let the subject drop. For now. And, since I'm no longer sitting next to a stripping Ben, I'm confident I can drive us to the bakery without accidentally running over any pedestrians.

"Thank you for sharing with me," I speak quietly as I maneuver the car through crowded streets.

"No problem."

"I mean it though. Your artwork is beautiful."

Ben's smile is tight, like it pains him to hear my compliment.

"Can I ask you for a favor?" Immediately, I regret my question. I don't deserve a favor after already demanding so much from him today.

"Anything."

"Never mind."

"Ask me, Holly."

Normally, I don't give in to demands easily, but Ben's smooth voice makes it hard for me to refuse him.

"Would you draw me something?"

BEN

"You want me to draw you something?"

No one's asked me to create anything for them in a long time. Now, here's this intriguing girl driving my car and asking that I draw for her.

"Yeah." She throws a smile at me before returning her eyes to the road.

"What do you want?" I want to ask her that question all the time. And not just about art.

What do you want from your life? What do you want to be happy? What do you want in a man?

But I'm also trying not to scare her away.

"What should I want, Ben? Draw me what you think I'd want." Holly delivers these instructions as she parallel parks on a street I'm not familiar with.

She wants me to choose?

The request suddenly sits heavy in my mind. Like, if I figure out the right thing, I'll win a magnificent prize. But, if I get it wrong, I'll lose out on the chance of a lifetime.

When she glances over at me and chuckles, I'm pretty sure it's because the worry sits clear on my face. "Calm down, Ben! First off, you don't have to do it right now. Just whenever you feel inspired. And I'm not gonna judge you. I want a Ben Gerhard original."

Before I formulate a response, she's out of that car, sprinting through the rain. I pop my door open and follow after her to a small storefront while trying to think of what in the world I should draw for this girl.

Walking inside, I'm surrounded by the scent of warm, fresh bread. Maybe this isn't such a good idea. I miss carbs, but my strict diet doesn't allow me to indulge often.

"Mmhmm. This is what I want heaven to smell like." Holly's voice is dreamy.

When I glance her way, I find her eyes are closed, and she's standing still in the middle of the shop. Some patrons are moving toward the exit, and she's right in their path. I put my hands on her shoulders and gently guide her to the side. She starts at my touch, but when she realizes the cause for her redirection, I'm rewarded with a grin.

"Sorry. Just got lost in the moment there."

"No problem."

Being in this shop seems to have relieved the last of Holly's jitteriness from earlier. She grabs my hand and pulls me to the counter. After placing her order for an almond croissant and a medium jasmine green tea with a dab of honey, she reaches for her wallet.

"Slow down there." I stop her searching hand before she can pull out money. "I asked where you wanted to go because I wanted to treat you."

"I can pay for my own food, Ben."

She's ready to argue. But so am I.

"There's no doubt in my mind that Holly Foster can and does pay for all of her own food. But you did me a huge favor today. So, now, I'm treating you."

"What are you talking about? You're the one who did *me* a favor by coming to pick me up."

"Well, you wouldn't have needed picking up if you weren't donating your kidney to me."

The barista watches our exchange like a spectator at a tennis match, head bouncing back and forth.

Holly stands with one fist on her hip, glaring at me, while I grin back. We're still holding hands, which I have no intention of pointing out to her.

"But the kidney exchange is happening because your cousin is donating to my brother."

"Aha! Exactly. That's two whole different people. They don't come into play."

"Of course they come into play!"

She is so fucking adorable; I want to drag her into my chest and kiss her angry mouth. Instead, I give her my snarkiest smirk and shake my head.

"Nope. This is between you and me."

She huffs out a dramatic sigh. "My croissant."

I raise an eyebrow.

She gestures to the cash register. "You can buy my croissant. I'm paying for my tea."

I make like I'm thinking over her proposal before nodding. "We've reached an accord."

She rolls her eyes and tosses a few singles on the counter. But I'm not fooled; I can see the little curve at the corner of her mouth.

After squeezing her hand, I let go to pull out my own wallet.

"How many ounces are in your small cups?" I try to approach my order as directly as Holly did hers, but apparently, my question confuses the young guy behind the counter. Or maybe he's still rattled from our verbal sparring session.

"Oh, um, I'm not sure. I'll go ask—"

"Small is twelve, medium is sixteen, and large is twenty."

Of course Holly knows. And she doesn't deliver this information like she's exasperated with the barista. Instead, she uses a teacher's tone, pleasant and informative. I smile at her, but she's fixated on the pastries in the glass display case.

"I'll take a small jasmine green tea. No honey or sweetener."

She glances up at me then, returning the smile, and then walks off to grab a table while I pay my part of the bill.

"You like green tea, too?" she asks when I sit down across from her.

"Haven't given it much of a shot. But I figure, someone who comes here all the time knows what's good."

"I'd love to come here every day, but I only treat myself on special occasions. Or when I'm badly in need of a pick-me-up."

"Why?"

"Money." She shrugs like it's no big deal. "Can't really budget for fancy teas and gourmet pastries on my salary."

I'm not sure how to respond, but luckily, our teas and food arrive before I have to.

For the next few minutes, I get to watch Holly slowly pick off pieces of flaky croissant and place them in her mouth. Each time, she closes her eyes and hums to herself. The precise way she eats her pastry shouldn't turn me on, but goddamn, it does. I'm focused on her mouth and her slim fingers, wanting both to be worshipping me the same way she is a piece of bread.

"Your turn."

I choke on the swallow of tea I have in my mouth and spend the next minute coughing the hot liquid out of my throat. When I focus on Holly again, she's no longer in the middle of a spiritual experience with her food. Instead, she's examining me with concern.

"You okay?"

I nod even though my throat is raw. "My turn?"

She pushes the plate across the table, offering me the last few bites of her precious treat.

"Oh no. That's yours."

I go to push it back, but she shakes her head. When I still don't move to eat it, she picks a piece off the plate and holds it in front of my mouth.

"Eat." Somehow, she glares at me but also pleads with me.

I consider getting into another debate with her. The first was so fun. Instead, I obey.

It's just one bite. No harm can come from something that small. Right?

When I open my mouth and lean forward, she blasts me with a grin. The buttery crust hits my tongue, and I go to bite down, only to feel my teeth gently nip the ends of her fingers. Holly's eyes widen. She pulls her hand back but does it slowly. Her skin slides against my lips during the retreat.

The pastry tastes delicious, but it's not what I want in my mouth right now.

Her hands wrap around her cup of tea, and she stares at me like I'm a puzzle to be solved.

I hope she takes the time to try.

"So, what do you think?"

"Best I've ever had."

6

HOLLY

"If you keep squeezing those balls so hard, there's going to be nothing left."

"Oh. Sorry."

Terra shakes her head at me as I drop the ground beef back into the bowl we're working from. We're almost done, and I don't want to mess everything up, so I let her take over and wash my hands in the sink. Before starting on the dirty dishes, I read over my to-do list for the day.

1. Weekly meal prep w/Terra.
2. Read digital marketing chapters 11–14.
3. Finish microeconomics PowerPoint.
4. Create Habitat for Humanity fundraiser flyer.
5. Go to spin class.
6. Don't call Ben.

Don't call him. There's no reason to call him.

It's been three weeks since I last saw Ben. The fact that I know that shows just how much it's nagging at me.

Whenever he texted, I would get silly butterflies in my belly. Then, I smothered those presumptuous bugs with delayed one-worded answers. Apparently, he took the hint because the messages have stopped coming.

Instead of feeling satisfied, I find myself staring at my phone, even when I shouldn't, like in the middle of class or when I should be looking for my bus stop. Or when I'm cooking with my roommate.

"Where's your mind?" Terra grabs the last handful of meat, carefully shaping it before lining it up with the others on a baking sheet.

For a moment, I just chew on my lip. Maybe talking about my inappropriate stomach butterflies will help to get rid of them. "Ben and I hung out a few weeks ago."

She finishes putting the tray of meatballs in the oven and then turns to lean on the closed door. Cats dance across her yellow apron, wearing little chef hats and holding spatulas. "What happened?"

I shrug. "Nothing really. It was friendly and fun. But a couple of times ... there were like a few moments ..." I struggle to describe what happened.

"Did he do something to you?"

"What?"

The scowl on her face makes it clear that I'm doing a bad job of explaining myself.

"Oh gosh, Terra, no! That's not what I'm saying."

"Then, what?"

"I-I think there was attraction. Like just a spark or two. At least, on my end."

Terra bites her lip as a grin threatens to overtake her face.

"Stop it!"

"Stop what?"

"Looking like I just made your day. This isn't a good thing!"

"Why not? He seems like a sweet guy. In fact, I think I like him more than any other guy you've dated."

"What's wrong with the guys I've dated?" I move to the sink and begin washing dishes by hand, scrubbing harder than is necessary.

"We're using a very loose definition of the word 'dated.'" She uses her fingers to create quotes before sticking her own hands under the faucet. "And the rare times I met a guy you were hooking up with, I got the feeling you weren't interested, which made me not interested in getting to know him."

An image of Roderick pops into my head. He took me cutting things off well. When I texted him that I wasn't feeling our setup anymore, I thought he might insist on calling me or meeting up. But he let go nice and easy, which was a huge relief.

Except for the fact that this just proves Terra's point.

"So, I haven't found someone I want to spend a lot of time around. That's not a problem. The issue is you thinking it's okay that Ben might be that guy." I grab a dish towel and start drying.

"Yeah, I'm still not understanding the issue."

"Are you kidding me? I'm giving him my kidney! The surgery is stressful enough, but just imagine the added pressure if there's a new relationship. What if we start something up, but then one of us wants to break it off? Who's to say he'd still want to do the exchange? Then, Marcus loses out again. Or what if ..." I trail off because I don't want to say it. The fear comes directly from the dark hole in my chest where all my childhood issues swirl and eat away at me.

"What if ..." Terra isn't grinning anymore; she's just listening.

"So, what if I tell him? And it turns out, he doesn't feel the same way, but he thinks I'll back out of the exchange, so he lies. Maybe we date. Maybe I feel differently about him, and I start to really like him. Then, I get the surgery done, and I wake up to find that he's gotten what he wanted. That everything else was a lie. How can I know if he actually likes me or if he's just keeping his organ donor happy?" It sounds so pathetic and full of self-loathing. But it doesn't sound impossible.

"Damn, Holly." Terra steps forward and wraps her arms around my shoulders. She's warm from standing near the oven, and I sink into her embrace. "Your mom really did a number on you, didn't she?"

I sigh and ignore the ache in my chest. "Maybe. But I still don't think my fears are unfounded."

She rubs my back in soothing circles. "Why don't you try getting to know him better? Maybe, one day, you'll be able to tell if he's lying or not."

I'm saved from answering when Terra's laptop lets out a ring.

"Faith!" That's Terra's girlfriend's name, not some declaration she's making. The two of them video-chat most days. She skips to her door but stops to glance back at me. "Think on it."

When she disappears into her room, I frown. My friend is too optimistic. She hasn't been lied to like me. Doesn't know how bad the fallout can be.

The food has some time to cook, so I climb up to the platform that acts as my bedroom and start on my homework. Our place is small, and I don't technically have my own room, but the rent is pretty cheap for how close it is to campus. We make it work.

Terra's conversation is just background noise as I attempt to focus on microeconomics. Spreading my notes across my mattress, I wait for my shoddy, secondhand laptop to power up. After the screen blinks to life, I actually make some headway before Ben saunters back into my mind.

First, it's just the thought of his goofy smirk.

I shake my head and force myself to work.

But then I see him pushing his glasses up the bridge of his nose with his long fingers. The same fingers that unbuttoned his shirt to reveal those inked images on his skin. The skin that felt hot under my touch.

I never got around to asking him when he'd gotten the tattoos.

Is he going under the needle right now?

That's risky, and I hope he's not that stupid. The way he described them, it sounds like a large portion of his skin is covered.

When did he start getting them? And what else does he have? I wonder how many more I might have seen if he had gone down one or two more buttons ...

"Ugh!" I flop back on my pillow, arm flung over my eyes, trying unsuccessfully to push the image of Ben disrobing for me out of my mind.

"Got boy on the brain?"

I yelp at the sound of Terra's voice, so close. Times like this, I regret not insisting on a two-bedroom apartment. I raise my arm and glare at her head, which hovers just at the entryway to my little loft. She must be standing halfway up the ladder needed to climb onto my platform

"Sorry. Should've knocked. But I heard your groan and thought you might be in pain."

My arm falls back in place. "You done chatting with Faith?"

"Yeah, she had to go eat. Stop changing the subject. Back to Ben."

In an overly dramatic sigh, I let all the air out of my lungs. "It's been three weeks since I saw him, but he's still in my head. Why won't he get out?" I sound like a whining baby.

Terra leans forward, so she can rest her elbows on my floor. "You miss him."

It isn't a question, but I answer anyway, "I shouldn't. We barely know each other."

"So what? You remember how we became friends."

Yeah, I do.

It was the first week of classes, and I was eating alone at the dining hall. My weekly planner was open, a green pen poised in my hand to begin tran-scribing all the assignments I had to keep track of for a semester, when I heard a loud click. Raising my head, I found a gorgeous brunette with torn-up jeans and a T-shirt with Calvin and Hobbes on the front, aiming a fancy camera at me. After snapping another shot, she put her camera on the table next to my notebooks and told me to watch it while she went to grab a plate of food.

"What if I had stolen it?" I asked when she got back to the table.

"Then, I would've chased you down and busted your kneecaps. But you

didn't. Good job on passing the decent-human-being test. I'm Terra Dono-van." She offered me her hand.

"Holly Foster." I took the proffered hand.

"Nice to meet ya, Holly. Wanna have a sleepover this weekend?"

"Yeah, you invited me to a sleepover like we were in seventh grade."

"And you accepted. That was after knowing me for less than five minutes. Now, we're permanent fixtures in each other's lives. So, is it really that strange that you care about a guy even if you've known him only for a little bit?"

"It's just not how I operate."

"Don't even get me started on how you operate. I'll be late for class."

"You don't have class today."

"Exactly."

I stick my tongue out at her, and she grins in response.

"Okay, then give me the CliffsNotes."

Terra clutches her chest, eyes wide. "Did I hear that right? Holly Foster wants to use CliffsNotes?"

I fling a pillow at her head, but she dodges it, pretending to fan herself.

"Oh, shush up."

"Language!" Terra mock scolds me, and I chuckle. Then, the humorous smile she wears fades into a sad one. "It's just that … I get you don't trust easily. And I'm not saying that you need to have hordes of friends. But I hate to see you wanting to connect with someone but holding yourself back out of fear. I think you should try hanging out with Ben again."

"I told you—"

"I'm not saying, date him! Of course, I'm also not saying, don't date him. But just consider that, sometimes, attraction is temporary. You could find that, in a few weeks, you don't feel that crush anymore, but maybe you have a new friend. Not a new best friend though. That job is taken." She rocks both thumbs at herself, emphasizing the gesture with a smirk.

"You're ridiculous," I mutter as I consider her point.

I'm not unaware of my distancing tendencies. But the part about attraction fading into friendship is a new concept I haven't considered. Maybe that could work.

"I see the wheels turning in your head. I'll leave you to it."

She disappears, and I lie back down in my pile of notes, staring up at the glow-in-the-dark stars stuck on my ceiling.

Friends with Ben.

That's what my original plan was. Then, my fluttering chest and heating panties got in the way. But those distractions could be temporary. I can tamp down those responses until they disappear. All it'll take is a bit of self-control.

Question is, does Ben still want anything to do with me?

BEN

"If you keep up this moping bullshit, I'm gonna stick your head in a toilet, so you really have something to be upset about." Jasper's exasperated voice drags me out of my self-contemplation.

"Fuck you." There's no heat in my words.

"You've been staring at that piece of chicken for, like, five minutes. Just put it in your mouth and chew. Don't tell me this girl has you so bent out of shape that you can't eat." He smirks at me before taking an exaggerated bite of his burger.

Normally, it's the dialysis messing with my appetite. But missing my donor doesn't seem to be helping.

Weeks. I haven't seen her in weeks. Since before fall break.

She responds to my texts hours after I send them with one-worded answers or emojis. So, I've stopped texting her. Doesn't mean I've stopped thinking about her.

What went wrong? After the bakery, I thought there was something happening between us. Now, I'm getting ghosted.

Just to get Jasper to stop harassing me, I shove the rest of my lunch down my throat, and we head out of the sandwich shop.

"I don't get it. You hung out a couple of times. I mean sure, Holly is cool and definitely hot, but so are a lot of other girls. So what if she's busy? Or not interested? It's not the end of the world. Find someone else. And she's still giving you her kidney!"

My roommate's arguments grate on my nerves. Mainly because they're rational.

Doesn't change the fact that, when my mind wanders, it goes straight to her pink lips, laughing eyes, and gentle hands. From the way she touched me in the car, I would've sworn that I wasn't the only one interested.

"I know it doesn't make sense. But Holly's different. I can't stop thinking about her."

"So you need—" He stops talking and walking at the same time, and I have to backtrack to keep from leaving him behind. Jasper stands, relaxed, on the sidewalk with a thoughtful expression.

"What's up?"

I'm not worried about his weird pause. Jasper is prone to random redirections and topic changes.

"Maybe this'll do the trick." Jasper puts on his pleasant but distant face so fast that I know I've missed something important.

"What—"

"Hey, Annabelle."

Oh shit.

Jasper directed his greeting over my shoulder, meaning that I just need to turn around to see her. Funny how, every day, I hope to casually run into a certain person, but the massive campus doesn't allow that to happen, yet it practically delivers my ex-girlfriend right into my lap.

"Hey, Jasper. Hi, Ben."

Yep, that's her voice all right. Soft, sweet, and shy, almost like a child's.

I'm not a jackass, so I turn around with a polite smile to return her hello. "Hey, Annabelle."

96

She hasn't changed much since the beginning of the summer when I broke things off. Her wavy sunshine hair still falls a few inches above her waist. The legs peeking out of her thickly patterned bohemian dress show off a solid tan. Annabelle is a naturally beautiful girl who looks like she belongs on some California beach, sitting around a bonfire, weaving jewelry out of twine and seashells.

Right now, she's approaching me like I'm a stray dog who might sprint away if she moves too fast. Perceptive, as I'm contemplating giving a quick wave and jogging off to safety. But that's the coward's move. It's just that the last conversation we had made it clear that we weren't right for each other, which I said. And then she cried.

I stand firm and embrace the awkward small talk. "How's it going?"

She beams like I've done her a favor. "I'm doing really well. Had a good summer with my family. And I've been working on a lot of new pieces."

"That's great. I'm glad to hear it." Not a lie.

Annabelle's art was the first thing that attracted me to her.

"And you? How are you doing?"

I have no intention of discussing with one of my exes my current unrequited infatuation, so I share the news she might care about.

"Summer was mainly working. You know, temping at my parents' law firm. And, just a month ago, an organ donor match was found."

"Oh my gosh, Ben, that's fantastic!" Annabelle clasps my shoulder and smiles up at me.

The gesture is nice, but my heartbeat doesn't pick up, and my skin stays the same temperature.

"We should celebrate! My roommates are throwing a party at our house on Friday night. You need to come." After a pause, she turns her smile to Jasper, probably just remembering he's there. "And, of course, you're invited, too, Jasper."

"I'm not sure—"

Jasper throws his arm around my shoulders, cutting me off, "Of course we'll stop by."

The irritated glance I give my friend doesn't go unnoticed.

Annabelle releases her hold to link her hands behind her back and stares up at me through her eyelashes, her mouth turned down in a heartbreaking pout. A pose I've come to learn is practiced.

"I know we broke up, but I still care about you, Ben. And it's just a small party." She clasps her hands together underneath her chin, her next words coming out breathless and excited. "And, if you come, I can show you some of my new pieces. You know how much I value your opinion."

By opinion, she really means praise.

I met Annabelle at one of the school's gallery exhibits last year. She had a couple of pieces on display that were beautiful. That was a remark I made out loud, only to find that she, the artist, was standing just a few feet away. I showered her with compliments, not knowing what it was about her paintings that I liked so much, simply knowing that I thought they were attractive.

Little did I know, that knowledge about art would not necessarily make me more appealing to Annabelle.

But we aren't dating anymore.

Still, I'm nowhere close to being with the girl I'm actually interested in. Maybe Jasper is right. I'm not planning on getting back together with Annabelle. That would be a disaster. But going out on the weekend instead of holing up with a book or my sketchpad is probably a healthier choice for my psyche.

"Okay, yeah. We'll stop by. Do you still live in the same place?"

"Yep!" Annabelle grins up at me, almost as if she expects something.

"All right ... see you Friday then." My hand curves in an awkward half-wave, and I make a move to leave as Jasper finally lets me go.

Annabelle's touch stops me as she grips my arm. "I'm glad you're coming. This'll be so fun!" She lifts up on her toes and presses her lips to my cheek. Then, she skips away to a group of friends I only now realize have been waiting for her.

"She's definitely still into you." Jasper claps me on the shoulder, smirk back on his face.

I resist the urge to wipe the back of my hand over my cheek. "So what? I ended it for a reason."

But, now, I'm going to a party she invited me to, probably giving her the wrong idea. We're not a possibility anymore. Took me some time to realize, but Annabelle isn't long-term for me.

"That was stupid. I shouldn't have agreed to go."

"That's where you're wrong. Just because she's the one who invited you doesn't mean you're going there for her. You need to have some fun. Parties are a good place to do that."

"Doesn't work so well when you can't drink."

Jasper shrugs and then winks. "There are plenty of other fun activities you can participate in."

I give him a shove before moving forward. "You know I don't just hook up anymore."

"Yeah, I still don't understand it though. Just because your kidneys are out of whack doesn't mean your dick is."

There's a gasp, and we both turn to see a freshman girl staring at Jasper with shock before she shakes her head and power-walks away.

"You just destroyed her innocence!" I grab his upper arms and shake him in mock outrage.

"Shut up." He's grinning as he shrugs out of my hold. "But really, man, there's sure to be plenty of girls there on Friday. Find someone to take your mind off her."

We walk in silence for a few minutes. It's a party. I don't have to go for Annabelle. Holly isn't interested.

Why not try to meet someone else?

My gut clenches uncomfortably, but the logic makes sense, so I give up.

"Okay, I'll go. It'll be fun."

"Awesome. Now, if you can say that without sounding like you're on death row, I might actually believe you."

7

HOLLY

"Wow, I guess it has been three weeks! Time flies, huh? Well, I thought I'd just stop by—no, that's so stupid." I roll my eyes at myself as I approach Ben's parents' house and practice what to say when I see him. "Hey! Just happen to be in the neighborhood"—if that's what you call riding two busses to get here—"and had this lying around"—or maybe spent twenty minutes in the shop, agonizing over which one to buy—"and thought you might like a visitor."

Still complete garbage. And I'll feel like a liar if I try spouting off that nonsense.

Now, I'm outside the Gerhards' intimidating townhouse on a Thursday morning, gripped with doubt.

Why did I think this was a good idea?

I could have texted him. Instead, I settled on this surprise approach.

But who knows if he's here? When you have your own dialysis machine, there's nothing mandating that you keep the same schedule. Maybe I'll ring the bell, only to find the house is empty.

And, even if he is in there, why am I so sure he wants to spend time with me? I practically ghosted him.

Normally, I'm so sure of myself, but just the thought of Ben pushes me off-balance.

So, now, I'm stuck here, gripping the strap of my bag that holds my peace offering while my other hand hangs in the air as I hesitate over the doorbell.

Before I can make a decision, the door opens.

"Oh!" I exclaim at the same time as Victoria Gerhard, who almost steps on me.

"Holly! You surprised me!" Ben's mom slips the phone she was staring at into her pocket and smiles.

Luckily, the abruptness of her appearance unfreezes my arm, and it drops to my side. "Sorry. I was going to ring the bell."

Was I though?

"Of course. Please come in." She steps back and ushers me into the house.

I follow her, my confidence rising with her positive greeting.

"How is everything with you, Holly?"

"It's good. Lots of studying for midterms, working—you know, all that."

"I'm sure you are performing fantastically. Would you like something to drink? Water? Wine?"

We've come to a pause in their beautiful kitchen, and I chuckle at her joke.

Then, I take a good look at Mrs. Gerhard. She's dressed in a power pantsuit, tailored perfectly to her body, with a set of ass-kicking heels. Her outfit exudes professionalism, but the way she wrings her hands and stares at me betrays a hint of desperation. And I realize she wasn't joking.

"It's nine in the morning. Also, I don't drink. With the donation and all."

The tension releases from her shoulders, and her smile becomes less strained. "My God. I don't know where my mind is today. I forgot my phone when I left for work, and now, I'm offering you a morning cocktail! Maybe I need a vacation. So, all your appointments are going fine?"

Ah, that's it. She probably thought I was here to deliver some bad news.

"Everything is on track. No problems so far."

"Good. That's so good to hear." She pauses and then places her hand on my shoulder. "I just want to thank you again. You are saving my son, and that is something I will never be able to repay you for."

The outpouring of thanks unnerves me.

She seems to pick up on my discomfort and lets her hand drop while changing the subject. "Are you here to visit Ben?"

I nod.

"That's kind of you. He mentioned you came before for a treatment." She lowers her voice. "He doesn't like his father or me sitting with him, so it's good to know he has a friend he'll let in."

"My brother pretended he didn't like anyone with him either. But I never listened to him. Little sisters can do that."

We share a grin.

"Well, he's already started, so you'll find him upstairs. I'm heading back to work. I hope I'll see you again soon, Holly." Then, with the quick snick of her heels, she departs, leaving me alone in the kitchen.

And I realize I'm an idiot.

What would I have done if she hadn't been here to let me in?

If Ben had been alone, I would have been forcing him to stop his treatment in the middle just to come open the front door, and then he'd have had to start up again. I berate myself for the oversight. Usually, I'm better at planning than this.

With nothing left as an excuse to stall, I climb the stairs. In a matter of seconds, I'm going to see Ben. Like a wanderer in the desert, I'm thirsty for him. Taking a pause, I let my craving roll over me. Then, I soldier on, confident the unwanted infatuation will pass with time.

Down the hall, I see light glowing from his treatment room.

There's also some noise, voices shouting. Pausing just outside the door, I try to figure out what movie is playing. Denzel Washington's voice is distinct, but that guy has made so many movies that I need more clues to narrow it down. It's not till I hear him complaining about being unable to read his newspaper that I get it.

"*Training Day!*" I proclaim triumphantly, bouncing into the room without considering if my dramatic entrance is a good choice.

Ben practically jumps out of his seat, the pencil and sketchbook he was holding clattering to the floor. He collapses back after realizing the intruder is a friend. "Holy hell!"

"Close, but you're missing an L. My name is Hol-ly." I drag out the L sound to exaggerate the joke while I move to pick up the stuff he dropped.

Strange, my anxiety from before has disappeared. Being with Ben now, I am centered and myself. No more nerves.

Ben, on the other hand, is still shocked.

"You—how—I—" He shakes his head, as if that'd help him start the right sentence.

I place the sketchpad in his lap and pat his hand. "Deep breath. Your mom let me in." Now, I pause and realize that, if Ben truly doesn't want to hang out with me, then this is a totally stalkerish move.

How the tables have turned.

Have we established enough of a friendship for me to show up, unannounced?

"We haven't hung out in a while. I thought you might want some company. I can leave, if you don't though." I gesture to the door and take a step back to show I'm serious.

"No!" He reaches out and clasps my hand, the warmth of his skin driving away any self-doubt. "Stay. You're always welcome."

His thumb brushes a few circles on my palm, sending pleasant chills up my arm and down my spine.

Well, that's not going to help smother butterflies.

I slide my hand from his. He frowns but lets me.

"Looks like you got rid of my chair. Be right back." I drop my bag on the floor and retreat from the room to grab a seat. The physical exertion of dragging the dining room chair up the stairs helps take my mind off how sensitive my skin feels after his touch. I stop at the top of the landing—not because I need a break from the weight, but because I need to take a deep breath before being in the same room as Ben again. These past three weeks haven't done anything to lessen his attractiveness. My errant imagination considers disregarding this chair and settling on his lap instead. Possibly running the backs of my fingers over his stubble. Maybe unbuttoning his shirt to discover more tattoos.

"Get yourself together, Foster," I mutter the words.

"You okay, Holly? Need any help?" his smooth voice calls down the hallway.

"No! I've got it. Had to readjust my grip." That isn't a lie. Apparently, the hold I have on my hormones is too loose. I do my best to lock down the fluttering in my chest and lower belly before picking the chair back up.

Time to test my willpower.

BEN

Holly stumbles her way back into the room, making me feel like shit because she had to carry her own seating again.

I can't believe she's here. It doesn't matter that I haven't seen her in almost a month; I still want to kiss her. Then, I want to give myself a swift gut punch. I'm pretty sure my obvious lusting after her is why she avoided me for so long. If I want her to stick around, I need to get my dick under control.

First step, try not to ogle her backside as she bends over to adjust the chair.

"I'm serious, Ben. If you don't want me here, just tell me to go."

"What?" When I whip my head up from my lap, Holly is sitting cross-legged in her chair, staring at me as if she could drill past my skull and dig into my brain.

Please don't let her be a mind-reader.

I mute the movie. "Why do you think I don't want you here?"

"Because you won't look at me. And, when you do, I get the sense that you're uncomfortable."

"I don't know what you're talking about."

Holly leans forward, eyes locking mine in place, so I have no option but to meet hers.

"Ben, I want you to know something about me. I make it a point not to lie to my friends. That doesn't mean I'm going to spill all my secrets and tell you every detail of my life. But, if you ask me a question, I'll be honest. I'll either give you the answer or tell you I'd rather not talk about it. Now, can you promise me the same?"

Shit. This girl won't stop knocking me on my ass.

I clear my throat, needing a second. "Yes, I promise."

That earns me a small smile, but the intensity remains in her eyes. "Good. Now, what's wrong?"

She gave me an out. She said I could claim I didn't want to talk about it and that she'd let it drop. But the thing is, I don't want to evade her. I like the idea of honesty between us, but it'll feel one-sided if I avoid the hard questions.

So, how to answer her without confessing my crush and ruining the fact that she showed up here today to see me?

"I haven't heard from you in a while. I guess I'm worried I did something that upset you. And I don't want to do it again."

Holly leans forward to grasp my hand, her face earnest and her skin warm. "No, Ben. That's all on me. I'm ..." She trails off.

"You're what?"

She releases me to gesture between us. "Bad at this." I raise an eyebrow, and she deflates on a sigh, trying again. "This is going to sound lame, but I don't have a lot of friends."

Really? Who wouldn't want to be friends with Holly?

"I've been told I don't let people get close easily. So, I guess, when we started hanging out, I panicked. I'm sorry. I shouldn't have avoided you."

Interesting. Maybe I wasn't the only one feeling that heat between us. Holly just isn't as receptive to it as I am. But she's here, so that's something.

"Okay. You're forgiven."

"Just like that?"

She gives me the start of a smile, so I push for more.

"Well, if you want me to come up with some type of punishment, I can do that." I give her my best evil villain grin.

She smirks. "And what exactly would that be?"

"Hmm, I don't know." I want to make it something dirty, like a spanking, but I keep the mood light. "How about thirty days in the stocks? Or you give me all your worldly possessions?"

The smile starts to grow, and I watch it with anticipation.

"Those sound a little harsh."

"Well, you did wound me deeply." I dramatically clutch my chest.

Holly grins. "That's true. What if I give you the gift I brought? Do you think you could forgive me then?"

Joking aside, I'm suddenly curious. She picks up her bag and rummages inside.

"You got me something?"

"Kind of. I got *us* something."

I like the way she says *us*, like we're a unit.

"Okay. What did you get us?"

Holly holds the mystery item up, and I see a heavy black hard-cover book with pages edged in gold. The format stirs memories of my grandmother trying to make sure I didn't grow up to be a heathen. Not sure if her efforts were in vain or not. Jury is still out.

"You brought a Bible?"

Her eyes hold mine for a moment before she nods solemnly. "Ben, I'm here to educate you on the good book."

"Uh ..."

Luckily, I don't have to figure out a response because her serious expression drops away.

"Oh my—oh my—oh my God! You should have seen your face!" she stutters out her words as she gasps with laughter. There's actually a tear leaking out of her eye.

My whole body tingles as the sound washes over me. This is how she should always be.

Still chuckling, Holly turns the book around, and I read the worn cover.

"*The Hitchhiker's Guide to the Galaxy.*" There's a picture of a goofy green ball giving the thumbs-up under the title. "Okay, so not the Bible."

She shakes her head, and her silky hair brushes against her flushed cheeks.

"Have you read it?"

"No. I've been meaning to though."

"Seen the movie?"

"Nope."

"Perfect!" She gives a little excited bounce and shimmy in her chair. "So, I was thinking about how you said you have trouble amusing yourself during dialysis. Then, there's this list of books I want to read, but I always feel guilty, sitting down for long stretches to actually read them. So, my solution ..." She pauses, and I get the sense her confidence has dimmed a bit. "I was wondering if you'd be interested in me reading to you?"

Holly's words seep into my chest and wrap me in a comforting embrace. She wants to read to me.

In the past, I tried to distract myself with a book, but the drum of the machine and the ache in my arm always pulled me out of the stories.

However, when Holly launched herself into the room, all of that faded so far to the background; it's barely registering in my mind. I could listen to her husky, sweet voice for days if she let me.

Apparently, she takes my silence the wrong way.

"It was just a suggestion. You can politely decline. We could do something else. Watch a movie or whatever you want."

"Hell no! Please read to me." To emphasize my point, I shut the

TV off and shift so that I'm facing her better. "This is one of the best things you could've suggested."

She sits straighter in her chair, wearing a pleased grin. "Good." Then, she pauses as her smile turns thoughtful.

"What is it?"

"Hmm? Oh, just wondering what the other best things I could have suggested are. If the reading doesn't work out, you'll have to tell me."

Not likely. The other things that could thoroughly distract me aren't something you normally ask a friend to do. Before my body can respond to my thoughts, I focus on the book she's holding.

"So, why'd you choose this one?"

"Well, of your tattoos I've seen, they've all been fiction, and few were fantasy. I know this is more science fiction, but it's got to have some fantastical elements. And Terra said it was really funny. What better way to deal with discomfort than to laugh it off? Anyway, if we don't like it, I can bring a different book next time. Oh, actually, I'll bring my list! Then, you can tell me which ones you want to hear."

Next time. Holly wants to make this a regular thing.

I want her to be a regular fixture in my life, not just when I'm in this room. But this is a start.

Somehow, I need to get Holly to see me as more than just the sick guy waiting on her kidney. And I need to do it without scaring her off. Obviously, she's interested in spending time with me. Now, I need to figure out how to show her I'm a person, not just a patient.

"Don't bring your list. I like being surprised. And I like all kinds of books."

"Yeah, I could tell from your shelves."

"Did you snoop in my room, Holly?"

"Maybe ..."

The mischievous turn of her lips makes me want to kiss her even more. Time for some platonic reading before I do something rash.

"Okay. Let's hear what you've got, Foster."

"Gladly." She flips the cover open, settles back into the chair, and gives a little throat-clearing cough.

For the next few hours, the two of us go on a hilarious space adventure together. Our laughter fills the room that I've always associated with misery.

And, whether she knows it or not, Holly does a hell of a job in making me fall for her.

8

HOLLY

Yesterday was a huge success. Not only was Ben excited about the whole reading-aloud idea, but he even commandeered the novel from me for the last hour when my voice started to dry out. Ben's soothing tone reciting the witty lines did silly things to my chest.

I try to remember the last time I've laughed so much and come up with nothing.

Unfortunately, despite the innocence of the interaction, there were times when I caught myself slipping into daydreams of Ben reading to me as we lay in a bed together. Clothes might or might not have been involved in said fantasies.

Not good.

Luckily, attending rigorous classes for the rest of the day took my mind off those inappropriate musings. Along with a vigorous spin class.

But, now, the morning after, those butterflies are invading my chest again the moment his name flashes on my phone.

"Hello?"

"Holly. It's Ben."

And there go the shivers down my spine at the sound of my name coming from his rumbly voice.

"Hey, Ben. What's up?"

"How do you feel about parties?"

"Birthday or drunken frat?"

His laughter drifts through the speaker, and I smile as I walk down the busy city street.

"Neither. Just your basic college house party. I agreed to go tonight, and I want company."

"What time does it start? I have to be at work by ten for my shift." This isn't a good idea. I know that, even as I make plans without hesitation.

"I can work with that. What if I pick you up at seven, and we can head over? Then, I'll drop you off at work."

"I don't want to make you leave your party early."

"Believe me, when you're the only sober one in the room, early is a perfect time to leave."

"You sure?"

"More than sure. I demand you come with me." The regal tone he uses makes me grin.

I'd be lying if I said I didn't want to go. I've been missing out on a lot of social opportunities because of my busy schedule, and now, my crush is asking me to attend a party with him. Ignoring the fact that I'm not supposed to have the aforementioned crush, I embrace what I want.

"Well, if you demand it, I guess I don't have a choice. But this had better be fun!"

"Trust me; I'll make it fun."

Those words from his mouth sound dirty. Or my mind is making them dirty. More likely, the second of the two.

"We'll see. I'll text you my address."

"See you tonight, Holly."

BEN

The worn button next to Holly's apartment number lets out a mechanic buzz as I press it. A moment passes.

"That you?" Even the crackling quality of the speaker can't fully extinguish the melody that is Holly's voice.

"Yeah." A second later, I add, "It's Ben," just in case I'm not the one she's expecting.

"Be down in a second!"

I back up, so I'm not crowding the doorway, disappointed she didn't invite me up. I just want a glimpse into her home. To find out more about her.

Holly hasn't been to my place yet, which I'd be happy to remedy.

We'd start with my bedroom. I can imagine escorting her in, watching her explore my private space. Maybe she'd sit at my desk, opening my laptop to see what I'd been browsing on the internet. Or maybe she'd settle on the bed, sinking slightly into the soft navy comforter. The bed is large, so there'd be plenty of room for us to lie down next to each other. We wouldn't even have to touch.

I'd want to touch her though, run my fingers along her neck and comb them through her hair. I'd cradle her face before pulling her in for a—

"Hey ya, Ben!" Holly bursts through the entryway, shoving my risqué thoughts to the back of my mind. But they push back when I take in her appearance.

She's wearing a green coat with golden buttons and a belt that ties at her waist. This comes to about mid-thigh, revealing her slender yet muscular legs, which travel down to a pair of black heeled boots that cover just to her ankles.

My mind, still not fully leashed in, takes a second to imagine me peeling her coat off and finding nothing underneath.

"You ready to go?" I try to use my mouth to keep my thoughts in line but no promises.

"Lead the way."

My car is only one street over, which is good because the cool night air causes goose bumps to scatter along Holly's exposed skin. A minute detail I try not to focus on. I hand her the keys, and once she turns on the ignition, I crank the heat up.

"Thank you," she whispers the words.

If I can always anticipate her needs, I'll be a happy man.

"No problem. Just head straight out of here, and I'll let you know when to turn."

I gesture ahead of us, and she nods. Holly driving seems natural now. Comfortable.

"Tell me more about this party."

Out of the corner of my eye, I watch her fidget.

Is she nervous?

"The girls who live in the house are mostly art majors, so I'm guessing that's what the crowd will be. But Jasper should be stopping by."

"Do you know them from class?"

"No, I've never gotten the chance to take an art class."

"What?" She brings the car to a more abrupt stop than needed at a red light before turning to face me. "You've never taken an art class?"

"No."

"But you're so good!"

Uncomfortable with her praise, I instead point through the windshield. "Light's green."

Her eyes roll as she presses the gas pedal. "I can't believe you haven't taken any classes," she mutters.

I want to correct her, to tell her about my granddad. But Holly likes asking questions, and that's a road with a depressing end. Thankfully, she lets it go, but the new topic isn't much better.

"So, how do you know them?"

The back of my neck itches. "I used to date one of the girls— Annabelle. Take a right here." My tone comes out casual ... I think.

The blinker flicks on, and we make a slow turn onto a busier street. Holly keeps her focus on maneuvering through traffic, nothing on her face showing any kind of reaction to my honest answer.

"Is she the one who invited you?"

"Yeah."

"Is she going to mind you showing up with another girl?"

Her question makes our outing sound like more than just two friends hanging out. More like we're on a date.

I bite my bottom lip to keep my grin from spreading.

"Well, she and I aren't dating anymore. So, she doesn't get a say." And, because it's been pounding in the back of my brain, I ask, "What about you? Any boyfriend who's gonna be giving me the stink eye for being your new best friend?"

Holly laughs and shakes her head. "Don't let Terra hear you say that. She's got the best-friend job on lock. And, no, I'm too busy for dating. Just booty calls and haven't had one of those in a while either."

"Sounds like I'm safe." I attempt a lighthearted tone, even as unhappiness bleeds into my chest. No boyfriend, but also no interest in one.

How can I convince her that I'm worth the time?

We spend the rest of the ride in silence, listening to the classic rock station I favor. I hand out a direction when needed, and Holly hums along to the songs she knows.

"It's going to be the last one up here on the left."

The townhouse I'm so familiar with but I never thought I'd return to sits lit up just a few feet back from the sidewalk.

We have to go down another block before we can find a free space to park, but I'm glad to have the short walk together. I want to take her hand, pull her toward me so that I can wrap my arm around her waist. But that's not how friends walk. Instead, we each keep our respective hands in our pockets. When we reach the front stoop, strains of soft jazz leak through the door. No top forty radio station for these girls.

"You ready?" My grip hesitates on the front handle as I glance back at Holly.

Part of me wants her to say no and suggest we go get dinner instead. The other part of me wants her to step forward, grab my hand, and confidently drag me into the party, as if I were hers to command.

Choosing neither of those options, Holly instead gives me a smile and a thumbs-up.

So, with a flourish, I pull the door open and grandly gesture for her to enter. As she passes, I catch a subtle honeysuckle scent drifting off her, and suddenly, I find those yellow flowers very arousing.

"You coming?"

If only, is about to slip off my tongue, but I stop myself from uttering the dirty wish and instead speak like a person who doesn't only think about sex, "Lead the way."

～

HOLLY

Ben keeps staring at me, and I have no idea if he's normally so tempting or if he's trying to have *fuck me* eyes.

And, now, he has me cursing! Even if it is only in my mind.

To try to clear the rising heat in my lady parts, I examine the house we're in.

These girls have money; that's for sure. The neighborhood's clean sidewalks are lined with well-groomed trees, and this townhouse is spacious for someone living within city limits. Even with the rising tide of partygoers, we have no trouble moving around.

"Do you want something to drink?" Even though the room isn't too loud, Ben leaned in close to softly ask the question near my ear. There's a scent of mint, like he just brushed his teeth.

Dental hygiene is a total turn-on.

I wonder if he would taste minty if I were to press my lips against his, maybe dip my tongue in his mouth. With me in my heels and him leaning toward me, the destination isn't that far away. I could slide my hands up his chest before wrapping my arms around his neck. He'd hug me to him, and as we kissed, I'd experience the warmth of his body all along mine, building enough heat until clothes wouldn't seem necessary anymore.

"Holly?" Ben gazes down at me with curiosity.

I realize I never answered him and that my eyes have probably glazed over as I was daydreaming about mauling him with my mouth.

"Drink. Yes. I would like one." And, now, I'm talking like Yoda.

Ben nods but doesn't move away from me. "What were you thinking about just now?"

Shoot.

I made a big deal about honesty, and now, he's asking for something I just can't give him. There's only one option, but I'm not sure it'll get rid of the subject.

"I'd rather not say."

A look of mild frustration crosses his face, but then he nods. "Let's go get a drink."

He let it go. What could have been awkward and uncomfortable just became a passing moment because Ben understood what I meant when I promised him honesty.

This guy just keeps getting more attractive. I certainly like the way he looks with his ruddy hair, easy smile, lithe and tall body with whips of muscle. He wears his clothes with precision, no wrinkles, well matched. Somehow, he makes his denim shirt look like business casual, tucked neatly into his deep gray pants.

He places his hand on my lower back and guides me through the cluster of strangers.

The kitchen is cute with white cabinets and colorful appliances. The counters are completely covered with food and what looks like the same amount of alcohol I have behind the bar at work. If I thought the artsy crowd was any less boozy than the frat crowd, I now know better.

"Don't worry. There's water in the fridge," he says with utter surety.

I can't help but note how familiar Ben seems with this place. The result is a slight twinge in my chest.

Could it be? No, please tell me I'm not ... jealous.

Dagnabbit, that's exactly it.

As Ben opens the refrigerator door, I lean back on a cabinet and try to sort through my feelings. I bring up a murky image of Annabelle in my mind, but I don't feel any animosity toward her. So, what is it then?

Ben straightens, a water bottle in each hand and a triumphant smirk on his face.

That's when it clarifies. I imagine him in my apartment. Right now, he'd be a stranger there, likely uncomfortable in the new setting. But I don't want my place to be new to him. I want Ben to confidently walk through my front door and scrounge around my tiny kitchen, looking for a few drinks.

Why didn't I invite him upstairs when he picked me up tonight?

Oh, yeah, because my vagina won't stop insisting that I show Ben my bedroom, too.

As I watch him shut the door with his knee, a set of slim arms wraps around his waist from behind. Oddly, Ben's face appears as shocked as mine feels as we meet eyes across the room.

Not knowing what else to do, I shrug and mouth, *I don't know who that is.*

Expression still confused, he mouths back, *Me either.*

His lost look is so stark that I find myself giggling, hand covering my mouth, as if I can somehow hide my laughter from him. No deal. He narrows his eyes as he fights his own smile. That drops from his lips the second the girl circles around in front of him.

On her route, I catch a glimpse of a pretty face. Tan skin and angelic features with cascading waves of golden hair. She's using a jeweled butterfly clip to hold some of it out of her eyes. I'm sure, if I stood next to her, she'd be a few inches taller than me, even with the heeled boots I have on tonight. And her statuesque, willowy figure is draped with an equally free-flowing white dress that seems like it's constantly shifting in a subtle breeze. The whole look suggests a bohemian innocence, and I have no trouble imagining this girl painting with watercolors or displaying a piece of handcrafted pottery.

"Ben!" Even her voice is sweet and high, like the glittering chime of bells. "I didn't think you'd make it!"

By her level of excitement at finding him here, I guess that this girl either is as infatuated with him as I'm trying not to be or she is the ex and wishes that weren't the case.

"How's it going, Annabelle?"

The ex it is.

This is one of those rare times when I have no idea what I should do. I tend to avoid these situations at all costs.

If I stay here, will Ben forget he brought me? If I walk over to them, will Ben be glad for the interruption or annoyed that I'm butting into their conversation?

If we'd been friends longer, I'd have a better read on him, like I do with Marcus and Terra.

I'm considering looking up the bus schedule on my phone, so I can leave and get to work early, but before I can take a step toward the door, someone calls out, "Holly!"

In a strange reflection of Ben's experience, a strong set of arms wraps around my own waist. Luckily, I recognize the voice, so instead of stomping on his instep and turning for a swift knee to the groin, I reach behind me and give Jasper an awkward hug around the shoulders.

"Ben told me you might be here."

When he lets me go, I turn to face him. It's not even eight p.m., but Jasper has clearly had a few.

"Class got canceled 'cause the professor had the flu, so got my weekend started early." He pulls a flask out of his back pocket and takes a long drag from it. "Figured I'd stop by here while you two were around and then go somewhere that actually has decent dance music."

"You can't dance to jazz? I'm disappointed in you, Jasper, and unimpressed."

He responds to my joking tone with his own mock offense. "I can dance perfectly to any tune. I highly doubt any of these stuffy shirts are capable of keeping up with me."

"Oh, really? I'll have you know, I have seen every dance move imaginable and could certainly apply them to whatever music is available." I'm doing my best to keep a straight face as I put Jasper in his place.

"You might be asked to prove that tonight, Miss Foster." He presents his flask to me, likely as a peace offering, but I firmly shake my head. "Oh, yeah, sorry. Didn't mean to tempt you. Gotta keep that golden kidney pristine for my boy Ben."

"*She's* your donor?" The exclamation comes from Annabelle, who is no longer clutching Ben but following close behind him as he steps up to join my and Jasper's conversation.

Ben glares at his roommate, and I wonder if he doesn't like people knowing about his kidney stuff. But it sounded like his ex was already aware of the situation, so his scowl confuses me.

"Yes. Holly, this is Annabelle. Annabelle, this is Holly. I thought you wouldn't mind if I invited my new friend to your party." Ben hands me one of the water bottles, which I accept with gratitude because I really want something to do with my hands other than have them shoved in my pockets.

"No, of course not." Her eyes run up and down my appearance.

I'm not sure what she's looking for or even if she finds it. However, what I am sure of is that Jasper loves mischief.

"Why are you still wearing your coat, Holly? Let me help you out." With adept fingers, Ben's roommate unfurls the bow and undoes the buttons that keep my coat as a protective shield from the world.

Not knowing exactly what type of party this would be, I let Terra help me search through my limited wardrobe for an outfit. We settled on something that would work in dimmer lighting and where there was more of a dance vibe. And maybe, in a few hours, this party will get to that point, but right now, it's more like a low-key get-together.

My dress will not fit in at this party.

Not that it keeps Jasper from revealing it.

With work later, I decided on black, sleeveless, and easy to move around in. The top is tight to my waist where sections of fabric have been removed on each side so as to show slices of my rib cage. Then, there's the skirt, which flows loosely to about mid-thigh. I'm not about to dance up on a stripper pole, but it's definitely more risqué than my normal shorts and T-shirt work uniform.

It takes a bit of juggling with my water bottle, but together, we're able to slide off my dark green trench coat.

"I'll go hang this up for you." Jasper gives my exposed side a light pinch before disappearing with my jacket.

I'm left with a quiet Ben and Annabelle.

"Yeah. So, I wasn't given a real detailed dress code. And I don't frequent parties too often, so this is what I ended up with. I'll make sure to keep the bending over to a minimum."

"You look fantastic, Holly." Ben keeps dragging his gaze over me, which results in waves of goose bumps running and skittering over the skin his eyes touch.

"Yeah. It's a cute dress." Annabelle surprises me with that compliment. I expected to be ignored by her. "I'm sure more people who show up will be dressed like you."

Was that a slightly snide undertone I heard?

Best thing to do is ignore it and rock my look. I've never actually gotten to wear this dress before; the tags were still on it as of an hour ago. Time to make the money I spent worth it.

"I look forward to the arrival of my fellow scantily clad women."

Ben snorts, Annabelle pouts, and I crack open my water bottle. Obviously done with the polite small-talk requirement, Annabelle turns to face Ben, completely cutting me out of their conversation circle.

"I have my new pieces hanging upstairs. Let me show you. I want to hear what you think."

Even though she's clearly only inviting Ben, he leans to the side, so he can include me. "Wanna check out some art, Holly?"

Honestly? No.

I'd like to be the bigger person in this situation, take a look at his ex's work, compliment it if I like it, and simply nod politely if I don't.

But, after spending a few minutes around her, I'm good on my Annabelle quota. Maybe, to the average person, she's genuinely pleasant, but my friendship with Ben is obviously setting off little jealousy bombs in her brain. Classic case of girl not over guy. My place in that drama is not comfortable. Instead of getting combative, I prefer to disengage.

My mouth opens before I've fully thought through my answer. Luckily, my savior appears.

"Sorry, you two. Holly promised to try dancing to this music with me." Jasper grabs my hand in his and tows me to the front room where there is literally no one dancing.

When I glance over my shoulder, I find Ben watching us with a frown while Annabelle tugs on his hand and talks animatedly. I give a mental shrug and return my attention to Jasper.

Would I rather it be Ben pulling me with him, so we can dance together? Duh.

But he has no obligation to do so and the same ability as Jasper to ask me.

Just because I find myself lusting after Ben doesn't mean I need to silently follow along behind him as he revels over his ex's art. I am perfectly capable of having fun with other people who want to spend time with me. Ben and I are friends. Jasper and I are friends. So, I let myself relax and even let out a laugh as I'm spun in an expert move before coming to a stop in the perfect position. Our hands are clasped together while my free one rests on Jasper's shoulder, and his grips my hip.

"Think you can keep up?"

This guy has a rogue's smile, meant to make both girls' and boys' hearts swell and break. Mine remains as it is, but he doesn't need to know that.

"Try me."

9

BEN

ANNABELLE TALKS for a straight ten minutes, and I don't pick up half of it. We're in front of a beautiful figure painting, but all I see is Holly laughing while she stands in Jasper's arms. Jasper is charming and funny, and even though I don't swing that way, I'd be lying if I said he wasn't one of the hottest guys I knew. So, I'm not surprised that she likes him.

That is exactly why I want to punch him in his douche-bag face.

He knows exactly how hung up on her I am. But what does he do the moment he sees her? Steals her away!

Holly would probably tear me a new one for saying someone is capable of stealing her. Probably say something along the lines of her not being a toy for boys to fight over. She'd want me to be honest with her, to tell her that I'd hoped we could spend the whole party together.

But what did my dumb ass do? I let my ex climb all over me and then abandoned the woman I really wanted to be with to my friend while I disappeared upstairs with said ex.

And we've been up here, going on fifteen minutes now. Holly

probably thinks I have no interest in spending time with her. Maybe that I only invited her to make Annabelle jealous.

As my brain works through the idiocy that is me, I don't notice at first that Annabelle has gone quiet. When I finish my brain cartwheels, I turn to find her gazing up at me with a content smile.

"I love watching you get lost in my work."

Because I feel bad about tuning her out, I give her something. "You've switched up your brushstrokes. Gives the pieces more fluidity."

She giggles and rolls her eyes. "Look at you, Ben. Trying to talk like an artist."

Wow.

Yeah, I'm done with this.

Like I thought, she brought me up here just for the ego boost, not to have a real conversation about her work.

Annabelle creates beautiful paintings, but her self-centered way of thinking is one of the main reasons I broke things off with her.

The other was that she didn't make my blood heat or my heart race, the way my dad had once described falling in love with Mom.

"I'm going to head back downstairs. Holly's probably looking for me."

"Wait." Her grip on my arm is light but still feels intrusive, especially because she's holding my left forearm, close to where I place the needles for my treatment. "Are you and Holly ..."

The vagueness of her question grates on my nerves, but it's also the fact that I know what she's asking and can't give the answer I want. Still, what we are and aren't isn't her business.

"I'm not sure why it matters." That comes out a bit harsh, but she's the one who decided to pry.

"Oh."

So familiar. Instead of clarifying or apologizing for being intrusive or even coming back at me for my tone, she uses that one word. As Annabelle so often did in the past, she pairs it with downcast eyes and bowed shoulders.

In the beginning of our relationship, that word and pose would bring on a strong wave of guilt, and I'd spend hours doing my best to make up for upsetting her. I thought she was fragile, possibly hurt from a past experience and in need of some coddling. Then, when we spent time with her parents, I watched her use the same pose on her father while giving me a sly smile behind his back. That was when I realized how skilled she was at lying with her body when she wanted to get her way.

But I'm not her boyfriend. We're not even friends really. So, I don't need to put up with her manipulations.

"If you have something to say, Annabelle, just say it. I don't want to play these games. My friends are waiting for me." I keep the anger of the past out of my tone and just speak straight.

Still, her mouth pops open, and her eyes widen. I'm not the same guy I used to be with her, and I don't feel like pretending.

"But not your girlfriend?"

She's asking me to spell out that I'm not with Holly. Like asking me to twist a knife in my own gut.

Well, I don't owe her that. I don't owe her anything.

"My relationship status isn't something I want to discuss with you. I get the feeling you're asking because of more than just general curiosity. I'm not trying to be mean, but we're not dating anymore, and I think that's the best. We didn't work."

"I just don't understand what happened. We were perfect together."

This only emphasizes my point. The fact that she has no idea how I felt about our relationship means communication really hadn't existed. We were just surface level.

"It wasn't perfect for me. This isn't going to happen between us, and it's not because there's someone else." That's mostly true.

When I broke up with Annabelle, it was for my own reasons. But, now, even after just spending a short time with Holly, I've glimpsed what real attraction is. Maybe, without her, I would have relapsed and gone back to Annabelle. Now, I know I never will.

"But what did I do wrong?" She still has her fingers curled around my arm, her grip becoming tighter and making my fistula itch and ache.

"Nothing. You were just yourself, and that's completely fine, but we don't work together. Don't change who you are. Just find someone who wants to be with you. I'm going now."

I disengage from her grasp and head downstairs before she can call me back to fix something that never worked right in the first place. I'm ready for something new. Something that feels right.

I'm ready for Holly.

~

HOLLY

Ben and Annabelle definitely aren't over. They disappeared upstairs twenty minutes ago, which I know because I keep checking the clock on the wall. Before, I was happy to sidestep spending more time around her, but now, even Jasper's constant stream of dry humor can't keep me distracted from the fact that the guy I've been silently stuck on is likely sticking it to another girl at this very moment.

Why did Ben even invite me? I get that we came as friends, but does that make it okay for him to go hook up with his ex after only being here for five minutes?

Silly me got excited about the invite. Thought I'd have some college-aged fun with my new friend. And, yeah, maybe the back chunk of my brain that always ignores reason developed a few different hopes. There might have been a fantasy or two about finding a dark corner, pressing myself against Ben as he ran his hands along the curves of my body.

Instead, I'm still here, dancing with Jasper. Not that he isn't a great-looking, fun guy. But, for some reason, his fingers wrapped around my waist are less arousing than the gentle brush of Ben's against the back of my hand.

Stupid hormones.

Embarrassment grows hot in my chest as I realize how ridiculous my unconscious expectations for the night were. Luckily, Jasper utters a naughty joke at that moment, so the heat rising in my cheeks can be explained away by his vulgar mouth.

"I doubt they're doing anything up there."

I pull my eyes away from the stairs where they strayed to yet again to find Jasper watching me with a sly curve to his mouth.

I shrug in a lame attempt to play off my vigilance. "Ben's his own person. If he wants to get back together with his ex, that's none of my business."

"Do you want it to be your business?"

Jasper isn't someone who chooses politeness over discomfort. It was a trait that made me gravitate toward him in class, knowing he'd make an honest classmate. Now, I wish I could just stuff his prying question back down his throat, so I don't have to admit my crush out loud to yet another person. Instead, I'm stuck, standing here, with his piercing gaze boring into my evasive one.

"I want to be Ben's friend." *And I also want to make out with him.* But I don't need to articulate that fact. "That's a good relationship to aim for. With our kidney exchange and all."

"So, because you're giving him your kidney means you can't be anything more than friends?" Jasper slips the hand on my waist up to clasp the one I have resting on his shoulder and proceeds to direct another intricate spin move.

I'm not sure if he just had the inspiration to step up our display or if he's giving me time to consider my answer. While unraveling from his arm, I notice we're not the only ones swaying to the music anymore. A few more couples have found the liquid courage to join us.

When I'm back to my original position, facing Jasper, his raised eyebrow demands an answer. I can't help the defeated sigh, a sound that emerges from my unfulfilled fantasies and the pressure of doing the right thing.

"It doesn't mean, we can't be. It means, we shouldn't be." As the sensible words emerge, I experience a vivid memory of a disappointing phone call that has me practically begging Jasper for his understanding. "This exchange can't fall through. Not again."

The amusement tickling behind his prying questions fades as true confusion takes its place. "What do you mean, again?"

That last bit slipped out. This is all too heavy for a Friday night.

"Never mind. Why are we even talking about this? We're at a party!" My forced enthusiasm only results in him frowning. "Come on, Jasper. Let's talk about something else."

We're both silent for a moment, but when he relaxes, so do I.

"I'll let it go. For now."

I stick my tongue out at him, and he laughs. Then, I laugh because it feels good to ignore the heavy things for a bit.

"Do you mind if I cut in?"

I repress a shiver at the smooth cadence of that voice.

Jasper smirks before literally bowing out, like he's a knight at court. "'Tis up to the lady, my liege."

Ben steps into view, pointedly ignoring the ridiculous antics of his roommate, and offers me his hand.

Despite the laughter, I still maintain the weight leftover from the reality reminder. I know, if I let myself fall into Ben's arms and dance the night away, I'll likely do something stupid. So, with a strength of will giants would envy, I shake my head, smiling to soften the rejection.

"I think I'm good on the dancing. But let's go see what else this party has to offer."

The disappointment in his eyes cuts at me. I want to step forward, clutch his hand, and wrap the other around his neck as we sway together. But he's already let it drop back to his side to slide into his pocket while Jasper straightens behind him, smirking at me.

Pushing through the discomfort, I turn back to the kitchen where I'm sure I saw people walking down a set of stairs earlier. With more effort than earlier, I weave through the growing crowd.

I trust Ben to follow me even if I can't trust him not to tempt me.

10

HOLLY

THERE'S a pool table in the basement.

Jackpot.

Ben and I dominate it for the next hour.

Playing as a team, we methodically take down each and every challenger. Of course, I look ridiculous the whole time, having to bend my knees and squat to get level with the table. If I went the more traditional route of bending at the waist, then all the competitors would get a nice view of my ass. Luckily, it's okay to look silly as long as you're winning.

And I always win.

"Eight ball, side pocket." My words are as steady as my hands, and with just a gentle coaxing, my prediction is made a reality.

"That's it!" Ben holds up his triumphant hand, to which I give a hearty high five. "So, who are we gonna take down next?"

He glances around the room, and a couple of guys approach the table with intent in their eyes. But two bottles of water mean I have some pressing matters that need attending to.

"Sorry, Ben. I've gotta take a bathroom break. You'll need to find another partner."

He places his hand on my lower back while handing off his pool cue to a curvy girl, who eyed him every time he bent over the table, like he was the one wearing an outfit on the verge of revealing his tight butt.

Not that I notice things like that.

"Can't do it. It would be unlucky to break up the dynamic duo."

I don't think he means to, but one of his fingers brushes against the exposed skin on my side. The contact tickles but in a good way. A way that makes me want to lean into his hand for more pressure on the spot.

Yeah, time to escape to the bathroom.

"Your choice. So, bathroom?" I point upstairs and raise my eyebrows in question because, from my quick scan, I don't see one on this lower level.

"Yeah, it's right by the front door. There's also one on the top floor."

I nod, but before I can turn to go, he gives my side a squeeze, like he wants me to look back at him. Helpless to give up the offer, I do as he directed.

Ben holds out his wrist to show the time on his simple silver-and-leather watch. "We should probably head out when you're done, right?"

It's just after nine. There's an uncomfortable pressure in my chest, reflective of the feeling in my bladder.

This has been so fun, bantering with Ben, throwing out insults to the other players, discussing shots. Now, the night is over, and I'm going to have to deal with drunken dancers for the next four hours.

Tips. Just think about the tips.

If the eyeballing I've been getting at this party is a good indication, I should expect my most lucrative shift. It'll be interesting to be treated like Terra for a night. I'll just focus on that new experience, and hopefully, it'll help me get past this disappointment.

Still, just because my fun is over doesn't mean that Ben's needs to be.

"You don't have to leave, Ben. I've still got time to catch a bus."

He rolls his eyes and walks with me to the stairs. "Yeah, right. I invited you here. I'm not about to abandon you to find your own way to work." He leans in close, lips almost brushing my ear. "Besides, now that Jasper's left, you're the only one in this house I actually like."

I pull back before I give in to the urge to turn my head to the side to kiss him. Instead, I give his rough cheek a pat. "Well, of course. That's because I'm the only decent pool player here."

We grin at each other, and then he shocks me by grabbing the hand I've left resting on his face and giving the meaty part of my palm a gentle bite.

My mouth is hanging open, I'm sure of it, but I can't seem to regain motor control of my face. Still grinning, he shakes his head and manually turns me back toward the stairs, giving me a guiding push.

"Didn't you need to pee, Miss Foster?"

I can't respond, so I just order my legs to move. Fortunately, they obey.

Ben is right behind me. I can practically bathe in his body heat.

Halfway up the stairs, he makes some inarticulate noise, almost like a groan. I pause and glance back to see if he hurt himself, but no. He's just a few steps below me, one hand threaded in his rusty hair, the other resting on the waist of his pants, and his eyes are looking anywhere but at me. Not finding the source of whatever made him grunt, I shrug and continue on my way.

Unfortunately, there's a line three people deep at the main floor's bathroom. While we were downstairs in our own little world of pool, the party up here doubled in size.

"I'm going to check the bathroom upstairs. You find wherever Jasper hid my coat."

"Aye, aye, captain." Ben gives me a salute and a smirk, and I stick my tongue out at him before sprinting up the stairs.

I really didn't want to use this bathroom. There's no valid reason why other than it's on the floor where Ben disappeared to with Annabelle earlier.

I mean, what do I expect to find? Her sprawled, naked, on a bed, fully satisfied from a bout of makeup sex? Even if they did the deed, she wouldn't still be recovering over an hour later.

Unless he's that good. And, if my hormonal reaction to his mere presence is any indication, he might be. I wonder if Ben would need as much instruction as Roderick did or if he could get me off on his own.

Nope. Stop it. Right now.

I can hear the *beep, beep, beep* of a Mack truck backing up as I retreat from my inappropriately naughty thoughts.

Upstairs is almost eerily quiet after the mass of voices on the first floor. The hallway is only lit by a night-light plugged into one of the outlets. I'm assuming the occupants of the house don't want their rooms messed up during the festivities because all the doors are closed. Problem is, now, I can't tell which one leads to the bathroom.

Luckily, I hear a flush at the end of the hall. I walk toward the sound, noticing all the artwork hanging on the walls on my way. That's slightly comforting—to know that there's actually artwork up here, and it's not all in Annabelle's bedroom. Maybe Ben did just come up here to comment on her paintings.

In the dim lighting, I can't really see them clearly, but even if I could, I'm no aficionado. I can say what I do or do not like, but that's about it. Ben's tattoos, for example. Those I like. A lot.

Before my mind can travel down that off-limits road again, the bathroom door swings open. And, of course, the occupant is none other than Annabelle herself.

Have I mentioned that I have fantastic luck?

"Oh"—her voice is lower now and slightly slurred—"it's you."

I notice the vodka clutched in her left hand. Not a cup. A bottle.

"Yeah. Just need to use the bathroom. There's a long wait downstairs." I don't like awkward situations. Who does? But I also don't tend to cower from them. I just bulldoze my way through till we're past it.

"By all means, take my toilet. You've taken everything else."

Well, that was uncalled for. And inaccurate.

"If you're referring to Ben, I haven't taken him from you. Because he's not an object to be handed around. Sorry if you're upset. He's a great guy, and it not working out probably sucks. But blaming me is silly. I didn't even know him when you two ended things." The speech spills out in a frantic rush because I'm getting awfully close to performing the pee-pee dance just so I don't wet myself.

But you can't reason with drunk girls.

"Why not me?" She glares to the side and talks like I can't hear her. "What did I do wrong? Is that what he wants? Should I dress all slutty?" Her fingers flick at my outfit, and I clutch my arms around my middle.

"I don't think—"

She talks over me, "We were perfect. The two of us." Her eyes grow wet, and I'm at a loss for what to do. "Have you two fucked? We used to, all the time. All over this house."

"Ugh! Stop!" I don't want to hear this. I take her by the shoulders and move her out of my way, so I can shut the bathroom door on her too-descriptive words. Still, I hear her moan through the door.

"Do I need to give him a kidney? Will he give a shit about me then? Is that how you got him?" Apparently, vodka destroyed whatever filter Annabelle might have had.

I want to sprint out of the house, but instead, I have to shimmy my underwear down to my ankles and take a moment on the toilet. I hide my face in my hands as I sit there, hoping to somehow erase the idea of Ben having sex with Annabelle all over this house. Probably in this bathroom.

After flushing and washing my hands, I prepare to power-walk with my ears covered. But the hall is empty when I leave the relative safety of the bathroom. It's creepy again, the air up here still, while I can hear the voices and energy muffled downstairs. I jog the length of the hall, half-expecting Annabelle to pop out of one of the bedrooms, brandishing nude photos of her straddling Ben.

When I get to the foot of the stairs, I'm once again surrounded by light and people, which help push away some of the discomfort of the confrontation. But not all of it.

"Ready to go?" Ben stands up from the couch armrest he was perched on and offers my coat.

While he holds it in place, I slip my arms into the familiar sleeves and welcome my layer of armor settling around me. I'm not so exposed anymore. Still, Annabelle's words are splinters, burrowing under my skin. I have trouble looking at Ben without imagining what she said.

And not just the sex part.

We walk out into a night chillier than when we arrived. Even more of an excuse for me to huddle into myself.

"Is that how you got him?"

There are some girls who've made an art of finding others' vulnerable spots and then just picking at them.

She practically read my mind, my fears of Ben only being nice to me because of what I could do for him.

Then, there's the shame of knowing that's what my intention was when I first decided to spend time with him. Keeping Ben happy means keeping cousin Fred happy, which means Marcus will get his kidney. But, now, I just want to be around Ben because of him.

That doesn't mean that Ben feels the same.

I flinch when his warm hand grasps mine. He opens my fingers and slides the cool car keys into my palm. Somehow, without me even realizing it, we're already at his car.

Just a short drive and a long night of work before I can go home and bury myself in my bed.

~

BEN

I can't get a fix on Holly.

At the beginning of the night, she gave me a look that I would have sworn was a result of naughty thoughts. Then, she went off to dance with Jasper, leaving me alone with my ex. When I realized that situation was partially my doing and I tried to make up for it, she didn't even touch my offered hand. But then we felt like a team, dominating the pool table, and I got to see her competitive side and earned multiple triumphant laughs. Things seemed better after that, and I was sure she returned some of the heat I felt. Maybe I shouldn't have bitten her hand, but I hadn't really thought about it. And I figured she'd slap me if I'd really messed up. But Holly just stared at me with her chocolate-brown eyes open wide and her pale pink lips slack.

I like surprising her.

One of the most conflicting moments of the night was on those stairs. I didn't want to be a perv, but goddamn, that short skirt swayed on her pert ass right in front of my face as she sauntered her way up each step. I actually had to adjust myself, so I didn't walk back into the party with a prominent hard-on. So, yeah, I was horny and considering ending the night with a confession of my feelings in hopes that I might actually get to taste those little pink lips.

But that dream got tabled when Holly returned from her short bathroom break. The cocky, slightly flustered woman who'd sent me off to find her coat was replaced by a distant stranger who now won't look at me for more than a quick glance.

I can't let the night end with her as that person.

"What happened when you went upstairs, Holly?"

She doesn't answer me immediately. A sick feeling cuts at my insides. Just because we weren't at a frat party doesn't mean there weren't guys there who liked to take what they wanted without asking.

I'm about to tell her to turn the car around, so I can fucking destroy whoever made her retreat like this when she answers me, "I ran into Annabelle. She was drunk. She said things that made me uncomfortable."

Anger tightens my chest.

"What did she say?" The words have trouble exiting through my clenched jaw.

Holly sighs, and some of the tension that's been holding her shoulders around her ears releases. But not all of it. "Just stuff about you two. Intimate things I'd have rather not heard in detail. And she cursed a lot. I don't like when people curse."

Thinking back, I can't remember a time when Holly has ever used profanity. I've noticed she mutters ridiculous words one might say in front of a child whenever it seems like an appropriate time to shout out, *Shit*, or, *Fuck*.

Good to know.

I wonder if the cursing is all that made Holly uncomfortable. A selfish part of me wants her to be jealous, too. But this agitated state Holly is in isn't what I want when I discuss my infatuation with her.

Instead, I focus on damage control. "I'm sorry she came at you. She's pissed at me."

Holly keeps her eyes on the road but gives a slight nod. "How long did you two date?"

Hell, are we really going to discuss my ex?

I want her in the past and to focus on getting Holly to be my future. But I promised honesty.

"A little over a year." Watching her profile, I pick out surprise.

"That long? What happened?"

Even though she's not looking at me, I still lift my shoulders and let them fall. Not because I don't know, but more because I'd like to shrug off my past stupidity. That time with Annabelle was a mistake, one I was embarrassingly slow to realize.

"I ended things." I sigh and continue before Holly asks me to because I know she will, "I went to a student gallery showing, and I was saying how much I liked some paintings that turned out to be hers. She overheard me. I loved her art and was flattered when someone as creative as her was interested in me. I think I kind of saw her as an embodiment of that artistic part of life that I loved. But she's a person with her own flaws, and when we got past the honeymoon stage, I realized she liked me more as a fan of her work than a partner." A sigh pushes its way out of me, and I reach back to scratch my neck. "Neither of us had really tried to get to know the other person, and when I started, she pushed back. She liked the surface type of relationship we had. But it wasn't working for me. We didn't work. But she thought everything was fine between us, so she was surprised when I broke it off at the beginning of the summer."

I tried to be gentle and explain how I felt, but when she started crying, it was hard to get her to talk to me. She told me to leave, so I did. I didn't like hurting her, but when it was done, I could finally breathe again.

"Well, she isn't over you."

Holly is hard to read at the moment. I want to tell her to pull the car over, so I can look her in the eyes as we talk. But I won't make her late to work. This isn't the right time for this conversation. But I need to figure out how to get out of this hole and have her smiling again.

"I said my piece. Now, it's her job to figure out how to move on. If I'd known she was still so hung up on me, I never would have gone to the party."

"So, you two didn't fool around when you went upstairs together?"

"What?" My voice shoots up into shouting range. I try to get it together. "You thought I'd slept with her?"

The car slows to a stop. We're already in front of the club, and she's about to leave me. Instead of immediately exiting, Holly puts the car in park and turns to stare at me.

"No, I don't. At the time, I thought that's what you were doing but not now."

The world still seems off-balance, and Holly doesn't appear settled as she goes to unclip her seat belt. Someone behind us honks.

"Look, I know you have to go. But I feel like you're mad at me, and I don't want you to be." I want her to ache for me the way I do for her.

She's got a grip on the door handle but pauses. With a shake of her head, she answers, "I'm not mad at you, Ben. We're good. I'm just …" She hesitates in a very non-Holly way while she brushes her hand down the front of her jacket, which she's buttoned all the way to her neck.

"You're just what?" That sick feeling is back in my stomach as I watch her fiddle with the top button of her coat.

"I'm just not excited to go to work after being told I'm dressed like a slut."

Before I can fully register the meaning of her words, Holly is out of the car.

I practically kick open my door, and I try to catch up with her before she disappears past the hulking bouncer. To get Holly to stop without actually grabbing her, I just jump in front of her, blocking the way.

She stares up at me, befuddled. "What are you doing, Ben? I'm going to be late."

"You're beautiful!" It comes out louder than I planned, and the people waiting in line find my display amusing. Chuckles drift from behind my back, but I only have eyes for the woman in front of me. "You're strong, confident, and sexy as all get-out. Anything you wear looks classy because you elevate it just by being the awesome person you are. She's jealous. You're fantastic." I'm rambling, but it's working because she's smiling. "You're going to run that bar like you always do." I step forward. Even though I want to sweep her up in my arms and ravage her mouth, I hold back and place a chaste kiss on her forehead instead. "Text me when your shift is over and you get home safe."

When I go to move back, Holly follows me and wraps her arms around my waist, hugging me tight.

"Thanks for a fun night," she whispers the words against my chest, and the warmth of her breath brushes through my shirt, accompanied by the heat of her soft body pressed against mine.

Keeping it PG, I just rub her back before she releases me.

With a grin and a wink, she pinches my side and skips to the club's door, calling over her shoulder, "Text ya later!"

If it wasn't for the jackass laying on his horn and yelling at me to move my goddamn car, I might have stood there, staring after her. Or even followed her in.

11

Holly: *Made it home safe and sound. Sleep tight, Benny.*

BEN

SHE TEXTED me at 3:14 a.m. I'd wanted to stay awake long enough to talk to her when she got off work, but past midnight is a no-go zone for me. My body doesn't function right without enough sleep.

I hope Holly's busy schedule still gives her time for enough rest. She was probably exhausted when she texted me last night, likely lying in bed when she typed out the message.

And, now, I'm imagining Holly in a bed. More specifically, my bed. Cuddled under the covers next to me. Smiling up at me with her head resting on my pillow. I'd want to do dirty things with her, but I'd hold back. Instead, I'd pull her in close to me and tell her to take a nap. Only after I made sure she was fully rested would I start to kiss her. Trailing my lips over her slim neck, finding out what noises she made when she was aroused.

Now, I'm sporting a partial.

I push the fantasy out of my mind as I get dressed. Time to focus on reality and how I can win over the real Holly.

When I walk downstairs, Jasper is passed out on the living room couch. He didn't even get around to taking his shoes off before he fell asleep. Seeing him there, totally relaxed as he snores, all my annoyance from last night rushes to the surface.

I creep close, circling around to the back of the sofa, and lean in until I'm right next to his ear. "YOU AWAKE?"

Without waiting for his reaction, I duck behind the couch. Jasper has been known to wake up swinging after a night of binge-drinking.

"Arg!"

The couch shakes, and then a thump vibrates the floor.

Standing up, I realize Jasper rolled off the couch. He clutches his head and moans pitifully.

"You're a vision this lovely morning." That comment gets thrown over my shoulder as I move into the kitchen, sights set on the teakettle.

"And you're a fuckface!" He struggles to drag his sorry ass off the ground. After a try or two, he succeeds and then stumbles after me. "What the hell is wrong with you? Why didn't you let me sleep?"

He pulls out a bag of bagels and pops one in the toaster oven, not even bothering to separate the halves first. Then, he pours a full glass of OJ and scowls at me over the rim as he chugs half the contents. I return his glare.

"Guess I wasn't feeling too charitable to the dick who was trying to hit on Holly—aka the girl who's giving me her kidney."

Jasper rolls his eyes, which only heats me up more. "I wasn't hitting on Holly. I was saving her from your manipulative ex while simultaneously doing some recon for you. Douche."

"Oh, really? Recon? What, you wanted to tell me exactly how her ass felt? Maybe what she tasted like?"

The teapot whistles as steam pours from its spout, a perfect reflection for the boiling emotions spilling out of me.

"You're fucking oblivious." He grabs a stick of butter from the fridge while shaking his head at me.

"Oblivious to what?"

He raises his eyebrows like it's obvious, and I can't keep from growling, "I know you fuck guys. But there's an equal amount of girls who do the walk of shame out of your room." The teapot swings in my hand as I gesture, risking covering both of us in boiling water.

"Not about me, dumbass." The toaster dings, and he removes the hot bread with his bare hand, cursing all the while.

Jasper is always a bear right after waking up, his talk littered with expletives. I take weird satisfaction in knowing that Holly would hate it. Even if she spent the night with him, she'd want to run out first thing in the morning.

Unaware of my thoughts, Jasper keeps lecturing. "If you'd watched us talk for even a minute, you'd have seen that she had zero interest in me. And, yeah, maybe, the first few days of class, I thought about trying to hook up with her. But, the second I found out she was your donor, I didn't even consider it again. Kinda sucks that you thought I would," he explains all this while slathering butter on the outside of his bagel, like some weirdo who's never eaten one before in his life.

As I pour my hot water into a mug, I let his words simmer in my brain.

Slowly, my anger cools, replaced with remorse.

Jasper won't meet my eyes as he takes a bite of his bagel, but at least he doesn't storm out of the kitchen.

"I'm an idiot. It's just ..." The chaos in my brain doesn't translate well into words, so it spills out in a frustrated sigh.

"She's not easy. To read, that is." Jasper chuckles, and my lips twitch involuntarily at his stupid joke. "At least, not for you. You're too blinded by your dick."

"No, I'm not," I grumble, fidgeting with my tea bag. Then, reluctantly, I ask, "What do you mean?"

Before answering, Jasper refills his glass and grabs another bagel, not even bothering to toast this one. He waves for me to follow him back to the couch, which he collapses on with a groan.

I choose to lean on the doorframe, too jittery to sit down.

If he chews any slower, I'm going to snatch his bagel away, holding it hostage until he tells me why I'm blind.

After swallowing another chug of orange juice, Jasper starts explaining, "She's into you."

"She told you that?"

Like we're back in high school, I'm about to demand an exact play-by-play of their conversation, but my roommate shakes his head.

"Not exactly. But I can tell. It's more in the things she didn't say. You've just gotta trust me."

When he's saying exactly what I want to hear, I don't need much convincing.

"Okay. Will do." My phone is out, a text open, and I'm brainstorming exactly how I want to ask her out. That is, until Jasper leans over and snatches it out of my hand. "What the fuck, dude?" Only the steaming cup of tea I'm holding keeps me from lunging after him.

"I'm not done. Put your dick back in your pants."

"My dick isn't out of my pants." My muttered comeback is lame, and I know it.

"Listen to me. Before you ruin everything." He glares at me until I nod, holding up my free hand in surrender. "So, yeah, she's interested in you. But she doesn't want to be."

Well, fuck me. Stab a guy in the gut, why don't you?

I've tried not to let on how different I've been feeling these past few years, but it's not like I can hide all the physical effects. I used to be in great shape. Like *run a marathon, climb a mountain, swim a few miles in the ocean* shape. But I've lost muscle and weight, now a reduced version of myself. Early on, I started to smell bad because of the fluids not being properly filtered through my kidneys. Thank the universe the odor went away once I began dialysis, but that came with its own body-image issues. Now, there's my fistula, an ugly, twisting bulge on my forearm where I have to hook myself up to the machine.

So, yeah, I'm not going to win any modeling contracts. But I've been hoping that, since Holly only knows what I'm like now, she might still find me attractive. She doesn't have the past version of me to compare this sickened form to.

Guess I was wrong.

"Okay. I get it. I won't make a move." I turn to leave.

"Fucking. Dumb. Ass." When I glance back at Jasper, he's glaring at me again. "It's not because she thinks there's something wrong with you. It's because of the exchange. She's probably worried, if anything happens between you two, that it won't work out. And then what happens with the kidneys? Does her brother still get one?"

"That's crazy. Fred wouldn't back out of the exchange."

That earns me a scoff. "You kidding? Your cousin would do anything you asked him to. He worships the ground you shit on." He shrugs. "Besides, she hinted that it'd happened before." He holds up his hand when I open my mouth. "I don't know the details. You'd have to ask her. But, if she's been screwed in the past, then she's probably being cautious. And having sex with the guy you're giving your kidney to is not exactly recommended." Then, he hits me with his evil grin. "Of course, if she's going to be inside you, it's only fair you get to be inside her."

"You're such an asshole."

Jasper just laughs, causing him to choke on his next bite of bagel, which in turn has me snorting. Then, we're both chuckling, and the tension eases out of the room.

"So, what're you saying? What should I do?"

I don't know why I expect Jasper to have the answers. He's not really Mr. Relationship. But he has this way about him where he seems to see everything that's going on.

"Play the long game. Show her you're reliable. Earn her trust. Be a friend. Then, maybe she won't be afraid to date you. But, if you try going all in right now, she's gonna bolt. And the only thing you're going to get from her is a kidney. No pussy."

I shake my head. "One minute, you're relationship Mr. Miyagi, and then you go and ruin it."

My roommate leans his head back on the couch, eyes closed, wicked smile on his mouth. "Gotta keep you guessing."

I mull over what he said.

Go slow with Holly.

I can do that. I don't want to; I'd rather pull her into my bed where we can spend the whole day exploring each other with our hands first and then our mouths. But, according to Jasper, Holly isn't ready for that kind of invitation. And I want more than just sex. I want all of Holly, including her friendship. So, I'll just start with that and keep my hands to myself.

Snores fill the room. I let Jasper sleep this time. Carefully, I slip my phone out of his slack hand before heading back to the kitchen to make breakfast. And I decide that a good friend would text Holly back.

Ben: *Glad u made it home safe. Have dialysis @ 2 today. Stop by if ur not too tired.*

There, that's perfectly friendly.
I can do this. I can be just friends with Holly.
And, if I repeat that enough times, I might start believing it.

HOLLY

The responsible thing would have been to go to the library, claim a table, and settle in for a serious study session. But I promised Pops I'd spend time on Saturdays doing something fun. Ben fits that category.

Not that I'm planning on doing *him*.

We can do fun things together. With our clothes on. Because we're friends.

I get off a city bus two blocks from the house, stomach light and fluttery from excitement. The air is crisp, even colder than last night when Ben dropped me off at work. I didn't experience the chill at all when he was shouting about how beautiful I was.

Working after that was easy. And lucrative. I don't think it was just my skimpy dress, though there were some comments from regulars.

What had people coming back to me repeatedly was the silly grin I wore all night.

"Is something wrong?" my boss, Curt, asked when he saw me.

Often, I don't see him till closing time, but he was making a round on the floor when I got behind the bar. I couldn't stop smiling, even with his confusing question.

"What? No." I shrugged. "I'm just happy, I guess."

A noncommittal grunt emerged from his bearded face, and he turned and moved through the crowd, which quickly parted for him.

Curt is intimidating that way. He's got intense facial hair, paired with over six feet of height and extensive tattoos creeping down his arms and up his neck. I'm pretty sure he's only in his mid-thirties, yet somehow, he gives off the air of being much older. But, when you get past his brooding exterior, the guy is a sweetheart.

I made a note to ask him where he got his ink done, so I could see if Ben had heard of the place. I felt a wash of contentment, knowing that, if Ben ever got a chance to meet Curt, the two of them would actually have something to talk about.

I check my watch, happy to see the time is one fifty p.m.

When I woke up a couple of hours ago and saw Ben's text, I made sure to check the bus schedule, so I could get here before he plugged in.

The doorbell ring has barely faded when the front door swings open, revealing a delicious view of a smiling Ben.

I mean, a normal, not-sexy view of my completely platonic friend Ben. I totally don't admire how good he looks while barefoot with his black sweatpants hanging low on his hips and a red thermal that fits a bit loose on him. And it would be silly for me to step forward and wrap my arms around his waist in order to smell him. So, I don't.

"You gonna stand outside all day?"

Shoot. I'm staring.

"Um ... no. Just a bit longer." I take a deep breath and peer up at the sky. Then, I focus back on an amused Ben. "Okay, I'm good."

When I step past him, he shakes his head.

"I knew it."

Crap. Did he realize I was ogling him? I'm such an obvious ogler.

Still, I try to keep the guilt out of my voice. "You knew what?"

He leans in close to my ear, brushing the scent of mint against my nose. "You're weird."

Ben leans back and grins at me, showing off a set of pearly whites. I'm like a Southern woman experiencing a fit of the vapors, needing to fan myself before the sight of his mischievous expression has me fainting.

"Holly! You're here!" Mrs. Gerhard saves me, appearing at the top of the stairs.

She waves for us to follow her into the kitchen, and I chase after her, Ben's presence a solid weight at my back. A laptop sits on the kitchen island where she must've been working before I arrived. Mrs. Gerhard grips my shoulders, and I get the sense it's her version of a hug.

"Good to know Ben hasn't scared you away yet."

"I'm not sure Ben could be scary if he tried."

I shoot him an exaggerated, disappointed look, and he returns with a mock scowl.

"You kidding me? I'm terrifying." He makes his hands into claws and tries a snarly face that just ends up adorable. "Don't wake the beast, Holly."

I snort and then notice Mrs. Gerhard glancing between us with an unreadable expression.

"You two want anything? Are you hungry? Thirsty?"

"You mind making us a pot of that new tea I got?" Ben releases his pose and gestures at one of the cabinets.

I'm about to tell her not to worry about it, but then I catch a glimpse of Mrs. Gerhard's face.

The light in her eyes and excited smile make it clear that she is overjoyed at the notion of making us tea. I wonder how often Ben actually asks her for something.

When I lived with Marcus, any chance I got to make his life easier, I jumped on. Every time we went in for his treatments, I could sense the discomfort rolling off him in waves, and there was nothing I could do about it.

What must that be like for a mother?

"Tea would be fantastic."

"Good, good. You two go ahead, and I'll put the water on."

"Yes, ma'am."

Ben gestures for me to lead the way, and I get a strange sense of comfort from the fact that I know where I'm going.

Before I've gone too far up the stairs, I remember something and stop to turn back around. However, my abrupt halt results in Ben running into my back and having to catch me before I topple forward on the steps.

"What's up?" His arm remains wrapped around my waist even though I've regained my balance.

I turn in his hold to face him but also so that I can head back downstairs. Standing a step up from Ben, I find myself in the convenient position of being exactly eye-level with him.

All I see is green. Dark green bordering on hazel but not quite there. The green of a dense forest with a canopy that sunlight has trouble penetrating. A place you go to for a sense of calm and stillness, so you can get lost and finally hear your own thoughts without the thunder of others around you. A green you can wrap yourself in and feel safe. A sturdy, reliable green.

The clang of a metal pot settling on a stovetop makes me flinch, and I realize I haven't answered Ben's question. And, what's more, he's simply standing still and letting me stare into his eyes, like the weirdo he's claimed I am. I shake my head and beat back my lady urges with a Fred Flintstone–sized club.

"Almost forgot my chair."

Ben still holds on to me and stops me as I move to step past him.

"Don't worry about it. There's one up there for you already."

A quick glance to the dining room table reveals a complete set, but when I look back at Ben, he just gestures with his chin for me to continue up the stairs. Then, his eyes drop to my mouth, and I'm tempted to bite my lip.

Not good. Time to move.

Only when I turn back around does he let his arm fall.

When I enter the room, my feet stutter to a halt. The machine and Ben's recliner have been shifted out of the middle, and there's a smaller yet still sinfully comfy-looking lounge chair beside his seat. It's angled so that the sitter can see the TV screen but also face Ben.

"That's your chair." Ben walks by me to pat the new furniture's armrest before taking his seat.

I want to ask him why there's suddenly a second seat in this room when there wasn't one before, but I'm afraid I'd like the answer too much.

Best not to question it.

As I go to take my place, I notice a small paper bag nestled on the seat.

"This yours?" I hold it up, about to hand it to him, when he shakes his head while wearing a half-smile.

"For you. Open it."

When I do, I gasp. "Seriously? When'd you get this? You didn't even know for sure I was coming over!" I pull out a lovely, buttery, flaky almond croissant.

Ben just shrugs like this wonderful pastry isn't a big deal. "I hoped you would but figured I could find someone to eat it if you didn't show up."

I don't know what to do, so I just settle into my new cushy chair and take a bite of the soft bread.

"Here, put this on. And look away until I tell you it's clear."

I slip the rest of the croissant back into its bag and then take the proffered medical mask. The fabric fully covers my mouth and nose with the elastic bands circling my ears. This brings me back to all those times I went with Marcus for his treatments. Need to make sure our faces are covered before inserting the needles. Those gosh darn needles.

Shame fills my stomach when I turn my back on Ben. There's no doubt in my mind that it's the best choice for me if I want to avoid triggering a panic attack. I just hope he realizes that I'm the one who's messed up. Not him.

"We're good."

I unwind to sit, facing him, grateful for the gauze he's placed over his arm yet again. I'm such a wimp.

"Tea's ready." Ben's mom appears in the doorway with a small porcelain pot and two mugs, which she sets on the table that rests between our lounge chairs. "You two need anything else?"

"We're good, Mom. Thanks."

With a smile and a wave, she leaves us alone.

When I first met her in that doctor's office, I saw her as methodical and a bit desperate, which was understandable, given her son's situation. Now, in her home, I'm getting to see a caring side of Victoria Gerhard, which is disarming. It's a new experience, receiving a glimpse of a devoted mother. Instead of letting resentment darken my reaction to her kindness, I decide to enjoy her nurturing while I can.

"So, movie or book?" I reach into my bag to tear off another piece of the feathery, sweet bread and pop it into my mouth after throwing out my question.

"Definitely book. I'll read first while you eat. We can switch when you're done."

As Ben flips through the pages to reach the point we last left off at, I pour us some tea. I'm sending out a silent prayer that it's not chamomile. Not that I don't like chamomile, but that'll send me straight to sleep, which is kind of rude when you're attempting to entertain someone.

The simple earth-colored mug warms my hands as I lift it to my nose. The subtle scents of green tea and jasmine tease my senses.

Ben bought my favorite tea to go along with my favorite food. I don't know what inspired him to get all this for me and then to have this soft sofa chair placed here. The idea of someone spending money on me has never been at the top of my list for picking out friends. But he gets major points for remembering exactly what I like.

"You ready?" Ben is wearing his glasses today. That, paired with the thick book in his lap, makes him resemble a sexy professor.

Big brains are high on my attractiveness list. This guy won't stop hitting my buttons.

Best to just push past it like I've been doing even if I have to struggle harder each time.

"Read on."

12

BEN

THE NEXT FEW weeks turn into a sort of routine with Holly coming to my Thursday and Saturday treatments to read to me. Though it normally turns out that we read to each other. Speaking for three hours straight is bound to dry out her throat, so I tend to take over halfway through.

For the first time, I start looking forward to my treatments, something I would have thought was impossible. I just wish she could come to all of them. But the Monday night ones are too late when she has early class the next morning, and Tuesday afternoons, I'm hooked up during her second job.

"Do you like your internship?" I ask my question as she hands over the novel for my turn at reading.

We finished *Hitchhiker's Guide* last week, and now, we're halfway through *The Princess Bride*.

By her wide eyes, I think I've surprised her. Slipping my finger in between the pages of the book to mark our spot, I give her my full attention. Reading is great, but I want to have her stare at me the way she focuses on the pages.

Holly shakes her head. "No. It's boring, and it only pays minimum wage. But working in an accounting firm, even if I am just answering their phones and taking notes at their meetings, looks good on a résumé."

"For what kind of job?" I know that she's working toward two degrees—BS in economics and an MBA.

"A managerial position. When I get done with school, I want to spend some time managing a work force before I look into running my own business."

Interesting but not surprising. I have no trouble imagining Holly as the boss. I'd let her order me around any day of the week.

"What type of business?"

"Haven't figured that out yet. Nothing big though. I want it to be compact and mine. Truthfully, my one-on-one time with Curt after my shift has been more educational than this joke of an internship. He shows me how he organizes his finances and directs all of us worker bees. We've discussed how he went about picking his location and his advertising strategies. I mean, you've seen how full the club gets. It's like that every weekend, and he has special themes and events on the weeknights, so those pull in some steady business, too."

"Would you want to own a club?" That doesn't seem like the right fit in my mind, but if it's what she wants, then I'll bet anything that Holly can achieve it.

She shakes her head. "Oh no. Curt is a total night owl, loves working those late hours. That would drive me crazy if I had to do it for the rest of my life. No, I want something with relatively normal business hours. I mean, it doesn't have to be nine to five, Monday through Friday. But I also don't want to be getting to bed in the a.m."

I nod but also cringe internally as I consider my future. My parents keep pretty normal hours now, but that's because they're well established. They've regaled me with stories from the trenches—when, as young lawyers, they slept in their offices because the big cases needed all the paperwork together or else the other sides could call foul. When they reminisce on their younger years, it's with looks of fondness, as if they enjoyed that stressful period. All that I experience at the thought is dread.

The only benefit this disease has had is pushing off my eventual immersion in the world of law. Well, that, and bringing me into contact with Holly. Being around her makes me not mind my crap kidneys so much.

As I unenthusiastically contemplate my future, she also appears to be lost in thought.

Her shrug brings us both back to the present. "So, yeah, I haven't figured it out yet. But I have time. Now's just about gaining experience and saving."

"Still, it sucks that you have to be at a job you hate for six hours each week." And sucks even more that she can't be here, sitting next to me, during that time.

Holly throws out a dismissive wave as she reaches for the teapot. "Gotta pay my dues. This is cold. I'm gonna make some more." Her footsteps are silent as she walks out of the room in her puffy green socks, clutching the porcelain pot to her chest.

I've made sure to have an almond croissant and jasmine tea ready for her every time she comes over. Even though it's part of the routine now, she never just takes them for granted. Instead, I get excited exclamations, a squeeze of my hand, maybe a hug or a kiss on the cheek. That last one is the holy grail. Her happiness makes the short trips to the bakery worth the hassle.

My mom's voice drifts up the stairs, the words indistinct. Holly responds to whatever she said, and I hear my dad chuckle. Whether she is trying or not, my parents are falling in love with Holly. She started off in their good graces just by having that viable kidney. Now, they're swooning over the fact that she visits during my treatments. Not to mention, they gravitate to her straight, honest way of talking. Lawyers tend to be around double-talkers during work hours. Holly must be a cool glass of water on a hot, dry day. Or at least, a couple of ibuprofen when you feel a headache coming on.

I'm alone for another five minutes or so, during which I have to keep from peeking at the next page. She stopped reading right as Westley and Buttercup were running into a place called the Fire Swamp. I itch to know what happens, having never seen the movie, which shocked Holly when I first admitted it.

"Hey, no peeking!" She's back, cradling a now-steaming pot of tea, scowling at me.

I love that she's comfortable with moving around this house, making her own tea. Now, I just need to get her as embedded in where I actually live.

"It slipped, I swear." I hold up my hands in surrender.

She sticks her tongue out at me as she settles into her chair.

Like always, I want to lean over and kiss her sassy mouth when she does that.

This waiting is making my skin itch. We're spending all this time together, but does she trust me yet? I'm ready to step things up. Problem is, I don't know how.

$\sim$

HOLLY

"Why are you laughing at me?" My voice is slightly muffled because of the surgical mask I'm wearing.

Ben's eyes crinkle above his own.

He's seen me in one of these things plenty of times. But, for some reason, on this Thursday morning, the sight of me has him chuckling. I swear, he even snorted.

"Tell you in a sec. You'd better turn around though."

Even though I want to keep interrogating him, I see his hand reach for the needles and know I'm beat. For the moment at least.

While he's hooking up, I slip my phone out of my pocket, turning on the camera and flipping the view so that I'm met with a reflection of my face. I'm worried I'm going to find bird poop in my hair or that the pen I was chewing on earlier leaked ink on my chin.

Nope. Instead, the surgical mask I'm wearing has a realistically detailed bucktoothed grin drawn on it. I look like a crazy cartoon character.

"You're such a jerk!" There's no real heat in my words because I'm laughing, too.

His hilarity spills out unabated now that he knows I know.

"What? You don't like your makeover?" Another deep chuckle. "You can turn around now. Let me see that pretty smile."

I slip off the mask and throw it at him, not that the small piece of fabric does any damage as it flutters into his lap.

"Mark my words, Benjamin Get-Hard the Fourth, vengeance will be mine!"

He pretends to scowl at me. "Don't tell me that name has stuck."

"Like superglue, baby."

With an overly dramatic sigh, he hands me our current book, Tina Fey's *Bossypants*. I decided we'd take a break from our epic sci-fi fantasy adventures every so often to read a nonfiction.

That doesn't mean it has to be academic.

An hour in, my phone rings. If I'm with Ben and I get a text, I always ignore it. I don't like staring at a screen when I'm with a friend or family member. I have the same No Checking Texts rule for Marcus, Terra, Pops, and Curt. But calls are different; they're more immediate, carrying a sense of urgency. And they aren't as common.

"Sorry. I'm just gonna take this real quick."

He nods and accepts the book when I hand it to him. My screen flashes Terra's name.

"Hey, Terra. What's up?"

"You with your man?" No greeting, just straight to embarrassing me.

I glance over at Ben, but I can't tell if his smile is just polite or if he heard what Terra said.

"I'm with Ben. Is that why you're calling?" No comment on him being my man, which he most definitely is not. I think my roommate and I might need to have a talk.

"Nope. Just asking. So, I have bad and good and bad and good news."

"That's a lot of news."

"Yeah, so here's the deal. Bad news: a pipe broke at the bar. Good news: we get the weekend off work while it gets fixed and they clean up the flood damage. Bad news: we don't work; we don't get paid. Good news: Curt has insurance and contractor buddies, so the bar should be good by next week."

My mind goes on a roller coaster with her as she reveals each of those news nuggets. Most people would be psyched for a weekend off. And, sure, I like having free time. But, now, I'm going to be lower on funds than I expected. Especially sucky with the holidays coming up. Guess that means more handmade gifts this year. Unless I want to give up a few meals.

"How bad is it?"

"Just some mild water damage on the first floor. And a hole in the wall needs to get patched. Still, it's enough of a safety hazard that he's decided to play it safe by closing."

"Okay. Got it."

"So, with the whole weekend open, maybe you can actually go out. Like, on a date or something. Do you remember what those are?"

"Thanks. You're a great friend." The sarcasm in my voice is thick.

"I'm just saying. Okay, I'll let you go. Give Ben a lingering French kiss for me." She hangs up, and I regret not leaving the room with my phone when I first saw she was the caller.

I can't tell if Ben heard any of the conversation. He's just flipping back through the pages we've already read, as if searching for something. I decide that he wasn't able to hear my roommate's inappropriate musings and feel a mixture of relief and regret.

"Everything okay?" Ben stares at me now instead of the book.

"Yeah. Well, kind of. That was Terra. Apparently, a pipe burst at Both Ways, and there's some water damage that needs fixing before Curt can open the place back up. Shouldn't take too long, but it looks like I have the weekend off."

"So, you're suddenly drowning in free time?"

"Seems like it. I'll have to decide what to do with my newfound freedom."

The change in my schedule is making me light-headed in a not-so-great way. I shuffle items around in my bag until I find my day planner. The two boxes I labeled as *Work* are written in bright purple pen because they were never meant to be erased.

Empty time, voids that need filling.

Not sure what to write in those spots, I grab for my striped note-book and flip to today's list, making sure to angle it, so only I can read the page.

1. Morning run.
2. Digital marketing class.
3. Dialysis/reading with Ben.
4. Don't sniff Ben.
5. Don't think about kissing Ben.
6. Don't imagine Ben naked.

Shoot, why did I write that down? That's just more likely to bring the thought to my mind.

I skip down to the end of the to-do list and write in another item.

7. Fill the schedule void.

With it on my list, I can put everything back in my bag and refocus on the present.

And I'm definitely *not* thinking about Ben naked.

BEN

This is it.

It's like the universe is working in my favor. Trying to give me a chance. Now, I just need to come up with a plan and get her to agree to it.

For the next half hour, I brainstorm, only slightly guilty that I'm not fully listening to Holly read. She always leaves the book here, so I can catch up later.

An idea finally forms, one that sets my nerves on edge. It'll leave me vulnerable, but I figure that's what you need to do to get someone to trust you. Show them the darker parts of yourself but also share the things you love with them.

At the next chapter break, I take advantage of her pause. "Holly." She glances up from the book, and I enjoy the warmth of her gaze on me before continuing, "Come on an adventure with me this weekend."

She blinks, obviously not expecting my invitation. I wait.

"An adventure? What kind?"

"An overnight adventure. A surprise adventure."

I grin, and she hesitantly smiles back at me. But her face is still full of questions.

"So, you won't be telling me where we're going?"

"Nope."

"That sounds kind of murder-y."

I chuckle. "Then, I guess you'll just have to trust me not to murder you."

Her teeth chew on her bottom lip as she regards me. I hold my breath. She opens her mouth to answer and then closes it, thoughtful again.

"How about this?" Obviously, something about the situation is making her uncomfortable, and I really hope the murder-y comment was just a joke. "I'll tell Terra where we're going. She can help you pack then. And, of course, you'll drive us, so when you get in the car, I'll give you the address. You can text it to Terra or your brother. That way, all my horror-movie plans will be ruined." I give a mock-frus-trated scowl, which successfully pulls a laugh out of her. The sound has my gut clenching in pleasure.

"Well, don't you have everything figured out? When were you

thinking we'd leave and come back? I have some things to do Sunday afternoon."

That sounds a whole lot like a yes.

"No problem. Friday to Sunday morning. When's your last class tomorrow?"

"Ends at three."

"Perfect. We can leave right after that."

"What about your Saturday treatment?" She waves at the machine chugging away beside me.

Fuck this dialysis.

I hate scheduling my life around it. Luckily, I have more control than those who have appointments at actual treatment centers, so I can manipulate when I get mine done.

"I'll hook up tomorrow after class and then Sunday when we get back."

Holly considers me again, but this time, while she chews her lip, the side of her mouth curves up into a half-smile. Like she's thinking good thoughts.

"Okay, Ben. I'll go with you on a weekend adventure. But, if I wake up in a bathtub full of ice, missing one of my kidneys, I'm going to be really angry."

"Don't worry. I plan to steal your kidney at a later date."

Holly sticks her tongue out at me, and my cheeks ache from the size of my grin. Maybe some guys would play it cool, act nonchalant about getting the girl they've been crushing on to agree to a weekend away. She asked me to give her the truth though, so I'm not letting my face lie.

Holly shakes her head at me like I'm crazy. Maybe crazy for her.

"Stop being weird and read. It's your turn." When she hands me the book, our fingers brush against one another, and if I'm not mistaken, her breath speeds up a bit.

Or I could be imagining things.

That's the problem though. I've been having trouble figuring out exactly how Holly feels about me. If Jasper's right, then she likes me but is worried about the exchange not happening if things start up with us and then go sideways. I doubt only hanging out with me during my treatment sessions is helping her forget those fears.

Time to get away from all these distractions.

Holly fishes some notebooks out of her bag, writes something real quick, and then puts it all away to focus back on me. "You gonna read to me or what?"

Maybe, this weekend, I'll get to explore the *or what*.

13

HOLLY

AGREEING to a weekend away with Ben is like eating a huge piece of chocolate cake. The whole time, you're fluctuating between loving the taste and chiding yourself for skirting your diet. And Ben is more tempting than desserts.

The buzzer lets me know he's here.

I press the speaker button. "Who, might I ask, is calling?" I use a prim tone, like he called on a fancy residence instead of a tiny apartment with two college students crammed into it.

"The renowned Ben Gerhard the Fourth. Here with his chariot." Some of the smoothness of Ben's voice is filtered out by the crackle of the speaker, but the sound still has chills skittering down my spine.

"Well, isn't that grand? We in a hurry, or do you wanna come up?" Ever since Annabelle's house, I've been imagining Ben in my space.

"I'll come up."

I click the other button by the speaker that unlocks the front door and try to calm my nerves, worried I'll start sweating. At least with the place being so small, it's easy to keep it clean. Terra hides her disorder in her own room, and I don't have enough stuff to get too messy.

The whole of my apartment could easily fit in the sitting room of Ben's parents' townhouse, but I like our little place. We have a tiny, round kitchen table with mismatched chairs that I reupholstered over the summer with funky floral prints. The overstuffed love seat Terra's mom donated to us sits by one of the two windows with a blanket Terra crocheted folded neatly on its back. My shiny orange pots hang from hooks on the walls because our cabinets are taken up by the food we buy in bulk.

Sure, my loft is a bit exposed and only has room for my bed, a lamp, and a dresser, but I have a soft mattress that Pops gifted to me for graduation. Plenty of times, Terra has climbed up my ladder to lounge with me on its comfy surface. Or I'll join her in her tiny bedroom for a Netflix marathon. It's not fancy, but it's home.

There's a knock on the door, and I don't dawdle in opening it.

Dang, Ben just keeps getting hotter. He has on dark jeans with boots, and his black winter jacket is unzipped, revealing one of the thermals he tends to wear. This one, interestingly enough, is purple. And he makes that deep plum work for him.

If we were a couple, I'd step forward to slide my arms around his waist. That way, I could hug his warm body against mine while also taking a long sniff of whatever subtle cologne he had on.

However, we are not dating, so I opt for stepping back and spreading my arms wide, Vanna White–style.

"Welcome to casa de Holly and Terra. Please refrain from flash photography and keep your hands inside the ride at all times."

"Yes, ma'am."

And there's that adorable grin that makes me want to melt into the floor or jump his bones. He follows me inside, shutting the door behind him.

"So, we've got Terra's bedroom on your right, the bathroom on your left, and the tiniest sitting area you've ever encountered straight ahead, and the kitchen is around the corner here." I lead the way, stopping at the stove because there is literally nowhere farther to go. Tour done. Wow, less than twenty seconds. I think that's a record.

"And where's your room?" The tone he uses when asking heats my blood and therefore my face. It's almost like he has plans for my room.

"Just gotta look up." I indicate the space above the bathroom where we can see short railings. I lean around the corner and point out the ladder that the front door hid when he came in. "I live above everything." I affect a haughty voice for this statement, covering my awkwardness with jokes.

"Well, this I need to see."

I praise the universe I made my bed as Ben grabs hold of the ladder and climbs his way up into my semi-private space. The idea of Ben in my sanctum is too tempting to miss, so I follow right after him.

At five-three, I can stand up with an inch or so above me when I'm in my room. Ben, on the other hand, clocking in at just under six feet, now hunches with the posture of Igor. I cover my mouth but not before a snort escapes. Ben smiles and plops down on my bed, so he can actually straighten his neck. Fortunately, he didn't knock down any of my glow-in-the-dark stars while pressed up against my ceiling.

"Nice space you got here."

To give a semblance of walls, I hung colorful thrift-shop scarves from the ceiling, draping them over one side of the railings. Unfortunately, because I don't have a closet, I had to install a rack along one wall to hang up my dresses and whatnot. That area is covered by a dusky-red shawl acting as a curtain. I basically look like I live in an Arabian tent.

"A bit different than I imagined though."

I raise an eyebrow. "You've been imagining my bedroom?"

His grin only grows. "Maybe."

"And what did you imagine?" This might be dangerous.

He shrugs. "Something orderly. Every bit of it organized. Not something so ..." He waves his hand, and I hold my breath while he searches for the right word. "Sensual."

I know I look shocked.

For the first time, I consider how this space might appear sensual. The fact that a bed takes up most of the room is probably a big part of it. The color scheme is all ruby and plum, matching Ben's current outfit. Making it seem like he belongs in this space.

It would be so easy to sink down next to him on the mattress—or better yet, straddle his lap. He could hold me against him as we explored each other, eventually lying back with me on top of him.

Sometimes, while lying in my bed, I've imagined being with Ben. And, a time or two, I might have brought myself to the finish line with those thoughts. But none of those fantasies were actually set here; they were just vague images my mind created of lips and hands and skin and pleasure.

This is real and potent.

"What are you thinking about?" Ben's question pulls me out of my fog.

Apparently, I've been staring at him again.

He stares at me with searching eyes, so I blurt out the first answer that comes to mind, "I've never had a guy up here before." At least, this isn't the dirtiest aspect of what was playing in my head.

Ben appears both surprised and pleased. "Really? None of your booty calls made the cut?"

"Nope."

I never liked the idea of Roderick in my space. What if he didn't want to leave when we were done? So, we stuck to his apartment.

I realize I haven't thought about my hook-up buddy in weeks, and I probably wouldn't have today if it wasn't for Ben bringing him up. Guess that makes it super clear that my decision to end things was the right way to go.

After spending all this time with Ben, I'm coming to realize that, when you want to make space in your life for someone, it's not that hard. And I'm thinking a hook-up isn't what I need anymore.

Things shouldn't go beyond friendship between the two of us. But maybe I should be open to a relationship with *someone*. Someone who makes me feel safe and comfortable yet also aroused, like Ben does.

I think I'm ready for more.

Trouble is, Ben's the one in my bed when I come to this real-ization.

∽

BEN

I'm the only man who's been in her bed before.

Like a caveman, I swell with primal pride.

Holly's bedroom is tiny, like her. And sexy, like her. I think it's the red-tinged lighting produced by the fabrics she's hung from the ceiling.

And the mattress is begging me to lie back, to lounge on its pillowy surface. I'd grab Holly's hand, so she'd land on top of me. Then, we'd kiss long and slow until we realized that too much time had passed for us to make our drive today. Instead, she'd invite me to spend the night here, with her, in her comfy little tent of a room. A night with Holly in my arms is vacation enough for me.

"Ben?" Her voice brings me back to reality. "You ready to go?"

Reluctantly, I nod and wait for her to descend the sturdy white ladder before making my own way down, worried about stepping on her slim fingers. When we're on the same level again, I get the sense that Holly is waiting for me to say something, like she's guarding herself against it. There's the beginning of a wall; she has put down a few bricks and is reaching for more.

I can guess why.

My parents are rich. They've worked hard for their wealth, and they're both fans of spending their money. We've only spent time in their luxurious townhouse, and now, I'm in Holly's small apartment, one most wouldn't think compares to what I grew up with.

But this is her place, so I love it.

"I'm all set." She grabs a duffel bag off the couch and indicates I should lead the way out the door. But I don't move yet.

"Your place is great."

She shrugs. "It's small."

"So are corgis. But they're great, too."

That gets me raised eyebrows and the chuckle I was hoping for.

"Very true. And bonus points for liking dogs."

"Of course. I mean, I have a soul, don't I?"

And so we leave Holly's place with smiles and traded jokes. Exactly how I want our trip to start.

"Can I have the keys, please?" Her hand, with its fresh green nail polish, stays extended as I load her bag into the trunk next to mine.

"Look at you, actually asking instead of just hopping into the driver's seat." I dangle the keys from my index finger.

She sticks her tongue out at me before snatching them. "Sometimes, I like to give the people around me the illusion of control," Holly explains over the top of the car as she shimmies out of her puffy winter jacket, tossing it on the backseat and then sliding into the front.

As we wait for the heater to start blasting its glorious warm air, I plug in my phone and type the address into a GPS app.

"Expected travel time: two hours, fifty-four minutes. Proceed five hundred feet and make a left," the automated female voice directs us from the car speakers.

"Three hours? Where exactly are you having me take us?" Holly sounds intrigued rather than put out by the distance.

"You'll see. You wanna text the address to Terra?"

"That's okay." She shifts into drive. "I trust you."

Boom goes the dynamite. Like a happy bomb has been dropped on my chest, an explosion of excitement and pride radiates through me.

Holly trusts me.

This is what I've been waiting for. But this doesn't seem like the right time to broach the topic of dating. I'll leave it—for now.

With a few swipes on my phone, the familiar voices of Preston and Steve and their morning crew fill the car.

Holly claps excitedly before returning her hands to ten and two. "You have their podcasts?"

"Yep. Downloaded a couple this morning. Figured they'd be good driving company."

"You figured right." She turns on the blinker and eases into traffic, leaving the city as the GPS directs.

"So, I need to apologize up-front. I'm probably going to fall asleep at some point." A twinge of shame pinches my gut. "It tends to happen. Like when I'm sitting for long periods ..." I trail off.

Holly reaches over, still keeping her eyes on the road, and gives my knee a squeeze. "You do you, Ben. Believe me, I wish I could sleep in the car. Just be warned, you might wake up with some new tattoos on your face, courtesy of my friend Mr. Sharpie." We're at a red light, and she flashes me a grin.

"You're evil."

"I'm imaginative." She turns up the volume as I chuckle.

Embarrassment eases from my chest, excitement returning. That's what Holly does for me—takes the bad and morphs it into good. That's why she's the perfect companion for this trip. There will be times on this adventure when sadness will try to push its way in and drown me.

Holly might believe this getaway is for her benefit. Selfishly, it's really me who needs her company in order to combat some dragons lurking in my past.

14

HOLLY

THIS ROAD IS CREEPY, lit only by my headlights, crowded on all sides by thick swaths of trees. At one point, I slow down to five below the speed limit because this place is just begging for a deer to jump out in front of the bumper. Then, I'd swerve into a tree, destroying the car, and the ax murder who had trained his pet deer to crash cars would have no trouble picking Ben and me off as we stood, stranded, on the side of this forgotten road.

I don't get out of the city much.

My overactive imagination goes to town on my nerves, and I need Ben to wake up to distract me. He lasted about thirty minutes into the drive before his head lolled to the side, his steady, slow breathing signaling he was asleep. I don't begrudge him his nap. Marcus gets tired easily, too. That's what happens when your organs don't function properly. It's like your body is constantly trying to reboot itself.

But nap time is over. The GPS claims we'll arrive in about twenty-five minutes, and I need reassurance there's actually a destination at the end of this winding road.

"Ben," I speak softly, hoping to draw him out of sleep gradually. "Ben?"

No dice. His face is still pressed up against the edge of the car door with his mouth parted. The pose is adorable. Doesn't mean I'm not going to wake him up.

"Benny, time to get up!" Now, I've transitioned into singsong.

He shifts a bit, and I think I'm successful. Then, he starts snoring.

Oh, heck no.

"Ben! The cops are on our tail!" My shout fills the car.

He shoots up, bleary, wild eyes searching for sirens or flashing lights. My chuckle brings his gaze to me.

"Glad you could join me, sleeping beauty. How was your nap?"

He grimaces at me, and I'm tickled to see him dragging his forearm over his mouth, wiping away a drop of drool that leaked out. Next, he massages his neck, discomfort clear on his face.

"Think I slept weird."

"You should have reclined the seat, cotton brains."

"Cotton brains?"

"Yep. Brains made of cotton. Now, take a look around and assure me that the GPS hasn't taken us the wrong way. Like to a haunted mansion or something."

Ben stares out the window, searching the dark forest. I'm not sure why I think he'll be able to recognize the uninhabited stretch of road, but I can hope. Glancing at the GPS, he manipulates the screen to read the upcoming directions.

"Yep," he says, sitting back in his chair. "We're right where we need to be."

I nod and then make sure I have my full attention on the road, still on the lookout for suicidal woodland creatures.

"Can I ask you a question?"

Even though I want to examine Ben's face after he throws out this query, I keep my eyes ahead.

"Sure. Doesn't mean I'll answer it."

Ben nods. "Fair enough." He clears his throat before going on, "Why do you need to drive the car?"

I figured this would come up at some point. Surprised he waited so long actually. I don't talk about this part of my life much, but with Ben, the words come easily.

"When I got my license, I honestly wasn't that interested in driving. I didn't have my own car, and I had the bus system pretty much memorized. Then, there was this one night, just a few weeks after I could legally drive by myself, when my mom picked me up from a friend's house. Problem was, she'd had a few drinks." And I'm almost certain something other than just alcohol was floating around in her system. "I asked her if I should drive, but she swore she was fine, and I let her convince me. It's just ... she wasn't around much. So, when she was around, I wanted to keep her happy. I didn't put up much of a fight."

I risk a quick glance at Ben, and he's watching me. No expression on his face.

"We were on the road for maybe ten minutes when she ran a red light. My side of the car got hit. Luckily, they weren't going too fast, but my door still got smashed in. I had a mild concussion, broken wrist, and a lot of cuts from the glass."

"That sucks. I'm sorry you went through that," Ben speaks softly.

"Yeah, so it was shocking. Scared the daylights out of me. Then, the next time I sat in the passenger seat, even though Marcus was driving, the minute he started the car, I began having a panic attack. And that's been the case ever since. I've tried a few more times with different people and different cars, but it's always the same thing. If I'm not driving, then I'm panicking."

"Make a right turn in one mile," says the GPS.

"Well, you can drive my car anytime you want. I don't mind." The easy smile in Ben's voice takes away my self-consciousness.

There's a slight pressure behind my eyes, and I think, if I wasn't driving, I would hug him. Or kiss him.

The road we turn onto is paved, barely, and the trees crowd in closer.

"You realize how creepy this whole situation is, right? There are dozens of horror movies that start in this exact same way."

"Wow. You a fan of the genre?"

Until he stops me, I don't realize I've been rattling off my list out loud.

"Terra is. I don't know why I keep letting her talk me into watching them."

"Well, you forgot the most obvious one: *The Cabin in the Woods*."

"Oh, yeah! That one's funny at least. But you're just proving my point."

"It's only scary because it's nighttime. Believe me, tomorrow, you'll think this is all gorgeous."

"If I live that long."

Ben laughs and chooses halfway through to morph it into a creepy, evil cackle. My only recourse is to punch him hard in the leg.

"Ow! Okay! I'll stop!" He's back to normal laughing, which has me smiling reluctantly. "We should have one more turn, and then we'll be there. And I promise there are lights we can turn on to scare away all the monsters and murderers."

Five minutes later, the GPS proves Ben right by telling me to make a left onto a gravel road. In fact, it's not a road at all, but instead, it is a long driveway ending outside a cabin.

"Welcome to my hideaway."

~

BEN

Four months. That's how long it's been since I last drove up to this place. I've come here a lot over the years, each time planning an extended stay. Invariably, I barely make it through one night before escaping back to the city. Whenever I pull up to the place, a strange cauldron of emotions boils in my gut, threatening to burn me. There are the old remnants of familiarity, excitement, comfort, but then there's also the new spectrum of despair and loneliness.

Holly shuts off the engine but leaves on the headlights. I don't know why I decided bringing her here would somehow make everything easier. But I'm willing to try.

"Are you renting, or is this your place?"

"It's my place. My grandpa left it to me when he passed away."

I've never thought *passed away* is an accurate way to describe how Grandpa Ben died, but Holly doesn't need to hear the harsh truth. At least, not at the beginning of what I hope will be a fun, relaxing weekend.

"Were you close?"

"Yeah. He lived here, and I'd stay with him for a few weeks during the summer and visit throughout the year." I know she's ready to ask more, and normally, I love her inquisitive nature, but if I'm going to talk about my grandfather, it's not going to be in a cold car after a long drive. "Come on. Don't want to be caught outside when the zombies start coming out of the woods."

"That's not funny," she grumbles the words but turns off the headlights and exits the car.

The distinct click of the trunk's latch sounds loud in this quiet space. Before I can grab her bag, Holly has the strap slung over her shoulder.

"You can't unlock the door if your hands are full. Now, please tell me this place has heat."

The moon is almost full, and in its dim glow, I watch her do a little dance to keep warm as her breath puffs out like fog. If we were a couple, I'd pull her into my arms, using my body heat to warm her, and probably take too much pleasure in having her soft curves pressed against me. Instead, I choose a more friendly arm-around-the-shoulders approach and enjoy the feel of her leaning into me as we walk up the stone path to the front steps.

"There are radiators in each room. We'll have to turn them on though. Sorry, but, to start off with, it's only going to be warm enough to keep the pipes from freezing. I have a local guy swing by every couple of weeks to check on the place. I asked him to bring by a few loads of wood." We're on the front porch, and I let go of Holly to pull back a tarp, revealing a generous stack of seasoned firewood.

"Oh, awesome!" Finally, she gives me that gorgeous grin. "I've never made a fire before! Can we make one tonight? Please?"

"You've never had a fire before?"

She shakes her head. "No. None of the houses I've lived in ever had a fireplace." Holly does a little happy jig that gets me chuckling.

"What a city girl."

She sticks her tongue out at me as I tsk in mock disappointment.

After unlocking the front door, I navigate with muscle memory alone until I find the first lamp. When I click it on, the interior of the cabin alights in a faint glow. White sheets cover all the pieces of furniture, giving the space a ghostly, abandoned feel.

That's not going to help Holly's horror-movie image.

I set down my bag before moving to the couch. As I grab one side, Holly joins me on the other, and together, we uncover the couch, a lounge chair, coffee table, a tiny, round kitchen table along with its two battered chairs, and the bookshelf. There's an old TV with only a VHS player hooked up to it. The narrow linen closet I store the sheets in is also where I take out multiple quilts.

When I glance back over at Holly, I notice her rubbing her arms despite her bulky sweater.

"Come on. I'll show you where the heaters are, and we can get them going."

The one in the main room is already on, so I crank it up. We go to the bathroom next, which is just an add-on to the building with basic white tiles, a stall shower, and a blue toilet and sink.

Grandpa Ben thought it was so funny that the department store sold colorful toilets. Before I started visiting, he didn't have a bathroom attached to the cabin, settling for an outhouse and washing off in the kitchen sink or a nearby river if it was warm enough. My parents demanded the addition before I could stay the night.

The small radiator gives a cough and shudder before sputtering to life.

"I think I'll wait for it to heat up before pulling my pants down in there. Sitting on that toilet would be like sticking my butt in the freezer." Holly shakes her head, an expression of horror on her face.

I snort. "Well, we wouldn't want to hurt your precious butt, now would we?"

"Definitely not. It is one of my most valuable *assets*." She wags her eyebrows at me while emphasizing that last word.

"Holly Foster!" I give a mock gasp. "Did I just hear you curse?"

"I don't know what you're talking about." With an innocent smile, she wanders to the other side of the room. Two closed doors sit almost side by side on the far wall. "Is this where we're sleeping?"

My body goes through a weird adrenaline and lust spike mixed with excitement and disbelief at her words. I rein it all in as best I can. Just because I want her lying in bed next to me doesn't mean that's why I brought her here. And Holly didn't mean sleeping together. She obviously jumped to the logical conclusion that both doors lead to bedrooms.

I take a deep breath to settle myself while doing my best not to imagine sliding under the covers with Holly, holding her flush against me, and making out until we're so hot that we don't need to worry about radiators.

HOLLY

Two doors. Maybe one is an office or something. Sure, it makes sense that they'd both be bedrooms, but can't I hold out a slight hope that there's only one bed, and we need to share it?

Obviously, my hopes need a stern talking-to. I'm not supposed to be lusting after Ben. I'm his friend, and I'm his organ donor.

And I'm in a secluded cabin with him that is practically begging me to snuggle up to him for warmth.

"Yeah, your room is on the left."

Balloon of inappropriate expectations popped.

The doorknob is cold as I grab it and turn, and the room behind it is just as chilly. Doesn't really inspire me to want to go to bed. Not helping matters, the full-size mattress in the middle of the room is completely bare.

"Here. I brought sheets. And the radiator is on the far wall." Ben gently moves me out of his way by placing his hands on my hips and directing me to the side. He flips the switch of a lamp on the bedside table and crouches down behind the bed.

I try not to watch the way his shirt stretches over his broad shoulders as he fiddles with something out of sight.

The now-familiar rattle and cough of a radiator sounds again, and I pray that means this room will be nice and toasty come bedtime. Just as we moved in sync when uncovering the furniture, Ben and I silently work together to make up my bed.

In the soft yellow light, I take in my temporary quarters. Simple furnishings, just like the main room, with a bed, side table with a lamp, and a heavy wooden dresser. The piece that stands out is an easel sitting next to the window.

"Was this your grandfather's room?"

He gives me a silent nod while tucking in a corner of the fitted sheet.

"Was he an artist, too?"

Ben glances up, surprise clear in his eyes. Then, he turns, following my indicating nod to the easel.

With his back to me, I have no idea what he's thinking or feeling, only that he's been quiet and still for a stretch. I'm about to try taking my question back when Ben clears his throat and meets my eyes.

"Yeah, he was. Taught me everything I know."

There's pain on his face, although I can tell he's attempting to hide it. Ben tosses me my side of the top sheet, which we arrange in silence and then finish by spreading a thick quilt over top.

When we're done with the bed, he doesn't immediately leave.

Instead, he slides open the shuttered closet doors. The top shelf holds a couple of pillows, which he hands to me.

I've started putting on the pillowcases when he speaks again, "This is some of his work."

Sitting on the floor of the closet is a stack of canvases. Ben removes one, stares at it for a moment, and then turns to show me. The image is of a mother deer and her fawn. The young animal grazes while the elder stands tall, on the lookout for danger. The detail is amazing.

I step closer, lean in, and notice the texture of the paint. I'm tempted to run my fingers over the subtle ridges, but I don't want to be disrespectful. "It's gorgeous. At least, that's my inexperienced opinion."

Ben nods. "All of his work is. He painted what he saw. Living out here." He settles the painting back in the closet and shuts the door.

For some reason, my heart aches. It seems wrong, almost criminal, to put that piece in the dark, like a forgotten item unworthy of the daylight. Maybe, if this trip goes well and Ben and I become closer friends, I could possibly ask to take the painting with me. I'd love to hang it right above the couch in our apartment. That way, I'd have a piece of this wild land with me back in the city.

My thoughts are interrupted by my stomach, which decides to make it known that I haven't eaten since the granola bar and yogurt I had for lunch about six hours ago.

Ben grins at me, having clearly heard my body's demands. "You hungry?"

"How did you guess?"

He chuckles. "I have a cooler in the car with food for the weekend. I'll go grab it."

I follow him out to the main room, and when he steps out the front door, I pick up the other stack of sheets. No reason for me to stand around, doing nothing, when there's another bed needing to be made.

The second bedroom is smaller, and there's only a twin bed. I feel bad that, even though I'm almost a foot shorter than Ben, he's giving me the larger bed. Maybe, before the night is done, I can convince him to trade with me.

Unlike the bare walls in the larger room, this one has paintings draped all over the place. Even my novice eye can tell these pictures aren't at the same level of the piece hidden in the closet. They're still very nice, but the detail doesn't seem to be as sharp, and the perspective in a few is a bit awkward. I imagine a younger Ben sitting in front of these canvases, working to match the advanced techniques of his grandfather. If the paintings in Ben's childhood bedroom are his, then he's clearly continued improving.

The car's trunk slams shut outside. I put aside my thoughts, hurrying to the bed. The sooner the chores are done, the sooner I can eat.

The twin bed is pushed up against the back corner, so after I tuck the fitted sheet's first three corners in, I have to crawl on the mattress to reach the final one. It's hard to lift up the mattress and settle the sheet in place while I'm kneeling on it, so I'm still struggling when the front door creaks back open.

I've almost got it right when Ben's voice snaps behind me, "What are you doing?"

15

BEN

THE MAIN ROOM is empty when I get back inside, but my bedroom door is open. After I set down the cooler, I move to find Holly, only to see her on all fours on my bed. Her tight black leggings show off the lovely, round shape of her ass, and she's practically wiggling it in the air as she messes with something.

"What are you doing?" The mental strength I use to keep all my blood from rushing down south also results in my words coming out gruffer than I meant them to.

Obviously surprised by my tone, Holly squeaks and flips over, bouncing when her butt hits the mattress. She slides off, revealing a partially made bed.

"Sorry. Am I not supposed to be in here?" She looks confused, but I'm relieved to see no embarrassment or discomfort.

"No, I'm sorry. You can be in here. I didn't mean to sound so harsh."

"Oh, okay. Weirdo." A small smile touches her mouth before she crawls back onto the bed to finish the job. "Turn on the radiator. It's freezing in here."

I gladly follow her orders because I also need to take a moment to adjust myself.

Who knew making a bed could be so sensual?

The way she crawls across the mattress slips right into my fantasies, and now, I'm thinking about me lying on the bed with her crawling toward me, lips curving, eyes heating, silently promising me wicked things.

"Are all these paintings yours?" she asks the question while tucking in the edges of the top sheet. As her fingers move, her eyes meet mine and then flick around to the crowded walls.

I'm not sure how I feel about her seeing them. I painted them when I was a kid, when I was just starting to learn. Not that I'm anywhere near a master now, but I'm much better. But, no matter how many mistakes I made, my grandfather praised me for each piece. Of course, he gave suggestions for improvement, but he insisted they all be hung on the wall to be admired. If Grandpa Ben could love them, then so could I.

"Yep. I started painting when I was around eleven, so they're not my best. But they're not too shabby either."

She's silent for a moment as she walks around the room, peering at each of them individually. I try not to follow behind her like a praise-seeking ghost.

"Mmhmm. I think it's this one." With a little wave, Holly points to one of the smaller canvases.

The winter break during my junior year, my parents let me spend half the time here with my grandpa. The image on the canvas is as close to a copy as I was able to make of the view from my window one early morning. In a vivid contrast, I painted a fat crimson cardinal sitting on a snowy branch, icicles dripping from the underside of the wood.

"You think that one is what?" My stomach clenches, and my nerves are raw as I wait for her answer.

Sharing my artwork isn't something I often do. Annabelle was a mistake; annoyance was in her eyes when I laid out a few of my sketches for her input. My parents show polite interest but don't tend to ask questions or encourage the pursuit. At least my tattoo artists gave positive feedback, but I was also paying them to apply my artwork to my body, so it wasn't like they were unbiased. Grandpa Ben was the only one who met my passion with his own.

I brace for the politeness or disinterest or possibly even the insult that will be injected into Holly's next words.

"I think it's my favorite ... nope." She glances around the room, shakes her head, and then hits me with her breath-stealing grin. "I know it is." With a light touch, she brushes her index finger down the sweep of the bird's back. "This is just so sweet. And gorgeous. And realistic. Did you actually see this bird?"

I nod. "He was sitting right outside my window one morning. I took a picture before he flew away and even had time for a quick watercolor rendering before he left. Then, I got to work and painted that. You really like it?"

"I more than like it. I *like*, like it. I have a crush on this painting. It's not just the bird. It's winter. You captured the beauty of winter." She goes to touch it again but then pulls her hand back.

For a moment, I can't speak. Somehow, this lovely woman perfectly interpreted the feeling I had been attempting to convey when making that piece. I want to gather her in my arms and brush kisses over her sweet lips as I thank her for understanding my work. Instead, I step beside her and slip the painting from the wall.

"You should take it then." Now, I'm hoping I don't find out she was just being polite.

That thought is quickly dismissed when she practically snatches it out of my hands.

"Really? I can have it? To take home with me?"

I cover up how much her excitement means to me by making a joke. "Well, since you *like*, like it. I wouldn't want to break up the happy couple."

Holly does a little hop dance, like an energetic puppy, while she holds my painting to her chest, as if I've given her some precious gift.

In reality, it's me who's just been given something wonderful. Then, shocking the hell out of me, she reaches her hand up to grab the back of my neck and pulls me down to her tiptoe level before planting a kiss on my cheek.

"Thank you, Ben." She releases me and slips out of my bedroom, eyes focused on her new artwork.

I, on the other hand, am still bent forward, dealing with the shock of having Holly's lips on me for even the briefest moment.

~

HOLLY

Dijon mustard drips onto my chin, and I quickly swipe it off with my finger but not before Ben sees.

He smirks and hands me a napkin. "I told you that was too much."

"You can never have too much mustard." I take another generous bite of the turkey, cheddar, lettuce, and tomato sandwich I assembled for myself from the different fixings Ben stocked the cooler with. "When I was a kid, I used to have mustard sandwiches."

"You don't mean ..." The horrified look on his face cracks me up as I nod.

"Yep! Bread and mustard. That's all I needed."

He mimes gagging, and I decide I'd better not mention how I resorted to that simple meal a few times this past year when money was tight.

"Don't tell me you've never eaten anything weird before."

Ben chews on his own sandwich, his expression morphing from disgusted to thoughtful. As he ponders his past eating habits, I take the time to study him.

We're sitting at the small kitchen table, and Ben's elbows rest on the worn plastic surface. He's wearing his wire-rimmed glasses. I'm betting it's because he knew he'd fall asleep in the car. Again, I can't help comparing him to a sexy professor. With them on, all he needs is a sports coat with elbow patches, and my panties would catch on fire.

Speaking of fire, the one he built roars behind him, bringing out the red in his hair so much that I can't even see the blond tones anymore.

My gaze moves from his face to his body. The purple shirt he has on completely covers his tattoos. I wonder if he wears long sleeves because it's cold or if it's a habit to hide the ink. I want to push them up his arms, so I can see more of his work.

But maybe it's not just his tattoos he's keeping covered.

I know Marcus is self-conscious about the raised ridge on his forearm needed for the dialysis treatment. He thinks it's unattractive. I, on the other hand, have always connected the twisting bulge with him staying alive. There's no part of my mind that views fistulas as ugly.

Maybe, if I told Ben that, he'd stop wearing so many long-sleeved shirts.

Maybe he'd stop wearing shirts altogether.

I jump and glance up when Ben finally answers, trying not to look like I was mentally undressing him.

"I've been eating sushi since I was three years old. Does that count?" Ben's eyes focus on me with a hint of hope in them, like he wants to be weird like me.

My smile is indulgent. "I'd say that's a bit odd. But it doesn't make me want to gag."

He smirks. "Sorry to disappoint. You want me to go grab a handful of dirt and try to choke it down?"

"Wow. You really know how to show off for a lady. I don't think a man has ever eaten dirt for me before. At least, not since kindergarten."

"There's not much I wouldn't do to try to impress you, Holly." The joking tone is gone from his voice, and when I meet Ben's gaze, a sudden flash of heat races over my body.

But that's probably just the fire.

I focus back on my sandwich, and we finish our meal in silence.

Ben cleans up the dishes as I go to sit on the couch, enjoying the gentle blaze. The flames shrank while we ate. Trying to be careful, I place a log in the fireplace before quickly retreating to my seat.

The heat from it is lovely, and the flickering amber and crimson embers are mesmerizing.

"How's your first fire? Everything you imagined?" Ben settles on the opposite side of the couch, turning to face me with his arm slung over the back cushions.

"I love it. It's so warm and soothing." Relaxed for the first time in a while, I sink back and let my body go limp.

These past few weeks have been tough. I've tried so hard to continue on my steady course, power through all the stress, never admit that there are nights I want to cry myself to sleep. With classes, work, internship hours, study sessions, club meetings, and doctor appointments, I've found it harder to keep away the ever-looming emotional storm.

Besides that one time, I haven't called Ben after my blood draws. Even while he tried to make me laugh, I could see the guilt as he watched me struggle to calm down. And it was too easy to rely on him. I need to do this on my own. So, each time, I spend close to a half hour in the restroom, working through a set of breathing exercises. Safe to say, my nerves are shot for hours afterward.

A few bright spots have kept me sane—talking on the phone with Marcus every other day, eating Monday night dinner with Pops, receiving texts from Fred about his tests going well, and visiting Ben during his dialysis sessions.

But those are just Band-Aids on a festering wound. This trip, a whole weekend away, is a healing balm.

"Thank you. For inviting me here. I've been ..." My throat clogs up, and to my horror, there's a sudden pressure of tears behind my eyes. Like my body wants to take advantage of my relaxed state to let go of all the tension I've been stifling in the form of a sloppy sob session.

Not gonna happen.

I breathe in deep through my nose, let the air sigh out of my mouth, and start again. "I've been stressed lately. Didn't realize how much I needed a few days off."

"Is it the exchange?" he quietly asks from his side of the couch.

I shrug. "Some of it's that. I just want it all to go smoothly. I need Marcus to be okay. He's my brother. He's everything to me." The desperation in my voice unnerves me but not as much as Ben shifting closer.

He reaches out his arms and wraps them around my shoulders until he can pull me into a gentle embrace.

At first, I tense but not because I don't want his hug. I want it too much.

Still, his warmth is so much more soothing than the fire. After a moment of hesitation, I surrender and lean into him.

~

BEN

We sit, wrapped up together, silently watching the logs crackle and spark. This weekend's adventure started with the simple goal of visiting this cabin without having the memory of my grandfather overwhelm me, and in doing so, I'm growing closer to Holly.

Apparently, I'm not the only one who needs some help.

She's starting to open up to me.

I've gotten the surface of Holly. Just a few pieces of her that she's willing to share. But I can tell, from offhanded comments and unconscious reactions, that there's more underneath her protective shield.

Twice now, she's been vulnerable with me.

There are no genuine words of comfort I have to offer because, until the donation happens, everything is just hoping. All I can do is be open and honest, like she is with me.

"My grandpa Ben, he was ... he lived here. By himself. Except for when I visited." The words don't come easy, but having Holly in my arms helps. "He committed suicide. That's how he died."

She lets out a small gasp before slipping her arms around my waist to wrap me in a tight hug. "When?"

"It was the summer before my freshman year of college. So, I guess it's been three and a half years now."

But I remember that day so vividly that it could have been last week. Mom picking up the house phone with a smile that was gone a second later. The way she stared at my dad, who was still reading the newspaper across the table from me. He didn't even notice her watching him, oblivious to the devastation that coated her face as some police officer relayed the news of her father-in-law's death. And I sat there, cereal forgotten, knowing that, whatever the call was about, it would tear my heart out.

"Doesn't matter how much time goes by. It still hurts," she whispers the words and rubs soothing circles on my back.

It's strange, revisiting the darkest part of my life, which was even worse than when I got sick, and at the same time feeling the highest level of comfort with Holly's small body pressed against mine.

After sitting quietly for some time, I'm ready to change the depressing mood. This is supposed to be a fun getaway, not a sob-fest.

I lightly kiss her silky, honeysuckle-scented hair and then use my grip on her to stand us both up.

"Enough with this sad talk. I promised you an adventure, and I'm gonna deliver. Put your boots on." There's almost a physical pain when I let my arms drop away from her.

"My boots? You don't expect me to go back outside, do you? It's below freezing out there!"

She rests her fists on her hips and glares at me like I told her we were going to run naked through the snow. Maybe, if there were snow, I would suggest it. The thought and her sassy reaction have me grinning.

"Don't worry, princess. We're not going out for long. And you'll be plenty warm. See?" I grab the stack of quilts. "I'll wrap you up."

She grumbles to herself as she stomps over to her boots. Laces tied, she glares at me from the front door. I'm not worried though; there's no real heat in it. Instead of just handing her the quilts, I take the opportunity to wrap one around her shoulders and then place the second over her head like a hood before tucking its corners into her palms.

"Hold the edges together. There, nice and toasty."

"I look ridiculous."

"Yeah, you really do." I laugh, and she pulls her trademark move of sticking her tongue out.

Does she know what that does to me? How my stomach clenches and my skin goes hot? The craving I get to cup the sides of her face and meld my mouth to hers, seeking out that tempting tongue with my own?

If she knew, would she still do it?

"You gonna tell me what we're doing or what?"

I reluctantly move my eyes away from her mouth to find her watching me. "Let's head out, and I'll show you."

After I cover myself in blankets, we walk outside. We're just twenty feet or so from the front porch when I stop her.

"Look up. Ever seen a sky like that in the city?"

Holly's stare follows my direction, and I get a rush of satisfaction when her mouth drops open. I move, so our shoulders brush and then look up myself.

Even though I know what will be there, the sight still rocks me, taking me back to my childhood when I was innocent. Full of wonder.

Luckily, we have a cloudless night, and the moon has sunk low. The dark, inky sky sprawls between the tops of the trees, filled to the brim with stars. Each one shimmers on the backdrop, making the universe seem infinite and daunting.

We stand silently, admiring the tapestry, until I can't fight the urge to hear her voice any longer. "Whaddya think?"

Holly gasps, as if she'd forgotten to breathe for the past five minutes. "This is so much better than my bedroom ceiling."

I'm confused for a moment before I remember the little plastic stars in her loft bedroom. Seems I chose well.

"Yep. Nothing beats the real thing."

For the first time since I told her to look up, Holly takes her gaze off the sky to reward me with a grin. "This is amazing. So far, I give this adventure an A-plus."

Success.

"Is the cold getting to you? Want to head back inside?"

She shakes her head and moves her eyes upward again. "Not yet. Just a few more minutes."

I keep my stare fixed where it is, finding the view on Earth more appealing.

16

HOLLY

My mind drifts on the edge of sleep. The last thing I remember is snuggling in my quilts on the couch. Now, I'm swaying gently with the sensation of strong arms cradling me. For a moment, I forget I'm twenty-one, thinking Marcus is carrying me to bed like he often did at Grams's. But the smell of my carrier is different. Marcus had a warm, deep scent, like baking bread. This person smells cool and fresh, like pine trees in new snow.

My eyelids crack just enough to make out a slim nose with glasses perched on the end and slightly curled hair falling over a concentrating brow.

Ben sets me down on my bed, pulls the sheet and quilts over me, and presses a firm kiss on my forehead.

I sigh and clutch the covers close as I ease into the mattress. Safe in my blanket cocoon, I let my eyes close, and sleep reclaims me.

When I wake up again, a dim digital clock at my bedside informs me that it's just after three a.m. Ben is gone, and everything is quiet.

The city never gets this hushed. Or this dark. No streetlamps or neon store signs shine in through the dense curtains. I'm shrouded completely in blackness and silence. But this isn't muffling, like when I cover my head with a blanket. This is expansive and daunting.

The quaint cabin might have been pleasant when we first arrived, but now, it sets my nerves on edge. I'm back in horror-movie mode. Especially because I have to pee like a racehorse, which means leaving the wonderful, warm safety of my bed.

I consider briefly the strength of my bladder but admit that, if I don't want to wet the bed when I fall back asleep, a trek to the bathroom is a must.

Pulling back the covers, I'm relieved to find I still have on my large sweater, leggings, and wool socks. A chill manages to travel through them, but at least I'm not putting my bare feet on the cabin's frigid hardwood floor. Only the muted glow of the alarm clock gives me any light. If I knew where my phone was, then I would use the flashlight on it, but apparently, when Ben carried me to bed, he didn't bring my phone along with him.

My bedroom door creaks as I turn the knob and pull it open. Out in the main room, I again have to navigate by the faint glow of a clock dimly shining from the kitchen stove. Ben's door is cracked open, so I make sure to walk on my toes, not wanting to wake him.

As I creep through the room, I get that sudden, panicked dread that comes with an overactive imagination. It's the same discomfort I experience when I go into Pops's dusty, unused basement or when I have to walk home after work, alone, late at night. Every shadowed spot is hiding a potential threat. Maybe a hand will shoot out from underneath the couch to grab my ankle. Or a looming figure is lurking just behind the door, ready to drag me to hell.

There's no visible danger, but my mind plays the what-if game until my heart picks up speed, and the beginning trickles of adrenaline enter my veins.

Before I can cause a self-induced panic attack, I'm able to maneuver around the few furnishings and reach the bathroom.

Problem is, I can't find the light switch. The walls are bare as my fingers scramble and search, coming up with nothing. Finally, I give up and resort to using my toes to feel my way around the confined space, eventually coming in contact with porcelain.

As I sit on the chilly toilet seat, I try to rationalize away my fears.

1. Ben's grandfather lived out here with no problems for years.
2. Our trip was so last-minute; no ax murderer would even know we were out here.
3. Ghosts aren't real.
4. Probably.
5. Ghosts probably aren't real.

This isn't helping.

Now, I'm stuck on ghosts and how likely one might exist in this cabin.

Ben's grandfather killed himself.

Did he do it in this house? In the room I'm sleeping in?

Suddenly, the haven of my bed doesn't feel so safe anymore.

Great. Toilet time was supposed to be *calm down* time, not *find new ways to freak myself out* time.

I flush and locate the sink to turn on a rush of cold water. That way, I can wash my hands and splash my face with it in an effort to shock the ridiculous nightmares out of my head. After drying off, I take a deep breath and place my unsteady fingers on the door handle.

Time to brave the unknown.

~

BEN

The sound of the toilet flushing wakes me up. A quick glance at the clock reassures me that Holly's probably just taking a nighttime bathroom break, and I haven't overslept. Unfortunately, I'm now fully awake, thinking about Holly sleeping one room away.

After stargazing, we hustled back inside and decided to watch one of Grandpa's old VHS tapes. Holly picked *Rush Hour 2*, and we chuckled our way through most of it, sitting side by side on the couch. At one point, her head rested on my shoulder, and I realized I was the only one watching the buddy-cop comedy. Carrying her to bed was easy; she's not that heavy of a person. What was hard was not crawling in beside her, holding her close to my chest, and falling asleep, pressed against her warm, soft body.

Instead, I covered her up and went to my own bed, which seemed like a chilly block of cement in comparison. Finally, after an unhealthy amount of tossing and turning, my mind relaxed enough to allow for a light, dreamless sleep that ended the moment it registered Holly up and moving around.

The old floorboards let out shallow creaks with each slow step she makes. Above that noise, I hear her voice. The words aren't clear, but she's definitely speaking.

Worried she might be sleepwalking, I decide to check on her. The decision has nothing to do with my constant craving for her presence. At least, that's what I tell myself as I slide from underneath my covers and grab my glasses off the nightstand.

Darkness coats the main room, and only from the dim glow of the oven's clock can I make out the vague shape of Holly tiptoeing across the room. In the silence of the night, I can hear her whispered words. Not that they make any sense.

"I don't want to bother you. I'm just minding my own business. You have a very nice house. Thank you so much for letting us stay in it."

Who is she talking to?

"Holly?"

Her shriek rips through the silence. A pillow from the couch comes flying at my head, which I dodge on instinct.

Before something heavier gets hurled at me, I crouch on the floor and call out to her, "Holly! It's me! It's Ben!" I scramble forward on my knees until I reach the closest lamp.

Light floods the room, causing my eyes to water and squint.

When I can see straight, I realize she's also blinking in the sudden brightness while holding a decorative wooden fish like a pitcher winding up.

That would've hurt a hell of a lot more than a pillow.

"Ben?"

She doesn't lower the fish right away, so I slowly stand up, hands splayed in surrender.

"Yeah. It's me. You okay?"

Her chest rises and falls on quick, short gasps. "You scared me!"

"Sorry. Heard you talking. Didn't know if you were sleepwalking or something." I step around the couch and cautiously approach her because she still resembles a deer in preflight mode. "Wanna put the fish down?"

Her head whips to the side, and she gapes at the knickknack like she's just realized it's in her hand. She quickly places it back on the table. "Oh gosh. Ben, I'm sorry. I almost bashed your head in!" She wipes her hands on her leggings and then wraps her arms around her middle.

"Don't worry about it. Happens all the time." That earns me a snort even though she won't look at me. I place my hands on Holly's upper arms and find she's shivering. "Are you okay?"

"Oh. Yeah. I'm fine. It's just ..."

I wait her out.

"I freaked myself out a bit. I'm not used to sleeping somewhere so dark and quiet." She shrugs.

"Who were you talking to?"

"What?" She avoids my eyes.

"Before screaming like a banshee, you were whispering. Like you were talking to someone." My hands slide up and down her arms, as if to warm her.

She sighs and rubs her forehead. Briefly, she meets my eyes and then seems to give up and lets her gaze drop to the floor again. Her answer clocks in at just above a murmur. "Your grandfather."

"My grandfather?" I'm so surprised that I let my arms fall and step back. "What does that even mean?"

Holly cringes and wraps her arms tighter around herself. "Sorry!

I'm sorry. It's just that my imagination was going haywire in the darkness. I couldn't stop thinking about how there might be an ax murderer outside the house. Then, I reasoned that an ax murderer wouldn't bother stopping by here because you're never here, and how would an ax murderer know to show up this weekend?" The words tumble out so rapidly; I'm worried she'll pass out from lack of oxygen. "So, that ruled them out. But then what about ghosts? This is just the type of dark, spooky situation where a ghost would pop out at someone in a horror movie. And, if a ghost were here, then it would probably be someone who died here. So, I just thought that maybe I should make a preemptive strike of kindness. Maybe your grandfather's ghost wouldn't jump out at me if I said nice things and thanked him and whatnot." Halfway through her insane explanation, Holly started pacing, and by the end, she's panting for breath.

I try to catch up with the mad train ride of her thought process. "You believe in ghosts?"

"No." She hesitates and then shrugs. "Maybe." A huge gust of a sigh leaves her, and finally, she holds my gaze. "I'm not saying I definitely do. But I thought it was better to be safe than sorry."

I think back on the things she was saying when I came out of the bedroom—complimenting the house, being thankful that we could stay here.

In a weird way, it's kind of sweet. Then, I imagine, if Grandpa Ben were actually a ghost, he'd probably grumble that scaring people was a waste of his time.

The thought has me grinning. Holly frowns at me, which only gets me laughing. She tries to glare, but a small smile tugs at the corner of her mouth.

"So glad I'm amusing you." Speaking is what breaks her stony expression, and a chuckle escapes.

I calm down, shaking my head at her. "I can't believe you were talking to my grandpa's ghost."

Her smile fades. "It was insensitive. I'm really sorry, Ben."

Stepping forward, I wrap my arms around her, not wanting her to beat herself up. "No. I'm sorry. I should've realized that sleeping here might be uncomfortable for you. New place. Out of the city. I get it. First few times I visited my grandpa, he put a night-light in my room." I don't mention that I was nine at the time. Don't want to wound her pride.

Holly relaxes against me and winds her arms around my waist. This result right here makes almost getting hit in the head with a wooden fish worth it.

"I'm such a ninny."

I rub reassuring circles on her back. "A ninny who's able to defend herself. So, there's that."

She gives my side a pinch, but I just chuckle again.

"You okay now? Think you can sleep?" I hate myself for the reasonable suggestion of her going back to bed. Getting to hold her, having her feel safer in my arms, eases a tension in my gut I didn't know was there.

To my relief, Holly shakes her head against my chest. I tilt my chin down, so I can see her face. The angle is too steep for my glasses, and they slide down my nose, almost falling off my face. Before I can reach to correct them, Holly lifts a hand and gently pushes them back into place while giving me a rueful smile.

"I'm too wound up to sleep. Could we put another movie on?"

She steps out of my hold, and the chilly cabin air stings in her place. I stoked the fire before carrying Holly to bed, so now, the room is a good ten degrees colder than earlier.

"Or ... I'm sorry. You don't have to stay up with me. You should sleep. I'll keep the volume low." She rubs her arms for warmth.

"No way. I'm up now, too. What are we watching?"

She grins and then chews on her lip. She casts her eyes down at her socked feet. "You pick since I'm the reason we're up past three in the morning in the first place. Be right back." With shuffling movements, she retreats to her bedroom.

While she's gone, I scan the movie selection even though I pretty much have it memorized. My grandfather loved cop and heist movies. But he also had a softer side. I slide a dusty VHS off the shelf and pop out the previous one in the player.

"So, what's it gonna be?" Holly's back, wrapped in the blanket from her bed, settling on the couch. She looks adorable, engulfed in the large quilt, her short brown hair mussed, an embarrassed flush lingering on her cheeks.

"You'll see. I figured we'd take a break from the action movies."

Holly pretends to pout, sticking out her bottom lip.

I want to bite it.

Then, surprising me in the most enticing way, she opens her arms, unwrapping the blanket from herself. "Get in here before we both freeze."

With an invite like that, I don't hesitate. Taking a chance, I wrap my arms around her waist and lean back on the armrest, pulling her with me. She squeaks in surprise but doesn't resist.

Once I'm reclined on the couch, Holly rests mostly on top of me, the quilt fully covering us both. I keep my arms loose for her to escape if she wants to. After a second of stiffness, she relaxes, snuggling in closer and laying her head on my chest.

This is a special brand of delicious torture. Every soft curve of her body is pressed against me. My arms rest high on her back, but my hands could easily slide lower to cup her round, perky ass. I could clutch her tighter to me, roll over, and have my body bear down on hers as I devoured her pouty mouth.

But I don't do those things. I'll only push the boundaries so far until she gives me permission to go the distance I want to travel. For now, lying here together is enough.

"*When Harry Met Sally.* Good choice," Holly murmurs while pulling the covers tighter around us.

"Don't know why you doubt me. I thought we'd already established that I could do no wrong."

In response, she pinches my side, but it's more like a ticklish caress than anything.

I take it as a good sign that she can be comfortable here, lying with me like this. That she feels safe now.

Each day, I'm more confident about Jasper's claim; Holly likes me, but she needs to trust me before I can ever hope to be with her.

17

HOLLY

THE STUPID, chilly weather is preventing me from fully admiring the sexiness that is Ben Gerhard. Of course, I wasn't complaining about the cold last night when it gave me an excuse to fall asleep on his lovely, warm chest. But, now, as we make our way through the woods, this late fall air is a real nuisance.

If it were summer, I imagine Ben would be in shorts and a tank top. I'd be able to see his long arms with those corded muscles shifting under his skin. And his calves would be on full display. People underestimate the attractiveness of a nicely toned leg. I'm not one of those people. And the tattoos! I almost forgot about the gorgeous ink illustrations on his skin that I've only gotten to peek at.

I want to see them again. All of them.

Instead, I get Ben in long pants, a shapeless navy North Face jacket, and a black knit hat covering up his ruddy-blond curls. Hiking behind him, I can barely even tell it's Ben. I could be following any random dude through the woods. Good thing I have an active imagination. As we hike up the narrow trail, I revisit images from last night.

That was one of the best sleeps I'd ever had. After the whole *talking to a ghost and throwing things like a madwoman* incident, of course. When Ben pulled me onto his chest, I was ready to stake a claim. That's my spot, no one else's. It's the comfiest place in the world, and I'm not a good sharer.

At least, with Ben, I'm not.

Thinking of Roderick, which I haven't done in a while, I remember the quick discussion we had a year ago about our arrangement. I was clear that, as long as he was using protection, I didn't care who he had sex with. He asked me if I was sleeping with someone else, and I answered honestly. I wasn't, and I didn't have any plans to. That was true at the time. The idea of dealing with more than one guy just felt like work.

But spending time with Ben isn't a hassle. More like a vacation I never want to return from. And the idea of someone else taking a vacation with Ben makes my face hot and my chest ache. Annabelle, the girl who so clearly wants to book a trip, shoves her way into my head.

And why in the world am I thinking about Ben's ex-girlfriend?

Stupid question. I know why.

I want to be his current girlfriend. I might even want to be his forever girlfriend.

Ben's the kind of guy who makes me ponder the future, not just the next hook-up. Not that we've had any hook-ups.

Sometimes, I get the sense that he's flirting with me, but then he's back to joking just as quickly.

In Ben's mind, we're just friends, which is how it should be.

My brain finishes its annoying loop of finding myself attracted to Ben, imagining being with Ben, remembering he sees me as a friend, and deciding it's best we stay that way. Every time, the realization hurts like little paper cuts on my insides.

It's a matter of minutes before the cycle starts again.

"How're you doing back there, princess? You've been pretty quiet."

The nickname sends those bastard butterflies ricocheting through my stomach.

"Just enjoying the view." No need to point out his firm butt is what

I've been staring at for the past fifteen minutes. "And trying not to hold you back."

He's been good about taking breaks regularly, reminding me to drink while taking sips from his own water bottle.

Ben stops and faces me. "If anyone is slowing us down, it's me. Not really at peak condition anymore." His comment comes out strained, as if he's trying for a humorous tone but failing.

"Could have fooled me. If I knew where we were headed, I'd offer to walk in front of you. Keep you at a gentle stroll the whole way."

He gives me one of those genuinely devastating smiles, like he thinks I'm the most amusing person in the world. "Believe me, I would love to follow behind you." A flash of something in his eyes causes my butterflies to riot. "But there's no real map, so I guess I'm the leader." He focuses a searching gaze on me. "But, seriously, tell me to slow down or stop at any time. You'd probably be doing me a favor."

My skin tingles as I take in his flushed face and crinkling green eyes. The sight of him is too much to deal with. I need more vigorous walking to calm down my clamoring hormones, which are currently demanding I shove him up against a tree and make out with his enticing mouth.

Where's a spin bike when you need one?

"Will do, oh fearless leader!" I mask my horniness with enthusiastic comments. "We must forge ahead. I want to see this glorious place of wonder!"

Before we left this morning, Ben claimed our hike would result in a beautiful view, making the two-hour trek there worth it.

"You won't be disappointed." Before moving on, Ben takes another sip from his water bottle. The markings on the side let him know how much he's consumed and how much more he can drink today.

As we continue moving, I consider how his life will change once the donation is complete. First off, no more dialysis. I'm giddy at the thought, but I realize I'm going to miss reading together.

Is that something friends can still do?

Although, maybe after both donations are complete ... I could ask him about being more than friends then. We won't owe each other anything at that point.

I bring up a mental calendar in my mind, wishing I had my physical one with me. Mapping out the upcoming weeks, I figure out the best time to bring the subject up.

The transplant will likely happen during our winter break, so obviously not before then. Then, there's recovery time, which will be longer for Ben than for me, so that gets us into mid- to late-February. After that, I'll get the chance to see if he still wants to spend time together as regular friends rather than as donor and recipient. And I could ramp up my flirting and observe how he responds. So, another month for that.

I envision flipping through my calendar. Looks like spring is when I should aim for.

When I get back to my apartment, I'll pull out my planner and pick an exact date.

With a plan in place, a swell of hope makes my chest lighter. I can suffer now, pine after him in silence, but it won't hurt so much, knowing that maybe, one day, there'll be a chance that something could happen. I don't like waiting, but for a shot with Ben, I'll sit on my hands and bite my tongue.

Like he knows I'm thinking about him, Ben glances back at me with a questioning brow raise.

Not ready to talk, I simply form my mittened hands into two thumbs-up and pair them with a cheerful smile. He grins and focuses forward again.

Yeah, Ben is worth the wait.

~

BEN

Tonight is the night.

I watch as Holly sidles up to the cliff's edge, and my heart rate increases. I want to snatch her back from the danger, but instead, I just keep close. Making sure I'm in grabbing distance.

When we broke out from the cover of the forest, her expression was worth every panting breath it had taken to get here. Trees spread in a russet blanket beneath us, and we can see for miles from our vantage point. But this view didn't come without a cost.

I ache in a way I never did before my kidney failure. When I came here with Grandpa Ben, we'd cross the distance in half the time it took today. Part of me wants to use Holly as the excuse for our slow pace. But, really, it was me.

When I look in the mirror now, I'm less than I was before. Literally. My body has less mass, less muscle. I try to keep in shape, but I'm restricted in what I can do. The strength I used to have is gone. In the past, I could hike for eight hours with only a quick break for lunch. Now, we've walked for two, and I know I'm going to need to sit here for a while before we head back.

"This is gorgeous, Ben. Can we eat lunch here?"

I nod, having trouble forming words when she turns her vibrant smile on me.

There's a flat rock, like a naturally formed tabletop, and the two of us perch on it while I pull the food out of my bag.

"What feast have you brought for me?" She rubs her hands together, and I laugh at her silliness.

"Well, princess, we've only the finest selections for your refined palate."

"Oh, do tell."

I put on my best haughty British accent and pull items from my bag with a spectacular flourish. "Our first course will be this lovely blend of nuts and dried berries, all gathered and assembled by blind nuns. Then, for our main meal, we shall explore a variety of Power-Bars, delicacies prepared around the globe. And, for dessert, our chefs have procured the rarest of fruits. This wonder is referred to by the locals as an *ap-pel*."

"It is glorious to behold!" Holly snatches the apples from my hands, as if they were made of gold, and does a great impression of examining them.

I'm the first one to break, letting out a snort. She giggles in return, tossing one back to me. We tuck into our meals, eating in companionable silence, the same way we hiked here.

When we're done, Holly stretches out her legs and reclines back on her elbows. Now that we're out of the woods, the sunshine finally reaches us. It warms the air and the rock we're sitting on to an almost-comfortable temperature. Both of us stare out over the treetops.

"I can't get over how beautiful it is here. Did your grandfather show this to you?" Holly continues to gaze out over the forest below.

"Yeah. He loved hiking. He's the one who first told me about the Pacific Crest Trail. Always saying how he wished he'd tried to hike it when he was younger and stronger." Bet he wouldn't have screwed it up royally like I did. Veering away from those negative thoughts, I focus on Holly's original question. "We'd come here in the summer and paint. Just watercolors mostly. Practicing. Or I'd draw. I'm better with a pencil over a paintbrush, but Grandpa was the opposite."

She nods and doesn't ask anything else.

But, suddenly, I have the urge to say more. I want to talk about him. I want to talk about him with *her*.

"He was the one who took me to get my first tattoo."

This gets her attention, and she gives a half-smile and raised eyebrow. "How'd that go over with your parents?"

"They were pissed when they found out. But I was eighteen." I shrug. "Nothing they could do."

"Which one is it?"

"Which tattoo was my first?"

She nods. I hesitate but then start to unzip my jacket, experiencing the same raw nerves I did in the car weeks ago when I went to unbutton my shirt for her. I'm revealing an important part of myself, and I want more than anything for her to understand it.

"Actually, my grandpa was kind of the inspiration for it."

Even with the sun, the autumn air chills my skin, working its way through my long-sleeved thermal when I shrug out of my jacket. It's going to get worse in a second.

"There aren't any books in the cabin, but that's because I took them all when he died. He read to me all the time when I was a kid. One book was his favorite."

I pull up my shirt, revealing my rib cage on the right side. There's a whole series of images there, but I point to the one I want her to see. It's of an old dog with shaggy hair and drooping tail but with one ear perked. Behind the dog is the shadow of a man.

"*The Odyssey*. There's a scene where Odysseus finally makes it home, and his dog is the first to recognize him right before he dies. That image stuck with me. So, I drew it. A bunch of different ways. Finally ending on this one. And, when Grandpa Ben asked me what tattoo I wanted to get, I felt like it had to be this."

After giving her another second to look, I let my shirt fall back into place and thrust my arms into my coat. But, even with my clothing shielding me again, I am exposed.

If she wanted to, Holly could really do some damage at this moment.

"That piece ... I don't want to say it's beautiful. Because that's not right. It's ... haunting. Yeah. Haunting." She leans forward and squeezes my arm, so I meet her eyes. "You're so talented, Ben."

With her face close and the warmth of her words, I'm at risk of becoming drunk on Holly. This would be the time to lean in and capture her lips, but she pulls back before I can focus my mind enough to make a move.

"I've never read *The Odyssey*. I'll add it to my list."

I watch as she stands and brushes some dirt off her tight jeans. My teeth bite into my lower lip as she smooths her hands over her backside, innocently looking for debris.

Clouds drift across the sun, lowering the temperature.

"Time to head back." I collect our trash, shoving it into my backpack, suddenly eager to return to the cabin.

Holly's smile is small and a bit regretful. She turns to face the overlook, spreading her arms wide, as if to embrace the whole scene.

"Good-bye!" Her call echoes over the expanse, fading as my grin grows. With a firm nod, she turns back to me. "Ready."

We fall into an easy, slower pace once we're on the trail again. I listen to her breathing behind me, the crunch of her steps, and imagine I can feel the heat of her on my back. I wonder if she looks off into the trees as we walk or if she stares at me. I know, if she were leading, my eyes would see nothing but Holly for as long as I followed her.

18

HOLLY

"I CAN'T BELIEVE we're cooking over a real fire. It's like The Oregon Trail!" I bounce on the springy couch cushions. "We'd better not die of dysentery."

Ben laughs while stirring the soup, his face flushed from being so close to the flames.

When we got back from our hike, I was surprised to find the return trip had taken longer than our way out. Then, my skin tightened with guilt, realizing Ben had to be exhausted. He'd probably pushed himself just to give me an adventure this weekend.

Of course, he doesn't know that every minute I spend with him is an emotional, wild ride.

But, before I could suggest a nap, Ben grabbed an armful of wood and told me we needed to get the fire going for dinner. Apparently, cooking over an open flame isn't as efficient as a stovetop.

Much cooler though.

"If you want the real Oregon Trail experience, we'd get this fire going outside. Sleep in makeshift shelters built out of whatever we found in the woods."

As background noise to his description, the wind blows through the trees just outside the cabin, knocking branches against the roof. The thought of sleeping on the icy ground and dealing with those chilly gusts all night sends a visible shiver quaking down my spine.

Ben chuckles at my reaction.

"No, thanks. Not now at least. Maybe when summer comes around."

Sleeping under the stars on a warm night sounds much more appealing.

When I glance Ben's way, I find him staring at me with a curious expression. I don't have time to interpret it before he turns back to the fire.

There's a metal arm with a hook that stretches out over the flames, and from it hangs a pot he dumped a load of ingredients into earlier.

"What's on the menu?" My stomach finished digesting our simple lunch a while ago and is starting to complain.

"Chicken and vegetable soup. Shouldn't be too much longer now."

As I sit on the couch and watch him stir the mixture, a sense of contentment flows over me. Every Sunday, I prep my meals for the week just to take some of the pressure off my busy schedule. Even with all my planning, it's still a lot of work and time-consuming. But, tonight, Ben is cooking for me. And in a ruggedly attractive way.

"You're a certified mountain man."

"You impressed?"

He grins back at me, and I realize he hasn't shaved in a couple of days. Suddenly, I get the urge to run my knuckles over his cheeks just to feel the coarseness against my skin.

I have to clear my throat before I can answer, "Maybe. What other secret talents are you hiding?"

Ben runs his eyes over me, slow and searching.

Now, I'm the one with flushed skin, but I don't have the fire as an excuse.

What's he looking for? Do I want to know?

In the spring. We'll talk about his hot gazes in the spring.

"Maybe I should show you some of them." One of his eyebrows rises, just cresting over the rim of his glasses.

Holy goodness gracious.

I think my panties just caught on fire. I don't know if he meant that to sound so dirty, but I'm on the verge of jumping off this couch to straddle him and beg for a detailed demonstration.

Instead, I struggle to find a witty response, ending up with a weird, strangled, "Mmhmm?"

His grin is back, making him appear wicked. But, when he talks, it's so casual that I question my entire interpretation of the situation.

"Dinner's ready." The spoon in his hand hovers above the open soup pot, and I can see the steam rising off the top. "Could you bring the bowls over?"

Trying not to look like I'm running away, I hop up and retreat to the kitchen.

When I grab the waiting bowls on the table, I notice one has measurements on the inside. Even when eating, he has to be precise.

As I hold them out, Ben spoons in our fire-cooked dinner, and excitement sets off little sparks in my chest again. This experience is so novel.

Wearing an oven mitt, Ben pushes the metal arm away from the fire and covers the pot with a lid before taking his bowl out of my grasp.

I settle in at the table, spoon in hand, ready to take my first bite, when Ben stops me with a chiding cluck.

"Careful. That's crazy hot. Also, you'll probably want this." After rummaging in one of the cabinets, he hands me a tiny saltshaker. "Sorry. Had to make the soup low sodium. 'Cause ... you know." He waves at his abdomen.

I wish I could just rip out my kidney, stuff it in him, and yell, *You're free! Eat whatever and drink however much you want!*

At least he doesn't have to wait much longer.

"No problem. I'd rather it be too bland than too salty. I can always add more salt but can't take it away once it goes in." I grin at him, but his smile doesn't reach his eyes. Time to change subjects. "So, you never answered my question."

"Which one?"

From his trusty bag of food supplies, Ben pulls out a loaf of crusty-looking bread. And, yeah, maybe the sight has drool pooling in my mouth. Looks like I found a new sexy image to add to my spank bank: Ben handing me bread.

What girl doesn't want a hot guy offering her carbs?

Pushing away the inappropriate thoughts, I try to keep the conversation light. "What other outdoorsy things can you do?"

Ben smirks before blowing on a spoonful of soup. Unfortunately, that brings my focus to his lips. I study their shape, how the upper lip is just a bit fuller than the bottom.

Would he like it if I sucked on it? Maybe gave it a gentle bite?

I pinch the back of my arm—hard.

Get it together, Holly! You're not in some low-budget porno where you can go around, biting people! He's not a piece of meat, so just try to act like a normal human being rather than a sex-crazed animal!

My inner tirade is broken off by him answering, "I can start a fire without matches or steel and flint. It takes forever, but I've done it a few times."

Takes forever? My panties are proof that he only needs one look.

Ben continues talking, unaware that I have absolutely no control over my hormones, "I can fish with just a line and a hook. We joked about the shelter, but I could actually make something that would keep us relatively warm through the night."

"I believe you. Still don't want to try it." Somehow, I keep my tone light.

He steals my move and sticks his tongue out at me. Not helping with my fixation. "Got it. I also know a bunch of different knots. That came in handy during rock climbing."

"You went rock climbing with your grandpa?" Doesn't seem like a common retirement activity.

"Nah. He was getting older and not really interested in that. I used to go with Fred all the time when he lived in Philly. Even road-tripped to Kentucky to climb in Red River Gorge. Grandpa Ben and I would stick to hiking and camping."

"So, he's the one who taught you all that stuff?"

"Yeah. He was in the military and learned a lot about survival from it before he became a lawyer, and the rest was self-taught. Mainly after he retired. He didn't have to live out here. Grandpa Ben was pretty well off. Could've set himself up nicely in the city. But, when he left the firm, one of the first things he did was buy this place and move into it."

"Do you know why?" Finally, I've stopped obsessing over my attraction. When Ben talks about his grandfather, I simply get the urge to settle in and listen.

"Said he'd spent enough of his life in an office. Wanted to breathe in the fresh air every day. He even quit smoking when he moved out here." Ben's smile melts away, leaving a dark, troubled look in its place. His soup forgotten, he leans back in his chair and stares out the window even though everything on the other side of the glass is solid black.

Curiosity scrapes at my nerves, but I don't want to pry into something that'll hurt Ben.

"So, you visited him out here a lot?"

He nods, still not looking at me. "Every summer. For a few weeks at a time. Sometimes, I'd come out on weekends. Spent a couple of Christmases here. We'd just hike and paint and watch movies. Wasn't anything spectacular, but those were some of the best days of my life."

When Ben turns to me, his expression makes me want to cry. His smile is laced with a deep pain. It's in the shine of his eyes and the twitch of his cheek muscle. The way his jaw clenches down after he's done speaking.

When did I get to the point where I could read his face so well?

"Sounds perfect to me."

Ben traces his eyes over me, but I don't get heat this time. Instead, it feels like an embrace. Comfort.

"He would've liked you. He was a no-nonsense kind of guy. Gruff and stubborn but caring. You remind me of him sometimes."

"You think I'm gruff?" I pretend to scowl.

Softness replaces some of the tension in his face, and the curve of his lips loses its forced nature.

"Maybe. After all those years of legal jargon and double talk and working with loopholes, I think he got tired of it. When he retired, he was all about being straightforward. No lying. Not putting up with liars and idiots. And you ... you're just like that. So, yeah, I think the two of you would have gotten along."

"I wish I could've met him."

In my mind, Grandpa Gerhard looks like Ben's father but with a few extra wrinkles in his face and a shock of white hair. I imagine him sitting in the bedroom I slept in, expression serious as he works on creating a beautiful painting of a mother deer and her baby. Then, I see him sitting on the couch with a little boy whose light-red hair curls around his ears and the edges of his glasses. In a deep voice, the man reads classic adventure stories to his adorable grandson before taking an old movie off the shelf and sliding it into the outdated VCR.

That's a man I would've loved to know.

So, why didn't I get the chance? What made him take his own life?

No matter how curious I am, I won't make Ben confront the pain of his past if he doesn't want to.

Still, it's like he reads the questions on my face because he goes ahead and answers them. "Grandpa was never the type to do what he was told. Always went his own way." His mouth quirks in a half-smile, half-grimace. "Even though he quit, the smoking still got to him. Lung cancer. Past the stage where much could be done. Doctors told him to move closer to a hospital. Start chemo treatments."

Ben glares at the table. Without thinking about it, I reach out for his hand, twining our fingers together. He returns my grip but still keeps his eyes down.

"What happened?" Silly question, as I already know the answer.

He's quiet for a bit before continuing, "My parents were planning on him moving in with them. Arranged everything, so he'd be as comfortable as possible. A few days before they were set to get him, we got a call from the police in the area that he'd been found about a mile from here. Sitting in the forest." A deep sigh echoes his pain. "When you have a lot of money like Grandpa did, you can get pretty much anything you want. Including a bottle of pills. They said it wasn't painful. Just like he went to sleep."

I notice a single tear trace its way down Ben's cheek. He doesn't seem to feel it, and I don't want to interrupt him. So, we just let it fall.

~

BEN

Holly places her free hand over top of our joined ones, and that gentle touch draws me back from the toxic darkness of my memories. I realize my face is wet, and I do my best to wipe away the tears. This wasn't my plan for the weekend. Yeah, I thought I'd tell Holly about Grandpa Ben because he was important to me. But I didn't think it'd hit me so hard. Not after all these years.

Now, she's got this look on her face, like I'm a wounded animal she has come across and has no idea how to help.

I try to smile, but I don't think it comes out right. "It's been a while. But I still miss him."

"Of course you do. God, Ben, getting that news, it must've been horrible." She rubs her hand over my forearm, soothing me with each stroke.

"Yeah. I mean, I didn't want him to suffer. So, if that's how he wanted to go, then okay. He could've told me. I don't think I would've tried to stop him." Who really knows though? The man was everything to me. Maybe I would've begged him to stay as long as possible. "It's just ... I never got to say good-bye."

That's what hurts the most. Him leaving without a word. And me never getting to tell him how much he meant to me.

I always thought I'd have more time.

"That really is the worst, isn't it? One minute, they're there. The next, they're gone, and you're left, trying to figure out how to keep living."

Something in Holly's voice draws my focus to her. She's got her eyes on our hands, a frown shadowing her mouth. Her shoulders bow forward like there's a heavy weight on them.

Sometimes, clarity comes without words.

"You lost someone, too. Didn't you?"

Her head flies up, and her expression gets guarded. For a minute, I don't think she's going to answer, but slowly, her defensiveness cracks until I glimpse pain and vulnerability behind her mask. She dips her chin.

"My grandma. I always called her Grams." Holly's normally cheerful, joking voice sounds watery.

Suddenly, sitting at the kitchen table seems too formal for this kind of intimate talk. I stand up, using my grasp on her hand to tug Holly after me. She follows without protest, hesitating for only a moment when I settle on the couch. The cushions next to me sink down, and I relax as her warm body presses against mine. With one hand, I hold hers, and I move the other to rub soothing circles on her back.

"What happened with your grams?" I whisper the question, but she still hears me.

Before responding, Holly leans her head on my shoulder, making my chest swell.

There hasn't been a time when I've felt more like a man than when Holly seeks me out for comfort and support. When she relies on me, when she trusts me, it's the greatest feeling in the world.

"You've probably noticed my family isn't exactly the normal setup." She fiddles with my fingers.

I give a small confirming noise from the back of my throat.

"My mom was never very responsible. She had problems with addiction. Apparently, she broke a bone or something while playing softball in high school, and the doctors gave her painkillers. Things kinda spiraled after that." Holly keeps her voice matter-of-fact.

I try not to react to the sad story, wanting to know everything about the girl at my side. Even the hard stuff.

"She met Pops, Marcus's dad, at a party. They dated for a bit. Then, she got pregnant. Pops stopped messing around. She didn't. When Marcus was born, he came out sick. Mom left him with her mother, Grams, to take care of. Pops helped, but he was barely older than a kid. Worked a bunch of jobs to cover the medical bills. Grams was a schoolteacher, so she didn't make much money. They figured things out though, the two of them. Then, six years later, Mom showed up, pregnant again, no father to be seen." Holly lets out a chuckle with no humor behind it.

I slide my arm around her shoulders, hugging her close.

She stares into the fire for a bit before continuing, "After what happened with Marcus, they did everything they could to get her clean, so I would be born a healthy baby. Mom even kept to the program after that, but we all still lived at Grams's. Well, the four of us. Pops had his own place by then. Marcus would stay with him on the weekends and with us during the week.

"So, when I was growing up, life was pretty good actually. I basically had two moms, and Pops was around enough that I didn't wonder too much about who my dad was." She tries to smile up at me, but I notice a tremble in her lip.

Then, she looks away, her shoulders going stiff. "When I was ten, Grams died. It was sudden. Sent Mom off the wagon. I'd never seen her like that before. One minute, I had two moms; the next, I had none." The deep breath she drags in stutters.

"I'm sorry, Holly."

She nods. We sit still together under a blanket of silence.

Now, I know how Holly felt when I told her my story. Helpless. There's a heaviness in the air, the weight from our pasts crowding the once-cozy cabin.

It seems wrong for us to stop here. The woman beside me deserves a happy ending.

"What happened next?"

Holly starts, as if she forgot where she was for a moment. After clearing her throat, she gives me the rest. "Marcus went to live with his dad full-time, but I stayed with my mom. The situation ... wasn't good. When he found out, Marcus convinced Pops to adopt me. So, the three of us made a new family." When she smiles up at me, this time, there's no quiver.

"Your pops sounds like a great guy."

"He's the best. You should meet him."

Now, I'm the one smiling. Holly wants me to meet her dad. That's the type of thing boyfriends do.

If I were her boyfriend, I'd also lean down to kiss her right now. With our faces only inches away, her big brown eyes locked on mine, it's tempting.

The silence grows thick between us as our breaths mingle in the close space. Hints of her honeysuckle scent tease and entice me, the warmth of her body turning my muscles into liquid lava.

Her lips part, and she gasps in a small breath. "Ben, I ..."

"Yeah?" My hand starts to rise to cup her face.

But then she turns her head and leans away from me. "I think our soup is cold."

That's not the only thing rapidly cooling down in this cabin. Still, I let her go.

"Don't worry about it. That's what we have a fire for." I walk over to the table, grab our soup bowls, and then crouch in front of the fire to return the contents to the original pot. Repositioning the pot over the flames, I realize we're low on fuel. "You give this a few stirs while I grab some more wood."

Her smile is toothy and excited as she eagerly reaches for the spoon handle.

I pull my jacket off the coat rack and slip my feet into my boots, not bothering to tie the laces when I'm only going as far as the porch.

The cool air hits my chest and creeps into the exposed seams of my shirt. Quickly, I gather an armload of split wood, balancing it on one arm as I pull the cabin door back open and shut it behind me, doing my best to keep the heat from escaping.

Holly is still by the fire, standing now, with her hands held out for warmth. The sight of her there, in her bulky sweater that hangs low over her leggings, cheeks flushed from the heat, short chestnut hair tucked behind her ears, I can't do anything but stare. This situation feels so right, like fitting that last little piece into the puzzle you've been working on for weeks. Spending time with her settles me but also sets my heart racing.

We've both cut ourselves open tonight. Been vulnerable with each other.

Greedy bastard that I am, I crave more.

I want to claim her as mine. I want to hold her at night when we fall asleep, kiss her in the morning, talk to her every day, worship her body, and have her explore mine.

Question is, does she trust me enough to give me a chance?

~

HOLLY

"You don't have to do that. I can get this." Ben comes up beside me at the sink, trying to take the sponge out of my hand.

I dodge him and flick some suds his way. "Nuh-uh. You cooked. I clean. Go pick out another movie." Besides, I need something to keep my jittery hands busy.

We almost kissed. At least, that was what it felt like to me. I barely pulled myself away from him.

He was probably just being kind. A good friend. Comforting me as I told him about my grams. That's all it was.

It would've been horrible if I'd leaned in for a kiss and he'd backed away, looking at me like I was a crazy person. Or even worse, what if he'd let me kiss him out of pity or because he'd felt obligated to keep me happy? Humiliating.

Good thing I have some self-restraint.

Instead of following my directions, Ben leans against the counter and grabs a towel. As he picks up dishes from the drying rack and starts wiping them down, he watches me.

I try not to fidget.

"What do you find attractive in a guy?"

The bowl I'm holding slips out of my hands, clanking around in the sink and splashing water onto my sweater.

Real smooth.

"What?" I try to recover my composure, concentrating on the dirty dishes.

"You know ... what makes someone attractive? To you specifically," Ben asks casually, like he's inquiring about what movies I like or how I take my coffee.

"That's a complicated question." I scrub vigorously at a specific spot that doesn't really need as much attention as I'm giving it.

"Really? I don't think so. Here, I'll go first." Out of the corner of my eye, I see him scoop up some utensils to dry. "Obviously, there's got to be something physical, but I like women in all different shapes and sizes."

I snort and can hear the grin in his voice as he keeps talking, "Then, there's the really important stuff. Like, do we laugh when we're together? Can we talk for long stretches without running out of things to say? Does my family like her? Is she passionate about life? Does she have a kind heart? Do I smile every time I think about her?"

I'm hanging on every word, applying his questions to the two of us.

Is that what he wants me to do, or is Ben just making casual conversation?

"Here, I think that one's clean."

Gently, he pries the bowl I was repeatedly rinsing throughout his description out of my hand. His skin brushes against mine in the exchange, and I give an embarrassing jump. Ben chuckles and leans in until I'm forced to meet his eyes.

"Your turn."

I can't help biting my lip. It's that or shout out, *You! All I want is you!*

Instead, I pick up the last plate, focusing on it while I work out an answer.

"You covered a lot of the bases. I guess I'd also want someone reliable. Honest. Someone I felt safe around. Like I could be *me* without being judged." The air gets heavy again, so I fall back on a joke. "And, of course, a pretty face to round out the package." When I grin over at Ben, I find him watching me. The eyes behind his glasses are emerald knives, cutting through my flimsy walls.

He steps in close, pressing me back against the sink but still leaving enough room for me to slip away if I want.

"Honesty. I can do that. Here's honest: I think about you all the time, Holly. Like an unhealthy amount. But I don't care if it's unhealthy because everything about you makes me feel good. You're my favorite person. Is that crazy?" His smile is sheepish but determined, and he shrugs. "Doesn't matter 'cause it's true. All I want is more of you."

Every bit of me freezes. Face, hands, body are all locked in place. For a moment, even my lungs take a pause from their normal duties. My brain needs to hit the restart button. He's scrutinizing me, probably looking for a reaction, but I'm sure my face is blank because I'm trying to figure out what to think.

"All I want is more of you."

"Like sex?"

Oh sheesh. That's the first thing out of my mouth?

Ben's cheeks get a ruddy glow, and his eyes heat up, but he shakes his head. "No. Not sex. At least, not just sex."

I'm usually great with thinking on my feet, but right now, my thoughts bounce around so much that I have trouble grasping them.

"More of me. What does that mean? What's *more*?" I sound breathy, probably from the lack of breathing.

"More is spending time together outside of my treatments. Like going on dates. More means holding your hand." He slips his fingers into mine and raises our joined hands. Then, keeping his stare locked on mine, he draws them to his mouth to brush a kiss over my knuckles. "More means more touching. I can hold you like I did last night all the time. That, once you give me the go-ahead, I can kiss you whenever I want. I feel like we're on our way to more. Like we've brushed against it." He rubs his thumb over the back of my hand, the rough pad of his finger sending tingles down my wrist. Then, with a sigh, he releases me and steps back. "If this is one-sided, tell me."

"One-sided?" I'm still floundering in all this new information.

"Yeah. If you just want to be friends, nothing has to change."

But that's not true. Ben just told me that I'm his favorite person. *Everything* has changed.

And my stupid mouth can't handle it.

"You're throwing off my entire schedule!"

19

BEN

Of all the possible responses, that wasn't one I'd planned for. "Huh?"

Holly brushes past me and starts pacing the length of the cabin. She mutters as she walks, and I'm not sure if she's talking to me or herself.

"Right now is all about surgery prep. Then, during the holidays, it's the surgery. Then, next semester is our recovery period. After that, you'd let me know if you still wanted to be friends. And *then* I'd ask you on a date. In the spring." She stops abruptly, staring at me from the other side of the room. Finally directly addressing me, her voice comes out desperate. "*That* makes sense. *This* does not. If it made any sense, then I would've done it already."

I think I'm following along. "You were planning on asking me out in the spring?"

"Well, I was before you did that!" She waves toward the sink, her hands fluttering and frantic like her words.

Cautiously, I approach her. This moment seems tenuous and

important. Still, I can't help grinning like an idiot. "Sorry. Next time, you'll have to let me know about the schedule."

She rolls her eyes. I empathize with her juicy bottom lip, pinched hard between her worried teeth. We stand, only a foot apart, silently staring at each other until I can't take it anymore.

"What are you thinking?"

She huffs out a breath and drops her gaze to her feet, which are covered in a pair of fluffy green socks. "I like you, but I'm worried about the exchange. For us, there's more than a friendship at risk."

My heart clenches. "Holly, do you think, if things don't work out between us, that I'd tell Fred not to give Marcus his kidney?"

Her grimace is telling. "When you say it out loud, it sounds cruel. But people can be cruel sometimes. A lot of times."

I reach out, brushing my fingers under her chin until she raises her head. "Do you think I'm cruel like that?"

Concentration furrows her brows and puckers her lips. Someone else might have wanted an immediate denial. But that would have rung false from Holly. Clearly, she's considering my question, so I know her answer will matter more.

"No. That just doesn't fit you." She gives me a tentative smile.

I beat back the excitement that threatens to spill over. She still hasn't agreed.

"Okay, so we don't have to worry about that. Anything else?"

A flash of some emotion flits across her face, there and gone too fast for me to identify it. Instead of answering my question, she leans closer, lifting her hand. Just at the point where I can feel the warmth of her skin, Holly pauses, watching me.

"So, *more* means, I can touch you?" she whispers, filling the heavy air between us with her hushed words.

My swallow is audible. If I open my mouth, I know I'll beg her to, so I keep to a silent nod.

With that permission, she rests her palm against my cheek. My face heats under the contact, and like a plant seeking the sun, I lean into her. I watch a light spark in her eyes as she runs her nails down my jawline, scratching the beginning growth of my beard, and then moves back up to finger-comb my hair.

A low humming sounds in her throat, and her eyelids sink until I can only make out half of her dilated pupils. Still, her hand moves. After finishing with my hair, she gently drags her thumb across my bottom lip.

I can't help myself. With a quick flick, I taste her skin with my tongue as it passes.

Holly gasps, pulling away. Then, she giggles, the sound setting off an explosion of exhilaration in my rib cage.

This is what I've been craving all these weeks. Playfulness between us that could lead to something more. Nothing other than this has to happen tonight, but just the promise of a future makes me grin so hard that my cheeks ache.

Still, I need to be sure. I run my palms over her sweater-covered arms. Then, I cup her neck and delve my fingers into her hair, the way she did with mine. The silky strands tease my skin.

"So, that's a yes? You're okay with *more*?"

"Yeah." She nods. "More sounds good to me."

HOLLY

I wonder if he'll grab my face and start kissing me. I'm actually looking forward to it.

Instead, Ben lets his hands fall away from my neck and laces our fingers together. He tugs me over to the shelf of movies and then moves to stand behind me, wrapping his arms around my waist and resting his head on top of mine.

"Pick one."

"Is this a test?"

His chuckle vibrates against my spine, and now, I'm sure I'm smiling as big as him.

"All of these movies are awesome, so you can't really go wrong."

I love it when Ben laughs, so I scan the titles for a comedy.

"This one."

"*Tommy Boy*? You a Chris Farley fan?" He reaches around me to slide my choice off the shelf.

It's odd how, one minute, we're trying to figure out our relationship, and the next, he's asking me about my favorite comedians. But I guess everything to do with us is a little weird.

"When Marcus went to Pops's on the weekends, they'd stay up late to watch *Saturday Night Live*. Monday night, he would tell me about the skits. I would be so bummed that I couldn't watch with them. Apparently, he told Pops because, one year, for Christmas, he got me the DVDs of the best of some of the cast members. Chris Farley's was my favorite."

I still have them. Whenever I need to smile, I pull one out.

"I knew you had good taste." Ben moves away from me to put the movie in, and I settle on the couch.

Once it starts playing, he turns but doesn't immediately sit down. The corner of his mouth curves up as his gaze traces over me. It's only then I realize I've brought my knees up into my chest and wrapped my arms around them like I'm a hedgehog curling in on itself.

I let go of my legs and try to sit like a normal person, but I don't think I'm doing it right. My back is stiff, and my legs cross and then uncross while my hands struggle to find where to go.

How do normal people sit again?

Ignoring my awkward movements, Ben plops down next to me. Then, without warning, he hooks me under the arms, and he half-lifts and half-shifts me until he's reclined on the couch while I'm sprawled across his chest. I appreciate his high-handedness because, suddenly, I'm extremely comfortable.

There's no quilt wrapped around us, but this feels more intimate than last night. Because, now, this is *more*.

The movie plays, and we chuckle at every classic joke thrown out by Chris Farley and David Spade. Ben's chest bounces me as he guffaws, making me laugh even harder.

Being together, like this, feels right. Letting go of the security of my timeline made me sweat at first, but for some reason, being around Ben eases my panic.

Even with the excitement of the night and the movement of his chest, I eventually drift off. Consequences of a long hike and a stomach full of good food.

When I wake up, it's because Ben is lifting me off the couch.

"Wha-what's happening?"

"I'm taking you to bed." He moves toward the bedroom, but there's a pressure in my bladder demanding attention.

"No, wait." I shake my head.

He looks down at me, befuddled, and then seems to come to some understanding. "No, no. Not like that, Holly. I mean, I'm going to put you in your bed. Then, I'll go to mine."

I roll my eyes and give his side a little pinch but not too hard. Don't want him dropping me on my butt. "Yeah. Got that. Appreciate it. But I need to use the bathroom."

"Oh. Yeah, sure."

Then, to my delight, I realize Ben is actually blushing.

When he sets me down, I stand on my tiptoes to plant a kiss on one of those rapidly warming cheeks, leaving him standing there with a goofy smile on his face.

The chill of the bathroom floor creeps through the wool of my socks. This spurs me on, and I finish peeing, brushing my teeth, and washing my face in rapid time. When I exit, Ben slips past me to take his own turn.

In my borrowed bedroom, I take stock of my appearance. Helping me pack, Terra said I'd want clothes for cold weather and being outside. In an effort to maintain friendship-like feelings toward Ben, I brought my most formless clothes. Luckily, they also happened to be my warmest—bulky sweaters, fleece-lined long underwear, thick socks. Now though, I want something that doesn't make me look like I'm preparing to be thrown out in a snowstorm. The best I've got is a worn pair of flannel pajama pants and a tank top I planned to use as the first of many layers. The ensemble still sits firmly in the category of comfy rather than sexy. But at least it's not frumpy.

There's a light knock on my door. When I open it, Ben leans against the doorframe, and I watch his body visibly relax when I smile up at him.

"Worried I was hiding from you?"

His arm flexes as he reaches back to scratch his neck while sporting a rueful smile. Then, I notice he's wearing short sleeves. The red T-shirt fits him snugly, the edge inching up as he raises his arm. I rack my brain but can't think of a time I've seen Ben in anything other than long sleeves. And I definitely would have remembered because, now, I can see more tattoos peeking out from under the fabric. But on his left forearm, there's a wide black armband covering the bump of his fistula.

So, he still isn't completely uncovered to me.

The effect is intense curiosity on my part. I want to pull the shirt off, so I can admire every piece of the artwork. Ben is such a calm, put-together, albeit snarky person for the most part. But, under that well-dressed armor, there's this hidden side. His passionate side. The concealed artist. I suddenly need to see that part of him even if I only get a glimpse tonight.

"I just wanted to say good night." He leans forward, like maybe he'll give me a chaste kiss on my forehead.

Brace yourself, buddy. I'm no delicate rose.

Stepping backward, I grab a fistful of his shirt and drag him with me. Off-balance, Ben stumbles forward.

My finger points to the bed. "You're sleeping here tonight. With me."

Quickly, I lean around him to push the door shut. Having told him the way of things, I walk to the bed and slip under the covers. Then, I hold up the blanket for him to join me. Ben stands in the middle of the room, eyes wide, mouth slack.

"Hurry. I'm getting cold." But the shiver that runs through my body isn't from the chilly air. The idea of having him pressed up against me all night is the source of the quivering.

Either way, it gets his feet moving. He sets his glasses on the table, and the bed dips slightly as he settles down next to me.

We lie, facing each other, not touching. Yet.

"Can you see me without those?"

We're less than a foot apart, and his green eyes seem like they're focused on my face.

Ben grins. "Nope. You're just a blurry mass. You could be Jasper or a grizzly bear for all I know."

"I'd hope my blurry mass is slightly smaller than a bear's." Then, I stick my tongue out at him and watch his eyes fall to my mouth, growing hot. I gasp in mock outrage. "You liar! You can totally see me!"

"No! I definitely can't!" He shakes his head, grinning all the while. "Is that you, Holly?" His hand comes out from under the covers and lands on my face.

I snort as he plays. Then, I grab his rough palm and place a firm kiss right in the middle of it. At the affectionate gesture, Ben goes still, watching me. The intense scrutiny makes me bite my lip. His playful expression turns serious with a wrinkle above his eyebrows that I want to smooth out.

"We don't have to do this, Holly."

I roll my eyes but smile at his reassuring words. "I know. I want to. Do you?"

"Do I want to do what exactly?"

"Hmm. Parameters. Good idea." Organization has always been my strong suit. I like clearly laid-out rules and plans. Why wouldn't I appreciate that in a relationship, too? "Tonight is just the exploratory phase."

"Exploratory phase?" He sounds confused, even as he grins at me.

"That's right. Exploration. For example"—I prop myself up on an elbow, hovering over him—"I want to explore your mouth."

Ben parts his lips as he stares up at me. Then, his eyelids grow heavy as my knuckles brush over the couple of days of scruff on his chin.

Even though I'm tempted to dive right in, I wait for his response.

Realizing this, his throat contracting, he swallows and nods.

That's all I need.

Our kiss starts out slow, just a gentle brush of my mouth against his. When I'm this close to him, the scent of mint and pine fills my nose, sending shivers of delight skittering over my skin.

His upper lip is just as soft as I imagined it.

The moment I peek my tongue out to swipe along the juicy treat, Ben bursts into movement. One arm wraps around my waist, the other hand tangles in my hair, and both pull me flush against his solid, hot body.

Ben is a good ... no, that's not right.

Ben is an Olympic champion of a kisser. He belongs on a podium with a gold medal dangling around his neck in the sport of worshipping my mouth.

His passion doesn't reveal itself in a hard, brutal claiming, but instead, he holds me firm against him for a slow, languid perusal. Some guys approach kissing like they're shotgunning a beer, only chasing the intoxication that comes afterward. Ben kisses me like I'm a top-shelf whiskey, and he loves the taste.

Only I'm the one who gets drunk on our kissing. My muscles liquefy, and I sink into him.

The hand he has in my hair remains where it is, but the other explores, traveling across my body. Through the kissing haze, I feel him stop in certain places. The tips of his fingers run over my shoulder blades before pressing each vertebrate on my spine, playing me like a piano. He circles his arm around my waist again, clutching me close for a moment and groaning low in his throat. He releases that hold, only to slide his hand to my backside. Through the thin soft flannel, his long fingers spread over one of my cheeks before giving me a firm squeeze. A gasp escapes my mouth, and he locks our lips together, as if he wants to swallow the sound.

His hard arousal presses against my stomach. There's a slight regret, knowing we're just exploring tonight, which means sex probably shouldn't happen. But, if Ben approaches sex the way he kisses, I'm worried he's in line to ruin me for all other men.

But would that really be so bad?

BEN

Her sweet mouth and sexy tongue put my fantasies to shame. I could spend the whole night in this *exploratory phase*, as she described it.

If exploring is what she wants, exploring is what I'll do. My hand has a mind of its own, touching every part of her I can reach. Then, there's the little happy sound she lets out when I give her ass a squeeze, which has me wondering what noises I'll get when I spread her legs and lick her.

Will she moan when I finally slide into her wet heat? Maybe she'll gasp my name.

Whatever happens, I know it'll drive me fucking crazy.

My fingers settle on the waistband of her pants, and I consider pushing past that barrier, exploring the smooth skin of her backside and then possibly dipping lower.

With herculean effort, I hold back. We haven't even gone on an official date yet. I'm not about to ruin this by going too far on the first night. Besides, I'm happy here, holding her against me, tasting her mouth, my brain going fuzzy with pleasure as I get high on her sweet, flowery scent.

Holly retreats from my lips, only to slowly kiss her way along my jaw, down my neck, and then to my collarbone where she gives me a playful nip.

I relax the hand I have wrapped in her hair, letting her head go wherever she wants it. My eyes close as I concentrate on the soothing effect of her soft mouth against my skin.

She works her way back up, but instead of returning to my mouth, her lips trail to my ear. A shiver racks my body when she gently bites the lobe and then runs her tongue along the outer edge.

"Ben?" Something—I'd like to think my kissing—has made her voice go deep and husky.

The sound of my name in that tone is like a stroke up my dick.

"Mmhmm?" Talking would require more brainpower than I currently have with all my blood rushing south.

"Can I take your shirt off?"

Some warmth leaves my chest, and when I open my eyes, I realize it's because Holly is sitting up straight, straddling my hips.

This view of her, the same one I'd have if she decided to take me for a ride, is all I need to get completely hard. An involuntary groan escapes my mouth, and she frowns.

"Am I hurting you?" She shifts, and the friction only brings more pleasure.

I grab her hips to keep her still, afraid I'll come in my pants like I'm a sixteen-year-old virgin again.

"No! No. You're fine." My words come out choked. I clear my throat. "You want to take my shirt off?"

She nods. "I want to see your tattoos. You keep teasing me with a glimpse or two. I want to see them all."

Fuck. Me.

No way will she be seeing all of them tonight because that would mean all my clothes would have to come off.

I'm trying to figure out if I can have her eyes all over my chest, touching me there, without me busting in my pants when she says exactly what she needs to in order to get me to give in.

"Please?"

Damn. She's got me.

"Okay. Just a second." I use my grip on her hips to shift her off me, and I can practically hear my dick cursing at me for getting rid of her lovely body against mine.

At first, she gives me an adorable pout, but it quickly transforms into a happy smile when I sit up and reach for the bottom of my shirt. In fact, she claps her hands together like she's about to see a fancy magician's trick. Not wanting to disappoint, I remove my shirt with a flourish.

"Ta-da!" It's corny, and we both laugh as toss it to the floor.

Then, her eyes go sharp, and she leans in closer, bottom lip once again pinched between her teeth. I sit still.

The weight of her gaze is heavy, and I'm suddenly self-conscious. These tattoos were always for me. They're a part of me as much as any of my limbs. And the same way I hope she finds my face attractive, I want Holly to like this piece of me as well.

"Can I guess?" She looks at me through her lashes, and my breath comes and goes a bit ragged.

"Guess?"

"You said they're all based on books. Can I guess which ones?"

Mute, I nod.

"*The Lion, the Witch, and the Wardrobe*." She points to the lamp-post in front of a snowy tree on the underside of my bicep.

I nod again, smiling at her triumphant grin.

Now, it turns into a sort of game. I lean back on my arms, so she has a better view.

"Hmm." She runs her hands over my skin, tracing some of my illustrations. And, hell, if this isn't one of the most erotic things she could do to me.

I want her to use her mouth.

"Darn. Your sexy chest is making me feel like I've barely read any books." She pauses at my hip. "Wait. Is this ... is it Snow White? Is that technically a book?"

The tattoo she's pointing to is an apple that's half-red, half-gray. "That's actually *The Giver*."

"Oh! I read that one. Where the whole world is gray at first? I get it now."

Her fingers continue over my stomach, which tenses under her touch.

"*Fahrenheit 451*?" She's at my other hip where I have an open book spilling out flames.

"You got it."

Another happy smile on her part. She removes her hand, only to cup my shoulder and give me a gentle tug. I lean forward, so she can review my back. After a moment, her finger taps a spot.

"Are these *Winnie-the-Pooh* characters? They look kind of like them but not as cartoony."

"Those are the originals. My mom read that version to me when I was younger." Those were some happy memories.

"That's sweet. Has she seen this?"

My gut tightens, and I shake my head. "My parents don't really understand my ... hobby."

Truth is, the images meant so much to me, that their dismissive attitudes ended up hurting worse than the needles.

"Well, I think it's sweet. And I think your artwork is amazing."

I know exactly where each and every tattoo is on my body, so when Holly presses her lips against my back, I can envision her kiss landing directly in the middle of the Hundred Acre Woods. My blood heats up, and arousal pushes at every inch of my skin. Time to settle down.

Reaching forward, I click off the bedside lamp.

"Enough exploring for tonight." I turn too quickly for Holly to react, wrapping my arms around her and gripping her wrists to her chest, so her adventurous hands can't continue with their torture. Pressed together, I slide us into the position I want, us spooning with her back against my front.

"No fair. I was just getting started." I can hear her smiling.

She squirms in my hold, pretending to get comfortable when, really, she's just pushing her tight butt into my very lonely groin.

I groan and bite her neck, just a playful nip. She gasps in response.

"Holly." Denied lust makes my warning sound more serious than I meant, but she just gives a big gust of a sigh in response.

"Okay. I'll be good."

I wait a moment and then release her hands. She keeps ahold of one, interlacing her fingers with mine, and plants a kiss in the center of my palm like earlier. It's such a sweet thing to do, and my chest tightens with some intense feelings I'm not sure I'm ready to explore.

"Night, Ben."

After brushing my lips over her shoulder, I whisper back, "Good night, Holly."

Whenever I've spent the night with a girl, I've always found a way to separate myself from them after sex, wanting my own space. Maybe I can blame the chill of the night, but here, in this bed, the idea of releasing Holly seems so ridiculous that I actually chuckle to myself.

"What're you laughing about?" Her whisper slurs with sleepiness, and I regret disturbing her.

"Nothing important. Go to sleep." I breathe in deep, getting drowsy, surrounded by the smell of her honeysuckle shampoo.

"You go to sleep," she mutters the command.

My lips curl at the edges, and for the first time in years, I fall asleep in Grandpa Ben's cabin with a smile on my face.

HOLLY

The door looms tall before me.

I reach up, turn the knob, and push. The hinges squeak as it swings wide, revealing the dark room beyond. My feet move forward on their own.

I'm in Grams's room. She should be asleep in the large bed I'm walking toward.

Someone is under the covers, but when I pull the sheet back, it's not my grandmother.

It's Ben.

He lies still, eyes closed, like he's sleeping, but his chest doesn't rise. I put my hand on his shoulder and find him ice-cold.

The darkness around me shifts and moves, closing in on us. Ben begins to sink into the bed, as if the mattress were quicksand. He's disappearing from my sight, and he doesn't respond when I scream his name.

There's a pressure at my back, pushing me toward the sinkhole in the bed where Ben has vanished. Terror crashes over me in waves.

I turn away, searching for the door. It stands there, closed again.

With fear clawing its way down my spine, I run. The darkness slows my legs, pulling me back, but I push my way through. My fingers clasp the doorknob, wrenching with a mighty tug.

I'm awake.

Something heavy is holding me down, and I cry out, flinging it off me. It's not until I've tumbled out of the bed, which sits a foot higher than the one in my apartment, that I realize I'm not at home. When I see Ben staring down at me in half-awake confusion, I remember where I am.

I'm in Ben's grandfather's cabin. We were sleeping in a bed together. That was his arm holding, not restraining, me. There's no terrible, creeping darkness.

"Holly? What's wrong?" He slides out of the bed and crouches in front of me on the floor.

Seeing him here, awake and moving, helps push back the panic of moments before. On pure instinct, I lean forward, clutching his face in both my hands just to make sure he's solid. When his scruff scratches my palms, I let out a sigh of relief.

"Nightmare. Just a nightmare," my voice sounds ragged when I whisper the reassurance, and I wonder if I was crying out in my sleep.

Remembering then all the effects of my nightmares, I glance down to see that I've sweated through my pajamas.

Gross.

At least I don't wet the bed anymore.

I drop my hands from his face and stiffly stand, moving over to my bag to search for something else to sleep in.

"That must have been a pretty nasty nightmare." He doesn't outright ask, but I can tell Ben wants to know what I dreamed about.

Usually, I only discuss it with Marcus. But my brain has never replaced my brother with someone else before.

What does that even mean?

All I have left in my bag are the clothes I planned to wear in the car tomorrow, which I really don't want to sleep in.

Maybe there are other benefits to *more*.

"I'll tell you about it if you lend me a shirt to sleep in. I have the unfortunate habit of sweating a bit when I have nightmares."

Ben doesn't hesitate to head over to his bedroom. I check the clock and find the glowing numbers read *2:23 a.m.* Second night in a row I've woken him up for no good reason.

When he returns with a soft white T-shirt, I tamp down my urge to kiss him. I want to change out of my sticky clothes first.

"Turn around." In the faint glow of the digital clock, I see him smile before he complies.

I peel off the tank top and pajama pants, tossing them in a corner to be dealt with in the morning, and then slip the clean cotton on. Much better.

"I'm decent."

The moment he turns back to me, I wrap my arms around his waist, still needing some more reassurance. Ben leads me back to the bed, tucking us both under the covers. He brushes my hair behind my ear and stares down at me. Waiting.

"Sometimes—not every night, only sometimes—I dream about the night my grams died. She had a heart attack when it was just her, Marcus, and me in the house. We found her when it was too late to do anything. She was just gone." I breathe in deep and slowly let the air back out. "I dream about that night, walking into her bedroom. Only, in my nightmare, I don't find her in the bed. I find my brother." Or at least, I usually do.

I shiver, and Ben pulls me closer, planting a kiss on my forehead.

"I know it's just a dream, but it guts me every time. Usually, I call Marcus, just so I can hear his voice. Know that he's okay."

"Do you want to call him now? I can grab your phone." He moves to get up, but I tug him back.

There's no need, seeing as how Marcus wasn't the one I left sinking into that hole of terror this time.

"I'm okay."

"Is there anything you need?"

I shake my head. "You got me a shirt. I'm good."

In the muted light from the clock, Ben's worried frown carves shadows into his cheeks. I use one of my fingers to push at the corner of his mouth until he gives me a reluctant smile.

"Seriously, Ben, I'm good now."

He sighs before tucking me in close under his chin. "Okay. Go back to sleep. And, if you have another nightmare, I have plenty more shirts."

20

HOLLY

THE OVEN LETS out an insistent beep, announcing to the kitchen it's preheated.

"Now, put this in and set the timer for an hour. Really though, you're looking for the cheese to be bubbling on the top. That's how you know it's done." Terra hands me a dish filled with all the components for chicken Parmesan.

I've just finished setting my egg-shaped kitchen timer when our apartment intercom buzzes.

My roommate gives me an impish grin before going to press the respond button. "Who may I ask is calling upon the Donovan-Foster residence?"

The crackling voice that responds matches her lofty tone, "'Tis I, Benjamin Gerhard the Fourth. Seeking an audience with Miss Holly Foster."

Terra turns to me, delight plumping her cheeks. Not everyone likes to play along with her teasing.

"Oh, I do declare!" With a flourish, she buzzes him up.

Even when wearing ratty sweatpants and one of her worn concert T-shirts, Terra insists upon dramatics. I love her for it.

As we wait for him, my pulse picks up pace, and a heat washes over me that has nothing to do with standing near the oven. I'm jittery. Almost nervous.

This morning at the cabin was uneventful. When I woke up, Ben was already out of bed, preparing scrambled eggs, shirt back on. While I was disappointed that we didn't wake up, wrapped together, I have to admit, I like my man in the kitchen.

One of the many reasons I invited him over this afternoon.

In the car ride, we threw *Tommy Boy* quotes at each other and listened to Preston and Steve's podcast. At least, I listened to it. Ben fell asleep about halfway into the drive again.

There's a knock on our door. Before I even take a step, Terra leaps from her chair and sprints to answer it. I lean back against the counter, letting her have her fun. Ben will need to get used to Terra if he really wants to spend time with me outside of his treatments.

"Benny boy!" She's definitely had more than one cup of coffee today. "Come in. Come in."

"Thanks, Terra. Good to see you." His smooth voice fills our tiny apartment, brushing against my skin like expensive silk sheets I wish I could afford.

The two of them walk around the corner, and our eyes find one another. His smile matches mine. While Terra resumes her seat, Ben crosses the room to stand in front of me.

"Hey there." He cups my face and leans down to brush a soft hello kiss across my lips. Mint and pine mix together and fill my lungs.

If Terra wasn't here, I'd let myself sink into him. Maybe try to unbutton his shirt, so I could get a better view of his artwork in the light of day. But my roommate watches us like we're a delightful romantic comedy, so I grip the counter with my hands to keep them from misbehaving.

After leaning into his kiss for a moment, I break it. The hazy, happy look in his eyes sets off tingles of satisfaction in my chest.

"Long time no see."

He grins. "Felt like it."

"You two are adorable." Terra has her elbows propped on the kitchen table, chin resting in her hands, as she gazes at us.

I roll my eyes and stick my tongue out at her.

Ben chuckles before pressing his lips to my forehead and then moves to sit across from her. "Put me to work. What can I do?"

"Ooh, I like you even more," Terra comments as I pull out our second cutting board.

"I'll give you the easy chore." I place the cutting board in front of him and then pick up the colander filled with washed potatoes from the sink. After a final shake to rid it of excess water, I place them next to Ben's elbow. "You cube these. We're making cheesy baked potato soup."

Once I hand him a knife, he sets to his task. Terra continues shredding cheese, the job half-done before Ben arrived. I work on dicing an onion, and for a moment, the three of us work quietly.

But Terra is here, so that doesn't last long.

"So, Ben, what are your life plans?"

My knife comes down harder than I meant before I throw a glare over my shoulder. "Terra," I chide, "that's not small talk."

She shrugs. "Small talk only gets in the way of actually learning about someone. I want to know the interesting stuff. Just be glad I didn't ask what his most embarrassing memory was." Her voice lowers to a mock whisper, and she leans in close to Ben. "That's my second question. So, brace yourself."

Even though I don't want to admit it, I agree with her. Still, someone needs to protect him from Terra's prying.

"You can tell her no. It's healthy for her to be denied every so often." I direct this at Ben, but he just glances between the two of us with an amused quirk to his mouth.

"I don't mind." He resumes cutting potatoes, and I turn back to my onion even though my attention is all on his words. "Let's see ... life plans ... being healthy again. That's top of the list. Thanks to Holly, I should be good there." A quick smile is thrown my way, and then he's back to his list. "I plan to land a position in a law firm and then eventually join my family's. It's good job security, good pay."

The lack of passion in his statement clings to me like walking through a surprise spider web. I try to brush it away but can't seem to manage it.

Terra shares my skepticism.

"Job security? Very practical of you. Is that something you worry about a lot? Losing your future job?" Her bowl is full of grated cheese, so she sets aside her implements and focuses completely on Ben.

My roommate's scrutiny can often make people uncomfortable, but Ben just appears thoughtful. His eyes are unfocused, and his hands have stilled as he considers her question.

"Not exactly." He brings his attention back to Terra. I still feel like I'm in his peripheral vision as he addresses her, "I made some selfish choices in the past. Went the irresponsible route and paid for it. I don't want to do that with my career."

"Hmm." Terra stares hard at Ben, and he doesn't let his gaze fall. She gives a small nod but still doesn't seem satisfied. "So, life goal number one is, get healthy. Life goal number two is, a good job. Any more?" Terra brings us back to her original question, listing off Ben's answers by counting on her fingers.

In a large pot on our stove, I begin piling in ingredients along with some boxed broth. When Ben doesn't respond immediately, I glance over to find him completely focused on the potatoes.

He clears his throat, eyes still on his work. "I'd like to find someone. A forever kind of someone."

I fully expect Terra to squeal, clap her hands together, and then mock us mercilessly. Instead, she gives a glimpse of her serious side, reaching across the table to grip his arm. At her touch, he glances up from his work.

"That's it, Ben. That's a good goal."

BEN

"Done. Finally." Holly collapses onto her mattress next to me.

"You do this every Sunday?"

She nods. "Deal with it now, and then, during the week, I can focus on school and work. If I waited till the last minute to come up with a dinner plan, I'd probably starve."

I don't know how she juggles it all. Just reading her day planner intimidated me. No wonder she'd claimed she didn't have time to date. Guess I'm lucky she found a way to fit me into her schedule. Especially since I'm already taking up some of her precious time by making her go to doctor appointments.

"Is the surgery going to throw you off?" My stomach twists as I realize how much more time I'm stealing from her. I prop myself up on an elbow. "What the hell is wrong with me? I can't believe we haven't talked about this. What's your recovery plan for after the donation?"

Holly reaches up to comb her fingers through my hair. "Dr. Williams says my recovery won't be as long as yours. I should be in the hospital for only a couple of days, and then I need to keep from doing anything more than walking for a few weeks. So, I'll stay at Pops's house for a bit. Probably just play card games and watch movies till classes start up in the spring."

"What about rent?"

She hasn't said it outright, but I get the sense that Holly and Terra don't make much between the two of them. Putting half the team out of commission for a few weeks isn't going to help.

"I've got some savings. And Curt said he'd pay me to take care of the scheduling and accounting for Both Ways, which I can do online while I rest in my bed." She fiddles with my collar, watching her fingers rather than me.

I'm such an asshole. This can't be how it's going to play out. No way am I taking Holly's organ and then delivering her a financial blow, too. For the first time since the lawyers told me about my inheritance, I'm grateful for the money Grandpa left me.

"You shouldn't have to worry about all that when you're recovering. I'll cover your rent until you're back at work."

"What?" That gets her to look at me. "No. I don't need you to do that. I can get by fine."

I stare her down. "Of course you can. You're like a freaking superhero to me. But, even though your surgery isn't as intense as mine, you're still dealing with a lot of risks." I cup her cheek, stroking her soft skin with my thumb. "Please let me help. If I know you're stressed about money, then I'm gonna be stressed about you making yourself sick, which will then make me sick. You don't want me to get sick, do you?"

She gives my shoulder a light shove and glares up at me. "You're suck a sneak! Of course I don't want you to get sick."

"Then, say yes."

"I just ..." She shifts, and I suppress a groan as her thigh brushes against my groin. I've got to focus. "I don't want to ask your parents to pay for me."

"You wouldn't even have to ask." She frowns, and I run my thumb over the curve of her plump bottom lip. "But it's not them. I have some money. Interning at my parents' law firm over the summer paid well. And Grandpa Ben left me more than just that cabin."

"No, Ben." Holly sits up, switching our positions, so now, she's the one gazing down at me. "There's no way I'm taking your grandfather's money from you."

This independence she has is equally attractive and frustrating. The fact that she can take care of herself, even when life is beating her down, is inspiring. But she needs to learn when to accept help.

I lie back on the bed, running my fingers up her arm and watching as goose bumps follow their path.

"When I found out Grandpa left me his cabin, I was numb. Then, they told me about the money, and all this guilt built up inside me. He's dead, and now, I have a cushy little bank account to show for it. I haven't touched it. I've never wanted to. So, it's just sitting there, useless." I take her hand in mine, lacing my fingers through hers and bringing them to my lips for a light kiss. "He might not have said it much, but I know my grandpa loved me. If he were alive today, he'd want to help out the girl who was saving my life."

Holly visibly softens, and I can sense her resolve weakening. She nibbles her lower lip while staring down at me. I want her agreement now, so we can move on to more fun things, like me biting that lip instead.

"You're giving me your kidney, Holly. Let me help you with a couple months' rent. Please."

Her shoulders fall on a sigh, and I grin at her physical surrender. "Okay. One month. That's it. I should be back at work by then."

Success.

I tug her hand, so she leans in close to me. Then, I pull harder until she's spread over my chest. "Thank you."

Her lips give a little smirk as her dark eyebrows quirk. "You're thanking me for letting you give me money?"

"Yep."

Finally, I capture her mouth, like I've wanted to do since I woke up next to her this morning.

She looked so tempting, wearing my shirt, one slim arm resting over the covers, the rest of her wrapped up tight. Instead of waking her up, I slipped out of the bed and retreated to the bathroom. In the shower, I stroked myself, massaging my hard dick as I remembered her fingers tracing over my tattoos and the way she'd gasped when I squeezed her ass. It wasn't long before I had to brace an arm on the wall to keep myself standing as I spilled on the smooth tiles.

Maybe another guy would have tried to seduce her into easing the ache, but I meant what I said about this being more than sex. Holly's used to flings, or *booty calls* as she phrased it. But, she won't get rid of me that easily. I'm planning on weaseling my way into her heart, just like I managed to push my way into her busy schedule.

Still, taking it slow doesn't mean I can't touch her.

My hands roam, starting at her shoulders and then sliding down her back. She arches into me. The natural curve of her spine guides my hands to her round bottom, which fits perfectly in my palms.

Gently, I grip her cheeks, loving the way Holly's hips start pressing into me in time with each squeeze.

Kissing her in a bed probably isn't the best idea. But I can't seem to stop things now that they've started, especially when she responds eagerly. Needing to have her firmly pressed against me, I roll us until I'm situated on top of her.

Mistake.

With a moan and a sigh mixed together, Holly lets her knees fall open. The core of her, where heat radiates even through her clothing, cradles me, and my cock presses against the fly of my pants. Now, I'm the one rhythmically moving my hips, unable to stop miming the action of thrusting into her. She pants into my mouth, little gasping breaths that boil my blood and stuff my head with lust-soaked cotton.

We should slow down.

How did we go from friends to dry-humping in twenty-four hours?

Somehow, I stop my body's movement and try to focus only on the honey taste of her mouth. But that's hard to do when she grabs my hand and guides it up under her shirt.

Beneath her thick UPenn sweatshirt, Holly's decided to forgo a bra. Luckily, Terra left for the library when the cooking was done because I can't stifle the animalistic groan I let out.

Her breast is small, not even really a handful, but it's soft, and her nipple is a tight little bead I pinch and tease as she writhes beneath me. My lips break from hers, and I make my way, biting and licking, across her jaw and down her neck, enjoying the silky texture of her skin against my curious tongue.

"Ah! Ben ..." she moans my name.

My hips give an involuntary thrust. I'm going to come in my pants if I keep this up. That doesn't stop me from sliding down her body while pulling Holly's sweatshirt up to reveal her naked chest.

For a moment, I just stare, relishing the view. The image of her prone beneath me will forever linger in my brain, demanding I find a pencil or brush to re-create the sight. But drawing this once won't be enough. I'm sure I'll never be able to lend anyone my notes again because the margins are going to be full of sketches detailing the perfect way Holly's breasts pool on her chest, pulled to the sides by gravity but still maintaining their natural curves. The minute my mind drifts, I know I'll be back in this moment, fixated on the exact button shape of her rosy nipples.

The glorious girl shifts beneath me, huffing out a frustrated sigh. About to tease her for the impatience, I'm surprised with the brush of a rigid nipple against my mouth as she tangles her fingers in my hair and pulls me down while arching her back.

"Lick me. Please."

Again, like an animal, I growl and then use my lips, teeth, and tongue to worship her breasts. Her little noises are only fuel to my fire, and she doesn't need to beg for me to continue. I hold her to me with one hand on the middle of her back while she presses her fingers into the spot where the skin of my neck disappears beneath my hairline.

I wish she would push harder, using enough force to bruise me. My skin should be marked by her, a permanent reminder of this moment.

I can't believe I have her in my mouth right now.

I can't believe it because it's too soon.

This time, I groan in frustration as I reluctantly release her nipple. In a form of good-bye, I let the sweet nub drag over my bottom lip before I tug her shirt back into place.

"Wha—"

I cut Holly off with a quick kiss and then sit up, pulling her with me.

Fuck, she's sexy.

Her short brown hair is all messy, curling around her swollen lips and pink cheeks. Slowly, her eyes come into focus.

My throat needs to be cleared a couple of times before I can talk, "I only planned on kissing you. Got a bit out of hand."

She stares at me. "So, you really meant, no sex?"

"We haven't even gone out yet. Like, on an official date."

Her one eyebrow curves high on her forehead as she leans back on her hands. "An official date? What does that look like?"

I shrug and try to adjust myself without her noticing. "Dinner. Movie. Walk on the beach."

She smirks and shakes her head. "No. Those are regular dates. I want to know what an *official* date is. Is there documentation? Do we have to dress all fancy, like prom? Do I get a corsage?"

"Of course. And there's the photographic evidence. Then, I'll send you a post-date survey, so you can rate your satisfaction with the experience." I maintain my best deadpan tone.

Holly giggles and then sighs, letting her eyes wander over me. "I guess I just kind of feel like we've been a couple longer than a day. Because we hang out so much. Is that weird?" Confusion flits through her eyes.

She's right. We might not have been calling it dating, but all those hours spent talking and reading together mean more to me. We've had a relationship longer than labels.

"Feels that way to me, too. But I'm still taking it slow with you."

Holly gives me an exaggerated pout. "So, no more hand-under-the-shirt action? Or mouth under the shirt?"

She's too tempting. I dip down for another kiss, needing a taste of her sassy mouth. But I pull back before it escalates.

"Not until after our official date."

21

HOLLY

"You really don't mind me heading out early?"

When I glance at Pops over my hand of cards, he's smiling at me. The dark skin around his eyes crinkles with it, and I know I'm done for.

"No, sweetie. I don't mind. And I believe that's rummy."

He sets down his final run, and I glare at him.

"That's not nice. You're supposed to let me win. Now, I'm going to be all bummed out on my date."

"Date?" Pops pauses in the process of gathering up our cards. "I thought you said you're hanging out with that boy who's getting your kidney."

Back when I was in high school, I'd always blush and get defensive when I brought up the idea of me going out with someone to Pops. He'd go quiet and just stare at me for a moment while I fidgeted. Then, he'd tell me to bring the boy by the house, so he could meet him, which I hated because Pops would proceed to stare at the guy until he fidgeted, too. Took me a while to realize my adoptive father was worried about me. That he was just trying to figure out how to be a dad to a teenage girl and how to keep her safe while also letting her have a life.

I think he did a good job. And, anyway, I've never been too interested in dating.

So, now, I nod and suppress my urge to shift around in my seat. "Yep. I am."

I wait for the staring, and I'm not disappointed. But, this time, I meet his eyes.

While we face off, I think about what it'll be like when Ben meets my dad. The fact that I have no idea how the rest of the evening will go should freak me out, but when I imagine the two of them in a room together, a smile creeps over my mouth.

Pops's eyes widen, and then he gives a slight nod. "You like him, huh?"

"A bit." I shrug, but I can't get rid of the smile.

"He picking you up here?"

"Yeah. Should be here soon."

He keeps watching me as he finishes gathering up the cards. "You're not gonna ask me to be nice to him?"

I lean back in my chair, my face cheerful as ever. "You can be whatever you want to him. I'm not the boss of you."

"That so?"

His eyebrow rises in disbelief, and I stick out my tongue.

The doorbell rings.

I hop out of my seat and start down the hall while my dad follows at a more leisurely pace.

When I open the front door, Ben's on the porch, waiting with a grin.

No glasses tonight, and the forest-green scarf wrapped around his neck sets off the matching color of his eyes. All the buttons are done up on his black peacoat, which matches an equally dark pair of jeans and a nice set of leather shoes.

I've never cared much about what the guys I go out with are wearing, but clothes on Ben are like shiny wrappers on a chocolate bar; they look great, but I just want to rip them off. My mouth waters.

"You gonna invite your guest in?" Pops's voice shocks me out of my ogle-fest.

Ben, still grinning, leans forward to quickly kiss my cheek, his hand pressing against my lower back during the exchange.

I step to the side, so he can slip past me, and then I close the door.

"Pops, this is Ben Gerhard. Ben, this is my dad, Isaiah Foster."

"Great to meet you, Mr. Foster. Holly talks about you all the time."

Ben reaches his hand out, and my father takes it without responding.

I brace for the awkward staring session to start.

But Ben has other plans. The moment their hands release, he's back to focusing on me.

"I got you something."

"You did?"

Before I have time to wonder what, Ben pulls out the hand I didn't realize he was hiding behind his back.

"Is that ..." My dad sounds confused.

I let out a half-groan, half-laugh. "A corsage. You got me a corsage."

Ben pops open the plastic container and pulls out the little cluster of pink roses. "Of course. This is an official date, isn't it?" The whole time, he never stops beaming down at me, his eyes flashing with mischief. "May I?"

It's too cute, him standing there, looking so handsome, and holding out the ridiculous floral piece. I give him my hand, and he slides the elastic band onto my wrist. Wanting to soak in every bit of the moment, I press my nose into the flowers and enjoy the tickle of sweetness they carry.

"Now, we need the photographic evidence. Mr. Foster, would you do the honors?" Ben holds out his phone to my dad, who watches my date with such obvious befuddlement that I can't help snickering.

After Pops accepts the phone, Ben pulls me into his arms. He wraps them around my waist, holding me from behind in the classic prom pose. I can't even fully bask in how his snug embrace eases away any remaining nerves. I'm too busy dying of laughter.

In every picture my dad takes, I'm sure my eyes are closed.

"Great. Thanks for that." My insane date accepts his phone back, sliding it into his pocket. He grins down at me. "You ready to go?"

Before answering, I have to take a deep inhale through my nose. "Just need to put my shoes on and grab my coat. Be right back."

Giggles still sneak out of me as I walk down the hall and give the two men a moment alone.

∾

BEN

Mr. Foster is staring at me.

Getting stared at is uncomfortable under normal circumstances, but Holly's dad piles a giant load of intimidation on top of it. The guy has to be at least half a foot taller than me and packing more muscle than I could hope to have, even when I was healthy. The man looks like he belongs on a football field, knocking men down so hard that they'd question whether they even want to get back up.

And I just walked into his house, expecting to take out his daughter.

He's got to know how beautiful she is, and he can definitely guess at some of the not-so-family-friendly thoughts I have rattling around in my head whenever I see her.

I try not to look guilty.

"So, you're getting my daughter's kidney?"

His question catches me off guard. I've been so excited about our date; I kind of forgot about that other aspect of our relationship.

"Yes, I am. And I'm extremely grateful. Holly's amazing."

"She is." Mr. Foster remains expressionless. "Is this standard practice? Dating your donor?"

Fuck me.

Seems like Holly's dad isn't a fan of me for more than just the normal reasons a guy might not like the person taking out his daughter.

That sucks, but I'm not about to back off just because he's being protective.

"Probably not. But, the way I see it, Holly's worth bending the rules for." I return his gaze, trying to let him know that I'm not some bum just looking to get in her pants. That I care about her.

He gives a noncommittal grunt as his daughter comes up behind him.

"You done with the intimidating staring? Told him he'd better treat me right or else he'd have you to answer to?"

She smirks at her father, and the guy's stony expression cracks with a half-smile.

"Nah, that's silly." One of his eyebrows creeps upward. "He does you wrong, and I've no doubt you can take care of him yourself." Then, he turns to me, his face splitting open in a blinding smile, his teeth shining bright against his ebony skin. "I'll just be around to help you hide the body."

I can still hear his booming laughter as we walk to the car.

"He likes you." Holly grins over at me from the driver's seat.

I'm not sure I agree with her, but I smile back. "What's not to like?"

She snorts, shaking her head, and then reaches over to interlace her fingers with mine, steering the car one-handed. "Where are we going?"

"It's a surprise. Take a left up here."

"You and your surprises." Holly follows my direction and then starts humming along to the radio.

As usual, I've got it set to the local classic rock station. The Police pump out of the speakers, "Message in a Bottle" filling the car.

She sings along when the song reaches the chorus. Her voice is sweet, and it combines with the lyrics to give me a solid punch in the gut.

Ever since I found out my kidneys were failing and that I'd need to get a donation if I hoped to live into my thirties, I've been silently panicking. When I'm around my parents and my friends, I smile and joke, but there's always a clock in my head, counting down. Only I don't know when it's going to run out. There are times the ticking gets so loud that I want to scream for help. Send out my own SOS, just like the song.

But all that panic fades away around Holly. She's a perfect match for me in more ways than I could have imagined. My cure and my inspiration. The future glows bright with her in it.

We come to a stop at a red light, and she beams over at me. My chest swells and aches in the best way.

"I think I know where you're taking me."

"What? No way. This is a secret little gem no one else knows about." I cover my onslaught of emotions with sarcasm, and she sticks her tongue out at me.

That's a move I can't ignore. The moment her tongue retreats, I dive in, firmly pressing a kiss on her mouth.

A car behind us honks.

Holly laughs and shoves me back to my side of the car. "Stop distracting me!" She accelerates through the now-green light.

I go back to admiring her, enjoying being with the girl who's saving my life and making every moment worth living.

HOLLY

My cheeks tingle from the cold and also because I haven't stopped smiling for the last hour.

"Come on, Holly! Catch up!" Ben taunts me as he skates backward around the rink.

Seems someone's dialysis treatment yesterday gave him an extra boost of energy.

"Well, aren't you fancy, Mr. Show-Off?" Laughter colors my words.

His grin grows, enticing me to move faster, so I can get a clearer view of his delicious mouth. But he keeps in front of me, just out of reach, with steady, sure movements. Nothing like my imitation of a drunken penguin trying to fly—aka lots of useless arm-flapping.

For years, I planned to go ice-skating during Winterfest. The outside ice-skating rink right next to the Delaware River with a beautiful view of the Ben Franklin Bridge always seemed magical. But, each year, I'd let the season pass without a visit, making excuses about other things I should be doing.

It's like I've been traveling at high speed, and Ben is a set of brakes. He insists I slow down and enjoy the view.

Even after an hour, I'm still wobbly, seeing as how the last time I went ice-skating was at a birthday party when I was eleven. But I'm determined to catch up to him and wipe that smirk off his face. Preferably by biting his smug lower lip.

Using the temptation of tasting him to drive me forward, I dig into the ice and pump my legs and arms harder.

Likely taking pity on me, Ben doesn't increase his pace. Instead, he opens his arms to wrap me in a hug when I reach him.

My momentum sets us off-balance, and Ben goes down first with me landing hard on top of him.

Worry rocks me, and I immediately turn into a mother hen. "Oh gosh. Oh, Ben. Are you okay? I'm so sorry. Crud! That must have hurt. Are you hurt? Do we need to go? You're not bleeding, are you?" My rambling spills out while I run my hands over him to check for any broken bones.

His legs seem fine, same for his arms and chest. But he doesn't respond to any of my questions, making me worry he hit his head.

When I reach my hands up to examine his skull, I find him staring at me with a strange intensity. There's humor in his eyes, but there's also something else, something not so lighthearted. Then, the mystery emotion is gone, and he leans forward for a swift kiss.

"You hungry?" His breath warms my chilled face.

I nod in response, wondering what I just missed.

He kisses me again and then leans back. "Let's grab something to eat."

We work our way up, one of us more graceful than the other. This time, Ben keeps my hand in his as we weave through the other skaters to exit the rink. After turning in our rented gear, he leaves me in the Chickie's & Pete's line because I'm fixated on the idea of getting some of their famous crab fries.

There are only two more people in front of me when Ben finds his way back to my side.

"I got you a hot chocolate." The cup he holds out steams and smells dreamy.

"You are perfection." My mittens grip the cup tight to keep it from slipping out of their penguin-like grasp.

"Careful. It's hot."

"Good looking out. I don't want to burn my tongue before eating my glorious fries."

The teenager at the counter leaves with his food, and I move one step closer to stomach satisfaction.

"No, we wouldn't want that. Nothing should come between Holly and her fries."

I stick my tongue out at him, and just like earlier, he steals a kiss the moment I stop, which only makes me want to do it again.

"I guess, since we're on an official date, I'll share with you but only if you fully respect their deliciousness."

"Oh, believe me, I am totally aware of their deliciousness. But those fries are all yours."

"You don't want any?"

Ben's smile dims just slightly. I realize why before he tells me, and I want to slap my own face.

"Those fries are exactly the opposite of what's allowed on the dialysis diet. There are the potatoes and the salt, not to mention that decadent cheesy dipping sauce. So, it's a no-go for me."

This night has been so normal and unrelated to kidneys that I forgot for a moment that he's sick.

"We'll just have to add these to the list of post-surgery feast items."

"Right under a whole pile of almond croissants."

"Oh, yes. We'll gorge ourselves on French fries and pastries!"

"Sounds like a date." Ben cups my chin, running a thumb over my cheek, as he smiles down at me. Playfulness sparkles in his eyes, capturing me in an almost-hypnotic state.

The guy at the counter has to clear his throat before I realize it's my turn to order.

Once my hands are full of crab fries and hot chocolate, we navigate through the lodge to find a place to sit. Since it's Monday night, Winterfest isn't too crowded, and we quickly claim an available couch. After placing my drink on the low table in front of us, I make sure to sit down close enough to brush against Ben but not restrict our ability to eat.

I'm halfway through my fries when I realize Ben is watching me.

"What?" I grab a napkin and wipe my face, sure I've dripped cheese sauce on my chin or something.

But he just shrugs as a smile tugs the corners of his lips.

"Come on. You're making me feel self-conscious. Why are you staring at me?"

Ben shakes his head and shrugs. "I was just thinking that I'm really weird."

"Why's that?"

His eyes trace over my face, focusing on my mouth. "Because watching you go to town on those fries makes me ..." He trails off, reaching over to slip a finger under the elastic of my corsage. Back and forth, he brushes against my skin, playing with the ridiculous gift I refuse to take off. Finally, he finishes his thought, "I just think everything you do is sexy."

My mouth, luckily currently free of fries, goes slack. I mean, I know he's attracted to me, but unless a girl is in a Hardee's commercial, there's really not a way to go about eating fries sexy.

"You're right."

He glances up, raising an eyebrow in question.

"You're weird."

His cheeks get red, a perfect color to match his devilish grin.

Then, slowly, with deliberation, I pick up a fry and hold his gaze as I take a bite.

22

Ben: *Official Post-Date Survey. Did you: A) Have a fantastic time with your charming date, B) Have an amazing evening with the funniest man you know, or C) Have a glorious night with a sexy weirdo?*
Holly: *D) All of the above.*

HOLLY

"Okay, I admit it. Having two ovens does make this a little bit easier."

"A little bit?" Ben doesn't even try to hide his smirk, so I pinch his side as I pass by.

"Okay. A lot a bit."

We're working together in Ben's townhouse, which I'm visiting for the first time. While nowhere near as large and upscale as his parents' place, this house still sits in an entirely different class than my apartment. Apparently, Sammy's parents own the townhouse and charge Ben and Jasper a pittance of rent.

The place oozes charm with its redbrick exterior and dark wooden floor. Black marble counters hold a spread of stainless steel appliances. It wasn't until I opened the fridge and saw a whole shelf devoted to beer that I accepted three college guys lived here.

Not that Ben gets to drink any of it.

When he invited me to do my weekly food prep at his place, I grabbed at the chance to be nosy. Even though I accepted because I wanted to see where he lived, I'm reaping some additional benefits. My Sunday cooking normally takes up an entire afternoon, but with Ben and his beautiful kitchen helping, we're looking at just about two hours of work.

So, yeah, I like the kitchen.

"Why would Sammy's parents let you live here for next to nothing? They could make a killing on this place by actually charging rent."

Ben shrugs. "I think they plan on selling the house when we move out. And it wasn't this nice when they bought it. The last owner let it go to sh—" Ben stops talking abruptly and clears his throat. "Let it go to crap."

I notice his stumble and correction, and my heart lightens. To thank him, I lean over to press a kiss on his shoulder and then rub my nose against the soft flannel shirt he's wearing.

In return, he kisses me on the forehead before continuing, "So, I think they got it at a decent price and then spent some money to fix it up. They don't need the cash from selling it though. I think they just like having a project. The Ches are both pretty handy. They did a lot of the work themselves. Along with Sammy." Ben picks up his cutting board and walks over to the stovetop to dump all the diced vegetables into a waiting pot. The hot olive oil already in the pan sizzles at the contact. After quickly washing his hands, Ben grabs a wooden spoon to stir the contents.

I admire his culinary skills out of the corner of my eye as I tear up kale leaves and toss them in a colander. "Still, it's nice of them."

Once he sets his spoon down, Ben moves behind me and wraps his arms around my waist. I know I'm grinning like a loon. His hugs are just that great.

"There's something else. We don't really talk about it though." His tone gets serious, so I set aside my lustful thoughts and listen in. For a moment, we stay quiet together. Only when I'm dying to ask does he finally share. "They want to control Sammy as much as they can."

"Really? Is he out of control or something?"

The brief interactions I've had with Ben's friend made the guy seem like an overworked stress ball who ruled the dance floor after a drink or two. Not necessarily someone I'd consider out of control. Pent-up is more like it.

"By their standards, I guess. They wanted him to go to medical school. Planned for it his whole life. But Sammy told me, the first time he observed a surgery, the minute they cut into the patient, he puked and then passed out."

My snort escapes unbidden, but I bite my lip and shake my head, trying to convince myself that the image of Sammy fainting into some med student's waiting arms isn't hilarious. Who am I to judge? One needle stick, and I'm in for the same fate.

Then, Ben chuckles, and I not only hear it, but I also feel his chest vibrate against my back.

My mind disregards images of Sammy and starts making up fantasies of Ben sliding his hands lower than my belly.

"Yeah, so, after that, he switched to pre-law. Even though it stresses him out like crazy, that's where he belongs. He loves it. He can't wait to be a lawyer."

"And what about you?"

"Me?"

"Are you excited about becoming a lawyer?"

We haven't really discussed Ben's major since the day he first showed me his tattoos. Bravo on his part for finding exactly how to distract me. Even now, my body yells at my brain to shut up, turn around, and rip his shirt off.

But that's what you do when you're hooking up. Not when you want to get to know someone.

"Sure." He retreats, unwrapping his arms from my waist.

The loss of his warmth is like stepping out of a hot shower and straight onto ice-cold tiles.

"You know, we've been friends slash 'more'"—I air-quote around the word before returning to my salad making—"for over two months now. We've talked about your art and tattoos plenty of times. But you've only ever talked about being a lawyer once."

Turning around to wipe my hands on a towel, I find Ben pouring broth into the soup pot, his shoulders tense.

"So?"

Trying to keep the conversation light, I reach for the croutons instead of making him look me in the eye like I want him to. "Why is that?"

He lets out a frustrated sigh. "I know what you're trying to lead me toward, Holly. Yeah, I find art more interesting than law. But I'm still going to be a lawyer. Work at my parents' firm. It's a good, stable job." When he says the word *stable*, there's extra emphasis.

I don't get why he's so worried about having a stable job.

And what's wrong with pursuing a career that's more about passion than money?

Even though I want to keep digging, I get the sense that, if I try, we might get into a fight. When I first walked in the door, Ben was smiling and relaxed. Now, his lips are pinched tight, and he's not looking at me.

I don't want to argue with him, especially not when he's in the middle of helping me cook all my meals.

Once the salad is done, I store it in the fridge and then turn to watch Ben stir the soup. He's still tense, so I move behind him and place my hands on his hips. Slowly, I slide my fingers forward until they meet on his belly. I rub my nose on his soft shirt again before peppering a couple of kisses on his spine.

"Thank you for helping."

The muscles on his abdomen twitch as I lightly run my fingers up to his chest and then down to his waistband.

"Anytime." There's a choked quality to his response, and I smile in satisfaction, knowing he's just as affected by the touching as I am. He clears his throat once, twice, and a third time before speaking again, "Happy to help."

"Mmm." The hum comes deep from my chest, brought on by the

delicious smells and the warm man in my arms. "Anything I can help *you* with?" My hands continue to wander.

Ben gets tense again, but this time, I doubt it's because he's upset.

"Holly ..." His voice is low and growly.

Shivers scatter over me, and I press in closer. "Mmhmm?"

Beneath my arms, his chest expands on a deep breath. "If you keep this up, I'm gonna burn the soup."

With my face pressed into his back, Ben can't see how wicked my grin is.

"Oh. Sorry. Am I distracting you?"

He huffs out a laugh before grabbing one of my hands and pulling it to his mouth for a swift kiss.

When he lets go, I back away but not before giving his round butt a squeeze.

~

BEN

I have to finish cooking, sporting a partial. Not that Holly seems to mind. She keeps giving me looks that make the blood pound in my ears before traveling south.

With the two of us working and my two ovens steadily chugging along, we speed through her list of meals. We even put together an extra lasagna for Jasper and Sammy, just in case they show up before Holly heads out with all her food.

I stack the last individual serving in the freezer as she fills up the dishwasher. This is all so domestic.

I love it.

I want Holly here all the time. We work well together, evenly dividing up tasks, joking and talking the whole time. The fact that she'll be heading back to her own apartment later casts a dim light over the rest of my night. Life is brighter when she's around.

"I can't believe how fast that went." Holly dries her hands on a dish towel before hanging it on the oven handle. "We have so much free time now!" She throws her arms in the air and spins around, her socks and the hardwood floor making the action smooth, like a dancer.

Her enthusiasm is contagious, and I laugh at her antics.

She slides up to me, letting her arms fall, and grabs my hands. "Come on. I've only seen your kitchen. Show me the rest of your house."

The rest of the house. Like my bedroom.

I breathe in deep and try to clear my brain of all its X-rated ideas and instead act like a civilized host. "Yeah, sure."

We start in the living room where a decent-sized TV acts as the focal point with two couches and a lounge chair facing the screen. Jasper's gaming systems are tucked inside the entertainment center, less because of a propensity for neatness and more because he'd turn into a full-on rage monster if someone accidentally broke one.

"This is where we hang out and do manly things, like play video games and watch action movies."

"Ah, yes. It's a very manly room." Humor flits through her eyes.

I lean down to brush my lips against hers. She tastes sweet, like a spoonful of warm honey. When I break away, her cheeks carry an enticing flush, and she smiles in a way that makes my cock twitch.

Trying to keep myself under control, I continue our tour instead of dragging her down onto the closest couch. The sitting room and the kitchen with its little dining area take up the entire first floor, so we head upstairs.

"On the left here is Jasper's room. On the right is the bathroom." I open the door to show her but leave Jasper's closed, trying to respect his privacy. "At the end of the hall is me. Sammy has the whole upstairs."

While I guide her along, Holly peers around, gaze wide and curious.

Trying not to be presumptuous, I turn back toward the stairs. "So, yeah, that's everything."

"Wait a minute." When I glance back, she's already halfway down the hall. "I want to see your room."

Hell. This will be ... torture.

I follow her, unsure if the churning under my rib cage is from anticipation or dread. After weeks of stroking myself to thoughts of Holly, she's going to be standing next to my bed—a piece of furniture that plays a supporting role in many of my fantasies.

I catch up before she opens the door. While pushing it open, she throws a wink over her shoulder. "Time to find out about the real Ben."

The shades are drawn, and when she flicks the light switch, only the overhead fan turns on.

"Here. It's this one." I slide past her and click on my bedside lamp.

The warm light from the bulb makes her skin glow golden. As she takes in my room, I watch her. I already know what she's seeing— books piled everywhere, my two bookshelves completely full, a desk with my laptop, and a few textbooks I don't spend enough time reading. Then, on the walls, I've pinned up some drawings I particularly like. My room isn't dirty, but it's not really tidy either.

Holly wanders around, running her fingers over the spines of my books, stopping at a few pictures to examine them closer. All the while, her mouth has an enticing upward tilt. I move back to lean on the doorframe, giving her every inch of the space to explore. With my arms crossed over my chest, I think I can keep my hands to myself.

"I like it. This is a very Ben room."

"Glad you think so. What with it being mine and all."

She sticks her tongue out at me. When the little pink tip disappears behind her lips, she watches me, as if she knows what I have the sudden, undeniable urge to do.

Why fight it?

With a hard shove, the door shuts, and in three steps, I'm in front of her. I cup the back of her head, dropping mine to her level so that I can taste her sugary mouth. Kissing her in my bedroom is not a good move if we want to take things slow, but the logical part of my brain takes a vacation when Holly gives me a push.

The backs of my knees connect with my bed, and I bounce as I half-fall, half-sit. At first, I chuckle, finding her playfulness funny.

Then, she straddles my lap, and my laughter turns into a moan. Now the one in charge, she presses her eager mouth against mine. One arm wraps around the back of my neck while her other hand rakes over my scalp and tangles in my hair. With one rolling movement of her hips, Holly presses her hot core into my groin, and I get a straight shot of pleasure up my spine.

I need more.

My hands come into play, wrapping around Holly, pulling her flush against me. Her every curve pushes tight to my chest, and my memory returns the image of her naked breasts. When I groan, it mixes with a happy sigh of hers, and she gives another mind-numbing roll of her hips.

"Holly!" I choke out her name, not sure if I'm scolding her or begging her.

With a last swipe of her tongue and nip to my bottom lip, Holly leans back, so I can see her devious grin. "Ben, I just want to say thank you for helping me today."

Another rocking of her hips has me growling with my eyes closed. She moves again, but this time, her hips don't push forward, instead sliding backward.

I tighten my arms, not ready to give up the sensation of her soft body against mine even if I should. If anything has felt better than this, us wrapped around each other, I can't remember it. With every other girl I've been with, touching has felt good, sometimes great. But, with Holly, it's like I'm missing something when she's not in my arms.

She belongs here.

A throaty chuckle and a hand firmly massaging my groin have me bucking so hard that the springs in my bed start squeaking.

When I meet Holly's gaze, she raises one eyebrow. "I want to thank you."

"You're welcome." My voice comes out choked, as if someone had their hands wrapped around my throat.

In reality, she's got a grip on something a bit more precious.

Holly shakes her head, still smiling. "No. I haven't thanked you yet. Let me go."

Unable to deny her anything, I let my arms fall to my sides.

She doesn't stand up, but instead, she slides to the ground, kneeling in front of me. Her hands push my knees open, so she can move in closer.

My mind is in a fucking uproar, and my dick wants me to beg her to keep the promise that's in her eyes as she stares up at me.

But I'm not an animal, so I let my heart take one last precaution. "Holly, you don't have to—"

"Ben"—she reaches out to give me another firm massage through my jeans, effectively cutting off my statement as I groan even louder —"I want to." She hooks a thumb around the button at the top of my pants but pauses. "Do you want me to?" She watches for my answer.

"Hell yes!" The words come out strangled and too loud, but she just gives me her sassy smile.

Then, with quick fingers, Holly undoes my fly. My cock springs free. She licks her bottom lip, and I know I'll be lucky if I last more than a minute.

At her gentle grip, I jerk involuntarily. A bead of pre-cum seeps out, and she uses her thumb to spread the moisture, caressing the sensitive crown and daring my heart to beat faster.

My brain cranks up to feverish levels. I think I'm going to have an aneurysm from the slow, deliberate way she's playing with me.

The temperature spikes when she drags her tongue from base to tip and then sucks on me like I'm a decadent dessert. I can't look anywhere but at her or think of anything other than the feel of her hot, wet mouth on me.

She draws me in as deep as she can, using her firm hold to make up for the distance. After experimenting with different movements, Holly settles on the perfect rhythm.

The sight of her pink lips wrapped around my dick is so sexy; it doesn't seem real. I reach out, gathering her silky chestnut hair into my fist, keeping it out of her way but also giving me something to hold on to, something other than her addictively skilled mouth, to let me know that this isn't all in my head. We're in the real world, and Holly Foster has me in her mouth.

I'm the one she wants, the one she's gazing at with all that hunger.

It's like we're back before I got sick. I'm healthy and strong and someone to be desired.

Her strokes push me closer and closer to the edge.

It's all I can do not to thrust into her like a savage.

There's a pressure at the base of my cock, and I know I'm about to come.

"Holly—hell—I'm gonna—"

She doesn't listen. Instead, her eyes lock on mine and hold as she goes as far down as her mouth will allow. So far that I brush against the back of her throat.

I'm so close.

Slowly, she drags her lips up my length and then swirls her tongue around my tip while her free hand cups my balls and gives them a gentle tug. That last bit of handling does it.

I explode. A shout rips from my throat as my whole body clenches and pulses. I curl upward as the pleasure rolls through my muscles in waves. Then, I fall back on the bed, all strength gone from my limbs. It spills out of me, into Holly's mouth. And, holy hell, she drinks it down.

HOLLY

I might have killed him.

"Ben? You okay up there?"

"Mmhmm."

I snicker at his dazed moan and then crawl up next to him on the bed. He turns his head to look at me, and I love the hazy expression on his face. Obviously, I haven't lost my fellatio skills.

"So, it was a bit of a drawn-out thank-you. But I thought you'd appreciate it." I want to kiss him, but some guys are weird about that right after a blow job. Instead, I press my lips against his neck.

"Mmm ... Holly ..."

"Oh, good. You haven't lost all brain function."

"You're amazing."

"Yep. You're definitely still sane."

Without warning, Ben rolls over on top of me, capturing my mouth and having his way with it. As our tongues tangle together, my cheeks grow tingly and warm.

A lot of guys get off and get out. Not that I've minded in the past, seeing as how I usually make sure to get off before them and I'm getting out at the same time.

But, this time, all I thought about was Ben and how I could drive him crazy.

After making sure I'm thoroughly kissed, he pulls back to stare down at me, wearing a naughty grin. "Your turn."

"What?"

I watch him stand and tuck himself back into his pants. Then, with a swift movement, Ben grabs one of my ankles and drags me to the edge of the bed as I squeak in surprise. One of my socks gets tugged off and then the second. His fingers slide into the waistband of my leggings, but he pauses, eyes locked on mine.

"Say the word."

Someone knows that consent is sexy, and it heats my lower belly in a delicious way.

"Go for it."

That's all he needs. My leggings get tossed to the other side of the room. He takes a moment to run his fingers over my lacy boy shorts but then sends those flying next.

I don't tend to be shy during sex, but I also don't usually sleep with guys I'm emotionally invested in. So, when Ben lowers to his knees in front of me, staring, I'm hit with a sudden bout of self-consciousness. There's a twisting in my chest, and my pulse picks up for all the wrong reasons. I'm having trouble with handling his intense gaze on the most private part of myself.

Unbidden, my knees move to close. He doesn't stop me but glances up with worry creasing his brow.

"Holly?"

"Sorry. It's just ..." I rub my eyes with the heels of my hands, as if that'd clear away the onslaught of nervousness.

What is going on with me?

The sound of Ben shifting causes my eyes to fly back open. He hovers over me, bracing his elbows on either side of my head. The kiss he brushes over my lips is unhurried and reassuring.

"Tell me what you're thinking."

I sigh. "You were staring at me. Like, really staring. I don't think anyone has ever done that before."

His nose rubs against mine before he whispers in my ear, "I was staring because I think you're sexy and beautiful. I want to memorize every single inch of you." He comes back to kiss me again, working slowly, hinting at how skilled he is with his mouth.

My discomfort fades, replaced with need. I sneak my hands up under his shirt to feel the shifting of muscles in his back.

Ben rocks against me, his jeans rough on the sensitive skin of my inner thighs. Everywhere our bodies touch is a source of raw pleasure. The heat of his arousal amplifies the scent of his pine-needle soap.

He breaks away from the kiss, panting. The desire in his dark green eyes turns my insides up a couple hundred degrees.

This man knows how to preheat my oven.

"You're a master at getting me hot and bothered. You know that?" I'm gasping, too, my lungs demanding I breathe him in.

His answering grin is boyish, full of happy excitement. "Really?"

Instead of answering, I grab his face and demand more scalding kisses. When we pause for another breather, I give him a gentle push down south. "Okay, hotshot, show me what you've got."

On his way down, Ben takes a pit stop, pulling aside the collar of my shirt and the cup of my bra, so he can run a thumb over my nipple. When I moan, he glances up at me, the corner of his mouth curling.

"Mmm. Missed these." After another swipe with his thumb, he leans down to suck the tight bud into his mouth. The rough surface of his tongue is almost too much sensation, dragging a cry from the back of my throat.

My fingers tangle in his russet hair as my back bows off the bed.

He lets me go with a wet pop, and I whimper at the loss of contact. Ben chuckles and then moves lower.

First, he uses his fingers, tracing them down my hips and through my curls until the pad of his thumb reaches my sweet spot. When he gives my clit a gentle rub, the sound I let out is a mixture of a gasp and a purr. It's intoxicating—being with a man who not only knows that my clit exists, but also knows exactly how to caress her.

"You like that? Want me to give you more?" His voice has gone low and dirty, and he firmly massages his thumb in a circular motion.

"Don't stop ... oh God ..."

As his one hand works, the fingers of his other explore. They run over my opening, teasing and searching. A groan flows out of me as he continues his steady rhythm. He blows on me, and I jerk in surprise. The shock of cool air contrasting with his warm thumb has me writhing.

Then, I get his hot tongue. Ben licks me like I'm his favorite flavor of ice cream, and I come to believe I'm just as delicious. His fingers spread me wide before he pushes that teasing tongue inside me.

My hips buck involuntarily, and I realize my heels are digging into his shoulders, urging him closer. Demanding he go harder.

But he just keeps to the same pace, slow and insanity-inducing.

Normally, I'm pretty quiet during sex, concentrating on finishing, usually by playing out some fantasy in my head that turns me on more than the guy I'm with. But I'm fully present in this moment with Ben, and he has me gasping and almost laughing in the sheer joy of the moment.

Even though my body is shaking out of my control, I've never been more comfortable. Ben is my safe place He holds me steady, so I can let go.

My cheeks prickle and go numb. My fingers and toes curl, my

whole body clenching, tensing, getting ready for the snap of a release. I'm light-headed and panting.

"Ben, please!"

My begging must be what he wants because he finally presses harder and moves faster.

Three ... two ... one.

The cliff edge comes, and I fall off, calling out his name. My muscles pulse with pleasure, finally releasing all that delightful tension.

Once the aftershocks fade, I sink, boneless, into Ben's mattress. Black spots dot in front of my eyes, and my throat has gone hoarse. The buzzing in my ears retreats until I can hear my own ragged breathing.

Ben appears in my line of vision, supporting himself above me, the way he did before he shattered me. He takes in my hazy, satisfied expression and gifts me with another of his heart-aching grins. If I had any control over my limbs, I'd drag his face down to where I could kiss him.

Instead, he leans down to kiss the end of my nose. "Let me know when you're ready for round two."

23

HOLLY

"H<small>AS</small> anyone offered to pay you for your kidney?" Dr. Carmine keeps his expression passive while he kindly interrogates me.

"Seriously? Don't you get tired of asking me that every time we're here?"

He just waits, pen poised over his pad of paper.

I sigh and avoid the urge to roll my eyes. "No. No one is paying me for my kidney."

A little voice in the back of my head whispers to me.

What about your rent? Ben's going to pay for that, isn't he? Rule breaker.

I shift in my seat. Maybe I should talk to him again. Tell him I don't need his financial help.

"Do you feel coerced in any way to go through with this donation?"

If he means threatened, then sure. I feel threatened by death with its scaly fingers wrapped around my brother's throat.

But I doubt that's what he's getting at.

"No one has coerced or bribed me."

"And you understand the risks of this surgery? You will be put under anesthesia, which can be very disconcerting for people."

Losing consciousness isn't high on my list of fun times, but I can deal with it. If anything about this process gets me sweating, it's the needles they'll be plugging into my veins. Best not think of it. And I have no plans to share my phobia with my temporary psychiatrist. I'm not sure if he'd call off the surgery because of it but better to err on the side of caution.

"I understand that. And I'm ready. I want my brother to be healthy. I want Ben to be healthy. I'd put up with a lot more pain and discomfort than this to make that happen."

Normally, as Dr. Carmine goes through his list of questions, he wears his classic therapist face. No emotions other than polite interest. But my last statement actually receives a small flicker of curiosity.

"So, you've had more contact with Ben?"

With great effort, I keep from shifting in my chair, a twinge of guilt rising in my chest.

Why though? Do I feel bad about dating the guy I plan to donate my kidney to? Or am I uncomfortable because I'm going to withhold the information?

Right now isn't the moment to dwell on it.

In theory, these sessions are meant to protect my interests, but every time I come in here, I'm on edge. If I give any indication I'm not completely for this exchange, they can call it off.

No way I'll let that happen.

"Yep. We talk sometimes. I'm looking forward to giving him my kidney. He deserves to be healthy again."

My answer is pleasantly bland and seems to satisfy Dr. Carmine.

Some of the tension eases out of my shoulders, but I know I won't fully relax until I wake up from surgery, short one kidney, with the nurse telling me that Marcus's procedure went just as smoothly as mine.

~

BEN

"I hope you don't plan on being on your phone this entire trip." My mom gives me one of her classic chiding stares she used all through my childhood.

When I was a kid, they'd fill me with guilt, but now, I just give her my most innocent grin.

"Who me? I was just checking the time."

"That's what watches are for." She reaches across the table to tap my wrist.

I've got on the chunky silver one my parents gave me for my last birthday. It's probably expensive. Mom said something about it being Swiss-made when I pulled it out of the box, but I've never looked it up. The thing that makes it priceless to me is the inscription on the back side.

Our best times are with you. Love, Mom & Dad

"Oh, right! Watches tell time. Totally forgot."

She shakes her head at me, but I notice the corner of her mouth twitch.

"Told you we should have spanked him as a child. Then, he wouldn't have such a smart mouth." This comment comes from my dad as he returns from the bar, carrying glasses of water for my mom and me and a measure of scotch for himself.

He's not a big drinker, but flying makes him nervous. Over his shoulder, a window looks out on the tarmac. In the distance, I can see a plane gracefully lifting off the runway.

"You might be right, honey. We were too soft on him." She continues to fight a smile as she takes a sip of water.

"Spank me? Can't believe you even considered it. I mean, just imagine the effect that would've had on my ass." Dad snorts into his scotch, but I keep going, targets set on my mom, "Probably flattened it right out. Then, how'd you expect me to get a girlfriend? The minute I turned around, she'd see I had nothing to grab on to and kick me out the door. Kick me right on my flat ass."

Mom's teeth bite into her lower lip, and she glares at me, but I can see her just about to crack. So, I turn around and glance over my shoulder, and with the most horrified expression I can muster, I grandly gesture at my butt.

That does it. She slams her glass on the table and uses both her hands to cover her face as she lets out the most ridiculous-sounding laughter that ever existed. It's like a donkey with hiccups, braying and snorting so loud that people at other tables glance toward us, probably concerned we're murdering an innocent farm animal.

Dad raises his drink to me, a silent cheers to my success. My mom hates her laugh, but the two of us love it. We constantly try to make her break.

"You are the devil!" She wipes at her eyes with a napkin and tries to glare at me as chuckles continue to sneak out.

I shrug and grin. "I am what you made me."

"Stop trying to embarrass me and tell me what's going on in your life. How are your classes?"

"They're fine. Finals are in a couple of weeks, so lots of studying and papers."

I don't tell them how mind-numbing I find my schoolwork. That it takes me twice as long to write my essays because all the facts get pushed out of my head by beautiful images I want to create. My notes from class are more doodles than words.

Not that I don't do the work. My GPA has never fallen below a 3.5. But the subjects bore me to tears. I'm surrounded by people who enjoy the classes while I'm just wishing I were somewhere else.

Holly probably would've latched on to my vague answer and pushed for more, but my parents let it pass.

"I'm sure you'll do great. You always do." Mom smiles reassuringly while Dad watches me over the rim of his drink.

After one last swallow, he finishes. "Gonna grab another, and then we can head to the gate."

As he turns toward the bar, my mom gives him a sympathetic pat on the back.

Because of my dad's fear, we normally keep our family trips to places within driving distance of Philadelphia. Even more so now that I need my treatments every other day. But my aunt Carol decided she wanted to visit her son—my cousin, Fred—out in Colorado and figured Thanksgiving would be a good time to go. Slowly, it turned into a whole family thing with my dad agreeing to fly and me finding a dialysis treatment center in Denver that had appointment times I could use while there.

All the plans were finalized months ago. Before I met Holly.

A trip I was originally looking forward to is now a week that I have to spend away from her. I'm doing my best not to turn into a dark storm cloud and ruin this family vacation.

As if she could read my mind, my mom starts up her questioning again. "What about dating? Ever since you broke up with that self-centered Anna girl, you haven't mentioned anyone."

"Her name was Annabelle, and I thought you liked her."

Dad gets back then, a new glass of scotch in his hand, and I catch his grimace.

Mom waves dismissively. "I tolerated her because you liked her. And I cracked open a bottle of champagne the day you told me it was over."

I start to snort in disbelief, but then my dad gives a confirming nod.

"Glad I didn't pop the question then. Good to know you two would've let me hang myself."

She reaches over to pat my hand. "We knew you'd eventually figure it out. And, now, you have a better idea of what to avoid. Time to look for a girl who cares about more than just herself. Someone with a good head on her shoulders. Like your donor, Holly."

I made the mistake of taking a drink when she said that, and half the water gets snorted up my nose in surprise. As I choke and cough, my dad gives me some unhelpful slaps on the back, and my mom keeps talking, like her son isn't dry-drowning in front of her.

"I mean, not *her*, obviously. But someone like her."

When I can breathe, I respond, though my voice comes out raspy, "Why not her?"

"Ha-ha. Very funny. You just can't stop with the jokes today, can you?"

My heart sinks at her response.

"But, seriously, any new girls catching your eye?"

After what she just said, I know telling her about Holly and me won't turn out well. Getting into a fight right when we're about to be stuck next to each other for hours isn't recommended.

So, again, I evade by using a vague version of the truth. "When I have a girlfriend, I promise I'll let you know."

Holly's technically not my girlfriend yet even though I want her to be, so this only feels a little bit like lying.

The overhead speakers announce the flight to Denver has begun boarding, saving me from further prying. As my parents fumble with their rolling bags, I take the opportunity to pull out my phone again and shoot off a quick text.

Ben: *About to board. Text u tonight.*

When I'm settling into my seat, my phone vibrates in my pocket.

Holly: *Have fun! And don't join the Mile-High Club without me! ;)*

Hell, I already miss her.

~

HOLLY

Pops's kitchen has never smelled so good. Just because there are only three of us doesn't keep me from pulling out all the stops. I run through my list again.

1. *Turkey*
2. *Mashed potatoes*
3. *Green beans*

4. *Cranberry sauce*
5. *Sweet potato casserole*
6. *Dinner rolls*
7. *Corn on the cob*
8. *Gravy*
9. *Applesauce*

"Marcus, are the rolls done?" I call out.

"Am I allowed back in the kitchen?"

I roll my eyes. "Of course. I never said you weren't."

My big brother walks through the doorway, a wary look on his face. "You didn't have to. Made it pretty obvious when you tried to dump a pot of boiling potatoes on my head."

A chuckle drifts from the living room, and I glare at the wall, as if Pops might experience the burn of my gaze through the plaster.

"I didn't try to dump it on you. You were in my way, so I told you to move."

He crosses the kitchen to pick up a timer I didn't notice on the counter. "You and I have different definitions of *told*." He holds the timer up for me to see. "The rolls have three more minutes. Are they the last thing?"

"Yeah. Help me move all this."

We both slip on oven mitts and carry the dishes into the dining room.

"Am I allowed in the kitchen?" Pops strolls into the room and grins when I throw my hands up at how dramatic they're being.

"Yes! Everyone is allowed in the kitchen! You'd think I'd put a sign up that said, *No Boys Allowed*, or something." I huff and go to grab the bowl of green beans.

Pops opens the fridge and pulls out two pies. My mouth waters at just the memory of that recipe. One I've never been able to master.

"Grams's blueberry pies. Thought I'd put them in to bake now, so they'll be ready for later."

Picking up the last few food items, I leave the two of them to work out the oven.

In the past few years, this has become our tradition. I'm in charge of most of the cooking, Marcus does the bread, and Pops does the dessert. Then, they handle cleanup duty, although I usually sneak back in to help dry some dishes.

My brother loves making dough from scratch, so I don't mind him covering that job. And every dessert I've ever tried to bake somehow goes to crap. Sweets are my kryptonite, so I finally gave up and passed the responsibility on to my dad. He's almost as good as Grams was.

Once the three of us are sitting around the table, Pops clears his throat. "I'm thankful for having you two in my life."

My throat gets tight when a sudden rush of emotion clogs it.

Marcus goes next. "I'm thankful that, even though I live in New York, I still get to visit plenty. And I'm thankful that I have a stubborn sister who's hell-bent on saving me."

He grins, and I take a deep, shuddering breath to keep from getting weepy.

"I'm thankful for the both of you and for paired kidney donations." My voice quivers.

Pops pats my shoulder. "There's a good girl. This looks delicious. Grams would've been proud."

As we dig in, my whole body aches with a strange mixture of happiness and loss. I can't help remembering all the Thanksgiving dinners from my childhood where there were five of us at the table. Back when Mom was clean and a part of my life. The days when I was my grandmother's helper in the kitchen. She'd have me read all the ingredients out loud from her handwritten recipe cards as she cooked. Now, I realize she probably had them all memorized but still wanted to give me a job.

Grams always made sure I felt useful. I was her ingredients reader, her wet-dishes drier, her dress-zipper-upper, and most importantly, her grocery list-maker. She was the one who gave me my first notebook, asking me to write down all the things we'd need to pick up at the store. And not just for holiday meals. Every day, she'd call out things that needed to go on the shopping list, and I'd pull out my handy notebook to write them down, so we'd be ready when it was time for a trip to the supermarket.

Now, with her gone, I find the practice of creating lists soothing. Because it gives me focus and reminds me of her.

My brother and dad are too busy stuffing their faces to make conversation, but they make plenty of approving noises. I beam at the both of them, loving my family even though it's smaller than it used to be.

I hope Ben is having a good Thanksgiving. We've been texting sporadically ever since he left, talking on the phone a few lucky times, and I'm surprised at how much I miss him. Normally, Thursdays are full of Ben—the two of us reading and talking during his morning treatment. But, with the holiday and his trip, I won't get to see him again till next week.

The chair next to me is empty. I wish it weren't. I want him here, getting to know my family, cracking jokes that would help take my mind off the pain of the past. If he were here, I'd reach for his hand under the table, just so I could hold on to him.

When did Ben become the person I most want to turn to when I'm feeling unsteady?

24

Holly: *Sorry, but I can't read to you today. Too much to study for finals.*

BEN

I GET her text just as I'm setting out all the materials I need to hook myself up. The words send my stomach twisting downward.

Another day without Holly.

It's the Tuesday after Thanksgiving, and yesterday, she told me, if I started my treatment after her work shift, then she'd come by tonight.

We haven't seen each other in a week, and I'm getting jittery. It's like, without regular doses of her, I go into withdrawal. I'm even considering if I can push my treatment off until tomorrow, so I can go find her right now. I just want to hold her against me, hear her scold me for being irresponsible, and then kiss her long and slow until she forgets my bad behavior.

But she needs to study, and I don't want her to think of me as a distraction.

I thought I'd have to be on my own in Denver, but Holly told me to call her when I was hooked up. So, I sat in that depressing place, surrounded by people in the same shitty situation as me, and followed her directions. She proceeded to read to me over the phone for almost the entire three-hour session. Then, she did it again two days later.

Even though I knew I was being a leech, I greedily accepted every minute of time she offered.

Now, I'm here, dreading the thought of sitting with these stupid tubes in my arms for hours with no Holly to talk to or listen to or look at. In a way, her coming to my treatments has made things worse. Now that she's shown me how easy it can be when she's around, getting my dialysis without her makes me want to tear my hair out and then take a bat to the machine.

I resign myself to the distraction of a movie, navigating through the digital downloads until I find *Die Hard 2*. Maybe some gun fights and explosions will drown out my restless thoughts.

Doesn't work.

Instead, my mind starts developing worst-case scenarios.

Does Holly really have to study? Could she just be looking for a break from me? Am I asking too much of her? When will she get tired of me? Has she finally realized I'm broken? Why do I think I deserve her?

I'm going in circles, asking myself these unanswerable questions, when I hear Holly's voice.

"Well, it looks like someone started without me."

And there she is, framed in the doorway with wind-mussed hair and an armful of textbooks.

"Holly! You're here."

Confusion and amusement sweep over her face as she unloads her bag and stack of books on the floor next to what I've officially dubbed Holly's Chair.

"Yeah. I told you I was coming." When her coat is off, she steps up next to my seat and leans down.

She's aiming for a kiss on my cheek, but after a week apart, I need more. My head turns at the last second, and I capture her lips. When she responds with a happy sigh, I wrap my free arm around her waist and pull her into me. Her lips curve in reaction to my antics, but she lets me hold her close, wrapping both her arms around my neck. Slowly, with great relish, I savor her mouth.

I swear, every time, the taste is even sweeter than before.

Holly eventually breaks the kiss with another sigh and untangles herself from my clutch. "You're not being fair. I told you, I need to study."

As she straightens, I realize her clothing is different than usual. Instead of the casual leggings or jeans, she has on a tight-fitting skirt with a dark green blouse. And heels. When she bends over to pick up a book off the floor, I'm treated to the glorious sight of Holly's pert ass encased in the charcoal-gray material, which ends just above her knees, and her shapely calves wrapped in sheer black tights. All this leads to black heels with little straps that wrap around her slim ankles.

"You're trying to give me a heart attack right now. You really are."

She glances over her shoulder at me in the same way she would if I had her on my bed, taking her from behind. Somehow, I suppress my groan as that mental image overlays with the very real one in front of me.

"What do you mean?" She straightens, book clutched in her hands, worry on her face.

"This outfit. You're like a business sex kitten."

Holly glances down at herself, smoothing her hand over her skirt. "This is how I always dress for my internship. It's a business office." She goes to sit in her chair but stops when she spots her treat.

Satisfaction fills my chest as she snatches up the brown paper bag, plunging a hand into it and coming out with a chunk of flaky pastry. Now, she sits, eyes closed and lips curled happily as she munches away.

"You're the best," she tells me.

At least, I think that's what she says, her voice garbled as she talks around another giant bite of croissant.

Fucking adorable.

"Glad you've figured that out. But back to this outfit. You look hot. Not that you don't always. But this is the first time I've gotten to see Sexy Business Holly."

She rolls her eyes and sticks out her tongue, and I growl in response because I can't lean over to kiss her without upsetting my tubes.

"You'll have to return the favor and show me Sexy Business Ben at some point," she murmurs, setting her snack aside to flip through her textbook.

I'd be happy to dress up for Holly. Maybe our next official date will be to a nice restaurant, and we can both get decked out. I wonder what Sexy, Expensive Dinner-Date Holly looks like. Maybe she'd wear that little black dress from Annabelle's party.

Next time I see her in that scrap of fabric, I'm not going to hold back. We'll find a pool table for her to bend over, and I'll push up the skirt and then slide off whatever lacy underwear she's got underneath it—

Shit. Now, I'm hard.

With her focused on her notes, I'm able to adjust myself without making it obvious that I was just picturing stripping her. This is a prime example of how different I feel when she's at my treatments. Before meeting Holly, I would have settled for just not being miserable while sitting in this chair. Now, I'm having vivid fantasies that completely block out the discomfort.

As Holly studies, I can't help but stare at her rather than the movie. Like the first day we met, she has a highlighter in hand, tapping it on her lip as she scans the pages in her lap. I don't want to interrupt her, but I get a strong urge to be connected with her, even when her mind is somewhere else.

"Give me your feet."

She flicks her eyes up to mine. "What?"

"Your feet. Put them in my lap." If I were able to move around more, I would just scoop them up myself. But, with the situation as it is, I need her to make the first move.

Eyebrows pinched in confusion, Holly shifts forward in her chair before placing her heeled feet on the top of my thighs. Instead of immediately returning to her reading, she watches me.

Slowly, I unbuckle the little straps, sliding each of the shoes off and setting them next to my lounge chair. Then, I set my free hand to work, massaging her arches.

Holly groans. "Oh, that's heaven."

I know my grin is smug, but nothing makes me feel like more of a badass than when I give my woman pleasure.

"So, this is just you being nice, right? You don't have some foot fetish I should know about?" Her expression is serious, but her eyes are laughing.

My grin widens. "What would you do if I did?"

She purses her lips in thought. "I guess I'd wear more open-toed shoes."

That surprises a laugh out of me. "I missed you."

"I missed you, too." Holly returns to her studying with a smile.

I'm able to watch my movie now, easily ignoring my arm when I have a set of warm feet resting in my lap.

~

HOLLY

"We've finished tallying up the money from the fundraiser, and we've ended up getting seventy dollars more than we hoped for. Great job, everybody."

Clapping fills the room, and pride swells in my chest. I debated on whether or not I should hand over the reins of the club this year, what with the surgery coming up. Even though Dr. Williams said it'd be fine for me to be back in classes by spring semester, she made it clear that traveling to New Orleans for the spring break Habitat for Humanity build was out of the question.

What kind of club president doesn't go on the biggest trip of the year?

But I decided to stick with it, and instead, I used my bossy organization skills to make sure everyone who could go was paying as little out of pocket as possible. This last fundraiser did just that.

Who knew that selling slices of pizza to drunk college students would be so lucrative? I don't mind taking advantage of their inebriated states when it's in pursuit of a good cause.

There are only a few more points on the agenda before we can wrap up our last meeting of the semester. Somehow, I'm able to make it through them all without stumbling even though a set of green eyes in the back of the room has my pulse stepping up its rhythm.

Ben decided he wanted to be more active in student organizations, apparently starting with Habitat for Humanity. He's lounging in his seat, a notebook on the desk in front of him, like he's actually writing down what I'm saying when I'm sure he's just doodling his random, perfect pictures. He's got a silly smirk on his face as he watches me speak. No glasses today and looking edible in his black thermal and fitted jeans. I'm not the only admirer Ben has. From my vantage point, I notice some of the female members casually turning in their chairs, attempting to check him out.

Normally, I'm a peaceful leader, preferring to solve problems with calm discussions. But, tonight, I'm about to challenge these girls to a street fight if they don't get their eyes off my man.

But is he mine?

I don't know, and that makes my skin itch.

Am I really going to be the one who brings up commitment first?

That's so out of character.

Then, I meet Ben's eyes, and he shoots me a wink.

Who gives a flying monkey's butt if it's out of character?

This is the fourth day in a row that we've hung out, and I'm speeding through my list just so I can go talk to him.

I want him. I want all of him.

"So, if no one has any questions ..." I hesitate, taking my gaze off Ben to scan the room.

Only about half of the members are here; most everyone else is either studying or has already left for winter break. No one raises their hand.

"Okay. Then, that concludes this meeting. I'll see you all in the spring."

People begin chatting or head for the door.

Slowly, I gather my notes, trying not to appear too eager even though I'm ready to sprint across the room. Turns out, I don't have to.

"Power looks good on you." Ben leans on the front of the podium, grinning down at me.

"Oh, really? You like seeing me tell people what to do?"

Ben's gaze heats up as he traces my face with his eyes. "I like it when you tell me what to do."

"Hmm." I make a decision then. We're going to talk. And then we're going to do more than talk. "Ben?"

"Yes?"

"Go get the car and meet me out front. We're going back to my place."

He doesn't even try to suppress the lust in his stare. "Yes, ma'am." With swift steps, he heads out of the room.

Suddenly, I'm too hot but in a good way. Like when I've been walking in the cold and then step into a steaming shower. My skin tightens, and my cheeks flush.

If just the thought of being more intimate with Ben does this to me, what's going to happen when we actually have sex? Will I faint?

Please don't let me faint during sex.

With that mantra running through my head, I weave around the few people left, mouthing good-byes to those who make eye contact, and head toward the front door. The evening air cools my skin, and I tug my coat tighter.

That's when I see *him*.

Roderick is leaning on his car just a bit of a ways past the building entrance. When he notices me, he gives a big wave and gestures me over.

Since I don't see Ben, I hesitantly walk to where my ex-hook-up is waiting.

"What are you doing here, Roderick?" The question pops out of my mouth, my tone colder than I meant.

But he just smiles at me. "Wednesday night is your club. I dropped you off a couple of times."

Yeah, months ago. Before Ben.

"Doesn't really answer my question."

"Right, yeah. Sorry it took so long. Work got crazy, and I finally figured out what you meant." Roderick stands up from his car, hands tucked in his pockets, giving me a rueful grin.

"What do you mean, what I meant?" My arms wrap tight around my middle, more to guard me from the awkwardness of this conversation than to keep me warm.

"When you said what we were doing wasn't working for you anymore. I totally get it. I want more than just hooking up, too. We'll start dating. You can be my girlfriend."

My first reaction is to laugh because the arrogance of that last statement is baffling. But I tamp down that response and try to remember the exact text I sent to Roderick. I thought I'd made it clear that it was the two of us that didn't work together, not the nature of our relationship.

The sound of doors opening and conversations drift from behind me. The last of the club members are making their exit, and even though I don't want what Roderick's offering, it doesn't mean I think a bunch of people should hear the rejection. So, I take a step forward in order to use a lower voice.

Unfortunately, he interprets this as an invitation.

Moving toward me, Roderick reaches out to put his hand on my waist. He barely makes contact before I step out of the hold.

This situation is one of the many reasons I've avoided relationships in the past. If we're not dating, then we don't have to go through a breakup. Or so I thought.

"Roderick, I wasn't trying to push you into a relationship or manipulate you. If I'd wanted us to start dating, I would have said that. I was being honest when I told you that I didn't think the two of us worked together. At least, it wasn't working for me."

The confidence leaves his face as my words settle in. And, of course, it's right at this extremely uncomfortable moment that I hear a familiar set of footsteps approaching.

25

BEN

THE VENTS BLOW out cold air at first, but I crank the heat, hoping to warm the car up fast. I don't want anything cooling the fire I just saw in Holly's eyes.

The memory of her command makes me shiver. She wants to go back to her place.

Pleasant thoughts of what we might do tonight get interrupted when I pull around the corner, only to see Holly walking away from where I planned to pick her up. She moves purposefully toward a guy with overly styled hair and a cocky-as-hell grin.

Instantly, I know he's not just a friend. The way this greasy-haired asshole runs his eyes over Holly makes it clear that he's got only one thing on his mind. But there's more than just attraction. He looks possessive.

Makes me want to punch that smirk off his face.

Why did Holly walk over to him? Why is she talking to him like they know each other?

Then, the obvious hits me in the gut.

Could this be one of her hook-ups?

My whole world tilts on its axis.

Are they still sleeping together?

I want to throw up.

My mind trips over the last few weeks, searching for something to deny what my eyes are telling me. This whole time, she could have been seeing someone else. Sleeping with someone else.

The cowardly thing to do would be to sit here, wait till she's done, and then pretend I never saw them together. Or worse, blame her for technically doing nothing wrong. We haven't talked about being exclusive. Just because the idea of her with another guy makes me want to spoon my eyes out of my sockets doesn't mean it's a betrayal.

So, I go with door number three.

It's time to make sure all parties are aware of the situation. This guy is going to know that he isn't the only one in Holly's life. And I'm letting Holly know that *more* isn't enough anymore. I want it all.

Time to crash their party.

The engine quiets as I put the car in park and remove the keys, praying I don't get towed from the No Parking zone. As I stalk over to them, the cold helps to cool some of my anger. So does watching Holly step away from the guy's reaching hand.

Maybe my first assumption was wrong.

When I come up behind her, something she says makes him frown. The agitation keeping my neck tense eases.

Glancing over her shoulder, the guy notices my approach, appearing startled at first and then glaring at me when I smile down at Holly.

Her wide eyes flick to me and then back to the jerk in front of her.

Time to lay it on thick.

"How's it goin'? I'm Ben Gerhard."

I hold out my hand to shake his, and reluctantly, he returns my grip. He squeezes hard, which just makes my false smile grow wider. Someone is not a happy camper.

"Roderick Harrison." Short and crisp, and his scowl remains.

"Cool, bro." Yep, totally just used my douche-bag, frat-guy voice. Just want to speak his language. "You two friends?"

The guy smirks, and I get that sickness back in my stomach.

"Kind of." This comes from Holly, and when I turn to look at her, she's all shades of uncomfortable.

"We're more than friends. Isn't that right?" Pompous ass has arrogance dripping off his words, and I'm back to wanting to smash his face in.

Instead, I plaster on the fakest grin I can muster. "More than friends? Whoa, you must be pretty special. Did you get a gold star? A note on your report card that says, *Plays well with others*?"

"Ben." Holly sounds exasperated but not particularly mad.

When I turn my smile on her, all the mockery is gone; just genuine affection remains. "Holly."

She rolls her eyes at me.

Still grinning, I grab her hand, setting the keys in her mittened fingers. "The car's ready when you are."

A laugh lacking any real humor comes from the guy. His smile is harsh as he transfers his glare to Holly. "Oh, I get it. You've found a new fuck buddy. So, what is it? Does he have a more flexible schedule than me or something?"

What. The. Hell?

Is this how he always talks to her?

I mean, I'm not happy about this situation either, but I'm not about to start tossing accusations around.

I'm ready to throw down to defend her, but instead, I get pushed to the side as Holly leans in close to Roderick, her eyes narrow.

"That's not what this is about." There's something in her voice, like a warning. If I heard it during an argument between us, I'd take a step back and reevaluate.

Not Ricky boy.

"Oh, really? Is this supposed to be a relationship or something? Does pretty boy here know how we used to go at it? How we fucked more than we talked? How it was so easy to get you to spread your legs—"

"Are you mental?" The rage in her voice makes me flinch even though it's directed at the asshole a few feet over.

Receiving the full brunt of her burning eyes, the guy is left standing with his words cut off, mouth agape. But she's not done.

"What's the point of this? I didn't lie to you. I didn't lead you on. And, now, you're trying to make me feel like a whore because I *don't* want to have sex with you anymore. Where's the logic in that?" Breathing in deep through her nose, there's an almost visible cloak of calm that she pulls over herself and her features.

Instead of hitting him with heat, all that's left is ice.

"You did a good job of convincing me you were a decent guy. Clearly, I was wrong. So, like I told you weeks ago, we're done. Do not contact me again."

I'm left to follow in her wake as Holly turns abruptly and strides to the car. Neither of us looks back.

It's not until we're on the road that Holly's icy exterior cracks. Someone cuts in front of us without using their blinker, causing her to slam on the brakes. Aggressively, she punches the horn.

"For the love of Pete! Look where you're going, you son of a biscuit-eater!" she shouts the words like they're the ripest curses in the book.

Knowing she's upset, I bite my lower lip to keep from laughing.

Her eyes stray to the side, and I turn my head too slow to hide my amused expression.

"What?" she snaps the word at me.

Again, I try to school my face. "Nothing. I completely agree with you. That guy is a"—I snort—"son of a biscuit-eater." Another snort.

Holly punches me in the arm, but it's not a hard hit, and she's clearly fighting a smile. "You're right; he is."

Carefully, so as not to startle her, I reach over and give her knee a reassuring squeeze. "Do you want to talk about it?"

The car stays silent for a few more blocks, but eventually, she sighs. "I ended things with him pretty soon after I met you."

Most of the tension leaks away from my shoulders. "Why?"

"He started hinting at having a relationship. And I didn't want that."

My heart and hopes take a nosedive at her words, barreling toward the ground. I brace myself for a fiery impact.

"But the bigger reason was that I couldn't stop thinking about you. Being with you. Roderick kinda paled in comparison."

I level out, holding off on utter disappointment. "Do you still not want a relationship?"

We've reached her apartment, and Holly concentrates on parallel parking, leaving me to sit in suspense. When the car is settled, she shuts off the ignition and turns to meet my eyes.

"I want you. I want you to be mine. *More* isn't good enough for me anymore. I want more than *more*." Though her words are open and honest, from the way she sits, with her arms crossed, leaning back against the door, it's obvious she's bracing herself.

As if I'd reject her.

Reaching across the distance she put between us, I pry one of her hands free and kiss her palm. A slight curve of her lips is my reward.

"I want to tattoo my name on your forehead, so every guy in the world knows you're mine."

The curve grows, but she keeps her gaze on our hands. "That wouldn't be very attractive."

"I'd use a really nice font. I swear." I lift her hand to my face, trying to get her to look at me. Time to get serious. "I'm already committed to you, Holly, but if you want the words, then let's go for it. You're my girlfriend. I'm your boyfriend. We're exclusive."

That earns me her eyes, and they glint with happiness. She drops her hand from my face, only to use it to push the armrests out of her way, so she can crawl over to straddle my lap. Then, she takes my head and kisses me slow, driving me mad with want. Our lips separate enough for her to whisper to me, "I'm your girlfriend. You're my boyfriend. We're exclusive." Another deep, searching kiss before she leans back, her gaze now full of excited mischief and a volcano's worth of heat.

We need to get up to her apartment. Right now.

～

HOLLY

We race each other to the elevator.

I stand on one side of the tiny compartment, my hands tucked behind my back, pressed flat on the cool wall, so I won't reach for him. Not yet.

Ben keeps to his side, leaning back against the paneled wood with his thumbs casually hooked in his pockets. But I can see his chest rising and falling with deep breaths, the pulse in his neck pounding. The same rapid rhythm pushes at my heart rate.

The urge to attack him, rip his clothes off, and climb him like a jungle gym has me digging my fingers into the wall for more purchase.

Ben might appear to be in shape, but I know better than anyone that his health's not one hundred percent. I should try to be gentle.

Hopefully, I can remember that once I have him naked.

The ding announcing our floor sounds, and I already have the apartment key in my hand. While I fumble to fit it in the lock, Ben moves to press his body against my back. He's like a warm, sexy blanket that came straight out of the dryer. All I want to do is wrap myself in him. When I finally turn my key and the knob, I stumble forward, my legs not wanting to move away.

My coat, purse, and shoes all get tossed to the side. When I turn back to Ben, he's leaning on the now-shut door, watching me with sparking eyes that set off a wildfire in my belly.

"Where's Terra?"

"Faith, her girlfriend, just got back from deployment. Terra drove to North Carolina to meet up with her."

"So, you're here, all by yourself?"

I nod. "Looks like I need someone to keep me company."

He lets out an exaggerated sigh. "I guess, as your boyfriend, that's one of my responsibilities." For a moment, he tries to keep a straight face, but a boyish grin cracks across it.

He's too delicious to ignore; I need a taste. Stepping forward, I weave my fingers behind his neck and pull him down, so I can kiss him. Taking what's mine.

Responding just as eagerly, he winds his arms around my waist and lifts me off my feet, so I have to clutch him tighter. His greedy reaction makes me smile as I enjoy his mouth. I suck on his lower lip, giving it a little nip.

He sets me down, breaking our kiss, but then turns me to face the ladder to my loft and gives my butt a firm squeeze. "I want you in your bed. Now."

"And you said I was bossy," I throw this over my shoulder as I make the climb, swaying my hips a bit more than usual.

I barely have time to step away before Ben lifts himself up after me, tossing his coat over the railing to land on the floor below.

Like last time, he has to stand awkwardly bent under my low ceiling. So, for his own good, I push him onto the bed. He lands with a grunt and a bounce but smiles up at me, his stare hungry. With him sprawled out on my plush bed, I feel like a conqueror, ready to stake my claim.

"Take your shirt off."

He smirks. "I will if you will."

There's not a shred of modesty when I hook my fingers under the bottom of my T-shirt and yank it over my head. Now standing in my simple white bra, I wait for him to return the favor.

But Ben doesn't make a move. Instead, his eyes roam over me, almost as heavy a touch as his hands.

No fair.

He reaches out toward me, but I step back and cross my arms over my chest.

"Nope. Your turn, buddy."

His half-growl, half-grin is sexy enough to make me melt as he whips his own shirt off. Finally, I get to see his sinfully tempting tattoos again. Last time, he only let me touch them. This time, I'm going to lick them.

"And the pants, too."

He raises an eyebrow at my demand, and I pick up on his silent request.

My fingers fiddle with the button and zipper on my own jeans until I can slide them down my legs and kick them to the side. Ben shucks his off, too.

The sight has me biting my lip. Hard.

Wearing only a set of black boxer briefs, Ben's artwork is almost fully on display. He has more designs on his thighs, obscured slightly by the reddish-blond hair covering his skin. The pictures are intricate, connecting and twining together in creative ways. I could stare at them for hours, just memorizing how the images stretch and flex over his straining muscles.

"Come here. Now."

When I glance up from Ben's legs, I realize his hungry gaze has turned ravenous.

Giving in to the need to touch him, I step forward and slide down to straddle his lap, just like I wanted to the first time he sat on my bed.

His warmth makes my head swim with lust.

I lean forward to trace my fingers over the dark lines etched into his skin. As I move my hands along his shoulders and then his chest, teasing him, his breath comes quicker, panting.

Ben clutches my hips, digging into my skin as he grips me close. He hardens underneath me, the swell of him pressing against my core. My body responds, my panties growing damp.

Unable to take my light touches any longer, Ben wraps a hand in my hair and drags my mouth to his. We kiss like we're starving for each other, lips exploring, tongues dancing. I rock my hips into him, and when he groans, I swallow the sound.

Then, his other hand slides from my side to my stomach, his fingers stopping to play with the waistband of my boy shorts. He uses his grip on the strands at the base of my neck to briefly separate us, his forcefulness ramping up my heart rate in the best way.

"Tell me I can." The sound of his deepened voice has the muscles in my thighs clenching.

"Please. Yes. Touch me."

Having gotten his permission, Ben resumes ravishing my mouth while also pushing past the thin cotton barrier. The pads of his fingers delve through my curls to discover my slick center.

He breaks away again. "You wet for me?"

"Obviously," I moan, and he smirks.

My clit begs for his attention, and he gives it. His skin is alive with electricity, shocking my most sensitive spot.

"That how you like it? Nice and hard?"

Speaking is beyond me now, so I just nod vigorously, my nose brushing against his.

His firm, demanding strokes have me gasping for air.

With each deep breath, I drag in more of his fresh pine-needle scent mixed with something that's unique to Ben. The man I trust enough to be out of control with.

He lets me enjoy the wildness. Makes me crave it.

My body starts to tremble. His talented fingers burn like a hot brand at my center.

"That's it, Holly. Come for me," he fiercely whispers these words in my ear, as if he has the power to decide when I break apart.

Turns out, he does.

"Ben!"

He bites my neck and gives another demanding stroke, and I'm gone.

Maybe I scream, maybe I black out, but I definitely follow his command. Delicious muscle spasms shudder through my body, making me twitch and moan. Every nerve ending tingles with shocks of pleasure.

When I come back to myself, panting and grinning, I'm bonelessly wrapped around my tattooed orgasm-giver.

His skilled fingers trace over my skin, promising that I've got more to look forward to.

BEN

We haven't even taken off all our clothes, and I'm on the verge of finishing.

Watching Holly orgasm has adrenaline pumping through my veins, pushing all my blood to my dick. I want to beat my chest like an ape and then make a novelty T-shirt to wear everywhere that says, *I made Holly Foster scream my name as she came!*

Her soft body is draped around me, her breath panting hot on my neck. As she recovers, I unhook her bra, sliding the straps down her arms. She lets me and starts to pepper small kisses on my neck.

Already, my girl is heating up again.

I move to lay her down on the bed, but she stops me, instead pushing off me to stand up. The loss of her warm skin against mine is like a Band-Aid being ripped off. I reach out to pull her back, but she dances out of my grip.

"Nuh-uh. I still haven't seen all the goods yet."

Hell, she's sexy.

Holly props her hands on her hips, not caring in the slightest that she's topless, only wearing a pair of tiny blue underwear with a little bow on the front.

I'm so distracted by her, the sway of her tits, and the damp shine to her inner thighs; it takes me a moment to figure out what she's saying.

"The goods?"

She crosses her arms, effectively covering her chest. I'm pretty sure I'm pouting or glaring. Doesn't matter. I just want to see her tight pink nipples again.

"Yeah. The goods. Your tattoos. I demand to see every inch of you before we ..." She peters off, biting her lip and fixating on my briefs.

Even though I'm so hard for her that it's starting to hurt, the cotton of my underwear stretched tight, I can't help teasing. "Before we what?"

Her eyes flick up to mine and then stay when she sees my expression. A slow smile, reminding me of that purple cat from *Alice in*

Wonderland, curls across her mouth. "Before we"—she hesitates —"fuck." The raspy tone of her voice as she carefully says that last word sets my brain on fire.

I should've known better than to mess with her. She plays to win. "You're gonna kill me."

Holly shrugs, still wearing her evil grin.

She wants to see all of me? Who am I to deny her?

Because of the low ceiling, I stay seated, shimmying off my last piece of clothing. I thought I might be insecure. I'm not in good shape like I used to be. But the way she stares at me, like I'm something she wants to consume, takes away any discomfort.

So, I lean back on my arms, knees spread, cock standing at attention, as my girlfriend drinks her fill.

"Lie back on the bed." Her voice, when it comes out, still has that deep, husky quality.

I do as she commanded, sliding backward on her silky comforter until I rest on the pillows.

But she doesn't move closer.

"Flip over." After I raise an eyebrow, she explains, "You said you have some on your … ass." The dirty word is placed gently between us, just like before. I saw the conscious decision she made to say it, which somehow makes it even sexier.

I roll onto my stomach, unable to contain a groan as I push my hard dick into the soft mattress. The bed dips. Propped up on my elbows, I glance over my shoulder.

Holly crawls toward me. As she moves, her fingers trail over the designs. Then, her lips do.

Starting at my upper thighs, Holly caresses, kisses, and licks her way up my body.

The whole time, I'm grunting and groaning, unable to help thrusting into the mattress, as if it were her I was fucking. I'll probably go insane if I can't sink into her soon.

Of course, I'm definitely going to lose my mind when I do.

When her breasts brush my shoulder blade and her teeth graze my neck, I'm done with holding back.

I roll over, wrap my arms around her slim waist, and press her hot body against mine. She gasps in delight right before I capture her devilish mouth.

"Take these off," I mutter in between kisses. My fingers tug at the scrap of cotton she's still wearing.

Smiling against my mouth, Holly pushes the panties down and uses her legs to shimmy them off. Then, the temptress throws one leg high over my hips, making it easy for my hand to slip down her backside. When I reach her swollen pussy, she's soaking wet.

Somehow, I tear my mouth from hers, even as my fingers push inside her. "Condom. We need a condom."

She whimpers, leaning down to lick my neck and place hot, open-mouthed kisses along my jaw. Her snug, slick opening beckons me to slide into her.

"Holly. Please. I need you."

She pauses, and in the brief break, I try to remember if I have any protection on me. I've got to have one in my wallet. Right?

I beg the universe that, at some point in the past, I was optimistic about my chances of getting laid. The minute Holly agreed to date me, I should've stuffed condoms in every one of my pockets. Just in case.

She reaches down to guide my fingers out of her, a gasp whispering over her lips as I slip free. When she rolls to the side of the bed, I prop myself up, worried I've killed the mood and still not sure I'm prepared if I didn't.

"Was hoping we'd get a chance to use these." Holly grins wickedly while holding up a variety pack of rubbers.

If possible, my dick grows harder when she has to take a moment to open the box. The *new* box. These are just for the two of us. A whole fucking box.

After selecting one and tearing the wrapper away, Holly shoves my shoulder. I land on my back with her moving to straddle my hips. My groan fills the small apartment as she strokes me a couple of times before carefully rolling the condom on.

We stay still for a moment—her gazing down at my body with a smug, heavy-lidded stare and me memorizing every gorgeous, naked curve of her.

She's pale and soft, tits sitting high on her chest with nipples pink like bubblegum that taste just as sweet. Her short brown hair is messy from having my hands in it, which only makes me want to grab her again.

Holding my gaze, she slowly leans down to brush a gentle kiss across my lips. Her fingers comb through my hair and then settle on my cheeks, cupping them, thumbs rubbing against the scruff I've kept because she said how much she liked it.

The affectionate gesture, in the middle of all this lust, has my heart expanding painfully in my chest. It's like she's reached past my rib cage and gripped the organ in her slim hand.

"You ready for this?" Her voice is just as tender as her caress.

I'm not sure the sound that comes out of my throat can be categorized as a word, but my nod is firm.

Holly sits back up and then raises herself on her knees. I hold on to her hips as she reaches between us to position me. Then, little by little, she lowers down.

The second my head crests her opening, black dots scatter across my vision. I buck involuntarily, my whole body wanting more of her. But she keeps to her own pace, burning me up with her little gasps and moans as she works her way down my length.

Finally, I sit fully inside her, and we're both breathing heavily. She moves, just a small shift to get used to the feel of me, but each slight adjustment sends hot streaks of pleasure through my dick and straight up my spine.

I groan. "This is perfect. I never want to leave."

"Really?" Holly grins down at me, her palms braced on my chest.

"Mmm, yeah. I—" My words get choked off when she wiggles her hips.

Then, she leans down, her honeysuckle scent brushing over me as she nips at my earlobe. "You'll have to leave for a little bit."

Slowly, she raises her hips, and I start to slip out of her.

I moan in protest.

She chuckles. "Don't worry. You can always come back."

That's when she really starts to move. Grabbing on to my shoulders, Holly sits up and begins to ride me, sliding up and down my cock.

As the friction builds, I meet each of her thrusts. I can't get enough of the sight of her on top of me. Her small tits bouncing as I pound into her, her lips parted, eyes hazy.

Soon, I can barely focus enough to remember my own name, pleasure coursing through me with each sway of her hips, fogging my brain. Pressure builds, a straining need at the base of my cock.

Holly has her hand between us, fingers working her clit as she bites her lip. I slide my fingers next to hers, nudging her out of the way.

"My turn." It comes out on a growl, and she adds a purr once I press down on her tight little nub.

We get a rhythm going—her riding me, me stroking her.

"Ben, I-I—"

"Yeah, princess. Give it to me!"

I demand her orgasm. She's mine, and it belongs to me.

A raspy moan leaves her throat as her slick walls clench my dick.

Like an animal, I thrust into her, fast and hard, chasing my own release. It doesn't take long.

I let out a shout of triumph as I climax, my fingers gripping her ass as I hold her tight against me. Ecstasy rolls through my body, seizing every muscle. I'm driven even further over the edge with the sight of my girlfriend above me, skin flushed with pleasure, still riding out her own orgasm.

This is what I've been fantasizing about for months—finishing as I'm buried in Holly's silky warmth.

No daydream even came close.

When I finally return to earth, it's with Holly spread across my chest and me still half-hard inside her. We stay like that for a while, letting our breathing and heart rates slow together.

I never want to move.

"We should do this all the time." She sounds sleepy, and I chuckle.

"I'm yours to command. Whenever you need me." I press a kiss to her forehead.

"I think I'm going to need you every day, Ben Gerhard. Because you make every day better."

Hell, there she goes again, digging into my chest.

My mouth opens to whisper back to her, but I stop myself before the words tumble out.

We just agreed to be exclusive and then had sex for the first time. This isn't the moment to be adding a certain three words into the mix.

Even if I know beyond a doubt that I'm in love with Holly Foster.

26

BEN

THE SUN CREEPING under the curtain hurts my eyes. More than that, it burns them.

I groan and roll over, realizing then that it's not just my eyes that hurt. Everything does. My muscles ache, my head's sore, and my throat tastes like iron or blood.

Not good. This is not good.

Where am I?

My bed. I'm in my bed.

Can I sit up?

Yes, slowly.

Can I stand?

Maybe ... no, not really.

Can I talk?

Whisper. Throat's too dry, and chest is tight.

Where's my phone?

The light of the little screen hurts as much as the sunlight, but I squint my eyes and suffer through it.

Who do I call?

I want Holly. I want her soft body pressed against mine, her soothing touch wiping away all this pain. She's always in control. She'll know what to do.

She'll come here and ... see how weak I am. How pathetic and sick.

She won't want me anymore.

Can't call Holly. Who do I call?

Jasper should be here.

The phone rings twice before he answers.

"Why are you calling me? Aren't you upstairs?" The sound of his video game plays in the background.

Good, he's in the house.

"Yeah." I cough, trying to force noise out of my throat. "I need"—more coughing—"hospital."

"Shit."

The phone line goes dead, and I let my arm fall to my lap. I want to lie back on the bed, find some way to sink into oblivion, but my barely functioning brain knows I'm going to need to stand up soon.

"Ben?" Jasper rushes into my bedroom, looks me over, and then presses his hand to my forehead. "You're on fire. Can you walk?"

Again, I try to stand but fall back after rising maybe an inch off the bed.

"Sammy!" Jasper yells over his shoulder as he kneels on the floor in front of me.

I don't understand what he's doing until I feel him slipping a sneaker onto my foot.

Sammy appears in the door, watching us with his eyebrow quirked. "What's going on?"

"Get the car. Ben needs to go to the hospital."

He doesn't hesitate. "Got it."

I try to lean over, put my shoes on myself, but the floor tilts at a weird angle, and Jasper's arm braced against my chest is the only thing keeping me from crumpling to the floor.

"Just let me do it."

My brain has trouble with the concept of time, so I don't know if

Jasper struggles to get me dressed or if he's done in a matter of minutes. At some point, he lifts my arms to slide them into a coat.

I make a weak protest. "Hot. Too hot."

"Too fucking bad, buddy. It's below freezing outside."

"Let's get him to the car." Sammy is back, and between the two of them, I hang.

Even though I try to put weight on my legs, the muscles just don't seem to be working right.

At some point, I stop trying to concentrate on my surroundings and just trust my friends to figure out what we need to do and where we need to go.

Finally, I'm able to lie down. But it's not a bed. My legs are bent, and I'm moving. Swaying, as whatever I'm lying on jerks around. I can hear Sammy, but it doesn't sound like he's talking to Jasper.

I'm in a car. I'm sprawled across the backseat.

It's embarrassing how long these facts take to register. At least, it would be embarrassing in a normal situation where I don't hurt so bad that my brain wants to run out my nose like water.

"We're five minutes out. Do you have Holly's number, or do you want me to call her?"

Holly. Holly. I miss Holly.

But no. Don't call her.

"Why would I call Holly?" My mom's voice sounds strange. Tiny and distant.

Is she in the car?

"Well"—Sammy's voice is much clearer than my mom's—"because they're dating."

"*They're dating?*" Her words crackle and hurt my ears.

Sammy is on the phone with my mom.

"Um, yeah. So, I guess I'll be the one calling her."

Don't call Holly.

My head pounds so loud that I don't know if I spoke.

"Ben?"

"Uhhhng."

"Did you bring your phone?"

"Here. I have her number." Jasper is here.

I crack my eyes open and see them sitting in the front seat of my car, Jasper handing Sammy his phone.

For a moment, a slice of clarity cracks through my pain-addled brain.

"Don't." My hand weakly tries to bat at the phone being passed. "Don't call Holly."

Before my eyes close, Sammy turns to meet them with his own bewildered ones. "Why not?"

"Please. Don't."

Then, I pass out.

HOLLY

I check my phone again. A selfie of me kissing Ben's cheek while he makes a goofy face at the camera stares up at me.

Just that, no texts or missed calls.

There's an itch, not a real one, just one in my brain, demanding I call him again. But I fight it because two unanswered texts and one voice mail are plenty to let Ben know that I've been trying to get in touch with him.

Still, it's weird. I haven't heard from him in over a day.

Okay, now that I say that in my head, it sounds kind of needy, but ever since our trip to the cabin, there hasn't been a day when Ben didn't at least text me.

Should I be worried?

This week has been crazy though. Finals meant late-night study sessions and hours of writing papers. Even though I'm sure he would've liked to blow them off and put a larger dent in my box of condoms, Ben's been good about respecting my full schedule. And, anyway, he's had his own classes to worry about. Maybe he put things off till the last minute and has had to use every one of the last forty-eight hours to catch up.

I consider texting Jasper. I have his number from when we exchanged messages in the past about digital marketing.

But I hold off. The idea just seems too clingy.

What kind of relationship do we have if I start texting his friends to find out where he is?

So, it's settled. I won't text Jasper.

Today.

Even though the radio silence from Ben chafes, I'm still filled with a sense of freedom. My last test was an hour ago, and I don't have to worry about school again until January. In just over a week, I'll be giving Ben my kidney, but right now, I have no plans or obligations. I don't even have to work at the bar tonight.

Taking advantage of this rare break in my normally hectic schedule, I brave the cold to stroll around the city. The chill in the air fogs my breath, but I'm toasty warm in my puffy winter coat. Deciding to treat myself, I stop in at my favorite bakery to buy an almond croissant and green tea. I've been rich in croissants lately. Ben always has one for me when I show up at his dialysis treatments. I think he sees them as a form of bribery, so I'll keep coming.

Guess he hasn't realized I'd sit with him for free.

Choosing to take my treats to go, I continue on with my walk, window-shopping and enjoying all the Christmas-themed displays. The rich crimsons mix beautifully with deep forest greens, the latter reminding me of Ben's irises. My favorite displays are the ones with pine trees covered in sparkling white lights. Grams never liked the multicolored strands. She said they were gaudy, and she'd rather have a display that resembled glowing snow.

Holidays always bring up the clearest memories of her, and the hurt in my heart pounds. But I've experienced the pain long enough that it's bearable now. So, I just press a hand to my chest, acknowledging the ache, and continue admiring the window displays.

Despite their loveliness, none of the colors are bright enough to entice me to crack open my wallet.

Money is tight again this year, even with Ben's promise to pay my upcoming rent. And I'm still not completely comfortable with that.

The idea skirts a little too close to me getting paid for my kidney. I tried to think of it as being bundled with my medical bills for the procedure, which are all being covered by Ben's insurance, but my conscious won't have it.

Next time we talk, I think I'm going to have to tell him paying my rent is a no-go.

With limited cash in my pocket, I had to get creative when it came to Christmas gifts. Luckily, I have a best friend who's a photography major. Marcus and Pops are not particularly materialistic, which is why I think they'll be completely happy with the black-and-white candid photos Terra took when she stopped by the house over Thanksgiving break. She showed me the negatives, and there was a perfect image of the three of us together. I've got my eyes shut with a wide grin and my finger pointing at my brother, whose head is thrown back, face contorted in laughter, as he clutches his stomach. All the while, Pops watches us, his hand half-covering his mouth but not enough to obscure the distinct curve of his lips.

I asked her for three copies. One I kept for myself; the other two I framed and wrapped.

Terra and I, fully aware of each other's financial situations, decided we'd keep it simple by picking out a Christmas ornament for one another to add to our plastic tabletop tree. The one I found for her is a palm-sized elephant, her favorite animal, wearing a little Santa Claus hat.

For Ben, I struggled a bit but was saved about a week ago while searching through a local used bookstore. Sitting on the shelf, like it knew I was coming, was a big, beautiful book about the histories of tattoos. Okay, so maybe it isn't *super* beautiful; the spine is creased, and some corners are folded. But I think he'll like it all the same.

So, my shopping is done. Who says the holidays have to break the bank?

Probably someone with more than four people to shop for.

When my nose turns numb, I decide to head home. I do have one thing I need to get done.

~

I'm arranging my clothes in neat piles on my bed and watching *SNL's The Best of Eddie Murphy* when my phone chimes. Diving for it, my initial burst of excitement dies when Terra's name flashes across the screen. Still, talking to her is way better than playing the same loop of questions over and over in my head.

I pause the video and answer the call, "Hey."

"Hey, roomie! How's it going? You crying alone in our apartment, missing me?"

I snort. "Yep. You got it. Already ran out of tissues. How's Fayetteville?"

"Boring. Faith had to go do Army stuff, so I'm just Netflix and chilling by myself at the hotel."

Now that she mentions it, I can hear the drone of the TV in the background.

"Only boring people get bored." That was a line Grams would throw at me whenever I whined for her to entertain me.

Terra's affronted huff bursts through the phone. "You shut your mouth! I've never been called boring in my life! If Faith were here, she could give you a detailed description of just how exciting our reunion—"

"Stop!" Even though she can't see me, I wave my hand, as if to ward her off. "I do not want a play-by-play of your sex life."

"Why not? I'm really good." From the tone of her voice, she's clearly grinning.

"I don't doubt it. But I'd never be able to look Faith in the eye again. If you start talking about you two, I'm going to lay out in vivid detail what Ben and I do in bed. You want to hear all about his penis?"

"Bleh. I don't know why you bother with those things. Vaginas are so much prettier."

"I'm sure he agrees with you."

For a second, we're quiet. I don't know who breaks first, but all of a sudden, we're both laughing hysterically. She might have been wrong about me crying, but my roommate was right about me missing her. Terra can make me smile, no matter how down I am.

As I catch my breath, I pick up my notebook and scan the list I wrote out earlier, ticking items off as I go.

"Did you ever give me back my blue scarf?"

"Nope. Should be somewhere in my room. You need it?"

Crap, not sure I'd ever be able to find something in the clothing hurricane Terra calls a bedroom.

"I guess not. I'm just packing."

"I thought you weren't going to your dad's until Monday."

With the surgery coming up, I decided to get settled at his house before the holiday.

"So? What's wrong with being proactive?"

I can almost hear her eye roll through the phone. "Come on, girl. Take a break. Watch some TV. Paint your nails. Read a book. Fool around with your man. You two hanging out tonight to celebrate the end of the semester?"

If she were in the room with me, Terra would know instantly that something was wrong. She can read my face almost as well as my brother can. But, today, I can give her the vague truth without being interrogated.

"Not sure. I'm waiting to hear back from him."

For a few minutes, Terra's silliness distracts me from Ben's silence, but the minute we hang up, I'm stuck on it again.

And kind of worried.

Could something have happened to him?

No, that can't be it. Someone definitely would have called me. Jasper knows we're dating, and Ben's probably told his parents at this point, too. They've all got my number.

So, it's got to be that he's busy.

Or maybe his phone broke, and he'll show up any minute, apologizing for leaving me hanging.

Or maybe he doesn't want to see me.

Stop it. Don't think like that.

But the insecurity weasels its way into my head.

I thought we were equally into each other. I thought he was as desperate to spend time with me as I was with him. The surety I have about our relationship, the understanding of how things stand, suddenly feels like trying to clutch a bar of wet soap as it slips out of my hands.

When did I give up all my control?

~

BEN

"Your temperature is down to normal, and all your vital signs have evened out since last night. We'd like you to stay for another hour, but as long as there are no changes, you'll be free to go home."

I shift uncomfortably in the hospital bed, wanting to leave now. But I'm not about to whine like a toddler, so I just give the doctor a nod.

"Thank you so much."

My mother extends her hand, and the doctor shakes it with a distracted smile before heading out. Once patients are dealt with, he's ready to move on. Efficient. I like that. It reminds me of Holly.

Hell, Holly.

I haven't texted her since Thursday morning before I crashed in my bed and then woke up with my body on fire. I have no idea what she's thinking. Hopefully, she'll just write me off as being busy with finals. My phone is still back at the townhouse on my bed, so I can't even check if she's tried to get in contact. If the doctor's timeline is right, I'll be home before my normal Saturday dialysis treatment, so I can ask her to come over for that.

And I'll just tell her ...

Well, maybe she won't ask.

More than anything, I want to keep this hospital visit off of Holly's radar. That's why I haven't asked anyone else to text her. She doesn't need to know about this. About how sick I am.

I hate the idea of Holly thinking of me as an invalid. She already gets a front-row seat to my treatments. No need for her to hear stories of my multiple hospital visits on top of that.

Right now, I'm the guy she wants to date. Someone she finds attractive.

I just want it to stay that way.

"You gave us a scare, hon." Mom combs her fingers through my hair and stares down at me with tortured eyes.

I hate that she's so affected by this.

"Sorry."

"Not your fault, son." Dad reaches from the chair he's sitting in to give my ankle a reassuring squeeze.

We lapse into silence—me worrying about what I'll say to Holly if she asks where I've been and my parents' thoughts a mystery.

Until my mom speaks up, "I want to talk about Holly."

Something in her tone makes my spine stiffen. I glance between the two of them. Dad keeps his gaze on his lap while Mom has on her determined expression that she uses with difficult clients.

"What about Holly?"

"Sammy said the two of you are together. That you are dating."

Her eyes search my face, and I get the strong sense she wants me to deny the claim.

Too bad.

"We are. She's my girlfriend."

Her shoulders bow inward as her fingers press the bridge of her nose. "Oh, Ben."

"What's wrong with that? I thought you liked Holly."

Her reaction hurts like a knife to the chest. This is the girl I love we're talking about, and my mom is acting like I just told her I'm dating a Nazi.

"I do like Holly. She's a very nice girl. Honestly, I want to kiss the ground she walks on. But, Ben, we're so close to the donation, and relationships can be messy. Emotions often cause us to make stupid decisions."

"What are you getting at?"

"What if you two have a fight? What if you say something that rubs her the wrong way? She can back out of this at any time." She paces at the foot of my bed. The steady *click, click, click* of her heels hitting the linoleum plays as background music to her worries.

"I know she can. And, if she decides to, that's her choice. But she's not the vengeful sort. I doubt us having a fight would affect her decision." My reasonable tone does nothing to remove the tension from my mother's shoulders.

"But why take that risk? This is your health, your life, that we're talking about. You need to do every—" Her lecture is cut off by the ringing of a phone.

And thank the universe because she is starting to piss me off. Logically, I know that her words are all coming from a place of concern. But her assumptions about Holly make my girlfriend sound like an emotional flake who's willing to toy with my fate.

Mom huffs in frustration but still reaches into her purse to retrieve the phone. Whatever name is on the screen deepens her frown, and her eyes flick to me and then away.

My stomach clenches, and I sit up straighter as she answers, "Hello, Fred. How is everything?" Despite the obvious unease on her face, my mom's voice is still pleasant as she talks to her nephew.

I can't hear his side of the conversation, so I instead watch my mom's reactions to his words in order to figure out what's going on.

At first, something he says softens her slightly, even getting her to crack a smile. I let go of the breath I'm holding.

But I relax too soon.

As she continues to listen, a sense of déjà vu settles over me. Her body language becomes so familiar until I'm struck with a harsh memory. We're back in the kitchen, the day she got the call about Grandpa Ben. But, today, she doesn't stare at my father with helpless devastation.

Her eyes are locked on me.

27

HOLLY

Finally, on Saturday, I get a text from Ben.

Ben: *Dialysis today 2 p.m.?*

I guess his phone isn't broken. The message leaves much to be desired, but I'm not about to be petty because I'm annoyed with him.

Holly: *I'll be there.*

Hopefully, when I show up, he'll have an explanation for why he ignored my messages for two days.

An hour and two bus rides later, I'm back in front of his parents' house. I wonder if, one day, I'll ever be comfortable enough to just walk in without ringing the bell. The idea makes me smile, and I'm still wearing the expression when Ben answers the door.

It falls away immediately when I take a good look at him. He's pale with dark circles under his eyes, and his lips are chapped and drawn tight. Without thinking about it, my hand immediately presses against his forehead. I expected to find him feverish, but his skin isn't more than pleasantly warm.

"You look sick, Ben. Are you okay?"

Instead of answering, he removes my hand and uses his grip to pull me forward. I let him, pressing up against his chest. Ben runs his fingers up my neck before cupping the back of my head. He angles me how he wants and then slowly kisses me.

All the while, the front door hangs wide, letting in cold air. While I enjoy his affectionate greeting, the impracticality of leaving a door open in the beginning of winter has me stepping away, so I can shut it.

When I turn back to Ben, he still seems off, but before I can ask him what's wrong again, he laces his fingers with mine and tugs me farther into the house. Instead of heading to the stairs, we move toward the kitchen.

It being the weekend, I'm not surprised to see Mrs. and Mr. Gerhard. This is their house after all. Ben's dad is leaning back against the counter, arms crossed, legs crossed, eyes on his shoes. Mrs. Gerhard is standing at the kitchen island, hands spread wide on the granite counter, watching me without blinking. Their agitation is clear.

"Hello." My greeting works its way through air so thick with tension that I'm surprised it even reaches them.

Mrs. Gerhard gives me a tight smile. She moves to pull out one of the tall chairs tucked under the island. "Hello, Holly. Please take a seat. We were hoping to speak with you for a moment."

This whole setup screams at me to cautiously back away and then sprint for the exit. Whatever this conversation is, I doubt I'll like it. When I glance up at Ben, I'm shocked to find him glaring at his mother.

What's going on?

Fighting my urge to flee, I take the offered chair. My body angles to face Ben's mom, but he swivels the seat so that I can only see him. In fact, he moves to stand between my knees, taking up my entire field of vision.

"I need to tell you something. I don't think you've heard yet. My parents asked to be here."

There's a pain in my stomach. A small, sharp pinch. Like a warning.

I nod for him to continue.

"We got a call from Fred this morning. He hasn't been feeling well for over a week. He was worried he might have the flu and that it would push back the exchange, so he went in for another checkup."

Two sharp pinches.

"He doesn't have the flu. He has Lyme disease. Got it from a tick bite while out hiking. There's antibiotics to treat it, but ..."

Three pinches. Four. Five. Six. More. More. More.

"Fred won't be able to donate to Marcus."

The pain grows until I have to wrap my arms around my torso to keep it from splitting me open.

"Marcus won't be getting a kidney." It's not a question, just a statement to make sure my brain registers the horror I'm living in.

Still, Ben answers, "No." His hands cup my cheeks. "I'm so sorry. I'm so, so sorry."

My mouth won't work, but even if it did, I don't have any words. Right now, there's just a solid wall of pain pressing on my chest.

I shut my eyes. Shut out the world. The cruel world that keeps giving me hope and taking it away.

A phrase does climb over the wall to plaster itself across my eyelids, pulsing and beating like a drum.

Not again. Not again. Not again.

But the words are useless. I could beg on my knees, but this would still be happening. Again.

"Holly. Please."

A voice pulls my eyes open, and I find Ben watching me with concern. But he wasn't the one who spoke. I look to Mrs. Gerhard. She fiddles with something in her hands.

"We know how hard this must be to hear. God, do we know." She takes a deep breath that catches like a hiccup. "But please ... please don't take away Ben's chance. You care about him, don't you?"

"Mom!" Ben's voice is sharp, whipping my head back toward him. He's glaring at his mother again, but his whole face softens as he turns back to me. "I understand, Holly. You don't need to feel bad about backing out. I know Marcus doesn't have many options."

Their words reach me on a delay. I see their mouths moving, but I need a moment to comprehend. A buzzing in my brain, a demand to sink into misery, does its best to drown out their voices. It takes effort to focus, but I try.

"You can. But, Holly," his mom is speaking again, "we can help you in other ways. We know you don't have much money. But you don't ever have to worry about that again." Mr. Gerhard steps forward to wrap an arm around his wife's shoulders, nodding as he stares at me. "Whatever you need, however much you want, we'll give it to you. Just please, save our son."

She slides a piece of paper across the island to me, and purely on reflex, I pick it up.

"Stop it. Both of you. This isn't what I want. You can't put this kind of pressure on her," Ben growls.

Why is he so angry? Should I be angry?

Right now, I'm just lost in the hurt. My skin is flayed open, all my nerves exposed and in agony. My heart breaks for my brother. The Gerhards must hear it cracking. The pain is too powerful to be inaudible.

"We have to! I don't ever want to get another phone call from Sammy, saying you're in the hospital! You could've died!"

"That's not the point!"

Hospital? Was Ben in the hospital?

With each beat of my fractured heart, the anguish inside me pulses. My brain wants to escape my head, growing and pushing at the confines of my skull.

I ache.

Focusing on something else might help me forget, if only for a moment. The first thing available is the paper in my hand. So, I hone in on it, studying each aspect to give my mind an escape.

The shape and layout are familiar. A small rectangle, lines filled in with written words. Some of those words look like my name. Then, there's a long line with no handwriting. An empty space waiting to be filled in.

This is a check. A check made out to me. A blank check.

"Has anyone offered to pay you for your kidney?"

Just like that, real time slams back into place. I drop the bribe like it's covered in anthrax, stumbling out of the chair and wiping my hands on my clothes, fearing the psychiatrist will somehow smell it on me.

"Are you insane?"

Whatever argument the three of them were in the middle of stopped the moment I moved, and both Ben and his mom flinch at my words.

Ben recovers first, reaching his hands out to me, palms up, as if I were a wild animal in need of soothing. In a way, that's what I am. Rabid, my brain melting, wanting to attack something, anything, as I grind my teeth.

"No, Holly, no. I would never expect you to. I know you need to find Marcus a kidney. It's okay."

He takes a step forward, but I fling my arms out to ward him off. The fact that I crave his comfort shows how little I deserve it.

"This wasn't supposed to be about you!" My voice reverberates around their stupidly large house. "I wanted to save Marcus!"

"I know, Holly. You still can." Ben's trying to reassure me with his calm voice.

But he doesn't get it.

Before, I was confused as to whether or not I should be angry. Now, I know.

I'm enraged.

"What the hell is wrong with you?"

Ben's mouth goes slack, and his parents watch me with wide eyes.

"You think I'm not going to give you my kidney? Of course I am, you fucking idiot! Of course I am! And your mother, with her stupid-ass check, is trying to ruin it all! And my—" I choke on a sob and do my best to push back the furious tears that want out. "My brother is dying. And it's all going to shit. And you think I'd let you get sicker? When I—when I—"

No. I can't say those words now. Not here. Not like this. Maybe not ever.

They're the reason I can't help Marcus.

I take another step back.

"Shh, Holly. Let's just go upstairs. Just you and me," he pleads with me, still holding his arms wide, tempting me to run into them.

A laugh spills out of me, high-pitched and manic. "Just you and me? So you can what? Make me feel safe? Tell me it's all going to be okay? You gonna lie to me, Ben?"

He grimaces.

My brain is on fire.

I see the three of them standing there. Together. A family.

It's too much.

"I have to go."

My sneakers squeak on their beautiful hardwood floor as I sprint from the room, down the hall covered in smiling family photos, and out their charming blue front door.

"Holly! Wait!"

I run, a full-on track-star sprint. I'm the healthy one. Even if he follows, he'll never catch me because I don't want to be caught. I just want to escape.

Once I pass the bus stop, none of the streets look familiar, but it doesn't matter because I just want to keep running.

And I do for some time until my lungs demand that I stop to catch my breath. But I keep moving, walking through the vapor clouds formed by my own panting breath. Now that I'm not running, a chill creeps over me, starting a persistent shivering that radiates out from the shattered organ in my chest that somehow continues to pump.

Spotting a city bus, I board it because the action is familiar, and in a way, it soothes me.

I sit in the back and curl in on myself. The pain claws under my skin, and I can't keep it inside anymore.

So, on a public bus, surrounded by strangers, heading in an unknown direction, I do my best to sob silently into my hands.

I'm very bad at it. Probably from lack of practice.

This goes on for a decent amount of time. Like a *make everyone else on the bus uncomfortable* amount of time.

At one point, when we slow down for another stop, I hear someone clear their throat next to me. Glancing up, I find a middle-aged woman with a kind, pitying expression watching me. She stands next to my seat, holding on to an overhead handle in order to steady herself. Without speaking, she hands me a package of travel tissues.

Numbly, I accept them, earning myself a small smile before she gets off the bus. Using the tissues to soak up my tears, I stare out the window, doing my best to figure out where I've landed in the city. It takes a good five minutes, but finally, I recognize a few storefronts. We're headed west.

I know someone in west Philly.

I have a destination now. A place to go where the pain might hurt a little less.

My hands search in my pockets, looking for my phone so that I can let him know I'm on my way. I come up with my wallet but nothing else.

I must have left it at the apartment. Not that it matters really.

Because who needs to announce themselves when they're going home?

~

BEN

Twenty-four hours and still no word from Holly. Maybe most people wouldn't think that's a lot of time, but to me, it might as well have been a month.

Over and over in my head, I play out the scene of her yelling at my parents and me. The devastation on her face. The sound of those harsh curses she normally avoids.

Holly was in a bad place, but instead of seeking comfort in me, she ran away. Too fast for me to catch her.

Now, I can't find her.

Well, I kind of did. When she didn't return my calls or texts, I drove to her apartment, but there was no answer. It being Saturday, I figured she might have gone into work early. Both Ways wasn't open yet, but when I knocked on the door, a huge guy with a thick black beard and more tattoos than even me appeared. Turned out, he was her boss, Curt, and Holly already asked for her time off. Apparently, she was worried about being exposed to so many people this close to the surgery. She didn't want to catch a cold.

Lacking any other options, I called her brother, whose number I still had from that first meeting.

The first time I had seen Holly.

Luckily, Marcus picked up just after the second ring. Fred had already talked to him about the problem, so I knew I wasn't going to deal with another round of being the bad-news messenger. Instead, I got straight to the real reason I'd called.

"Yeah, I just got word from my dad. She's at his place. She doesn't have her phone on her. I'm getting on the train to Philly now."

There was a lot of background noise and the sound of departures being announced.

Some of the panic twisting my stomach eased. At least she wasn't wandering around the city.

"She's upset. Just ... she was cursing."

"She what?"

Even over the phone, I could tell I'd shocked him.

"Yeah. She yelled at us. Then, she ran away. I want to make sure she's okay."

Marcus didn't answer right away, but I could still hear the sounds of the station, so I knew he was there.

"Just give her some space. I'll talk to her. If she wants to see you, I'll text you. But she usually needs some time to come to terms with everything when this happens."

I was pacing around my bedroom, but those words had me tripping to a halt. "When what happens?"

His sigh pushed through my phone speaker, and the background noise faded. I assumed he'd made it onto a train at that point.

"When my transplants fall through."

"Transplants? As in plural?"

"Yeah."

My head started to ache, and I sat down heavy on my mattress, suddenly exhausted. "Marcus, how many times has this happened?"

The other man hesitated before responding, "This'll be the third."

His answer was like a punch to the gut. My doctor had warned me that lots of things could go wrong when trying to schedule a donation with a live donor, especially if it was an exchange situation. But I'd never really spent much time worrying about it.

Now, Holly's frantic response made even more sense.

How desperate must she be feeling after having something go wrong for a third time?

I couldn't remember what else we said other than his promise to text me about Holly. Then, I spent the rest of the night trying to wrap my mind around Marcus's and Holly's consistent disappointment.

Later, after I finished my dialysis and drove back to the townhouse, my phone dinged from a text. Scrambling for it, my pulse sped when I saw Marcus's name, but my hopes plunged after the message.

Marcus: *She's asleep. Don't want to wake her. Maybe tomorrow.*

But, now, it's tomorrow, and the day is more than half done with no word from Holly or Marcus. I'm living on the edge of insanity. There are things I need to tell her.

I'm sorry.

Forget the kidney.

I love you.

Fuck it. I can't do this anymore.

Sitting around isn't going to solve anything.

28

HOLLY

"HOLLY, put the plate down. You've done enough," Pops scolds me, his voice gentle and low.

"I don't mind cleaning up."

"No. You made dinner. I'll do the dishes. Talk to your brother."

Ever since I was a kid, I've been convinced that Pops is a mind reader.

I arrived at Pops's house Saturday afternoon, still recovering from my public-bus sob-fest, and the first thing my adoptive father did was pull me into a tight hug. If I could hand out awards for the best hugs, Pops would get the blue ribbon every time.

Apparently, Marcus had already called him, so he knew what my surprise visit was about. Pops made me a strong cup of tea, and we spent the rest of the evening playing chess before ordering Chinese takeout. The familiarity of the situation calmed me. Until my sophomore year of college, I lived at home, and there were plenty of nights Pops and I filled the time with board games and greasy food.

Exhausted from the day, I went to bed early. In the morning, I was greeted by Marcus and a bag of bagels. The moment I saw him, I had to fight back tears, and just like our father, he gathered me into his arms, holding me close. His face was stoic, accepting of yet another bad turn of luck.

And, every moment since then, I've been trying to figure out how to tell him my decision.

We spent the day catching up, mainly Marcus talking about his job and me about my classes. Nothing deep. Avoiding the looming storm cloud darkening the room. Then, we cooked together like old times, and I didn't want to ruin the moment.

But, now, the food is all gone, and it's time for me to poke the storm cloud and bring on the rain. He deserves to know.

Pops collects the dishes, balancing them on his arm like a pro. Before working as a mechanic, he waited tables, and apparently, the skills stuck with him.

"Thanks, Dad." Marcus leans back in his seat, eyes focused on me. "What do you want to tell me, sis?"

The two of them are too perceptive for their own good sometimes.

I breathe in deep to brace myself and then let the truth flow. "I'm still giving my kidney to Ben, which means that I won't be on the exchange list for you anymore. And I'm sorry. I'm so unbelievably sorry about that. But, when I think about Ben suffering through everything you deal with and having the opportunity to help him ... I can't just stand by and do nothing."

Both of us sit in the quiet for a moment before he responds, "Good."

"Good?" I sputter over the word.

"Yes. Good. It's good that you've found someone else you care about. It's good that you can put a stop to that person's suffering. It's good that you realize my entire well-being does not rest solely on your shoulders."

"I-I don't think that." This is not at all how I thought he'd react. I expected frustration, maybe the silent treatment. Classics from our childhood when I'd pissed Marcus off.

Instead, I got, "Good."

"Come on, Holly. You're more invested in my health than I am.

And I'm grateful. I really am. But it's not your job to cure me." He holds me with his eyes, but I don't shy away. "Tell me you understand that."

I huff. "Maybe it's not my job, but—"

The doorbell ringing cuts me off.

"My hands are kinda full. Could one of you ..." Pops calls out from the kitchen where the water is running loudly.

I don't know if he really can't get to the door or if this is his way of de-escalating what was probably going to turn into an argument. Either way, I'm the closest, so I push up from my seat and try to guess who could be coming by this time on a Sunday. Probably one of the single women in the neighborhood. A lot of them like to flirt with Pops and bring him food. One time, I heard a lady whispering that he looked like Idris Elba. He just turns on his Southern charm and keeps them at a distance.

I'm prepared to politely greet a middle-aged woman when I open the door, so the sight of my boyfriend standing on the front porch has my mouth popping open like a dead fish.

"Holly," he sighs my name out along with a heavy dose of tension from his shoulders.

I, on the other hand, don't really know how to react. Ever since I ran away from his parents' house, I've been dealing with a toxic combination of devastation, anger, anxiety, hopelessness, and regret. My coherent thoughts have all consisted of plans on how to tell Marcus my decision. I didn't let myself think about Ben.

But Marcus knows now, and I need to figure out the rest of my issues.

"Ben." The way I say his name sounds harsh to my own ears, and I try to take the bite out of my voice. "What are you doing here?"

He runs his eyes over me, frowning. "Looking for you. I wanted to make sure you were okay. And to talk to you." His hand lifts, as if to reach for me, but then it reroutes to land on the back of his neck. "I needed to tell you the donation is off."

I flinch at his words. "Yeah, I know. I might have gone a little nuts the last time you saw me, but I didn't forget. Fred's not viable. No kidney for Marcus."

Why doesn't he just squeeze lemon juice in a paper cut while he's at it?

"No. I mean, our donation. I appreciate that you're willing to stick it out, but I'm going to respectfully decline. Okay?" His satisfied expression reminds me of a cat that's just brought you a dead bird and expects you to say thank you.

"Okay? *Okay?*" Now, he's the one who flinches as I shout at him.

What is it with the Gerhards and their ability to make me want to scream?

Up until this point, we've been talking in the open doorway. Wanting some privacy, I move to push Ben back, so I can step out on the front porch with him. Then, I get hit with an icy shot of cold air and change my mind. Wrapping my hand in the front of his jacket, I tug him into the house.

"You wanna talk? Let's talk. Upstairs. But don't get any ideas. This is a front-porch discussion that's happening in my bedroom only because it's colder than a snowman's butt out there."

I glare at him and then turn to stomp up the stairs, hearing him following behind me. When we reach my room, I shut the door behind us and round on him.

Ben watches me with wary eyes.

"You want to respectfully decline my kidney? Fine. That's your right. But, just know, if you do, we're done."

"What?" His stare goes wild, and he steps toward me, reaching out a hand that I brush away.

"You and me. We. Are. Done."

~

BEN

Panic sends shards of glass shooting through my veins. She can't mean it. We can't be over.

"Why would you even say that?"

322

"Because it's true." Holly leans back against her bedroom door, crossing her arms and glaring at me. "If you don't accept my kidney, then we're over."

Now, I get a burning in my chest, some righteous anger of my own. "So, you're going to hold our relationship as ransom?"

Apparently, I stole my fire from Holly because she loses her defensive posture with a full-body sigh.

"No, Ben. This isn't some game I'm playing with you. I'm telling you what I need. From a partner. If you don't let me help you, I'll go insane. It's the only thing I'll ever think about when we're together. Is that what you want?"

"No." Unhappiness fills me, making me pace around her small bedroom. The purple carpet muffles my footsteps, but the beaded bracelets on her dresser rattle with each step.

If this were any other situation, I'd love to have the chance to explore Holly's childhood bedroom. But I can't spare any thoughts for the posters on the walls or the knickknacks on the dresser. My brain is too busy, trying to think of different scenarios, some kind of solution where she isn't picking between her brother and me.

None come to mind.

With a defeated exhale, I give in, self-disgust roiling through my gut. "Okay. We'll do the transplant."

"Thank you," Holly whispers the words, her eyes closing and head falling back against the door.

Even with the dark emotions churning inside me or maybe because of them, I need to hold her.

When I cross the room and place my hands on her upper arms, she softly asks a question, "What did your mom mean about you being in the hospital?"

I wince. I thought, in the high emotions of the moment, she'd missed that. Should've known better when it comes to Holly.

"It's nothing. Just forget it."

She goes rigid in my grasp. "Your mom was practically in hysterics. That's not nothing."

"She was overreacting."

"You're lying." Holly shrugs my hands off and stalks away from me, putting distance between us. "I don't have much experience with relationships, but I'm pretty sure you don't hide important parts of your life from each other. Like, oh, I dunno, a medical emergency!"

This whole situation is getting away from me. I'm desperate for a fix, something to get the anger off of Holly's face. I don't think the truth will help, but it's the only option left to me unless I want to throw out an even bigger falsehood.

"Fine. Thursday, I woke up with a fever. Jasper and Sammy took me to the hospital. It wasn't much worse than a cold. Any normal person wouldn't have needed professional care, but my body couldn't handle it. But I'm better now. In the clear."

She watches me with stunned eyes and a hand over her mouth. "Why didn't anyone call me? Or at least text me?"

"I told them not to."

"Why?" The question comes out on a hurt gasp, and the betrayal in her stare feels like someone is carving into my chest with a melon baller.

So, like an idiot, I get defensive. "Because you already get a front-row seat to all my other medical issues! I hate you seeing how weak I am! So, forgive me for wanting to maintain just a shred of my dignity."

My fingers claw through my hair. I watch her face go from shocked to ice-cold, and I know I've fucked up.

"Weak? You think that I think that you're weak?" Holly speaks slowly, like an executioner giving a gentle practice swing of their ax.

My jaw clenches as I shrug.

"So, by that logic, you think I think my brother is weak?"

"I didn't say that."

"You didn't have to." Those words come out whip-fast. "To clarify, I've never thought of you as weak or less than because of your illness. If anything, I admire your strength when it comes to dealing with all the crap life has piled on you. So, this issue you have is yours, not mine. And it doesn't give you the right to lie to me."

"You're making this bigger than it has to be," I growl, frustrated

324

that she doesn't understand. That I can't make her understand. "I didn't tell you. So what? I'm fine now. It's over."

Holly stares at me for a moment, no expression on her face. I thought I wanted the anger in her eyes gone, but this blank look is even worse. Silence sits heavy between us, pressing on my chest, making me wish I could take back everything I shouted at her.

"Do you know why I'm afraid of needles?"

For a moment, I can't speak, the abrupt topic change throwing me off.

Apparently, she doesn't need me to respond, continuing to talk in an almost-conversational tone. But sitting in the bottom of her voice is a hint of some emotion I can't place.

"I've told you about my mom. Her problems with addiction. It started with pills and booze, but when those stopped giving her what she needed, she moved on to bigger things. Like heroin."

She pauses to take a breath, and that's when I realize what the emotion is.

Pain.

"She'd tell me she was done. Say she wasn't going to use anymore. Then, that needle would slide into her arm, and my mom would disappear. Instead, I'd get a stranger. She'd forget I existed. Or remember and curse at me for existing. Then, the drugs would wear off, and my mom would come back. Again, she'd tell me she was done. Then, she'd get another needle." Holly's tone doesn't change, but her eyes shine overly bright.

Every word of her sorrowful story digs into me, and I ache for her. If I thought she'd let me, I'd pull her into my arms, have her rest her head on my chest, and tell her to let the tears gathering in her eyes fall.

"The last thing she said to me was, 'I'll see you next week.' That was two years ago. So, yeah, your lie might not seem like a big deal to you or anyone else. But I've had more dishonesty than I ever need from someone I care about." While she talks, Holly keeps her gaze just over my shoulder, and now, she raises it to the ceiling, blinking rapidly and visibly swallowing.

"I'm sorry, Holly. I promise I won't do it again. I'll tell you everything."

When I move to step toward her, she holds up a staying hand.

"We should probably take some time."

The shards of glass are back, cutting up my insides as I try to stifle the panic. "What do you mean?"

She talks while keeping her face tilted upward, "This whole situation is stressful. There's a lot of pressure. Let's just put things on hold for now."

My first urge is to shout, *No!*

I have to breathe in deep a few times before I can respond without yelling, "I disagree."

There's steel in my voice, and it gets her to finally look at me.

Holly frowns, obviously frustrated that I won't just follow along with her dictate. "We can talk after the surgery."

I shake my head.

"I made a mistake. I was stupid. But I'm not your mom. And it doesn't matter if it's before or after the surgery; I'm still going to want you." This time, I ignore her staying gesture, moving to stand in her personal space so that she has to crane her neck to glower at me.

Her palms press flat on my chest to push me away, but I capture them in my hands and hold her close.

"I need time," she growls at me.

If the words didn't hurt so much, I'd find her fierce scowl adorable. All I want is to kiss her plump mouth, so she'll stop saying things that tear up my insides.

"More time to what? Convince yourself that I'll screw up again? Well, I've already got an answer for you. I will." Through my desperate anger, I still find a way to smirk down at her. "I'm an idiot a good portion of the time. But no one's perfect."

"I didn't say you had to be perfect." The hint of uncertainty in her declaration lights a spark of hope under my rib cage.

"Good to know." Watching the tangle of emotions on her face, I take a risk. Her hands slide from mine as I step back. "You want time?

Fine. Take it. I'll leave you alone until the surgery, if you promise me one thing."

Holly gives me a wary look that almost melts my own irritation. "What?"

"I get to drive you to the hospital the day of the transplant."

Her lips purse, and she glares. "I need to drive the car."

I glare right back. "Deal."

Then, I storm out of her house before she can change her mind.

HOLLY

He tricked me. I never actually agreed to ride with him, but he left before I thought to point that out.

My head hurts, a pounding pressing against the backs of my eyes. Probably from the tears I held back. I can't believe he lied to me. That he withheld something so important.

What if it had been more than just a cold? What if he had died, and I hadn't gotten a chance to say good-bye?

I try to ignore the rational voice in my brain pointing out that breaking things off with him because I'm mad that I might not have gotten the chance to tell him how much he means to me is a twisted mess of idiocy.

Once I'm sure I won't start crying, I head downstairs to find Marcus and Pops setting up Monopoly. Some of the tension eases from my chest.

"I get to be—"

"The banker," they finish my sentence in unison, grinning at each other as I roll my eyes.

"Am I that predictable?"

Marcus smirks. "When it comes to being in control? Yes."

I stick my tongue out at my older brother, and he chuckles while passing me the fake money.

We've gone around the board a few times before Pops addresses the big, fat elephant sitting at the table with us.

"So, your man left here in a bit of a huff. Something go wrong between you two?"

I grimace, getting the urge to brush the topic off. But then I'd be doing the exact same thing I'm mad at Ben for.

"We argued. But the transplant is still going forward."

I shoot Marcus an apologetic look, but he just smiles and rolls the dice.

"What did y'all argue about?"

"Gosh, Pops. Nosy much?"

Instead of answering, he stares at me. Waiting.

I sigh before giving in, telling them the gist of what we yelled at each other about.

"And then he tricked me into agreeing to drive to the surgery together."

Pops coughs, but I would swear it started out as a snort. "Just so I understand, you're mad at the boy because he got sick and didn't tell you?"

"No. I'm mad that he lied about it when I asked him." My roll comes out of my hands harder than I intended, and the dice go bouncing onto the floor. I huff in irritation, crouching beneath the table to retrieve them.

"Hmm. Okay. I agree that was a bad move on his part. But, sweetie, I think you might be going a little hard on the boy."

His words shock me, and I swing my head up to tell him just how wrong he is. The only problem is, I haven't cleared the table, so I end up whacking my head so hard that the game pieces rattle.

"Ow," I wail, clutching my throbbing skull.

Pops clucks his tongue in sympathy, kneeling down in front of me to gently take my head in his hands. He skims his fingers over my scalp, and I hiss when he reaches the sore spot.

"Didn't cut yourself, but you're gonna have a knot the size of a chicken's egg."

I settle back in my seat, Marcus running his eyes over me in concern, and my dad leaves the room, only to come back with a bag of frozen peas.

"Hold this on there."

The icy vegetables help take away some of the tenderness, but my mood is officially as sour as a whole bucket full of lemons. A box of lemons? A tub? I don't know how large quantities of lemons are transported, but let's just agree that it's a gigantic amount of lemons.

"You're wrong. I'm not being too hard. He lied to me, and I don't put up with liars."

Marcus frowns, and Pops shakes his head.

"I'm not saying you should. You were right to tell him he hurt you. But, baby girl, the world isn't black and white. Just 'cause someone makes a bad decision doesn't mean they always will. If that's how things worked, I wouldn't be sitting here today. I'd be drunk at some bar, forgetting my name and drowning my worries." He reaches across the table to squeeze my shoulder, holding my gaze with his. He looks so deep into my eyes; I think he sees more of myself than I can. "Now, you want people to be honest with you. How 'bout you be honest with yourself? Why're so mad at the boy?"

"I told you. He lied."

"Nah, sweetie. That's why you're *mad*. But why're you *so* mad?"

The game is on pause while Pops forces me to push past my barriers. As the peas make my hand go numb, I think back over everything Ben told me, trying to figure out what my dad is getting at.

And I realize my anger was there before I even asked Ben about his hospital visit. Before he had a chance to lie to me.

Finally, a slice of understanding splits through my fog of pain and betrayal.

"If he doesn't tell me when he's hurt, I can't he-help," I whisper the revelation, the effort of holding back my tears making me stutter on the last word. My teeth bite down hard on my lower lip to keep it from quivering.

"You can't control the things you don't know about, huh?" Pops raises his eyebrows in question, and I nod. "But, see, there are lots of things in life you won't be able to control. Especially people. And, if you keep letting that get you riled up, it'll eat you up inside."

I fiddle with my plastic houses, worried that, if I try talking again, I might start crying. Besides, what do you even say when all your insecurities get laid out on the table?

"We don't have to talk about it anymore. Just think about it." He waits for me to nod again before placing the dice in front of me. "Now, let's get back to it, so I can beat you both."

Marcus scoffs. "Yeah, right, old man. Prepare to be bankrupt."

The game goes for another couple of hours, and I'm able to push aside thoughts of my unhealthy approach to relationships by systematically bleeding my dad and brother dry.

29

HOLLY

Luckily, the surgery doesn't require me to have working-order hands because I'm pretty sure Ben is crushing my finger bones.

"Ben."

He doesn't look down at me as we make our way through the parking garage, and the distance between us is starting to scare me.

When he showed up at Pops's house this morning, all he gave me was a kiss on the cheek and a tight smile. I spent the whole drive over trying to figure out how to explain all the thinking I'd been doing. How to apologize for letting the issues in my past affect how I see him. You'd think, after having a week to work it all out, I would've found the right words at some point. But, whenever I went to open my mouth, nothing came out.

Ben just stared out the window, his knee bouncing and his hand scratching the back of his neck. So, the car ride was silent.

Now, his eyes are distant, as if watching a scene playing only for him.

This can't be how we go into this thing.

I stop walking, digging my heels into the concrete. When Ben reaches the end of our arm lengths, I hold him in place, and he stumbles to a stop, glancing around, confused, like he's waking up from a heavy dream.

"What—Holly, what's wrong?"

"You looked like you were going catatonic on me. Also"—I raise our joined hands and see my fingers have started turning white —"this has morphed from a reassuring hold to a ninja death grip."

His hold immediately loosens, and he looks ashamed as he massages my digits back to life. "God, I'm sorry."

"Name's Holly. You must really be out of it." My lame joke earns me the barest hint of a smile. But I'll take it. We're alone in the garage at the moment, so I step in close to Ben, crowding him before his mind can retreat again.

"Kiss me." It's been so long, and if I can't explain what's changed in my mind, maybe I can show him.

"What?"

When I see the shock on his face, I realize something.

Ben thought we were over.

I can't blame him. The only message I sent him since he stormed out of my dad's house was a quick, *Merry Christmas*. Why wouldn't he think I decided to end things permanently?

Clearly, I need to correct him.

"Here. Like this." My hands slide up his chest to wrap around his neck. I rise up on my toes, pressing my body fully against his as I draw his mouth down to mine.

Then, I ravish him.

The kiss is heady and passionate. I show him how far we are from being over by worshipping him with my lips.

With an agonized groan, his hands dig into my backside, so he can pull me closer.

I missed the feel of him. Solid, warm, and comforting but also maddeningly intoxicating. My head fills with thoughts of his mouth all over me. Every inch of my skin tingles and tightens, begging for his attention. One thought slips through the haze, crystalizing until it's as solid as a diamond in my mind.

I need Ben.

Not just right now. But always. Whatever happens today, whatever pain I might experience, it will be nothing compared to the agony of not having this man in my life.

A car honking the level below us ends our frantic mauling of each other. At some point, Ben backed me up against one of the support columns. The cement's chill begins to work its way through my coat.

He rests his forehead on mine while working to calm his labored breathing.

"I'm sorry," I whisper, tracing my fingertips over his cheekbones and down his chin.

"Me, too." Ben leans in for another swift kiss before backing away. He grabs my hand again, but this time, he's careful not to crush anything.

There's still a strained element to his smile, but with what we're walking into, it's the best I can hope for.

I take the lead, tugging Ben along after me. It's not long before we're walking through the sliding glass doors into the hospital, and some helpful nurses direct us to the proper waiting area.

Mr. and Mrs. Gerhard are already seated. His mom jumps out of her chair when she sees us, and the older Benjamin follows close behind. My family, on the other hand, takes a more relaxed approach. Pops and Marcus stay sitting and simply wave at me, knowing I'll make it over to them in a moment.

"Holly! How are you? Thank you so much for the flowers, but you didn't have to do that. I'm the one who needs to apologize." Mrs. Gerhard wrings her hands as she stands in front of me.

After my freak-out-fest at Ben's parents' house, the guilt of having shouted curses at them was giving me heartburn. So, I sent them a bouquet of daisies with a note telling them how mortified I was.

"It was a bad moment. I think we can just forget it and move on."

"Still, I'm very sorry. And how are you feeling today? Both of you doing all right?" Mrs. Gerhard runs her eyes over us, probably ready to have a conniption if there's even a paper cut visible.

"We're fine, Mom. You're going to need to calm down. You can't keep up this level of frantic for the next however many hours."

We both told our family members that they didn't have to show up at the appointment time. There's checking in, then surgery prep, and then the actual surgery, which normally takes a few hours. So, they could easily be sitting here for close to an entire workday. Showing up in time for the recovery process would've been fine.

All of them chose to ignore us.

After checking in, I make sure to introduce Pops to Ben's parents. When they start telling my dad how he raised a "miracle for a daughter," I hide my blushing face in Ben's chest. His hand cups the back of my head, and I enjoy the rumble of his laughter at my embarrassment. The familiar, spicy pine scent of Ben's soap helps to ease some of my nerves. If only I could stay here forever.

But, a short ten minutes later, Ben and I are called back. I try to ignore the fact that Mrs. Gerhard is crying as I give my brother and father quick hugs.

"Next time you see me, I'll be anesthetized, so it's your job to make sure I don't say anything crazy."

They both smile with affection, and Marcus musses my hair.

"See you soon, sis."

"You ready, Holly?" Ben stands beside me, reaching out his hand.

I know, when I walk through those doors, I'll be putting myself in a dangerous situation. There are the needles that terrify me, but more than that, there's the surgery. It isn't an uncommon procedure, and the newer laparoscopic technique means I'll only be getting three small incisions instead of one large one. But it's still surgery. I'll be under anesthesia for the first time, trusting these people to keep me alive as they remove one of my organs.

To cover my fear, I paste on an overly enthusiastic grin.

"You bet I am." I grab Ben's hand and march us forward. "Let's get you a kidney!"

BEN

After I'm prepped for surgery, I get to see Holly one last time.

They wheel my bed out into a wide hallway, arranging the foot of mine against hers, so we face each other. Like me, Holly has on a pale blue hospital gown and a surgical hat that looks like something you'd wear in the shower to keep your hair dry.

And there's a needle in her arm.

"How are you doing?" My voice comes out strained.

She looks small, barely taking up any room on her bed.

Why haven't I ever noticed how tiny she is before?

There's no way her kidney can be big enough for me.

How can these idiot doctors think it's okay to cut into such a delicate body?

"I'm good. Ready to go."

"Even with the—"

She cuts me off with a firm shake of her head. "Let's not talk about what might or might not be sticking in my arms right now." I watch her breathe in deep and then slowly let the air out. "Besides, I've been practicing."

"Practicing?"

"Yeah. I've been visualizing it happening. Working on meditating during it. Watched a bunch of YouTube videos just to get used to the sight of it in a neutral setting. Even practiced holding some needles that Dr. Williams gave me. It's helped." Her triumphant smile shines out, glorious in this depressing setting.

Still, this situation is freaking me out.

Like she can read my mind, Holly turns my question around on me. "What about you?"

Me?

I'm lucky they haven't hooked me up to a heart rate monitor yet because that shit would be going haywire, screaming warning bells like there's a fire. I'm ready to rip my IV out, followed by hers, throw her over my shoulder, and sprint out of this white-tiled nightmare.

But I shouldn't tell her any of that. She needs me to be strong for her.

To tell her everything is going to be fine.

Right?

The second I open my mouth to give Holly some bullshit answer, I meet her soft brown eyes, wide open and honest. And I realize she's not asking me to comfort her. She just wants to know the truth.

And I remember my promises—that I wouldn't lie anymore, that I'd tell her everything.

Time to put up or shut up.

"I'm fucking terrified." I cringe. "Sorry! I meant, flipping. I'm flipping terrified."

Instead of glaring at me for my slip, an adorable smile wrinkles her nose. "Don't apologize." She bites her lip and then admits, "I'm flipping terrified, too." Before I can tell her to back out then, she gets a determined expression on her face. "I have no control. That freaks me out. But I don't need to control something for it to turn out all right. I can let go, and things will still be okay in the end." Holly beams at me now, the sight so beautiful that I can barely think. "It's just like one of your surprise adventures."

I don't have time to respond because a set of nurses walks through the double doors behind her bed.

"Time to get you two set up. Let's go."

I'm still struggling for words as we're rolled into a large room filled with everything needed to take out Holly's kidney and put it in me. The team is efficient, hooking up all the wires and wrapping blood pressure cuffs around our arms. It's only when I see one of the medical team members plug a syringe into Holly's tubing and tell her to count backward from ten that I realize my time is up.

"Ten, nine—"

"Holly!" I'm frantic for her to meet my eyes, but when she turns her head, her pupils don't really focus on me.

"Eight—"

"I love you!"

Her lids are still half-open, but her mouth has gone slack. She doesn't say, *Seven*. She doesn't say, *I love you, too.*

Instead, the doctor adjusts her head and fits a breathing tube in her mouth.

"Okay, buddy, I'm gonna need you to count backward from ten."

I tear my gaze off Holly and meet the eyes of the guy holding the syringe meant to knock me out. Before I can rage at him for not letting me know I lost my last seconds with her, he pushes the plunger down.

They all expect me to follow the rules, rattle off numbers until I pass out.

But I'm busy. Every part of my rapidly fading brain is begging the universe not to take Holly away from me just when I've found her.

HOLLY

Head fuzzy. My head is fuzzy.

I blink slow. Real slow.

This room is fuzzy. Those lights are fuzzy.

And bright.

I'm awake.

"Good morning."

"Holly!"

Did I say that?

"I'm Holly."

Laugh. Someone is laughing. His face is fuzzy. His teeth are bright.

"Sorry. I'll shave closer next time, so my face isn't so fuzzy."

Oh, good. He knows he's fuzzy, too.

"How do you feel, little sis?"

His face is near my face.

"You're Marcus."

Bright smile again.

"Yes, I am. And you're Holly. You're done with your surgery. You're in the recovery room."

"Am I sick?"

"No, Holly. You're not sick."

"Okay, good."

"Hey, sweetie." Another face. Darker but still fuzzy.

"I don't think she realizes how much she's actually verbalizing."

"Pops!"

More laughter. Deep, deep laughter.

"That's right. Take your time, baby girl."

"I love you." I try to reach my hands up to squeeze their fuzzy faces, but my arms are heavy.

"We love you, too."

"I love Ben, too."

"You do?"

Neither of the fuzzy faces is speaking.

Who's talking?

"Oh, sorry, dear. That was just me."

Ben's mom. She's fuzzy, too.

Did they decide to have a fuzzy party, and I wasn't invited? Or was I invited?

More laughing.

"Ben. I love Ben. Where's Ben?"

Fuzzy faces frown.

"He's still in surgery, sweetie."

"Why? I want him."

"I'm sure he'll be out soon."

"Tell him. Tell him I want him."

"Okay, Holly. We'll tell him."

"Good. That's good."

I shift and squirm. This mattress sucks. I hate this mattress. I want my mattress.

"Pops. Pops. Pops."

"Yes, Holly?"

"I want my mattress."

"I know, Holly. You've been saying that for the last five minutes."

"Did you tell Ben I want him?"

"Why don't you rest your throat, Holly? It must be sore from the breathing tube."

My throat? My throat is sore. My throat is sore.

At some point my thoughts begin to stitch together properly. Everything loses the blurry edging, and I stop blurting out every random string of words that flows across my mind.

That doesn't change the fact that I want to see Ben. His parents are in my room. I don't mind, but shouldn't they be with him?

Why isn't he in a recovery room like me?

I can't remember asking anyone how much longer his surgery would be than mine.

My four visitors deal with the time in their own way. Marcus has his sketchbook propped on his knee. No surprise there. Pops reads a book. Likely, it's some historical biography. He never has been a fan of fiction. Mr. Gerhard has a file open in his lap, but I haven't seen him flip to a new sheet of paper since I became lucid enough to notice things like that. Mrs. Gerhard has an iPad in her lap, but like her husband, she hasn't touched it. They watch the clock and the door.

"Pops?"

He uses his finger to mark the page and turns to look at me.

"How long since I've been out of surgery?"

He checks his watch. "Close to two hours now."

Two hours, and the Gerhards are still here. My mind might be stuttering by at a slower rate right now, but that doesn't mean I can't feel fear.

If I had my striped notebook, I'd write out a list. That always helps to calm me down. Instead, I try to make one in my head.

When Ben and I are better, we will:

1. Eat delicious food, like croissants and crab fries.

2. Go on more official dates, and I'll buy him a boutonniere.

3. Visit the cabin and go on a long hike.

4. Find a new reading spot. Maybe in his bed.

5. Do other fun things in his bed.

6. I'll teach him to play gin rummy and beat him in Monopoly.

7. I'll get him to draw me beautiful pictures.

I asked him to draw me something, and he never did.

The painting of the red cardinal is hanging in my kitchen, and I love it, but he never drew me a picture like I'd asked.

What if he never gets the chance to?

A memory of Ben creeps into my mind.

I was studying in the library, and he came to sit with me. I thought he was studying, too, with his textbook open and a notebook beside it. My concentration was split, and I covertly watched him. He seemed distracted, his eyes drifting from the moving pencil in his hand to staring absently around the room and then returning again. The whole time, he wore a half-smile.

"What are you thinking about?"

Ben jumped in his seat. I guessed my question had brought him out of some deep thought.

"Oh. Uh, just the book we're reading." He grinned at me and leaned over to kiss my forehead before focusing on his textbook for the first time in twenty minutes, the happy, thoughtful expression fading from his face.

That was when I caught a glimpse of his notes, only they weren't notes at all. On his lined paper was a detailed sketch of two men dueling with swords.

Just like a scene in the book we'd been reading, The Count of Monte Cristo.

Growing up with Marcus, I always thought drawing meant bending over a piece of paper and concentrating on every little detail.

That day, I discovered Ben almost appeared to be daydreaming when he sketched.

I want him to look like that more often. Maybe I could even make him a color-coded schedule like mine. And, like Pops did with me, I could demand Ben pick some time each week to devote to drawing.

He deserves to do something that makes him happy.

Question is, will he get the chance?

Please, let me leave here with Ben.

Panic boils up my throat, searing away the calm from making my list.

"Pops?"

"Hmm?" He glances up from his book again.

"Read to me. Please. I just ... I need you to read."

"Of course, sweetheart. Should I start at the beginning?"

"That's okay. Wherever you are now is fine."

My father's deep, normally soothing voice fills the room. I try to pay attention, but the words don't make sense to my ears. He doesn't sound anything like Ben, and that somehow makes my anxiety worse.

A knock interrupts Pops a moment before Dr. Stevens enters. He's not in the lab coat and business-casual attire of our first meeting. Instead, he has a full set of blue scrubs on and some funny-looking white Crocs-like shoes.

"Ben is out of surgery. He's in recovery next door. Everything went well. You can see him now."

The world rocks. And shifts. And settles.

Mrs. Gerhard gasps and sprints from the room, her tablet clattering to the floor. As always, Mr. Gerhard is just a step behind her. Marcus and Pops grin at me.

And I start crying.

The determination that gave steel to my spine isn't needed anymore. I'm released from the worry and the fear. It all drains out of my eyes as I hiccup and sob. I'm convinced that the drugs are making my reaction over the top because, hard as I try, the flood has been released and can't be contained.

Marcus slides up on the bed next to me, maneuvering through my wires and tubing so that he can gather me in his arms. And then he rocks me and hums nothing words in my ear, just the way he did when I was younger and woke up from my chaotic nightmares.

Only, now, I'm not terrified. I'm just overwhelmed, and I have no strength left to work through these emotions. So, I cry until his shirt is soaked.

When my sobs die down, I realize Marcus isn't whispering

nonsense to me. It's a good thing I've used up most of my tears because the words he murmurs squeeze my heart until I want to weep all over again.

"You're my hero, Holly. You're amazing. You're so brave. I love you. I love you so much."

30

HOLLY

THE DOOR LOOMS tall before me.

I reach up, turn the knob, and push. The hinges squeak as the door swings wide, revealing the dark room beyond. My feet move forward on their own.

This is Grams's room. She should be asleep here, in her bed.

Someone is under the covers, but when I pull the sheet back, it's not my grandmother.

It's Ben.

He lies still, eyes closed, like he's sleeping, but his chest doesn't rise. I put my hand on his shoulder and find him ice-cold.

The darkness around me shifts and moves, closing in on us. Ben begins to sink into the bed, as if the mattress were quicksand. He's disappearing from my sight, and he does not respond when I scream his name.

There's a pressure at my back, pushing me toward the sinkhole in the bed where Ben vanished. A feeling of chaos seeps from the black space.

I turn away, searching for the door. It stands there, closed again.

But the door isn't an escape. Just a different hell.

Fear is a living thing, pulsing from the dark hole on the mattress.

Wading through it, I throw one leg and then another over the edge to dangle in the abyss. There's nothing but black beneath me.

But Ben is down there.

I let myself fall.

I'm awake.

As always, my clothing is soaked in sweat, the hospital gown sticking to my skin. But, for the first time, I don't wake up from the nightmare, panting for breath, terrified that I just let someone die. Instead, a sense of peace settles over my shoulders.

I didn't run from the darkness. I jumped into it.

BEN

When I sleep, it's in short bursts. The pain medication helps with the aching in my abdomen, but it can't get rid of the discomfort of lying in a strange bed. Of being back in a hospital. I've spent a lot of bad nights in these places, and it's hard to separate myself from those memories.

So, when my eyes crack open to a dark room, I figure it's because my body is complaining again.

Then, I hear the click of the doorknob.

A beam of light spills in from the hallway as the door pushes inward. Someone slips in through the gap, immediately shutting the door behind them, casting the room back into darkness, except for the faint glow of the machines monitoring my vitals. Everything past a certain point is out of focus, so I reach for my glasses, sliding them on.

The blurry figure solidifies.

Holly.

When our eyes catch, she grins, and my whole body clenches with happiness.

"What are you doing here?" My voice still sounds hoarse from the breathing tube they had down my throat during surgery.

"Came to see you." She leans against the wall, as if this were a casual visit.

Then, I notice the deep breaths she's taking. Like she's having trouble catching them.

"You should be in bed. You're going to tear your stitches. Or pass out on the floor." I try to push myself up, but my bones are as supportive as liquid.

"I'm okay. Look." Holly shuffles across the tiled floor toward me.

As much as I want to hold her, the painfully slow movements urge me to press a button to call the nurse in here, so someone can force her back to bed. Before I make up my mind, she reaches the foot of the bed.

"Ta-da!" Somehow, she's still got a silly grin on her face, even as air whistles in and out of her nose.

"Impressive. Thanks for the show. But I think it's time someone takes you back to your room."

However, when I reach for the remote, Holly takes another stumbling step forward and grabs my hand. The shock of her soft skin against mine freezes me, and I almost groan in pleasure. She's better than pain meds, her touch finally easing all my discomfort.

"Wait, Ben. Please. I just want to sit with you for a bit."

How can I say no to that?

When I nod, she lifts herself onto the bed, sitting with just an inch between us. Her thumb rubs over my knuckles before she lifts our hands to place a kiss in the middle of my palm. Gentle waves of calm flow through me. I want to give her the same.

"Why're you up in the middle of the night?"

She shrugs. "Couldn't sleep. A dream woke me up."

I remember the night in the cabin. "Another nightmare?"

"No. Not a nightmare. Just ..." She trails off, a curious look on her face while she fiddles with my fingers. After a moment, she shakes her head and focuses back on me. "Just a dream."

"Hmm." I pull her hand to my mouth and press my lips against her knuckles. "Was I in the dream?"

"Maybe." She watches my mouth move against her skin.

"Maybe? You trying to tell me you were dreaming about some other guy?" My tone is light and playful, but there's a pinch of fear in my chest.

A week ago, Holly told me she needed time. Said we'd talk after the surgery. Then, she kissed me like it meant something in the parking garage and told me she was sorry.

But sorry for what?

Sorry that she put space between us?

Sorry that she made me live a week of my life without her?

Or sorry that she's ending things?

Sorry for making me fall in love with her?

I don't know if she heard me before the drugs kicked in, and I don't know how to ask. My chest stings suddenly—and not from the aftermath of the surgery. Instead, I wonder if she's snuck in here to break things off with me once and for all.

"Oh, yes. So many men," she continues to joke, unaware of the chaos in my mind. "Practically an orgy. Just imagine how disappointed I was when I woke up in an empty bed." She keeps a straight face with only a slight twitch at the corner of her mouth.

"Must've been heartbreaking." I mask my fear with humor. As long as she's bantering with me, nothing is over. "So, that's why you staggered over here? Trying to make your dream a reality? Should've grabbed some male nurses while you were out there."

Another lip quiver, but she doesn't break yet. "Darn. See, this is why I need you, Ben. How else am I going to plan a proper orgy?"

This conversation is so ridiculous, but when she says she needs me, I get a heady rush. Maybe that wasn't part of the joke.

"I'm at your service. Anyway, I don't really care what got you in here. I'm just enjoying the view."

Holly's hair is pulled up into a messy bun with random strands coming loose and falling around her face. She's got on a shapeless hospital gown with a robe thrown over it that she's left untied. In the faint light of the medical equipment, her skin glows an eerie blue.

And she's so beautiful that it makes my bones ache.

Holly sticks her tongue out at me before sighing. "Yeah, yeah. I'm a sight; I'm sure."

"You are." I drag my lips across her knuckles again. "I call this look Sexy Hospital Holly."

Her free hand covers her mouth, but I can still see her eyes crinkle and hear her snort of laughter. Got her.

"You're weird." She shakes her head and reaches out to finger-comb some hair off my forehead. "I love it."

"I love you."

Her hand pauses, hovering so close to my skin that the heat of it is a touch itself. She stares down at me, and again, I wonder if she heard.

It felt so good to say; I don't mind repeating myself.

"I tried to tell you before the surgery, but you'd already passed out. So, I'm saying it again. I love you, Holly. I know I messed up and that you might not trust me right now, but I promise, if you give me another chance, I'll never lie to you again. Starting now by telling you that I'm so in love with you that I'm happy my kidneys failed. I'm grateful. Because, without that happening, you never would've come into my life. And the idea of not knowing you hurts worse than any of this." I nod at the machines before locking my gaze on hers.

Holly's teeth sink into her bottom lip while she contemplates me. A moment passes, and then a smile breaks out across her face.

"I thought I'd dreamed you saying that." She caresses my cheek before leaning down to give me a light kiss. "I love you, too." Those priceless words come out in a whisper against my skin before she leans away to gaze at me with shining eyes.

In my mind, I'm wrapping my arms around Holly, pulling her down on top of me, so I can claim her mouth and body. I want to worship her for loving me. But the best I can do is grip her hand tighter and grin up at her like a doofus.

"Kiss me again."

347

She snickers but gives me what I want. The tender way she presses her mouth to mine only makes me crave her more.

"Say it again," I demand.

Between kisses, she responds, "I love you ... I love you ... I love you, Ben ..."

Each time is better than before, and I've never felt stronger than in this moment. I have the love of Holly Foster, and all she asked for was honesty.

This sense of freedom, of knowing that I'm not lying or hiding anything from her, that we're completely open to one another, gives me a wild head rush.

This is how all life should be.

Later, when Holly gets too tired to sit up, she stretches out next to me on the bed. I keep her fingers tangled in mine, clasping them to my chest.

With her head resting on the pillow next to mine, the small puff of her breath brushes my neck when she asks the question, "How are you feeling?"

"My body is tired and kinda sore. But, other than that, I'm amazing."

"Amazing, huh?"

I turn my head to grin at her. "Of course. You love me, and I just got a grade-A Holly Foster kidney installed."

"You make it sound like I manufacture car parts." She pretends to scowl at me, but humor hides just beneath the surface.

For a minute, I stare at her, falling into her dark brown eyes. When she blinks, her lashes brush against the top of her cheeks. Creases form beside her nose as a hesitant smile appears. Stray pieces of hair curl at the edge of her face.

Every bit of her is perfection, and she gave some of it to me.

All the awe I feel for her seeps into my voice. "I have a piece of you now."

She traces her thumb along my bottom lip. "You had a piece of me before the surgery, too."

31

Ben: *On our way. See you soon. Love you.*
Holly: *Hurry up. Love you, too.*

HOLLY

I SIT ALONE IN THE GERHARDS' front room on the pristine white couch. Both of his parents went to pick Ben up from the hospital, and I'm jittery, waiting for them all to arrive back here.

After finding us asleep in the same hospital bed, Ben's parents extended the offer of having me stay with them during my recovery period. They figured we'd probably want to spend our time healing together. My father seemed put out by the idea, but they also pointed out how their house was closer to the hospital, and they'd hired a nurse to check up on Ben, who could also monitor me.

The decision was left up to me, obviously because I'm a grown woman. I made it clear to Pops that I in no way doubted his ability to take care of me but that I would be less stressed if I could be in the same place as Ben. When the Gerhards added that he and Marcus were welcome over anytime of the day, that did a lot to placate him.

I've been here for a week, only able to see Ben during visiting hours. But, today, he's getting out.

The sound of the front door opening has me standing, but I hold myself back, not wanting to crowd them.

"Holly?"

All reasoning for waiting where I am flees at the sound of him saying my name. Ben is here. I'm hustling forward when he rounds the corner. It takes a decent amount of willpower not to throw myself at him. Instead, I step into his open arms, gently sliding my hands up his back as I hug him close.

"You're here. Finally."

Under my cheek, his chest vibrates with a chuckle. "Sorry to keep you waiting."

Ben combs his fingers into my hair and then gives the strands a gentle tug. I grin as I tilt my head up.

Our lips meet, and a sigh of utter contentment flows from me to him. He tenderly handles me, kissing in a slow, deliberate manner— and not only my mouth. No, he ventures further. To my nose, my forehead, my cheeks, my jaw. His sweet caress reaches my neck when there's a deliberate throat clearing behind him.

My face flushes a deep red, which is ridiculous. Over the past few days, Ben's parents have helped me in all types of extremely tedious ways. I can only attribute my current embarrassment to the fact that I was in the middle of imagining stripping their only son of all his clothes and ravishing him in their foyer.

Or maybe it's because the simple action of kissing the man I love is the most deeply intimate act I've ever performed.

Whatever the case, I have the complexion of a tomato when I lock eyes with the Gerhards.

"We're always happy to see him, too, dear. Only I don't think he enjoys our greetings near as much." His mom relays this comment in a deadpan tone.

I can't help myself. Laughter spills out of me as I bury my face in Ben's shoulder. He chuckles right along with me and presses a kiss in my hair.

"How are you feeling?" He moves us out of his parents' way as he asks the question.

They head upstairs, leaving us to catch up on our own.

"Oh, I'm good. I feel much stronger. For the most part. There will be random times when I'm good and then—*boom!*—I'm exhausted. Your parents have been great," I whisper the last sentence, having found that Mrs. and Mr. Gerhard tend to shrug off praise unless it's about their son.

"Good. So, you still wanna stay here?" His hands remain wrapped around the back of my head, massaging my neck.

I become a puddle under the tender touch.

"Of course." I happy sigh and then shake myself because I'm not the one who needs caretaking anymore. "What about you? How are you doing? You should sit down."

I slide my palms up to grasp his, so I can lead him to the couch. But, when I bring them in front of me, I freeze. There are dark lines tracing over the back of his hand. Marks that definitely weren't there before.

"Is that—did you get a new tattoo? On your way home from the hospital? After having surgery?"

Ben laughs, and if he wasn't recovering from his operation, I'd shove him for being so stupid.

"What is the matter with you? That's so irresponsible! I can't believe you would do that!"

"Holly, calm down. It's just a pen drawing. It's not a real tattoo." His fingers massage mine, helping to soothe my heated mind so that his words can penetrate.

The hot air that built up so fast leaves in a huff, and my indignant chest deflates.

"Well ... it looks real." That's a crappy apology. It actually wasn't even an apology at all.

Still, Ben stares down at me with amusement and excitement and love. So, he can't be too upset at my brief freak-out session.

"It's supposed to look real. Dr. Stevens said he wants me to wait at least six months before I get any more ink. And I will. But, when he clears me, this is the first tattoo I'm getting."

He moves his hand higher, indicating I should take a closer look. When I do, I realize that he's drawn some type of plant, its many branches extending from his wrist to spread out across the back of his hand. The shape of the leaves looks familiar, and it doesn't take long to figure out why.

"It's holly."

"Good girl. Got it on your first guess."

My throat tightens as I blink away oncoming tears. I've cried way too much these past couple of weeks. "But I thought it was bad practice for a lawyer to have visible tattoos."

"Good thing I'm not going to be a lawyer then."

Ben keeps dropping bombs left and right, and I'm doing my best to keep up.

"Wha—what do you mean?"

He kisses my knuckles before pulling me over to the couch. When we're sitting side by side, his arm around my shoulders, our fingers twined together, he explains, "When I pushed off college to hike the PCT, part of that was a tribute to my grandfather. A way to deal with his death. But another part of it was because I was struggling to figure out what I wanted to do with my life. Family business or follow my passion?"

I settle my head on his shoulder, watching his throat move as he talks and breathing in the comforting pine scent of him.

"Then, I got sick, all because I'd made that selfish decision. And I felt like a burden on my parents, like I'd let them down. So, I chose the responsible path. The safe one."

My heart clenches, and I press my lips together to keep from interrupting.

"Then, you came along." He grasps my chin, tilting it so that I'll meet his smiling eyes. "And my whole perspective changed. What seemed like a stupid decision suddenly turned into the luckiest accident. And, honestly, if I could go back in time, I wouldn't change anything that happened. Because, in the end, it got me you."

He says that like I'm some amazing treasure, and I've never felt more cherished.

"So, yeah, maybe going into law makes more sense. But it's not what I want. You told me I needed to be honest, so I'm going to stop lying to myself. I'm going to stop trying to convince myself that the practical choice is the right one."

"So, what does this mean?"

I love the eager smile on his face, like he can't wait to face the world with this new outlook on life.

"When I go back to school full-time, I'm going to transfer from political science to the art program. Might take me a few more years to finish my degree, but it'll be worth it."

"And your parents? When are you going to tell them?"

His grin grows wider. "I already did. Went surprisingly well actually. I think seeing their only son in a hospital bed kinda softened them up. Probably could've asked for a yacht, too, now that I think about it."

Ben pretends to look put out, and I bury my face in his shirt as relieved laughter spills out of me.

Until this moment, I didn't realize how much his career choice had bothered me. Like a biting fly, it'd buzzed around me, causing small, sharp twinges of pain whenever I thought about Ben stifling his creativity to pursue a job just for the stability of it.

As he shrugged the burden of lying off his shoulders, he also freed me from my not-so-silent disapproval.

Now, we can start living.

"I can't wait to see everything you create."

Humor still flashes in his eyes.

"Well, I might need your help. You know, for inspiration."

"Inspiration, huh?"

There's a devious quality to his expression, and I know he's going somewhere with this.

"Yeah. You're my muse. You'll have to be around me all the time, so I'll always have those creative juices flowing." He plucks at the shoulder of my sweater. "And maybe model for me. You know, when I have to draw nudes."

"Ben!" I go to shove his chest but stop myself just in time. Can't forget he's still got a lot of healing to do. Instead, I wave my finger in his face. "This was your game from the start, wasn't it? Just trying to get me to take my clothes off."

He catches my finger and gently bites the tip in a very suggestive way, and then he waggles his eyebrows. "If memory serves, you're the one who begged to take my shirt off before we even went on a date."

I do my best to copy his classic smirk. "Well, when Benjamin Get-Hard the Fourth gives a striptease, it's hard to think about anything else. What's a girl to do?"

EPILOGUE

HOLLY

Four Years Later

"Have you figured out what you want yet?" Ben is sitting at his drawing table, ready to transfer whatever design idea I've come up with onto paper.

He's so handsome, dressed in his black jeans and T-shirt, tattoos snaking down his arms and onto his hands. Before answering, I step in between his open knees, slide my fingers into the hair at the nape of his neck, and kiss him thoroughly. His mouth tastes like mint, and he always smells a little bit like the forest. We need to go back to the cabin soon. I'm craving some long nights of lovemaking in front of a warm fire.

I hum in the back of my throat as I end our impromptu make-out session. Ben stares up at me with a drunken smile but soon shakes his head, so he can focus again.

"You're stalling. You don't have to do this." Even as he scolds me for distracting him, his hands settle on my backside.

355

"I'm not stalling. Your sexiness just drives me to distraction."

Even after years together, I'm still madly in love with this man. He'll move in a particular way or say just the right thing, and it's like a bonfire lights in my chest, and I need to touch him.

"Anyway, I've figured out what I want."

Ben nuzzles his nose into the space between my breasts, humming his own satisfaction. I use my grip on his hair to pull him back even though I can't keep from laughing.

"Stop being ridiculous!"

"You started it. So, what do you want?"

I give him my most innocent smile. "I want a surprise."

His mouth pops open, and I enjoy how befuddled he looks.

"You can't be serious."

I nod. "Yep. You're getting too comfortable with me just telling you what to do. This is your area of expertise, and I trust you completely."

Ben scowls up at me, opening his mouth for another point that won't change my mind. Before he can lecture me, I place my finger on his lips.

"Our love."

His eyebrow rises in question.

"That's as much direction as I'll give you. You have this." I scoop up his left hand, running my fingers over the intricate holly branches.

Ben kept his vow. He waited until Dr. Stevens gave him the go-ahead, which was almost eight months after the exchange. The next day, he was under the needle again.

"I want one of my own. Something that, when I look at it, I'll immediately think about how much I love you."

"Holly." There's happiness in his voice, but still, he pushes back. "You should get something for you."

"This *is* for me. Now, I'll just sit over here and act as inspiration. Let me know when you're done." After another quick kiss, I return to the front counter and pick up the paperwork I was reviewing.

The first time I glance up, he's still staring at me, so I give him a big grin paired with an enthusiastic thumbs-up. He simultaneously rolls his eyes and shakes his head.

The second time I take a break from my work, Ben has on his distracted, thoughtful look while his pencil dances across the page.

Over an hour goes by before he finally stands up to crack his back. "Okay. Come take a look."

"Nuh-uh." I wag my finger at him and know there's mischief in my smile. "I'm committing to this trust exercise. I'll take a look when it's on me."

"Come on, Holly. That's crazy." Ben's arms cross over his chest, as he's ready to fight me on this.

But I'm not backing down.

"Crazy would be handing your tools to a homeless man on the street and asking him to tattoo me. But you know what's fun and romantic?" I stand from my seat and saunter toward him. "Asking my handsome, talented, amazing, trustworthy partner to design a surprise tattoo for me."

This morning, I dressed for war, knowing this might come down to trickery. Ben always gets turned up hotter when I slip on one of my shapely pencil skirts and pair it with a set of heels. Sexy Business Holly he calls it.

I watch my efforts work. His scowl drops away as his eyes trace down my approaching figure. He's biting his lower lip when I stop in front of him. But he still doesn't give in.

"You shouldn't get something permanent on your body without seeing it first."

Instead of answering, I reach out my hand, sliding my fingers along his waistband, gently caressing the warm skin of his midriff. His ab muscles clench at my touch.

"Then, it wouldn't be a surprise."

He scrubs his hands over his face, and then he grabs my wrists and drags me to his chest. "You're sure about this?"

I smell mint again as his question brushes over my face. Immediately, I nod.

"Okay. But it's your fault if you don't like it."

Before he can turn back to his table, I slip my hands from his hold and wrap my arms around his waist, giving him a squeeze. "You drew it. So, I'm going to love it."

He harrumphs but kisses my forehead and directs me to sit in the dentist-like chair. In an effort to keep from glimpsing the design, I don't watch him as he preps everything even though I really want to. Seeing my guy in his element is the best kind of foreplay. He doesn't hesitate or dawdle; he's all business.

"You said your wrist?"

"Yes, my left one." I display the area by stretching out my arm on the padded armrest.

Ben coats my skin with a layer of deodorant and then reaches for the stencil he just printed. By turning my head, I avoid ruining the surprise. Apparently, the movement makes Ben doubt this whole exchange once again.

"You don't need to do this, Holly."

"I know that. But I want to. I've been thinking about doing this for a while now. I want our love to be permanent on my body." I continue even though the second reason is sillier, "Also, no way can I own a tattoo shop and not have a tattoo of my own."

"Sure you can. You can do anything you want."

His words make me grin, even as I keep my face turned away.

"You're right. And I want you to tattoo me. If you don't, then I'll have to ask some other random tattoo artist to do it."

He gives me a sexy growl in answer, and I know I've won. Ben isn't some raging alpha male who gets jealous at the mere sight of me talking to another man. But no way would he be happy about someone else's needle touching my skin.

"If anyone is going to mark you, it's going to be me."

"Agreed." I turn just enough to capture his eyes. "I trust you."

All uncertainty leaves his face, and he gives me one of his wicked grins.

My chest warms as I smile back before turning away again. Goose bumps race over my skin at the whirring sound of his machine, and with the stinging pierce of it hitting my wrist, I'm finally able to relax.

Except not really because, *Ow, ow, ow, ow, ow!*

This hurts like someone is digging their fingernails into a fresh sunburn. I want to complain because I'm a wimp, but I clench my teeth and keep my whining to myself. I'm not giving Ben any reason to stop.

I wish I had thought to put on some music or something. This would be more bearable with a distraction.

As if reading my mind, Ben pauses. "You want me to put on the radio?"

"Yes, please." That sounded completely normal and not at all like I'm trying to hold back a whimper.

There's a stereo near Ben's desk, so he just leans back and flips the power button. The familiar voices of the Preston and Steve morning show crew fill the studio. Their crude, hilarious conversations are exactly what I need to take my mind off the discomfort of my arm. Soon, I'm able to block out the persistent ache.

A commercial is playing when Ben lowers the volume. A glance at the clock shows it's been a little over an hour.

"All done." He wipes the area with a wet paper towel, and the cold is a shock against my sensitive skin.

"Should I look?"

He lets out an exasperated sigh. "I've wanted you to look from the beginning!"

I turn and stick my tongue out at him because it's what he deserves. Then, I gasp when I finally examine his creation.

What was once a pale, bare wrist now has a beautiful scene etched into it. A tiny replica of our cabin sits, surrounded by delicate pine trees, and rising from the chimney is a stream of smoke that forms a wistful little heart. My own heart clenches and stutters at the gorgeous piece of art that is now a permanent piece of me.

"So ... is it okay?"

When I gaze up at the man I love, he's leaning away from me, hand scratching the back of his neck.

How could he doubt, even for a moment, that I would be in awe of his talent?

"There is nothing more perfect in the world than this picture. I love it almost as much as I love you." I'm tickled to observe a slight reddening of his cheeks as he smiles at me.

I want to run my fingers over the tattoo, but I know I'll just hurt myself if I do. So, instead, I stare down at the picture, taking in every detail. In the delicate work, I see Ben's love for me.

He's inspecting me when I raise my head. Making sure not to jostle my arm, I slide off the chair and settle myself in his lap.

"I love you, Ben Gerhard."

When he opens his mouth to respond, I cut him off with a kiss. I don't need to hear him say the words when I have them displayed on my wrist.

~

BEN

Holly peels back the gauze I loosely taped over her wrist earlier. Marcus swore, she was playing a joke on him when she called to tell him about the tattoo. He showed up at the shop just a minute ago, demanding proof.

"Isn't it the most precious thing you've ever seen?"

"The perspective and structure are all formatted correctly. But that's not how smoke works."

His analytical review of my piece makes me laugh, but Holly shoves her brother's shoulder, scowling at him.

"Of course not, you dummy. Ben knows that! It's a heart because we love each other."

"Yeah. I got that. I still can't believe you willingly had a needle touch you."

We talked about that exact concern back when Holly brought up the idea of purchasing a shop together. She had a fantastic business plan laid out that addressed all the logistics; she'd even talked to two other artists about joining the team. But none of that addressed how a girl who was terrified of needles would be able to work around them all day.

When I brought it up, she explained that her mind didn't see medical needles and tattoo needles in the same way. Holly even picked up my tattoo gun, easily holding it in her palm, to demonstrate the lack of a panicked reaction in her body. Once I was sure of how calm and at ease she was, I stopped doubting. After two years as an apprentice and two more working in other people's shops, I was ready to create my own space with Holly.

Combining the rest of Grandpa Ben's money with a small business loan, we bought this place. Holly adores the red brick walls, and I'm a fan of the giant storefront window that lets in plenty of natural light. Pops was a huge help with refurbishing the place. Two months in, and business has been steady.

Over the years, I've accumulated some regulars—fans of my work who don't care which studio I'm in. Holly's marketing skills bring in new customers daily. Jamie and Ridley, the other two artists who joined our studio, have styles all their own, making sure we can serve a variety of clientele.

Some days get hectic and unstructured, but Holly just gives the reins a tug, and everything falls back into place. My girl is amazing, the way she makes sure everything runs how it should. Her mastery of the business side of this situation means I can concentrate on the customers and making their dreams a reality.

I love it.

I love her.

I finished up with my last appointment of the day a few minutes ago, giving them their tattoo care kit before letting them go. Ridley took the last walk-in, and the shop is set to close soon. As I set my station to rights, I observe Holly and her brother laughing together. He's relaying some story as she adjusts a framed picture that has tilted off-balance.

The painting depicts a gorgeous forest scene. A Benjamin Gerhard the Second original. In fact, the shop houses a large amount of my grandfather's art. Not all of it. Some we sold, donating the proceeds to a charity that supports cancer research. Holly's idea. But many we haven't put price tags on because I want a reminder of him when I walk into this shop. I wouldn't have any of the things I love today if it wasn't for him.

He taught me a love of art, which I've found a way to make a career of. And, in my grief over his death, I injured myself, which at first seemed like a cruel twist of fate but ended with me finding the love of my life.

I owe him everything.

Holly flips the front sign to inform everyone that we're closed for the night. Then, she reaches for her purse under the front desk and walks over to me. I grab my water bottle and have my hand outstretched before she even asks. The daily pill container gives a little pop as she pushes the Thursday lid open and dumps out the colorful tablets into my palm.

I can handle my medications on my own, but Holly is calmer when she's sure beyond a doubt that I've taken them. Gives her a sense of control.

After the transplant, we still had to deal with the waiting to see if my body would reject the donation. Luckily, nothing went wrong. Her little kidney is still chugging away nicely in my abdomen. Maybe it's weird, seeing as how I've had it for years now, but I still think of the kidney as Holly's. I always have a piece of her with me.

"Marcus wants to take us out to eat to celebrate my bravery." She puffs out her chest in an overly exaggerated display, making me chuckle.

"By all means, let's take advantage of your brother's generosity."

"Nice to know my family appreciates me," Marcus calls out before stepping through the front door.

"He's gonna meet us there." Holly smiles after her brother.

After she gave me her kidney, I worried that Holly might come to resent giving up the chance to help her brother find one. I should've known better. Just because she couldn't offer her organ up in exchange didn't mean she would stop looking. In fact, using some creative methods, Holly was able to locate a donor for her brother not too long after our surgery.

That anonymous donation saved Marcus's life and relieved Holly and me of our guilt.

Thank the universe for generous people.

I check on Ridley to see that she's finishing an eagle in the classic American style—thick black lines, bright and vivid colors.

"Nice work. Holly and I are headed out. You good to close up?"

"No problem. See you tomorrow."

Holly shuts down the front desk's computer, and we're set to go. Before stepping outside, I twine my fingers through hers, making sure to take her right hand, so I don't jostle her tattoo.

The night air is cool, and I'm glad I wore my jacket. Holly shivers, so I let go of her hand to wrap my arm around her shoulders. With her gripping my waist, she tugs me to a stop and turns us, so we're facing the front window of our shop.

The name is displayed in simple flowing script—Colorful Scars Tattoo Studio.

"Let's see." She stretches out her hand and holds up a finger for each item as she starts to make one of her lists. "One, we got you healthy. Two, we earned our degrees. Three, we worked our butts off to save up for this place. Four, we opened up the coolest tattoo shop in Philly. Five, we continue to be insanely in love with one another."

"Don't forget that we tattooed ourselves on each other." I smirk down at her as she grins up at me.

"Is that weird?"

I shrug. "Who cares? I love being weird with you."

Holly sticks her tongue out at me, and I follow it to her mouth, giving her a scathing kiss. When we surface, she's wearing a triumphant smile, probably because she knows I can't resist her. As she stares up at me, her shining eyes turn just a shade serious.

"Look at us, living our dreams," she whispers, as if someone might try to snatch them away if she talks too loud. "Anything else you want to add to the list?"

Suddenly craving the warmth of her body, I pull her fully into my embrace. As I cup the back of her head in my palm, her lips part slightly in anticipation of the kiss she knows is about to come.

"Anything else?" Our breaths mingle as I lean in close. "No. All I want is more of you."

<<<<>>>>

THANK YOU!

Thank you for taking the time to read this book. This means a great deal to me, especially because it is my first published novel. I hope that you fell in love with Holly and Ben in the same way I did!

If you would like to hear about new releases or just stay up-to-date with what is going on in my writerly world, please join my newsletter at www.laurenconnollyromance.com.

You can also follow me on:

Twitter: @laurenaliciaCon

Instagram: @laurenconnollyromance

Facebook: www.facebook.com/LaurenConnollyRomance/

I would also love to hear from you! Please send me an email at laurenconnollyromance@gmail.com.

ACKNOWLEDGMENTS

This book would not be what it is today without the help of some magnificent people. I read a great deal about kidney failure and dialysis, but it was the human perspective that enabled me to bring Ben and Holly's experience to life. Thank you, Janay Freebery, for being so open about your and your father, Jack Freebery's, donation story. Also, I appreciate Mark and Ann for talking to a complete stranger about such a personal topic. To my two wonderful aunts, Maureen Cambier and Patricia Porta, you not only gave me your love and support, but also provided me with a glimpse into a medical professional's viewpoint.

Then, there are the lovely women who took the time to read my story when it was still in rough shape. Thank you, Kate, Allyson, Heather, Dana, Jamie, and Crystal. Through your honest commentary, I was able to approach the editing process with a new perspective and hopefully do justice to the characters on my page.

I have to give a major shout-out to Jovana Shirley at Unforeseen Editing. My book would have been riddled with an embarrassing amount of grammar errors if it wasn't for your sharp eye. Thank you for working your editing magic.

If I have forgotten anyone, I am truly sorry. But know that I appreciate you all.

AUTHOR'S NOTE

Kidney failure, also known as renal failure, affects hundreds of thousands of people in the United States. The main form of treatment is dialysis, of which there are two forms: hemodialysis and peritoneal dialysis. However, the most effective form of treatment is receiving a kidney donation.

I first became interested in this subject after watching an episode of *Last Week Tonight with John Oliver* that discussed the state of dialysis treatment in the United States. After my curiosity was piqued, I began researching on my own, which was how I learned about paired donations. The idea of giving one of your organs to a complete stranger in order to help a loved one inspired me, and from that inspiration arose Holly, Ben, and Marcus.

A great many things can result in kidney disease and eventual kidney failure, meaning no one person will have the same experience. However, if any of my readers have dealt with this disease and believe I misrepresented it, I apologize.

If you wish to learn more about kidney disease or if you are interested in the donation process, I encourage you to read up on the subject. A good place to start is www.kidney.org.

ABOUT THE AUTHOR

Lauren Connolly works as a university librarian when she's not crafting love stories. This means she's used to researching random topics—from revitalizing rural communities in Japan to the stigma held against horse slaughter and consumption in the United States. (That last one was a bit difficult, what with her being a vegetarian, but she did it!)

In her free time, Lauren wrestles with her grumpy cocker spaniel, named after her favorite pop culture librarian; drives or flies long distances to visit family and friends around the world; reminds herself she should do something healthy, like lift weights or yoga; and stays up past her bedtime to read "just one more page."

Lightning Source UK Ltd.
Milton Keynes UK
UKHW010646100822
407113UK00001B/30